DECADES

RUTH HARRIS

SIMON AND SCHUSTER · NEW YORK

DESIGNED BY EVE METZ
MANUFACTURED IN THE UNITED STATES OF AMERICA

1   2   3   4   5   6   7   8   9   10

LIBRARY OF CONGRESS CATALOGING IN PUBLICATION DATA

Harris, Ruth.
   Decades.

     I. Title.
PZ4.H3159De [PS3558.A655] 813'.5'4 74-4127
ISBN 0-671-21799-2

FOR MICHAEL HARRIS

PART ONE

THE SEVENTIES

Men and Women:
The Games People Play

1 BARBARA ROSER HAD A
theory that you could tell a lot about the man who ran a
company the minute you walked in the door. It didn't matter
if the company was IBM and the man was Thomas B. Watson or if it was Sammy's Radio & TV Repair and the man
was Sammy. The principle was the same: a man's office was
his Rorschach.

Barbara Roser was interested in the men who ran companies: they had money, which she herself had and which she
considered essential in a man. They had power, of which she
had some and wanted more. And, because they had power
and money, they were invariably sexy. Money and power
were the all-time turn-on.

It was August 1971, and Barbara had just walked into the
reception room of Alpha Records. She was there to meet its
president, Nat Baum. Barbara herself was a vice-president—
of the Jared & Spolin Publishing Company—and she was at
Alpha to present promotion plans to introduce the tie-in
that had just been negotiated between Alpha and J&S.

While she waited for Mr. Baum's secretary to appear and
lead her into his office, Barbara looked around the room,
trying to figure out Nat Baum.

The glove-leather sofa was from Atelier, the steel-and-glass
Parsons table was an expensive one and the carpet, a gray-and-navy hexagonal, was a David Hicks—a real David Hicks
and not a cheap knockoff from an outlet in Long Island City.

So far, so good. Nat Baum had taste and Nat Baum had
money.

On the other hand, dusty proof sheets were thrown into

old Four Roses cartons, a plastic Christmas tree was propped against one arm of the sofa and the glass top of the Parsons table could have used some Windex.

The dichotomy between the expensive decor and the sloppy housekeeping tantalized Barbara's imagination. Maybe Mr. Baum was a man who disdained trivial details. Maybe, though, it was more ominous: maybe he had a serious character flaw.

Barbara knew she was being dramatic, but she always liked to make the most of everything: even the few minutes spent waiting in a reception room. You only lived once, she said, and she wanted to go all the way even if it sometimes meant going too far and getting in over your head.

"Miss Roser?" asked the young secretary who had appeared silently in the door of the reception room.

"Mrs. Roser," said Barbara although she was thinking of changing to Ms.

"Nat will see you now."

Barbara followed the girl through the maze of corridors that led to Nat Baum's office. Maybe it would reveal more about him. Barbara had concluded that the reception room was too schizzy. Maybe her theory was for the birds—or maybe Nat Baum was just Rorschach-proof.

Nat Baum's large, corner office was painted charcoal gray and furnished with burled-ash pedestal tables. There was no desk, and a burgundy felt-upholstered banquette stretched the length of one wall. Several chrome-and-cane Breuer conference chairs completed the seating, and wall-to-wall carpeting in a gray that matched the walls created the ambience of a womb. The room was extremely comfortable.

"Nat," said the secretary, "Mrs. Roser."

Barbara saw him before he saw her. He was sitting on the banquette looking over mechanicals for an album cover. He was the right age, thought Barbara: about fifty. She was thirty-four. He was handsome, with a perpetual suntan that had attractively deepened the laugh lines around his eyes. He had the body of a tennis player, and he was wearing one of the great Saint Laurent silk Art Deco shirts.

"Hi," he said. "Come in."

"Hello, Mr. Baum," said Barbara.

"Nat," he said. "Everyone calls me Nat."

"So I notice," said Barbara, sitting down purposely in one of the Breuer chairs. She didn't want to sit on the banquette next to him. Let him work a little.

"Ed Vallett," said Nat Baum, introducing the young man who was handing him the mechanicals. Ed Vallett was wearing a body shirt opened to the waist, shaded granny glasses and skin-tight bell-bottom jeans. He looked like every art director under thirty that Barbara had ever seen. "He's our art director," continued Nat. "A boy genius."

"I can tell by looking," said Barbara, letting Nat Baum know she was hip. "Hi, Ed."

Ed nodded.

"Well, what do you think?" Nat Baum handed Barbara the two mechanicals, casually, on purpose, letting their fingers touch. She glanced at the two versions. The album was called *Yoga For You,* and one version showed a model in a leotard doing the Lotus, the Lion and the Shoulder Stand. The second showed a model in a bikini looking happy and skinny.

"I don't think anything," said Barbara. She put the mechanicals back down on the pale ash table, making a point of not handing them back directly to Nat Baum. He was playing a game and she knew the rules and he knew that she knew. They might as well get as much fun as possible out of it.

"No opinion?" asked Nat Baum with mock shock.

"No opinion." Barbara certainly had no opinion about *Yoga For You* covers. That was Nat Baum's problem. And she also had no opinion about Nat Baum—except that he was sexy and trouble. The trouble was that he was married. The Nat Baums of this world always were. Barbara had found that out the hard way. All the desirable men in New York—the ones who ran things, who had money and power and charm—also had wives. Too bad.

"No opinion!" said Nat Baum again. "You're fired!"

"I don't work here," said Barbara. "I'm immune." What she was telling him was that she was immune to him. He got the message and he knew that she was lying.

Ed Vallett just stood there. He heard them, the undertones and the overtones. He had heard them every time Nat met a new, good-looking woman. They always responded, too. Ed didn't care. He just wished Nat would cut the crap and make up his mind about the album cover.

"The positions look like murder," said Nat. "The women won't go for them."

"But we've got to look different from the competition," said Ed, accurately pointing out that all the competing yoga albums had models in bikinis looking ideally thin and idiotically happy.

Nat looked at the mechanicals again for a moment and then he shrugged. He flipped them back to Ed and dismissed him. "Whatever you think is best, Ed."

Barbara got the point: up front, Nat Baum wanted to make sure she knew he was running things. He was right in there, testing, testing.

He knew the game all right, and he was good at it. So was she. Each had met a worthy competitor.

Barbara Roser was the promotion director and a vice-president of Jared & Spolin, one of the biggest book publishers in America. She was the only woman with vice-presidential status, and it had taken her eleven years to get her executive title and executive salary, and even though she loved them, she hadn't planned it that way at all.

Barbara had grown up in the fifties and she had done everything the times had dictated: she had married at twenty; had two children, a girl and a boy; gotten divorced and achieved professional success, sexual liberation and emotional independence all in the correct sequence.

Nat Baum, although he was lower-class Jewish as opposed to Barbara's upper-class WASP, had also done all the right things. He had married the daughter of a rich man. He had started in the record business on a shoestring in the late forties, concentrating at first on jazz and swing. As rock emerged and his company couldn't compete financially with the major labels, Nat had turned to making self-help records. Alpha Records promised health, wealth and happiness: *Weight Loss Through Hypnosis*; *How To Triple Your Money In Real Estate In Your Spare Time*; *Stop Smoking In Thirty Days*; *Sexercises for the Sensuous Woman* and a selection of personalized zodiac interpretations by an astrologer named Igor Puligny. Alpha's ads had run in *Cosmopolitan*, *Redbook*, *Good Housekeeping*, *McCall's* and the *Ladies' Home Journal*. Business had been good, and Nat Baum had become a paper millionaire. He had a daughter he adored, all the money he could ever need and only the vaguest memories of the Essex Street tenement he had grown up in.

Barbara Roser and Nat Baum, each starting from a different point in time and space, had both achieved the American dream.

They each had only one problem and it was the same one: what next?

"He's the art director, right?" asked Nat, referring to his decision to let Ed Vallett decide which cover to use.

"But you're the president," Barbara pointed out.

"Only when I'm forced," said Nat Baum. "Frankly, I'd rather be drunk under a palm tree."

"Oh, Christ," said Barbara. "One of those."

She knew a hundred men with the same hang-up: they lived for their work, for money and success and going-to-the-office, and all the time they clung to adolescent fantasies of a tropical island, dusky maidens and no responsibilities.

"The fact is," she said, "you'd be bored to death."

"Try me," said Nat Baum.

He was pushing too hard this time. He had overstepped the rules of the little match they had been playing. And so Barbara called the game.

She got down to business, outlining the promotion she had planned: announcements to wholesalers, posters and window streamers for retailers, descriptive brochures with order forms for jobbers. When she finished, she paused, waiting for Nat's reaction. There was none. He sat there, lighting one cigarette after another, puffing on each a few times, grinding it out and lighting its successor.

Barbara wondered if she had turned him off completely. She hoped not—she hadn't intended to; but there was nothing she could do about it now. In a very businesslike way she continued. She quoted the costs per thousand, prices for color separation, the expenses of printing, stuffing envelopes and mailing.

"J&S will pay the initial expenses and we'll bill you at cost for half in thirty days." It was all in the contract. Barbara had said everything she was there to say. Nat Baum lit up another Kent.

"I'm trying to quit," he said.

"What about *Stop Smoking In Thirty Days?* Or don't your records work?"

Nat Baum shrugged. "It's a living."

"You're probably very romantic under all that cynicism," she said, deciding to play the game again—for a while, anyway. He was too attractive just to write off.

"You're probably right," he said, and because he smiled, she did. The tension between them had evaporated and they were comfortable with each other.

"Do I have your OK to go ahead?" asked Barbara. The contract specified that Nat Baum had to agree to all advertising and promotion that went out from J&S.

"Sure," he said. "Why not?"

"I'll leave these with you," said Barbara referring to the mock-ups she had brought along. "Look them over if you want."

"I don't want."

"Don't you want to see what you're spending your money for?"

"I'll trust you."

"Thank you," said Barbara.

Then she got up to leave. The meeting was over and so was the game. She picked up her bag and the Vuitton envelope she used as an attaché case and headed toward the door. It was almost twelve-thirty. The game had ended in a draw.

Suddenly Nat Baum stood up. He was slightly shorter than Barbara had imagined.

"Have lunch with me," he asked. "We can talk some more."

Barbara knew perfectly well that Nat Baum wasn't asking her to lunch. He was asking her if she'd sleep with him.

The Barbara Roser of the fifties wouldn't have understood his question. The Barbara Roser of the sixties would have fallen into bed with him the same afternoon. But this was the seventies, and all Barbara said was "Yes, I'd like to have lunch with you."

The game wasn't over at all, and by the time they got to the elevator Barbara was already wondering who the winner was going to be.

PART TWO

THE FIFTIES

The Transitional Woman

"There's no reason a woman can't have a family and a career. All it takes is organization."

—Barbara Roser
September 1959

1 "I'M PART OF THE LAST American generation that had a small-town childhood," said Barbara. "White church steeple on the town green, cheerleaders at the high school games and a phone operator who listened in."

If you were to ask her what it was like, she'd say: "It's like a foreign country you lived in when you were little. You can remember some of the vocabulary but you don't know the language anymore."

Her name then was Barbara Drooten. Her family was heavy on background and light on cash. Her ancestors on both sides had been among the Dutch farmers who had settled the Hudson Valley in the early eighteenth century. Her mother had grown up with tutors and a pony cart, and her father was good at sailing and croquet but not so good at running the local insurance and real estate business his father had left him. Her parents could remember what it was like to be rich in the twenties, and they feasted on their memories of caviar in the past and economized on meat loaf in the present.

In a small town like Pawling economic divisions didn't matter too much, and Barbara went to the right number of pajama parties, sock hops and pep rallies. She was a little too pretty to be really popular with the girls and a little too bright to be really popular with the boys. She had had, however, a best friend with whom she exchanged telephone confidences by the hour and, by senior year, a steady who took her to the Senior Prom in June and tried to lay her every Saturday night for the rest of the summer.

She wore circle skirts with elastic waist cinchers that

rolled down from the top and up from the bottom. She wore ankle socks rolled down three times and held up with rubber bands that left marks on her legs for hours. She wore pennies in her loafers and cardigan sweaters backward and white piqué dickeys with Peter Pan collars. She used chlorophyll toothpaste and Revlon's Fire 'n Ice lipstick; she wanted to be hep but she was afraid of the hoods—the boys who souped up their cars and wore greasy d.a.'s. She knew that Peggy Sue Diskby got caught in junior year. Her "visit to her aunt in Chicago" was, Barbara knew via study-hall gossip, really a trip to an abortionist in southern New Jersey.

Give 'em hell Harry, lovable Ike and his golf scores, Joe McCarthy and the Senate hearings, Sputnik, the Cold War and H-bomb testing in the South Pacific didn't interest her. She cared about who was going with whom and who had broken up with whom; whether or not French kissing made boys uncontrollable and if you could use Tampax even if you were a virgin.

Barbara went to Wellesley because her marks in high school were good, because her uncle on her mother's side had endowed the Wellesley library with a collection of rare seventeenth-century illustrated manuscripts on European herbs and botanicals—and because college was the best place to meet a man.

In the fifties, as the saying went, the boy got his Ph.D.; the girl got her Ph.T.—Putting Hubby Through.

Barbara entered Wellesley in the fall of 1954 with a wardrobe of cashmere sweaters, pleated plaid skirts and several pairs of Bermuda shorts. She knitted argyle socks for her boyfriends, played endless games of bridge, sat up long into the night discussing how far to go after you were pinned and how many children made the ideal family.

Barbara believed in love at first sight and she was positive that she'd recognize her future husband the moment she set eyes on him. All she had to do was be available and compliant and have freshly set hair.

She met Dick Roser on a blind date in October 1955. Toby Griffith, who lived in Barbara's dorm, had offered to fix Barbara up. Dick was a fraternity brother of Toby's fiancé, Toby explained, and he was really neat. He was getting his Ph.D. in marine engineering, was cute-looking and came from the Far West. Toby was cleaning her two-point-four diamond engagement ring with jeweler's rouge and an old toothbrush as she filled Barbara in on the details. It was a ritual with Toby: every morning and every night she polished her round-cut stone until it gave out blinding sparkles; and Barbara yearned to have one like it. She longed to ask Toby if she could try it on, but she didn't dare. Many girls had a thing about letting someone else try on their engagement rings. It was like a betrayal or like gambling with the devil: too risky.

"He started in marine engineering to keep out of the Army," said Toby. "He didn't want to get stuck in Korea— and now he's getting his Ph.D. He's second in his class. He'll have a good future."

Even though it wasn't love at first sight, Barbara liked Dick Roser the minute she first saw him. He wore gray flannel trousers with a tweed sport jacket, an oxford button-down shirt and a red-and-black-striped rep tie. His white bucks were properly dirty, and he was clean-cut.

"Where would you like to go?" he asked. He couldn't believe his good luck. He had been told that she was good-looking, but she was a real doll. He hadn't expected that.

"There's the greasy spoon. All the kids hang out there," said Barbara. There was also the Wellesley Inn, but it was expensive, and it wasn't nice to suggest an expensive place on the first date.

Dick opened the door of his gray Oldsmobile and helped Barbara in. She arranged her crinolines around her, loving the starchy, crinkly sound they made. She thought it was sexy without being obvious. It made a boy aware of your underwear without actually revealing anything. She was glad she had washed her hair that afternoon. It was parted on the right side and held in place with an oval sterling silver barrette.

She thought they made a nice couple: Barbara and Dick.

Over Cokes and hamburgers, they found out about each other. Dick came from outside Aspen, Colorado, was in his last year of grad school and was planning his future.

"I've already been approached by McLaughlin Steel and Apex Shipbuilding."

"Which one will you go with?" Barbara was very much impressed. Everyone knew that the campus recruiters made their offers to the best boys in class practically a year before graduation.

"It depends on salary and benefits. They haven't made their final offers yet." He ordered more Cokes. "What are you majoring in?"

"Lit. I love Salinger and I just hate Kerouac. I read *On the Road* last week and I can't stand the Beats. They're so dirty and they have no goals. Existentialism is just an excuse for laziness."

"I don't have too much time to read, but I thought *Franny and Zooey* was terrific," said Dick. He was afraid Barbara would try to get into a long discussion of Existentialism; he hated intellectual girls—although she was certainly too pretty to *look* like one.

"Do you think Franny was pregnant?"

"Oh, definitely. There's no question about it."

"My Lit professor says she was having a religious experience," said Barbara tentatively. She didn't like disagreeing with a boy, but her professor had half convinced her that Franny's experience had not been a physical one.

"There wasn't anything religious about it. She was pregnant," said Dick. He was a scientist and didn't like hazy, metaphysical theories. To him they didn't count as explanations.

"Most of the kids think she was pregnant too," said Barbara, and changed the subject. She told Dick that she had gone to public high school (she wanted to get that over with quickly in case it mattered to him), that she thought Elvis Presley was disgusting and that she hoped Princess Margaret would get her sister's permission to marry Group Captain Townsend.

"It would be terribly romantic, wouldn't it?"

"It would be romantic," said Dick. "But I don't see how the Queen could go against hundreds of years of tradition."

Barbara sighed in agreement. Still, maybe the Queen would surprise everyone and consent to the marriage.

"I think True Love always wins, don't you?" asked Barbara.

"True Love can cause a lot of pain," said Dick, counting out the tip.

Barbara shuddered.

"I just can't believe that," she said, "and I won't believe it."

"Well, it won't happen to you, anyway," said Dick. The conversation had gotten too serious and he wanted to change the subject.

"Which?" asked Barbara, pursuing it. "True Love or pain?"

"Pain," said Dick, saying what he knew she wanted to hear.

"I don't think so either," said Barbara.

She was still young enough to think that she was immune.

On their second date, Dick took Barbara to the movies. They saw *Bad Day at Black Rock,* and although Barbara let Dick hold her hand, she was careful not to let him put his arm around her. On the third date, she let him kiss her good night, although she kept her lips closed and he, knowing the rules as well as she did, didn't try to go any further.

It wasn't long until Barbara began saving Saturday nights for him and then weekends. They ate hamburgers and pizzas, went to the flicks, studied in the afternoons, held hands in the day and necked at night. In the fifties, the rules of sex were as formally choreographed as the steps of an eighteenth-century gavotte. After a month, Barbara began to let Dick touch her above the waist and over her clothes. Gradually, she allowed him to unbutton the top buttons of her Peter Pan–collared blouses and touch her breasts outside, then inside, her bra. Just before Thanksgiving, Dick gave her a red-and-white-striped Harvard scarf to wear over her camel's-hair coat and she knew that he was getting serious.

In January, when they saw each other for the first time after Christmas vacation, Dick told Barbara that he was sure he was in love with her and asked her to wear his pin. Barbara was so moved that she couldn't speak and so she nodded. With trembling hands, Dick pinned it on her pink sweater just over the left nipple. It was on the part of her nearest her heart. Barbara and Dick kissed with open mouths and searching tongues and Barbara said the magic words to herself: engaged to be engaged.

She had completely forgotten about love at first sight. She had found something much better: True Love.

In 1956 the world's largest stock issue was floated when the Ford Motor Company went public with an initial offering of 10.2 million shares. In the first week of trading, Americans spent six hundred and fifty-seven million dollars to own part of the future of the American economy. In that same year, Martin Luther King, Jr., organized a bus boycott in Montgomery, Alabama; President Dwight D. Eisenhower condemned Israel, Britain and France for the use of force in the Suez crisis; Mickey Mantle won the American League batting championship; the Swedish Academy decided that no Nobel Prize in the area of peace would be awarded and, late in the year, Elvis Presley, shown only from the waist up, sang "Hound Dog" and "Heartbreak Hotel" on the Ed Sullivan show.

Barbara's father didn't take advantage of the Ford offering; he thought that Martin Luther King was stirring up unnecessary trouble; he met the man his daughter was going to marry and approved of her choice and none of the rest of it mattered to him because in the late spring, he died. He did it as politely and considerately as he had lived.

He had just set his tee in place on the start of the third hole of the golf course of the Pawling Country Club when he began to gasp convulsively for breath. The skin around his mouth went white, then blue as he collapsed on the new spring grass, breaking the right lens of his sunglasses on the wooden tee. His partner and the caddie both ran to the clubhouse and called the hospital.

"I'm sorry to be such a nuisance," said Peter Drooten as the driver and the attendant placed him on the stretcher, slid it into the ambulance and, siren wailing, drove him to the hospital.

Those were Peter Drooten's last words, because he was dead on admission to the emergency room. His death certificate accurately cited the cause of death as heart failure.

Barbara and Dick spent the week following his death with Barbara's mother. Evangeline Drooten was now a fifty-four-year-old woman with no husband and no money. Although Peter Drooten had been in the insurance business, he had not left a cent of insurance. All his widow had to her name was the house she lived in, the clothes she wore and thirty-two hundred dollars in cash. For a week she wept and refused to eat and wouldn't dress. Barbara and Dick stayed with her, trying to cheer her up and reassure her.

"Everything's going to be all right," said Barbara.

Her mother looked at her and wondered if Peter Drooten's impracticality had been inherited by his daughter. If so, it was the only thing she'd inherited. It made Evangeline cry again.

"Oh, Mama," said Barbara. "Please don't cry. Everything will be all right. It really will." This time Evangeline forced herself to believe her daughter.

"What do you think you'll do?" asked Dick. Mrs. Drooten could have blessed him for his down-to-earth attitude.

"I don't know," said Mrs. Drooten. "I guess I'll have to get a job."

Later that evening, after Mrs. Drooten had gone to her solitary bed, Dick said to Barbara, "I'm going to see to it that you never have to work."

For some reason that she didn't understand, Barbara began to cry for the first time since the funeral. She buried herself in Dick's arms and cried until his shirt was soaked to his chest.

"Don't," said Dick. "I only said that I want to take care of you."

He hadn't meant it as a criticism of her father, but the implication was clear: her father hadn't taken care of her or her mother. Why not? Barbara was sure that he had loved them both, and they had loved him. Peter Drooten just hadn't been very practical, that was all. Barbara blew her nose on the handkerchief that Dick handed her and smiled at him. It made her feel very safe to know that the man she was going to marry wasn't at all like her father.

Barbara was surprised that Dick's parents weren't there to meet them at the Denver airport. It was Christmas vacation and Barbara had flown home with Dick to meet his parents for the first time and she had assumed they'd be as anxious to meet her as she was to meet them.

"It's my father's busy season," said Dick. He guided Barbara quickly through the airport crowds. Crowds disturbed Dick and he was always in a rush to get away from them. Crowds evoked Barbara's curiosity: she wanted to stop and see what was going on. "He doesn't like to take time away from business. It's a short season." Dick's father owned and operated the ski-rental and food concessions at several lodges. He had from October to Easter to earn enough money to support his family for the year. Dick led Barbara to the Hertz counter, where he filled out a form, presented his license and, in return, was given the keys for a blue Dodge.

The scenery on the drive to Aspen was spectacular: a jagged, brutal mountainous contrast to the gentle rolling hills of Dutchess County. Everything was covered with snow, even the branches of the tall pines, and the small, nondescript villages they drove through consisted of a grocery store, post office and gas station all in one wooden shack with a tarred driveway in front.

26

"Do you think your parents will like me?" asked Barbara for the hundredth time.

"Of course. Don't worry about it." Dick paid attention to his driving and Barbara knew better than to pursue the conversation. He disliked speaking while he drove; he said it upset his concentration. Barbara decided to let his parents take the initiative: if they embraced her, she'd embrace them; if they kissed her, she'd kiss them back; and if they shook hands, she'd be contented with that too.

The Rosers' house wasn't visible from the entrance to their driveway, which was unpaved—a dirt road, badly pitted and potholed. When Barbara finally saw the house, she was disappointed, although she didn't know why. She hadn't really expected a Swiss chalet, but the Rosers' house was just an ordinary American house that needed a paint job, just like one you'd see in a suburb of Long Island, Minneapolis or Sacramento.

Barbara followed Dick on the dirt path that led from the parking area to the back door. Through the window, Barbara could see a woman standing at the kitchen sink. Dick opened the door and Barbara went in. She found herself in a short hallway with the kitchen to her left, a living room to her right and a stairway directly in front of her. She waited for Mrs. Roser to say something. She knew that she was expecting her. Just the week before, Barbara had listened while Dick spoke to his mother and told her that he was bringing home a girl. "Someone special, Mom. I'd like you and Dad to meet her." But the woman didn't move from in front of the sink, and Barbara wondered why Mrs. Roser wasn't as interested in her as she was in Mrs. Roser.

"Hi, Mom," said Dick. He put his arm around her, but Barbara noticed that mother and son didn't kiss. "This is Barbara. The girl I mentioned."

"How do you do?" said Mrs. Roser. The sink was filled with water and potatoes. Some of them were peeled and some were unpeeled. Mrs. Roser went on, using the small metal potato peeler. Barbara wondered how she could see what she was doing; it was after five and the kitchen was dark.

"Hello, Mrs. Roser. I've been looking forward to meeting you. Dick has told me so much about you."

"I'd shake hands," said Mrs. Roser, "but they're wet." She indicated her hands still in the sink, peeling potatoes underwater.

At least she wanted to shake hands. At least she didn't hate her on sight. Barbara stood there not knowing what to do with herself, feeling awkward in the Dalton dyed-to-match sweater and skirt she'd bought especially for the occasion.

"You ought to put the lights on," said Dick, doing so. The room was small and practical, with a linoleum floor that was old and worn but spotlessly polished. The refrigerator was the old-fashioned kind with the coil on top, and the stove was a large, black wood-burning model. Barbara had never seen one like it except in New England antique stores.

"We were five minutes ahead of time," said Dick. "Must have had some good tail winds for a change."

"That's good," said Mrs. Roser. Now that the lights were on, Barbara could see her gray hair twisted into a practical knot, the cheap printed cotton housedress she wore and the neatly darned brown cardigan sweater. She felt a moment of deep pity for her: she seemed to be so worn down by life. Barbara knew about her other son, Dick's elder brother, Bud—about how much hope she had had in him, and about how those hopes had been so abruptly ended when he died in a place she had never heard of called Pork Chop Hill.

"I've never seen anyone peel potatoes that way," said Barbara.

"Stops 'em from turning brown," said Mrs. Roser.

"Where's Dad?" asked Dick.

"Out at Number Two Lodge," said his mother. Barbara felt hurt because Mr. Roser evidently hadn't considered her important enough to come home early for, but she pushed the feeling aside. Dick had warned her that his family was undemonstrative.

"How's business this year?"

"Too early to tell," said Mrs. Roser, filling a large enamel pot with cold water and putting all the peeled potatoes into it. "Now they'll stay nice and white till suppertime."

"Can I help with anything?" asked Barbara.

"You could set the table. Dick, show her where things are." Mrs. Roser turned to Barbara and for the first time looked directly at her, meeting her eyes, and she smiled.

Barbara laid the tinny, unmatching knives and forks on the bare table with military precision. She folded the paper napkins and put them to the left of the forks and, finally, she arranged glasses, the kind that gas stations gave out as premiums, along the top edges of the knives.

"There's your father now," said Mrs. Roser. Dick looked out the kitchen window and so did Barbara. She couldn't believe her eyes, but the car he was getting out of was a light blue four-door Cadillac.

Christmas week the pretty town of Aspen glittered and twinkled around them. Every time Barbara wished that she could put on a long skirt and a cashmere sweater and have drinks with Dick in front of a roaring fire at one of the inns, she sternly put the thought aside. Instead, she spent her time with Dick's parents. His mother was a woman who rarely spoke and never showed emotion. Barbara felt constantly ill at ease with her and much preferred Alex Roser—who, at least, talked. He explained his inventory systems to her, told her how the customers had no respect for the equipment they rented and returned it in pitiful condition and complained about the college students he was forced to hire to staff his various businesses.

"None of them want to give an honest day's work for an honest day's pay," he said, and Barbara nodded agreement while Dick looked blank. Business bored him, he said; only the certainties of engineering satisfied him. Either a system worked or it didn't—there were no fancy accounting theories to play with, no dishonest employees to keep an eye on, no unreliable weather to ruin a whole season's profits.

"He never did have a business head," said Mr. Roser. "Too

bad—" and he stopped his sentence short. Barbara wondered if he was going to add something about Dick's brother, Bud, but he said nothing more.

"The world needs engineers too," said Dick in his own defense.

"I suppose so," said Mr. Roser, who didn't seem convinced.

Barbara spent a whole week trying to make Dick's parents like her. She felt that she failed with his mother. Mrs. Roser was a devout Mormon. She didn't believe in drinking, dancing, reading fiction or going to the movies. The reason the house was always so dark was that Mrs. Roser also didn't believe in waste. It was a sin, she said.

Alex Roser, on the other hand, was opinionated, lively and responsive. He was an outspoken atheist, equally contemptuous of Catholics, Jews, Protestants and Mormons.

"Religion's for stupid people. It keeps them down and the churches get rich," he'd say. *His* religion seemed to be money. He added up the day's receipts every night after dinner, and it never seemed that business was as good as Alex Roser thought it ought to be. Between the dishonest and incompetent college help and the voracious appetites of the IRS, Alex Roser said, life was a struggle to survive.

Barbara was drawn to Alex Roser's energy, and she was even interested in his business. He made it into an action-packed entertainment filled with victories and defeats, hated enemies and loyal friends. It was a soap opera with a cast of thousands, of whom Alex himself was the main character. Ultimately—and ironically—Alex Roser would have more influence on Barbara's life than Dick himself. But that was for the future. . . .

"If I had the nerve I wouldn't pay any of the sons of bitches," he said, referring to the Federal income taxes. "Goddam country is run by Commies anyway."

"Alex, your language," Mrs. Roser would say.

"My language is my own business."

"It's the Lord's business too."

Alex and Sarah Roser seemed to share little except a belief in hard work and the importance of frugality. Sarah Roser washed, scrubbed, bleached, scoured, polished and cooked from early in the morning to the time she went to bed. She showed Barbara with pride the subcellar whose shelves were lined with the corn, watermelon pickle, beets and limas that she had canned at the end of summer when produce was plentiful and cheap.

"Do you think they like me?" asked Barbara as soon as she and Dick got back into the rented Dodge and drove away down the rutted driveway. She was positive that Mr. Roser did; she was less sure about Dick's mother.

"They like you," said Dick.

"How do you know?" Barbara yearned for proof, for something concrete.

"I know." Dick was being evasive. It was very unlike him.

"Is it a surprise?"

Dick's smile told her everything.

"When will I find out?"

"Soon enough."

"Meanie," said Barbara. She moved over on the front seat and put her left hand on his right thigh and wondered what the Rosers had said or done.

There was nothing about Dick Roser that Evangeline Drooten could complain about: he was obviously in love with her daughter; he was sensible and sensitive; he had graduated from Harvard with honors; he would certainly have a good financial future. Dick Roser was everything a woman could wish for in a son-in-law.

Yet Evangeline was troubled. He was so staid. And although she hated to admit it, she thought her daughter staid too. They acted like a couple who'd been married for forty years. They were content to watch television every night after dinner; one evening they played bridge with another engaged couple; one night they took Mrs. Drooten to see *Around the World in 80 Days*. She wondered whether they ever had any fun.

Her husband's death had changed Evangeline tremendously. She had learned how to run Peter Drooten's business. In the beginning, she did it because she had no choice: she needed to support herself and decided to learn about real estate and insurance rather than work in the local Woolworth's. It didn't take long for her to discover that she not only liked working but was good at it. She was good at selling properties to hesitant buyers, and she found out that selling the insurance to go along with the house and grounds took almost no additional work. Within half a year she earned as much as her husband had in the whole year before his death.

She bought new clothes, she had her kitchen remodeled and she could even recall the happy moments of her marriage without crying. She particularly liked to remember the days when Peter had courted her: it was in the early twenties and they had necked in the open Duesenberg touring car that Peter's father had given Peter for his twenty-first birthday. They had put the top down on a bitter November night to see the harvest moon and had paid for their pleasure with colds bad enough to pass for pneumonia. She also remembered how they had drunk champagne at parties and awakened with headaches and how they had learned to Charleston with just enough Prohibition gin in them not to feel stupid. She remembered crepe-de-chine underwear and Chypre perfume by Coty and that it had all been a lot of fun.

Every time she saw Dick and Barbara together, their seriousness disturbed her. But she said nothing. After all, she had grown up in the Jazz Age and times had changed. The fifties was the era of Togetherness.

"My mother gave it to me to give to you," said Dick. Dick and Barbara and her mother were still at the dinner table when Dick pulled the small, tissue-wrapped packet out of his jacket pocket. Barbara opened it and began to weep when she saw the two-carat diamond sparkling in its simple Tiffany setting. Her hands were shaking as Dick helped her put it on. Third finger, left hand.

"That's how you knew she liked me?"

"When she gave it to me she said to tell you that she hopes you and I will be as happy as she and my father are."

"I hope so too." Barbara sniffled. Not only was she now engaged, but her new parents-in-law approved of her. She held her left hand away from her so that she could admire her ring from the same distance a stranger would. Then she held it up to her mother.

"It's just beautiful," said Evangeline Drooten. And it was. A perfect, flaw-free blue-white diamond. "It was very touching of your mother."

"It's hard for her to say things in words," said Dick, who was unaware that he shared the same quality. Unspoken gestures were easier for him too.

"I love you," said Barbara, and kissed him in front of her mother.

In the course of that night Barbara woke up several times and switched her light on. She took off the ring and held it directly under the bulb so that the colors—red, yellow, blue, green—flashed and twirled in sequence as she turned the stone. She kissed it and put it back on. It felt so heavy on her finger. She wondered if she'd ever get used to the feeling. She hoped not: it was too precious ever to take for granted.

So enchanted was Barbara with her own happiness that she never stopped to wonder what Sarah Roser's definition of a happy marriage might be. Nor did she even wonder how a woman like Sarah Roser, whose life was predicated on self-denial, had acquired such an expensive diamond ring.

"We can now. Now that you have your ring." It was nine o'clock on the Tuesday after New Year's. Milton Berle's Texaco show had just gone off the air and Dick and Barbara were alone in the living room. He put his left arm around Barbara and he stroked the diamond with his right index finger. While Uncle Miltie had dressed up in women's clothes and mugged outrageously, Barbara and Dick had been petting heavily. Barbara's blouse was unbuttoned and her skirt was pushed up to the top of her thighs. It was lumpy under her bottom and the crotch of her panties was pulled to one side. She was uncomfortable, but she hadn't noticed until Dick spoke.

"I know," said Barbara. Long ago, in the Wellesley dorm, she and her friends had agreed that it was OK to go all the way as long as you were engaged. Still, the prospect made Barbara's heart skitter. Once you Did It, Went All the Way, it was irrevocable. There was no going back. It was the most important decision Barbara had ever had to make—more important, even, than the decision to marry Dick. That could always be changed: engagements were made to be broken.

"I love you," said Dick. "I want you."

"Are you sure it's OK? Really OK?"

"Of course."

If Dick said it was all right, then Barbara believed him. He had never yet lied to her; she knew he never would.

"Let's," said Dick. He kissed her, opening her mouth with his tongue, resuming the petting where they had left off. Barbara lost herself in the kiss and in the stroking of her breasts. She lost herself in sensation, and when the time came she didn't have to say anything. Her legs opened by themselves. She helped Dick remove her panties by lifting her hips at the right time. When he inserted his penis in her, she wasn't sure whether or not it was really in. She touched the juncture of her body and his to make sure that he had really penetrated her. It surprised her that his penis didn't feel any different from the way his fingers had. In fact, it was smaller and didn't reach all the way to her cervix. And yet, this was It. She was a woman now. She had gone all the way.

"Don't worry," said Dick. He withdrew his penis, and Barbara felt angry and empty. "I've got something," he said. He tore the aluminum-foil packet of the rubber with his teeth and Barbara lay back and shut her eyes, trying to maintain the mood, while he slipped the Trojan on. Then he eased himself back into her and began to move. At first the rubber was too dry, and then it became slippery with the remnants of her passion. There was no difference to Barbara, rubber or no rubber; she appreciated Dick's thoughtfulness, she knew he had been thinking of her, but the interruption had broken the spell. She faked it while Dick finished.

2 MRS. RICHARD ROSER.
Barbara Roser.

Barbara loved her new name and practiced different ways of writing it. She couldn't decide between a tailored printing and a flourished scrawl, and when she wrote checks she had to stop and think which signature she had given the bank. She ordered printed stationery and used it to thank people for her wedding gifts and even to order sheets, towels and bath mats from Altman's.

Although Barbara hadn't planned it that way, she was the first girl in her class to become a Mrs. when she and Dick got married Thanksgiving of 1957.

"How many children are you going to have?" asked Toby Griffith just before classes broke for the four-day Thanksgiving holiday. Barbara was packing to leave Wellesley forever and Toby was sitting cross-legged on Barbara's bed.

"Four," said Barbara. "I'm an only child and I'm dying for a houseful. I always wanted a brother or a sister." Barbara had never asked her mother why she had never had more children. She was afraid that she already knew: children were an expense and an inconvenience and her parents could afford neither.

"Four is a good number. I want four too. I don't think I could cope with five, and three is icky. An odd number—you know what I mean?" Toby was polishing her engagement ring on the Stewart tartan skirt she wore. Barbara wondered if Toby would wear out her ring, but so far it showed no signs of overattention.

"We're going to start right away, too. It's nice to be young when your children are young," said Barbara, snapping shut the second suitcase. She really didn't know that for a fact, but the authorities—*McCall's,* the Sunday *Times Magazine*'s child-care section and Dr. Spock—all seemed to agree that young mothers made the best mothers. "This is the last time I'm packing as a Miss," she said. "Do you realize that the next time I pack it will be for my honeymoon?"

"Oh, you're so lucky!" Toby positively squealed.

Barbara and Dick got married in the small Dutch Reformed Church in Pawling on the Friday after Thanksgiving. Barbara wore a long white gown, and even though she wasn't technically a virgin she felt that she wasn't really cheating because she had saved herself for her husband and her husband only. The fact that they had jumped the date by several months was incidental in the face of her love and her commitment. After the wedding, Barbara and Dick drove to Manhattan for a short honeymoon and Evangeline Drooten drove the Rosers to Idlewild for the flight back to Denver.

"Your son is a lovely boy," said Evangeline.

"A ten-thousand-dollar-a-year man," said Alex Roser. He had always thought that Dick was the impractical one while his brother had had the business head. Showed how wrong a man could be. . . . "Wasn't that way when I started out. No, sir."

Evangeline didn't tell the Rosers that she and Peter Drooten had started out rich. That when she was twenty-three she had had mink jackets and that she and her husband had crossed first class on the *Ile de France* for their honeymoon. Peter's father had left his son not only a going business but a cash inheritance of two hundred and fifty thousand dollars. Evangeline Drooten also didn't say that when the two hundred and fifty thousand dollars was gone in vintage champagne and mink jackets and shiny touring cars, Peter Drooten hadn't known what to do. They were equal now, Evangeline supposed. Average Americans with average incomes.

Alex Roser, in his turn, didn't tell Evangeline Drooten, nor had he told anyone, excepting his lawyer, that he was now worth one and one-half million dollars. When Dick's brother had died, he had rewritten his will . . . oh, well, what the hell. He liked his new daughter-in-law. Maybe he'd rewrite it again. It was no one's goddam business. The main problem was keeping it out of the hands of the IRS.

The new in-laws smiled at each other, saying goodbye at the American Airlines terminal. They had done their share —raised, fed and educated their children—and done a good job of it. From now on, it was up to Dick and Barbara.

When Barbara and Dick arrived in New York, they checked into the Plaza and spent their wedding night making love and drinking a bottle of Mumm's champagne which had cost Dick thirty-five dollars from Room Service. On Saturday night they had dinner at the Chambord and saw *My Fair Lady*. They both loved it and, later on, when Audrey Hepburn was picked over Julie Andrews to play Liza in the movie version, they both thought it terribly unfair.

After a day and a half of indulgence, love and champagne, they began to look for an apartment. Since McLaughlin's offices were on Pine Street, the Village was the obvious place to live. But 1957 was a bad year for apartments. There had been little building in New York in the early fifties, and finding a place to live was depressing and expensive. After looking longingly at a large three-and-a-half room apartment at Number Two Fifth Avenue which cost two hundred and seventy-five dollars a month, they settled on a much smaller three-and-a-half in a brand-new building on West Tenth Street. Its rent was a hundred and ninety dollars a month, its walls were paper-thin, its view was of a barren courtyard —but it was the best they could do, and Barbara thought that with clever decorating it would be a pleasant place to

37

live until after her first child was born. They signed the two-year lease on the Monday after they were married and moved in on Tuesday.

There was no furniture at all, and so they ate Chinese food from cartons and slept on blankets. That first night, they made love on the floor.

"I'm buying a bed first thing tomorrow," said Barbara. "This is murder on my back." They laughed, made love again and fell asleep in each other's arms.

The honeymoon was over. Real life was beginning, and Barbara couldn't wait.

Barbara's mother and the Rosers had each given them a thousand dollars as a wedding gift. While Dick went to the office, Barbara spent her days in Macy's and Altman's buying dishes and kitchen equipment, eyeing the Village antique and secondhand shops for furniture and learning to cook and keep house. Every Thursday she read Craig Claiborne, and she learned to use a whisk instead of an eggbeater, that cheese should always be served at room temperature and that roast beef came out browner if you used the high-temperature roasting method.

She liked setting the table, cooking, polishing the silver her mother had given her, seeing to it that Dick always had enough shirts and socks and that his suits and ties went regularly to the cleaner. She hated cleaning the oven, defrosting the refrigerator, using Ajax in the bathtub and changing the bed. When she complained about it, Dick pointed out that while he enjoyed drawing blueprints, he disliked budget meetings and that while it was possible to talk to other engineers, the P.R. people drove him up the wall. It was all part of the job. Barbara stopped complaining and thought for the millionth time how lucky she was to be married to someone with such a calm perspective on life.

Another thing Dick liked about his job was his boss: Commander Edward Stilson.

"He's just like an officer in a movie," said Dick. "White hair and a dark suntan. You'll think he's sexy. You know, he got the Silver Star with an oak-leaf cluster for his service during World War Two."

"Oak-leaf clusters are sexy," said Barbara. "Never could resist them."

"You'd better," warned Dick, pulling her out of the kitchenette, where she was washing salad greens. "Or I'll spank you. You belong to me. Private Property. No Trespassing."

Now they were on the bed and Barbara had completely forgotten that sometimes—and she hated to admit it, even to herself—she felt that Dick was more married to McLaughlin than he was to her.

"Operator? I want to place a person-to-person call. To Mr. Richard Roser." Barbara gave the Annapolis number Dick had left with her. He was at the Naval Academy for consultations for work that McLaughlin was performing for the Navy. Barbara was in a phone booth in the Schrafft's on Seventy-seventh Street in the Parke-Bernet building. It was a bitter, sleety day, January 5, 1958. Eisenhower was just starting the second year of his second term, *Dragnet* was still going strong on NBC and Liz Taylor, according to the movie magazines, had found true love with Mike Todd. It took ages for the operator to place the call. Despite the cold, Barbara was hot and flushed with excitement. Finally, a male voice, blurred and indistinct, answered.

"Richard Roser?" asked the operator, spelling out the Roser, just the way Barbara had.

"Dick?"

"I am sorry," said the operator's mechanical, wind-up voice, "but on a person-to-person call you are not permitted to speak until the party has been located."

Barbara knew the rule, but she hadn't been able to contain herself. Where was Dick and why didn't he hurry?

"Hello?" he finally said.

"I love you," said Barbara. She hadn't planned it. It just came out that way.

There was silence on Dick's end.

"I love you," said Barbara again, "and our baby loves you."

It took a second for it to sink in. "You're pregnant. That's great! When?"

"July. I just got the test back from the doctor. I didn't want to say anything until I was positive."

"July? That's just great!" Dick was delighted. He was looking forward to being a father. More than he had ever looked forward to anything, even marriage. But of course he had never told Barbara that. He was afraid that she would take it the wrong way.

"Do you care if it's a boy or a girl?"

"As long as it's healthy," said Dick, although he hoped it would be a son. Every man wanted to have a son. It was only natural.

"Sometimes I think I want a boy and sometimes I think I want a girl. I can't decide," said Barbara.

"You won't have to," Dick pointed out.

Barbara laughed and relaxed for the first time that day. Then she thought of something.

"Will you still love me when I'm fat and have a big stomach?"

"More than ever."

Barbara's mother was happy about her daughter's pregnancy, although she privately wondered why Barbara and Dick wanted to tie themselves down so soon. The Rosers also seemed to be happy, but they were so far away that they didn't seem very real. Barbara wondered how they'd react to a grandchild. It would be their first.

While she waited for July, Barbara called the Salvation Army and had them pick up the dinette table and four teak chairs that she'd bought at Bon Marché. Now that the one-half room was empty, Barbara began to furnish it for her baby. Her mother gave her the crib and high chair she herself had used as a child. She purchased a bassinette from Macy's and a cabinet from a medical-supply house with a lot of drawers and a flat top for changing the infant. She stocked up on diapers, Q-Tips, cotton balls, undershirts, flannel sleeping suits, a baby scale, an infant's thermometer, a sterilizer and two dozen bottles with nursing nipples. Barbara wasn't planning to breast-feed, no matter how healthy and natural the doctors said it was. She had heard from a friend that it could hurt and that sometimes the baby even bit your nipple.

Barbara read Dr. Spock, and she practically memorized a pamphlet her doctor had given her called "Healthy Motherhood." She watched her belly grow and her breasts swell and was overwhelmed with love every time the baby kicked. Big blue veins appeared on her breasts in the last months of her pregnancy and she was worried that Dick would find them ugly. She was wrong.

When she asked him about it, he traced the path of a vein with his tongue. "I told you," he said, "that I would love you more than ever when you were pregnant."

"I love you more now too. Doesn't that seem just crazy?"

"Crazy but true," said Dick.

"Maybe I'll stay pregnant forever."

"I won't object."

Up until the last three weeks of her pregnancy when it got too cumbersome, they made love every single night. Barbara had never felt such intense sexual desire. She couldn't get enough.

"I'm turning into a nymphomaniac," she told Dick one night, when they were sweaty and tired, their arms and legs wrapped around each other on the wrinkled sheets.

"That's what I always wanted," said Dick.

"A nymphomaniac?"

"A pregnant nymphomaniac." And they began the act of love all over again.

Barbara's labor pains began at eleven on the morning of July 10. That evening at six-thirty Barbara gave birth to a little girl. She had had a spinal block, but she was conscious at the moment of birth and heard her baby's very first cry. She held out her arms, and the doctor, after swabbing out the infant's eyes, noticed.

"You can't hold her now. She has to go into the nursery for identification."

Barbara felt a sharp disappointment, but it lasted only a second and then the euphoria swept over her. She was a woman—she had given birth. She had justified her existence.

"You're a good girl," said the doctor. He patted Barbara on her exposed behind and checked his watch. "Plenty of time to make the eight-thirty curtain. My wife and I are going to catch Robert Preston in *The Music Man*. I wish my other girls were as considerate as you."

Barbara smiled at him. It made her feel good that she hadn't caused him trouble. Her father had always been so pleased when she was neat and obedient.

Barbara had been worried about postpartum depression. She had asked her mother about it.

"We didn't have it in my day," said Evangeline. "But, of course, in my day we had nannies and nursemaids."

They both knew that Evangeline's experiences didn't apply to her daughter.

Barbara then asked Toby, who had just had twins.

"Postpartum depression? Are you kidding? With twins you don't have the time."

As it turned out, Barbara's apprehension was unfounded. Rather, she felt like an Olympic athlete in the peak of condition who had just won a gold medal and now, still strong and fit, gloried in the victory.

Annette was an adorable child. Pink and cuddly and smily. She had alert blue eyes and seemed to smile from the moment Barbara first took her in her arms. The books had warned that the new father might show signs of jealousy toward the infant, but Dick seemed as fascinated by Annette as Barbara was. He even forgot that he would have preferred a son—there was always time later for a boy. Meanwhile, he took movies and photographs and sent his parents air fare to New York so that he could show off his new daughter.

Alex and Sarah Roser were transformed by Annette. They hugged her and kissed her and even Mr. Roser cooed baby talk to her. It was the first time since Bud died that either of them had given expression to emotion, and it poured forth in waves. When it was time for them to return to Aspen, they not only returned the air fare to Dick but left a thousand-dollar check with Barbara and Dick "just to help out."

The books had also warned that a new father might be less sexually interested in his wife than usual. The opposite was true of Dick. He seemed more in love with Barbara than ever, and she was in absolute awe of his penis because it had the power to give her such a wonderful gift as Annette.

They decided to have another baby just as soon as possible.

In 1958 the space race began in earnest. The Soviets were far ahead with three Sputniks and the space dog, Laika. The next thing, there'd be a Russian on the moon. The resulting competition caused a sharp increase in appropriations for space exploration and for national defense. McLaughlin received a number of large Navy contracts and Dick Roser shuttled to and from the Pentagon with regularity. In fact, he was there, attending a Top Secret lecture on spy planes and overflights, when Barbara called to say that she was pregnant again. Dick told her that it was wonderful and that he had to get back to the lecture, and he crossed his fingers and wished for a son.

In the spring of 1959, the Rosers moved to a six-room rent-controlled apartment just off Gramercy Park. A fifteen-dollar bribe to the super got them a key to the park. It had decorative iron gates, and its green plantings were carefully planned by gardeners hired by the Gramercy Park Association. It was peaceful, English and elegant. Barbara was happy to say goodbye to Washington Square Park with the old men playing perpetual games of chess and the winos sleeping it off on the benches. The difference between the two parks was a perfect symbol of the upward mobility the Rosers experienced as the economic climate at the end of the fifties soared.

Even though Barbara obeyed her doctor's instruction just as carefully during her second pregnancy as she had during her first, she had morning sickness. She discovered that eating a Jacob's Water Biscuit before arising controlled it. During the seventh month of her pregnancy, large purple veins began to throb in her legs and made walking Annette's carriage to the park a painful experience. Even standing hurt. She complained to her doctor.

"Don't worry," he said. "It often happens the second time around."

"But the books recommend having your babies close together. That way the children don't experience sibling rivalry. They look on each other as allies, not enemies."

The doctor smiled. "They're absolutely right from a psychological point of view. But sometimes carrying the second baby causes excessive physical strain. I wouldn't worry. Lots of women have varicose veins. It's something to be proud of."

This time it was Barbara's turn to smile. The doctor had said exactly what the books did. Except, said part of Barbara's mind, what was she going to do in the summer, when her legs would be exposed on the beach? Another part of her mind reassured her that Covermark would make everything just fine.

"Sometimes," said the doctor, "the varicosity goes away spontaneously after the delivery."

Barbara left his office certain that that was what would happen to her: her veins would disappear by themselves.

When her pains began, Barbara went right to the hospital. But she stayed in labor two and one-half days before, finally, on July 13, 1959, she delivered a son. She was exhausted and unconscious at the moment of birth. She had bled so heavily that she required two transfusions. There was no medical reason for the difficult delivery.

"Sometimes it's just like that. No reason that we can see. Nothing wrong that we know of," said her doctor on the day she was to be released. "It's nothing to worry about."

He patted her, on the shoulder this time, and left her room with a joke about seeing her next year, same time, same place. Barbara dredged up a wan smile.

She felt so wobbly that when she left the hospital, Dick had to carry his son, named Christiaan after Evangeline's father; hail the taxi with his free hand and help Barbara in. The Gramercy Park apartment was more than twice the size of the old one and each child had its own room. Yet Barbara, as soon as she got home with her new baby, began to have fearful attacks of claustrophobia. She felt that the walls were closing in on her, crushing her, taking away her oxygen. She would ring for the elevator and, impatient and overwrought because it hadn't reached the eighth floor quickly enough, run down the stairs and through the lobby and out into the street, where at least there were no walls. She couldn't stand being at home and she couldn't leave, and the reason was Christiaan.

He had colic. He cried and whimpered all night long. He threw up his food. There was a stale smell of baby vomit clinging to the apartment that wouldn't go away no matter how much Barbara washed and scrubbed and disinfected. In the daytime, if the weather was nice, she could escape to the park, but at night she was trapped. Somehow, Dick slept through it all. Not Barbara. She heard every cry. She tried to rock him, to croon to him, to sing lullabies to him. Once she even masturbated him because she had read that it was a common practice among illiterate Victorian nursemaids. But nothing helped. Christiaan wailed and fretted. It affected Annette, who turned from a winsome child into a fretful whining monster, shrieking when Barbara paid more attention to Christiaan than to her. If she ignored him, he cried, and if she tried to calm him, he cried. The whole time Annette, who was beginning to toddle, would sit on the floor and pull at Barbara's ankles demanding affection. If she didn't get it immediately, she began to scream.

This time when the Rosers came to see their new grandson, they said all the polite things. They tried to share their time equally between their new grandson and their granddaughter, but Barbara noticed that they played much more with Annette than with Christiaan. She also noticed that when they left, there was no thousand-dollar check. She was too depressed even to mention it to Dick.

Barbara began to think seriously that she was losing her mind. Her claustrophobic attacks got worse, and she couldn't remember what it was like to have a normal night's sleep. She was haggard from too much weight loss and she had dark circles under her eyes. She snapped at Dick for no reason and had no interest at all in sex of any kind. Sometimes, when she lay tossing and turning, trying not to hear Christiaan fretting and mewling, she could feel the bed move and she knew that Dick was masturbating. She didn't care. She couldn't help it. She was sorry, but she couldn't help it.

The wiring of the building was too old for air conditioning, and the heat and humidity increased Barbara's sense of confinement. She wished that Christiaan were dead. Several times she put him to sleep on a table that she had pulled near the open window and left the apartment to go to the A&P. She hoped that he would accidentally fall out the eighth-story window and die. But just as she reached the street, the guilt would guillotine her and she would run up all seven flights of the dark back stairs with the steel risers, hoping not to trip, and would open the door and snatch Christiaan off the table. She'd hug and kiss him despite his sour vomity smell. He'd cry and thrash, and not even her guilt made him better.

Barbara's doctor told her not to worry. He told her that colicky babies always outgrew it. It was just a matter of time.

Hot and humid July and August dragged by, one endless day after another. Dick was obsessed with designing a new hydraulic system for nuclear submarines. Barbara was obsessed with the fear that her life was over before it had really begun.

"Maybe it's the city," said Dick one evening. "Maybe we ought to think about moving to the suburbs."

Dick was in the living room while Barbara was washing the bottles and sterilizing the nipples in the stuffy kitchen. One of the advantages of having your babies close together, said the books, was that you would economize by using the same equipment for both children. They hadn't referred to the number of times the same washing and drying and sterilizing had to be repeated.

"The Stilsons love it in Westport. Maybe you wouldn't feel so shut in in the suburbs." Dick was trying to be helpful. Barbara had described her claustrophobia to him. She realized that he thought the cure was as simple as a change of locale.

"We can't afford Westport." McLaughlin was now paying Dick fourteen thousand dollars a year. It was a good salary but not enough for a place like Westport.

"What about Long Island? One of the guys I work with just bought a nice place in Nassau County."

"You mean Levittown?" Barbara tried to keep the conversation on the reasonable level that Dick preferred; inside there were visions of infanticide and suicide, devastation and destruction. "And be an identical family in an identical house?" She had so often laughed at the snide *New Yorker* cartoons of men arriving home at night not knowing which house was theirs. Her laugh sounded like a madwoman's.

"Well, not Levittown," said Dick. He was on guard now. Her laugh had given her away. "Something nicer. Green. With trees. The children could play in our yard. You wouldn't have to go to the park."

He was trying to make her life more bearable. He had just taken away the one thing that did make it bearable.

"I like the park," she said, her laughing fit over, her voice, like the rest of her, dead.

"At McLaughlin they approve of the suburbs. They believe McLaughlin families should have all the advantages—"

Barbara's dead voice had fooled Dick into thinking the Alert was over. Suddenly becoming aware of the sounds he was hearing, he stopped in mid-sentence and went into the kitchen. Every baby bottle was smashed on the kitchen floor. Shards of glass glittered in the fluorescent light and Barbara was sitting on the floor sifting the broken glass through her fingers. She looked up when Dick came in. Two slow tears ran from her eyes.

"Would you mind cleaning it up?" she asked quietly. She brushed a strand of hair away from her forehead and left a sticky blood mark where she had cut her palm.

"I'm sorry," she said. "All I want to do is go to sleep."

He watched his wife make her way through the living room and wondered what was going on. He got the dustpan and brush out of the broom closet and began to sweep up the glass.

Dick was spending the third week of October in Montauk. McLaughlin was having a "think session" and, in order to assist its employees in thinking more effectively, McLaughlin had decided to sequester them at Gurney's Inn for a week.

"Why don't you join me?" said Dick on the phone. "Come out on Friday night and I'll take the next week off." It was the first conversation about anything other than necessities that Dick had initiated with Barbara since the broken-bottles incident. He was afraid of her; he thought she was unstable and didn't want to risk anything that might push her over the edge. He was also afraid of losing her. Even if she didn't like their life, he did. He loved his routine, he loved his children and he loved his wife.

"What about the kids?"

"Your mother is always asking to see them. Why don't you ask her if she'll take them?"

Evangeline was delighted. She drove into Manhattan on Friday, early in the afternoon. She was wearing an Italian cotton knit shirt and a wraparound denim skirt and she looked very chic and very attractive. When she kissed her daughter hello, Barbara smelled fresh cologne. Barbara couldn't remember the last time she had put on scent.

"I was wondering when you were going to get away," said Evangeline. "The fact is that you look terrible."

Barbara looked down at the faded madras shirt dress she had on. It was left over from college, and it hung on her now since she had lost so much weight. The only makeup she was wearing was a slash of lipstick which only emphasized the gray cast of her skin. Her mother was right.

"I know. I feel terrible. I wish I were going away forever." The words slipped out before Barbara could censor them. Her mother's tenderness and concern had melted her barricades.

"Is everything all right between you and Dick?" It was one of the rare times Evangeline Drooten had allowed herself a personal question. She had always made a point of not prying.

"I don't know. He has his job and I have the children . . ." Barbara didn't care anymore about how she sounded. She had no pride left, no desire to cover up, to show everyone how happy she was.

"But you wanted children so badly."

"I know."

"You must have known that they'd be work."

"I didn't think about it," said Barbara, who was thinking about it for the first time. "I wanted children because everyone wanted children. A big, happy family. Like all those pictures in *McCall's*—Mommy and Daddy and the children always together, always doing things, nice things." Barbara paused. Then she shrugged. "I guess I fell for the propaganda."

"So young, so bitter," said her mother. "Don't give up so easily. Here," said her mother, and handed Barbara two one-hundred-dollar bills. "Fight back. Spend it all on yourself. Buy some new clothes, get a decent haircut. Don't give up without trying." She folded the bills and put them into Barbara's handbag. She wondered what would happen. Her daughter felt her life was falling apart and all she could offer was new clothes and a becoming hairdo.

"Thanks." Barbara fastened the clasp on her bag.

"Seduce Dick," said her mother, spelling it out. "And if you can't seduce him, seduce someone else."

Evangeline took the two babies and closed the door behind her, leaving Barbara alone for a moment before it was time to leave for Penn Station. All she could think about was that her mother was fifty-seven and she was twenty-two.

Only twenty-two.

3 THE SPECIAL LONG ISLAND Rail Road Friday-afternoon coaches had plush-covered swivel armchairs with crisp, starched white cotton headrests. Obsequious waiters served drinks, and the air conditioning made the air dry, odor-free and breathable. Barbara felt sure that Scott and Zelda Fitzgerald had traveled like this. She had two gin-and-tonics with fresh lime and started the year's biggest best seller, *Exodus*. She thought about her life and decided to follow her mother's advice. Tomorrow, first thing, she would have her hair cut and set. She would act like a wife toward her husband; she would regain a sense of womanliness. She also resolved to think about herself and what she wanted to do with her life. She was too young to let it lurch away on an unguided course. By the time the train reached Montauk, Barbara had decided to meet fate on equal terms.

Dick was there to greet her, and he looked very good—tanned and rested—and Barbara was surprised at how nice-looking he was. They had a civilized dinner with adult conversation about how strange the flag looked with fifty stars now that Alaska and Hawaii were states; they planned to go to the controversial new Guggenheim museum; they decided that one night a week they would hire a baby-sitter and Dick would make a point of getting home early from the office, and they agreed that the movie they most wanted to see was *Hiroshima, Mon Amour*.

Afterward, in the impersonal room, with spotless sheets, a shower that gushed hot water and a long, illuminated mirror over the twin basins, Barbara, unaccustomed to the wine they had had with dinner, stripped off her clothes and announced that she felt like a whore.

"Prove it," said Dick. "Act like one."

"I'll do the best I can," she said, and she did.

It was a week of Indian summer, sunny, unseasonably warm with bright, preautumnal skies. Every day they took long walks along the deserted beaches and every afternoon they went into the old-fashioned ice cream parlor and had double hot-fudge sundaes. Each evening they gorged on lobster or steak or roast beef, and every night they made slow, lascivious love. Everyone who saw them thought they were honeymooners.

"I'm not going back."

They were sitting on a dune, late on Friday afternoon, watching the Atlantic roll onto the shore in long, lazy waves. It was six-thirty, and the sun was just beginning to fall. The warmth of the day still hung in the clean, salt air.

"What I mean is I'm not going back to the way I left. I'm not going back to diapers and Dr. Spock. I'm going to get a job." She held her breath and waited for him to refuse her.

"What about the children?" Dick said carefully. He didn't want to upset her. He didn't want to go back either to the way things had been. But he didn't know how to go forward.

"We'll hire someone."

"I can't afford full-time help." Dick was trying to tie a series of knots into a blade of dune grass.

"I'll have a salary. We can use that."

"You won't clear a nickel."

"So what?"

Barbara looked at him, and then she got up and began to walk along the dune, away from him. He let her go for a moment and then got up and followed her until he, with his longer strides, caught up.

"Honey," he said, "I didn't know you felt so strongly about it."

It turned out that New York wasn't precisely seething with jobs for Wellesley dropouts who had majored in English, couldn't take shorthand and could barely type. Barbara's request for employment was turned down by the house organ of Metropolitan Life, the house organ of Socony Oil, the editor of a quarterly specializing in dance funded by an obscure foundation whose name Barbara never did get straight and by *Look* magazine, where the Personnel staff said they would hire her as a receptionist but then turned her down when they learned that she had to wear reading glasses. They didn't want a girl with glasses to be the first person visitors saw when they got off the elevator at 488 Madison Avenue.

Finally a *New York Times* ad for an editorial assistant led her to the surprisingly unchic offices of *Harper's Bazaar* in an old building at Madison Avenue and Fifty-sixth Street. Her prospective boss was the sportswear editor.

Edith Steinetz was in her fifties. She wore her gray hair pulled back in a severe knot like a ballerina's, tortoiseshell glasses were perched on the tip of her nose and she wore a large, square man's wristwatch. Barbara had never seen a woman wearing a man's watch before and she was very much impressed with the originality. Throughout the interview, Mrs. Steinetz stitched away on a needlepoint cushion cover. She asked Barbara where she came from, commented on the landscape around Pawling and said that "those old barns are divine." She asked Barbara where she had gone to college and told her that the new dean of Wellesley had been a Vassar classmate of her older sister's. She asked Barbara if she had children and if she had a good housekeeper to care for them and finally said that she thought the Gramercy Park Bakery was one of the best in the city. Particularly its rye bread.

She informed Barbara that her duties would consist of helping out at photography sessions, going to cover the market as an assistant and keeping the accessory information straight for the copy department. She concluded by telling Barbara that she liked her and that, if she wanted it, the job was hers.

Barbara thanked her and said, yes, she wanted it and that it sounded like fun.

"Fun, hah!" said Edith Steinetz, clipping off an end of yellow wool. "It's a fucking salt mine."

Hiring someone to care for Christiaan and Annette was harder, it turned out, than getting hired. When Barbara got home from job hunting, she interviewed prospective housekeepers.

She rejected a Puerto Rican woman who smiled constantly but spoke no English; a surly black woman who smelled of gin and tutti-frutti chewing gum; an elderly woman who arrived with a cane and heating pad, explaining that they were for her arthritis; a gorgeous Swedish girl who wanted to be a model but would consider child care until she got established. She asked if she could start at noon, since she stayed out late most nights meeting people who might further her career.

Then there were the people who rejected Barbara: one, the very picture of a British nanny, firm, kind, competent, who asked how many other servants the Rosers employed, since she did only child care and refused to clean, cook, do laundry, take messages or walk dogs; another, a black woman from Barbados with a lilting accent who said that she worked only for families who lived on Fifth Avenue in the Seventies because all her friends did and they met every day at the Seventy-second Street playground. There was also a middle-aged homosexual who seemed pleasant but who informed Barbara that he couldn't possibly work for her since he found the furnishings of her apartment dreary beyond words and he knew that he wouldn't be able to survive in such a depressing atmosphere.

Just when Barbara was beginning to think that she would never be able to organize her life the way she wanted, Vera Souchak appeared. Mrs. Souchak spoke English with a slight accent and explained that although she had been born in Poland of well-to-do farmers, she had been evacuated to England during the war. Her parents and two brothers had disappeared into a German concentration camp, and their farmland had been confiscated for the benefit of the Führer. While in England, she had met and married Pavlov Souchak, a Czech. They had moved to New York, where Mr. Souchak worked for a prestigious custom tailor on Fifty-seventh Street. They had no children of their own and Mrs. Souchak dearly loved them. She had had experience caring for others' children: her previous employer had been a divorced buyer at Bloomingdale's who had since moved to Texas when Neiman-Marcus hired her. She presented excellent letters of reference, and Barbara hired her on the spot for eighty dollars a week—the precise amount of her salary from *Harper's Bazaar*.

Barbara's decision to get a job had been a question of survival. She had never stopped to wonder what other people might think and she was surprised when she discovered that some, like Toby Griffith Wells, were jealous of her. She had lunch with Toby early in the spring of 1960. Toby was hugely pregnant, wearing a two-piece lime green outfit with an accordion-pleated overblouse and a skirt with a hole cut out and an elastic waistband. They met at an inexpensive French restaurant in the West Fifties, just off Fifth, and Toby was fascinated by Barbara's job, by anecdotes about the models and photographers and, most of all, because Barbara could buy designer clothes at wholesale prices.

"It's so glamorous," said Toby. Her apparent envy shocked Barbara. She hadn't planned on making her friend feel bad.

"It's not that glamorous," said Barbara. "I baste a lot of hems and press a lot of skirts. Most of the time it's like being a high-class laundress."

"You don't look like a laundress." Toby admired Barbara's Donald Brooks dress and her newly bouffant hairdo. "How are the twins?"

"Terrible two. Just like the books said."

They ran out of conversation. Toby didn't want to tell Barbara that her husband, now an account exec at BBD&O, had confessed to having an affair with his secretary and that the baby-to-be was a gesture at reconciliation. Barbara didn't want to tell Toby that she felt guilty because she loved leaving the apartment and her children every morning. She was worried because her children were, in essence, being brought up by a stranger, and she devoured every magazine article by a psychologist that said it was the quality of time a parent spent with a child rather than the quantity that mattered.

Barbara and Toby said good-bye out on the sidewalk, and although neither admitted it, both knew that despite their vague promises to "do this again soon," they wouldn't. Argyle socks, all-night bridge games and diamond engagement rings were too far in the past, and the reality of each one's present was too worrisome a secret to be confided.

Evangeline Drooten was amazed by her daughter's capability. She was impressed by the fact that Barbara still served fresh vegetables instead of frozen, and she was relieved that Barbara's air of desperation had disappeared.

"I don't see how you do it, but I'm very impressed," her mother said.

"I'll tell you my secret: I have lists. Grocery lists, chore lists, job lists, children lists, shopping lists. I even have lists of lists." Mother and daughter both laughed, and Evangeline Drooten wondered how long Barbara could keep up her hectic schedule.

In July of 1960, in their slow season, Alex and Sarah Roser came East for their yearly visit to their grandchildren. Barbara was afraid that they would disapprove of the frivolous nature of her work; but on the contrary, Sarah Roser and Vera Souchak found a lot to talk about, and Alex Roser was full of unsolicited advice about how Barbara should manipulate her boss to get her job plus a raise and a better title.

"What are you going to do if you have more babies?" Sarah Roser wanted to know.

Barbara was taken off guard by the question. She had forgotten that she and Dick had promised his parents four grandchildren just after Annette was born, and so she evaded the question. She didn't know how to tell her mother-in-law that she wasn't going to have any more. The fact was that she hadn't even told Dick—the subject had never come up.

Alex Roser was full of confidence. "Next time I see you, you'll be a vice-president," he said and, for the first time, kissed Barbara. Sarah Roser followed and Barbara felt real affection for her in-laws. They had begun to come alive when Annette was born, and now that Barbara had her own career they seemed even more involved. Barbara kissed them both good-bye and for the first time in her marriage she looked forward to their next visit.

The only person who was unaffected by Barbara's job was her husband. She planned it that way, because the only condition he had imposed was that her job in no way affect their marriage. Barbara made a point of getting home before Dick did. She straightened up after Vera Souchak, who invariably left a trail of candy wrappers and magazines; put on fresh makeup; started dinner and had a Scotch-and-water ready when Dick walked in the door. As far as he was concerned, Barbara had been at home all day, waiting for him, and he was satisfied again with his marriage.

He didn't know it and neither did Barbara, but their whole life was fiction—carefully planned and strenuously maintained, but nevertheless fiction. They were living in never-never land.

Time in never-never land sped by. John F. Kennedy was elected and his wife conquered Vienna and Premier Khrushchev, while his children, Caroline and John-John, captured the fancy of the nation. The Peace Corps was created and the Bay of Pigs was an unmitigated disaster. Pablo Casals played at the White House and Marilyn Monroe died of a combination of pills and alcohol with a telephone in her hand.

Dick Roser got regular promotions at McLaughlin, and if dinners with the Stilsons were a drag, they were part of the job and Barbara accompanied her husband gladly, happy to be able to meet her obligations as a wife.

She worked for Edith Steinetz and was fascinated by her. Edith knew how to turn a gum-chewing semiliterate teenager from the Bronx into a goddess for an afternoon photography session, and she knew what angle made a twenty-dollar dress look like a two-hundred-dollar creation. She knew immediately whether different makeup, hair or underwear was needed to make a color page jump. The whole time she worked her wonders, she stitched away at her needlepoint, barely looking up at the activity she set in motion.

Barbara was mesmerized by her and copied her. She bought the same kind of T-strap sandals that Edith Steinetz wore every day; she bought a man's wristwatch and pulled her hair back into a severe ballerina's knot. She copied Mrs. Steinetz' clipped, idiosyncratic way of speaking and never noticed that Edith Steinetz never spoke of family, children, friends or any life outside the confines of *Harper's Bazaar*. When Barbara heard from another editor that Edith Steinetz had been divorced for seventeen years and was rumored to be a lesbian, Barbara refused to believe it. She continued trying to absorb Edith Steinetz' identity until the day she left *Harper's Bazaar* for a better job as film acquisitions editor for Charter Books, a paperback company.

Edith Steinetz said she was sorry to see Barbara leave but that she had expected it. "You're too bright for the *shmatte* trade," said Mrs. Steinetz, who took Barbara to the Côte

57

Basque for a farewell lunch and presented her with a Victorian shell pillbox as a going-away present. Barbara had no way of knowing that the shell had come from a Madison Avenue antique shop and had cost one hundred and seventy-five dollars. Twelve years later, when Edith Steinetz died by jumping from her eighteenth-floor window overlooking Park Avenue, *The New York Times* ran the obituary on the first page of the second section, citing Edith Steinetz' contribution to the world of style and fashion, calling her "a major influence." No theory was published about the reason for her suicide, and Barbara wondered what would happen to all the needlepoint. She herself still had the shell, by then had learned its value and kept it on her desk filled with paper clips. Edith Steinetz would have approved.

When Charter Books offered Barbara the new job, Barbara consulted Dick, telling him that the salary would be one hundred and twenty-five dollars a week, that she would have a title—assistant editor—and that she would be co-ordinating the books based on movies. She asked Dick if he thought she ought to take the job.

"If you want it," he had said. "You don't need my approval."

"But I wouldn't do anything without asking you."

"As long as you can meet your responsibilities at home, I'm proud of your successes."

"One hundred twenty-five a week. You know, I'll finally be making some money," Barbara said. She was feeling the champagne Dick had brought home to celebrate her first day at her new job. She still paid Vera Souchak eighty dollars a week, although she felt that since she had had a raise, she ought to give Mrs. Souchak one too.

"I'd better watch it," said Dick, "or pretty soon you'll be supporting me." The overtone was humorous. Barbara reacted to the undertone.

"I'm still your wife and the mother of our children, first."

"I'm not worried," said Dick, and he wasn't. He was confident that Barbara understood the priorities. That she might understand them but not accept them never dawned on him. It was not to dawn on Barbara until much later.

In the sixties everything changed.

Music changed. The Beatles chanted Yeah, yeah, yeah and the Stones snarled a surly defiance.

Politics changed. Barbara joined the March on Washington in August 1963, and she heard the "I Have a Dream" speech broadcast on amplifiers. She thought that it would really do some good. Three months later Lee Harvey Oswald shot John F. Kennedy and Jack Ruby shot Lee Harvey Oswald. Marina Oswald said that her husband had been impotent, Marguerite Oswald insisted that he had been innocent and responsible people wondered if there had been a worldwide conspiracy with tentacles reaching into who knew what low and vile places.

Clothes changed. Mary Quant designed the mini, Vidal Sassoon created the geometric haircut and André Courrèges looked to the space programs for inspiration.

War changed. Soldiers were called technical advisers, and in the early sixties no one paid very much attention to Vietnam.

City life changed. In the hot summers, black ghettos in Detroit and Watts burned and raged while young blacks looted and screamed obscenities.

Women changed. They read Betty Friedan's *The Feminine Mystique* and they wondered if woman's place was really in the home.

Men changed. They bought clothes designed by Pierre Cardin and began to feel insecure about the dimensions of their erections.

Barbara was affected by all of it. She cut her hair and shortened her skirts and in 1964, at the age of twenty-seven, began to think that she was getting old. She was afraid of her thirtieth birthday and it was just around the corner.

She looked at Dick, in his gray flannel suits and short hair-cut, and marveled that the sixties had left him untouched.

When she was offered a job by Joseph Levine's film company she asked what the salary was. One hundred and fifty dollars a week. And she asked what the job consisted of. Publicizing the stars in Levine Productions. She accepted the offer on the spot and informed Dick of her decision that evening. She thought he seemed hurt that she hadn't consulted him first, but since he said nothing, she said nothing.

She catered to a film star who dieted on organic food washed down with one-hundred-proof vodka; to a bisexual motorcycle idol who told her where to buy the best leather boots in New York and the best silk underwear in Paris; to an older actor who played distinguished-lawyer roles and who liked young black boys and to the most famous cowboy of them all, who gave Barbara a plastic replica of his golden six-shooter in thanks for all she had done for him.

Barbara tried to pretend that the contrast between her glamorous days and domestic nights were hugely funny. She joked about spending the day in a five-room suite at the Plaza spoon-feeding caviar and champagne to an Italian film star's French poodle and then coming home and putting the potatoes in the oven and rinsing out her bra in the bathroom washbasin. By day she shopped in Tiffany's with a sex symbol and at night she helped Annette with her arithmetic. She talked dirty, knowing talk at the office and pretended she didn't get her husband's boss's off-color jokes at night.

It lasted for seven years—from 1959 to 1966. America fell apart and so did Barbara's marriage.

One Wednesday evening early in October 1966, Barbara rushed home from work, showered and changed into a black suede miniskirt, a silver Lurex skinny-knit sweater, black panty hose and black-and-silver evening sandals.

"What in hell do you call that?" Richard walked into the bedroom as she finished dressing.

"What is this? An inspection?" Barbara knew what they were going to fight about. It was an instant replay of a million other fights they'd had.

"That skirt is up to your ass." It was rare for Richard to use slang. The warning flags were all out.

"So is everyone else's."

"Not at McLaughlin they're not."

"McLaughlin never heard that the sixties are here."

"I want you to change into something more conservative."

"I don't have anything left over from college. That was the fifties, in case you forgot."

"Change into something more conservative." Richard's lips were pursed. He refused to pursue the byways Barbara wanted to open up.

"I don't *have* anything more conservative." Barbara smoothed her left knee where the panty hose bagged slightly. She looked up at her husband and the contempt that she usually repressed flooded over her. He was worried about McLaughlin. About what his boss would think. He was still making his way up the corporate ladder. What a fool he was. What an outdated fool. "Unless you'd like me to go topless? Maybe your boss would like that?"

Dick slapped her, so hard that her cheek stung and tears came involuntarily to her eyes. She stared at him for a moment.

"You asshole," she said.

"I'm sorry," he said.

"Go fuck yourself."

They went down in the elevator in silence, and in the taxi Dick tried to make up by taking Barbara's hand. She pulled it away from him.

The Stilsons lived in a conservative cooperative building at Park Avenue and Seventy-fourth Street. By the time they rang the bell of the apartment, they both had smiles plastered on their faces. Nancy Stilson opened the door.

"Hello, Barbara," she said. Although Mrs. Stilson had known Barbara for almost ten years, she had never asked

Barbara to call her by her first name. Dick had explained that in the Navy, wives of inferior officers never addressed the wives of superior officers by their first names. It was just Navy custom, that was all.

"Hi, Nancy," said Barbara. Mrs. Stilson frowned. "How are you, Nancy?" Barbara stopped. She dared anyone to say anything.

"Hello, Mrs. Stilson," said Dick. Silently, everyone agreed to ignore Barbara's faux pas. Everyone except Barbara.

Commander Stilson appeared and led Barbara and Dick into the living room. It was furnished in beige: beige carpet and beige curtains, beige slipcovers and reproduction early American maple lamps with beige shades. The Stilsons served weak, beige drinks with Pepperidge Farm Goldfish in a reproduction pewter dish. They discussed Annette's and Christiaan's progress in school, the superiority of Campbell's products over Heinz's and the wonderful things that were being accomplished at McLaughlin. They avoided the Commander's hawkish position on Vietnam and Mrs. Stilson's opinion of the Pill, Pot and Permissiveness, and no one looked at the length of Barbara's hemline.

The Stilsons took them to the Passy, an old-line restaurant for those who were rich and secure enough to undertip without embarrassment. Commander Stilson ordered another round of drinks without consulting anyone and asked Barbara how she was keeping herself busy.

She began to tell him about plans for a new Mike Nichols film to be called *The Graduate*. Dick kicked her sharply, and she was so shocked at the second physical assault that she shut up in midsentence. She realized that Dick wanted her to talk about the children, about Annette's math or Christiaan's athletic ability. The Stilsons didn't notice a thing and the Commander ordered another round. He and Dick indulged in some boring office gossip and Barbara picked the rice out of the curried chicken. It was gluey.

"And how old are the children now?" asked Mrs. Stilson, doing her bit to be social and include The Wife.

"Thirty-five and forty. Respectively," said Barbara.

Nancy Stilson gave her a strange look, and a psychopathic shadow gleamed in Dick's eyes. Edward Stilson didn't notice a thing; Barbara realized from the pink flush on his face that the old goat was half crocked. Suddenly, the Commander leaned across the table and, upsetting a water goblet, patted Barbara on the stomach.

"Anything in the oven?" he slurred, and leered at the same time.

Barbara looked at the three people she was with. Edward Stilson, too old and too drunk; Nancy Stilson, dried-up and WASP-like, and Dick Roser, a man she had married once upon a time.

She picked up her evening bag and without a word, surprising the waiter, the busboy and the maître d', got herself a taxi and went home.

"I am being considered for a big promotion." The tight creases around Dick's mouth told Barbara that he had decided to be firm but rational. He had apologized for Barbara's behavior, stuck out dessert and coffee and, when he got home, found her in bed, waiting for the Carson show to start. Viva was going to be a guest, and Barbara had heard that she was witty. She was looking forward to seeing her.

"I said . . ." Dick began again, and Barbara leaned forward and turned up the volume. Tex Antoine was predicting sunny skies and unseasonably warm temperatures for the next day. "I said," he started again. Barbara stared at the screen, making a point of ignoring Dick.

"Why are you being like that?" he asked.

Barbara didn't know why, except that it upset Dick and upsetting him gave her pleasure. It was one way of making him pay attention to her. Dick couldn't bear it when things got out of control. He wanted everything neatly drawn and labeled on a blueprint.

"Honey, don't you care about me?" The tone of Richard's voice broke down her barricades.

"Of course I care." It was only a half lie.

"I'm being considered for the Commander's job," said Dick, unable to keep the pride out of his voice.

"You are?" Barbara was surprised and impressed. It was a big job with a lot of responsibility and a large salary. "Why didn't you tell me?"

Dick paused before he answered, "I didn't think you'd be interested."

Barbara didn't reply. There was nothing to say.

As she fell asleep, Barbara realized what she had already known for some time: her outrageous behavior and Dick's stubborn persistence didn't add up to just another fight. There wasn't going to be a winner—not this time. They were involved in the death of their marriage and they were both going to lose.

The only question was, How long was it going to take?

4 THE ACQUISITION OF Mc-Laughlin by Nikko was officially announced to the business community in February 1966: a hundred-million-dollar transaction involving transfers of stock, capital assets, deferred earnings and careful analysis of projected cash flow. It was brought about by a California-born American of Japanese parentage, who as a result of his conglomerate, Nikko Industries, ranked as the twenty-seventh-richest man in the United States. Yamaki Nikito had started in 1961 with a small agency licensed to handle imports into the West Coast markets of Japanese-made automobiles, television sets, radios and electronic components. Borrowing against the projected profits of that distributorship, Yamaki Nikito had then bought orange groves in and around the Salinas Valley, subdivided them and leased—not sold—them to real estate

developers. Subsequently he purchased a plywood company that sold prefab shells to the entrepreneurs who were developing retirement communities there. In rapid succession, Nikito bought a plumbing-fixture supplier and a large appliance outlet, and four years later he was selling the developers to whom he leased the land virtually all the equipment needed to complete the development.

By 1965, Nikito had interests in automotive-parts suppliers, fiber mills, oil storage and refinery complexes, heavy trucking, minielectronics manufacturers, shipping and dockage facilities and, finally, the takeover of McLaughlin. Nikko systems, executives and philosophies were introduced. Longtime McLaughlin executives were kicked upstairs, paid off or retired. Nikito did not believe in firing men, no matter how incompetent: he adhered to the Oriental preoccupation with saving face. When all the reshuffling was completed, a process that took the amazingly short time of four months, Commander Edward Stilson found himself giving speeches in high school auditoriums informing students of the wonderful future in marine design and engineering and Dick Roser found himself head of the entire marine-engineering division, supervising the work of two hundred and twelve draftsmen, naval architects, R&D Ph.D.'s and a raft of Navy men assigned to McLaughlin. Dick was virtually blushing with pride. Even his father was impressed, and said so.

"I've got everything—and more—that I ever worked for and it's all worth it." Dick shook his head, hardly able to believe not only that his dreams had come true but that they were better in real life than they had been in fantasy. He spent eighteen hours a day at work and loved it.

Annette was approaching eight, and her marks in the private school that they could now afford were excellent, but Barbara was informed by the school psychologist that the child needed a father figure. Annette, it seemed, was extremely seductive with all the male employees, from the principal to the English teacher to the janitor. Christiaan, nearing seven, never said a word about missing his father, who now spent more time than ever in Washington and Annapolis, but he refused to go to sleep unless Barbara let him wear Dick's pajama tops.

In June of 1966 Barbara took fate into her own hands and made two important changes in her life: she took her first lover and got her first important job. In July of 1966 fate itself took over and changed Barbara's life in a way that she could never have foreseen.

In New York, everything happens at lunch, even adultery.

Eugene Stannett was a literary agent who looked like an accountant, took risks like a horseplayer and had a clientele that was a Who's Who of the best-seller lists. At a time when most men were trying out their Cardin suits and wide ties, letting their sideburns grow and cultivating a rich-hippie look, Eugene Stannett wore dark gray chalk-stripe suits with vests and wing-tip shoes.

Since the Joseph Levine office was constantly negotiating for properties represented by Eugene Stannett's office, Barbara had met him often and lunched with him frequently. In all the times she had met him, she had never once speculated on him sexually. In the Swinging Sixties when every man was always coming on, looking for easy sex, Eugene Stannett was a gentleman, courtly and correct. Barbara nearly died when he propositioned her one day after lunch in the Spanish Pavilion.

"I'm very attracted to you," he said in the same tone he might have used to describe the pignolia cake. "I'm married, you know."

Barbara hadn't known, but she said nothing. He continued.

"I'm married. I've been married for eighteen years and I have no intention of getting divorced. But I want to take you to bed."

Stannett had never touched her, and he didn't touch her then. He waited for her to consider his wishes. Barbara noticed how firm and clean his skin was and she remembered, perhaps irrelevantly, that she had always thought his voice sounded very sexy over the telephone.

"You're right," she said. It didn't occur to her to be surprised at the ease with which she assented to adultery. All she felt was desirable. It was a long time since she had felt desirable.

"Come," he said, signing the check and adding the tip. "We'll go upstairs."

He led her out the front door of the restaurant, down a few steps on Park and into the lobby of the adjoining Ritz Towers. They took the elevator to the fifteenth floor, to a suite that was permanently rented by a client who spent most of the year in Marrakech, and looked at each other and solemnly kissed.

Eugene Stannett turned out to be a thoughtful and imaginative lover. They met one afternoon a week and it was the only time, other than on strictly business occasions, that Barbara ever saw him. She never fancied that she was in love with him; it never occurred to her to want to spend more time with him or to query him about his wife or his children; she didn't care where he lived or what he did on weekends. She asked him only one personal question:

"Have you had many mistresses?"

"No," he said. "Very few." From the way he said it, she knew he wasn't lying.

Being an adulteress changed Barbara. She bought new underwear—Rudi Gernreich's No-Bra; she began to wear pants to work, discreet false eyelashes and tons of Le De perfume. She was positive that Dick would notice. She was afraid that he would say something. But no. Nothing.

"As I get older and older I wear more and more makeup and less and less underwear," she said. It was 1966 and Barbara was twenty-nine years old.

Dick didn't respond.

She tried the line again, this time on Eugene, for she had liked the sound of it.

"Don't be vulgar," he had said. "It doesn't become you."

"But this is the sixties," said Barbara. "It's wild. Don't you love it?"

"I love you," said Eugene. It was the only time he said it, and he said it so softly that Barbara realized what he had said only when it was too late to answer. But it didn't matter, because she didn't love him. She didn't love anyone and that made her feel very free. The best thing about having the affair with Eugene Stannett was that it was the only secret Barbara Roser had ever had in her life. It gave her a feeling of power.

Barbara had known Ned Jared professionally for several years, and she had speculated about him sexually and dismissed him as nice but neuter. Ned was the promotion director of Jared & Spolin Publishing, one of the few privately owned book companies. When its president, Leon Kravat, had been interviewed by the *New York Times* Sunday business section, he had said that as long as he ran the company, it would resist the trend toward amalgamation and conglomeration. There was still a place, he had said, in the business community for a small, independent firm. J&S might have been small compared with the giants, but it was rich. For years it had been making substantial profits on reference books and textbooks.

"What we want," said Ned Jared over *moules marinière* at Le Mistral, "is to get into trade publishing. We want to take on the big boys—Simon and Schuster, Random House, Doubleday. We want to be where the action is."

"You mean you want to go commercial?" asked Barbara.

"Exactly. We have the money, the staff. What we need is a good promotion and publicity specialist." Ned Jared said that J&S, which, by the way had been founded by his grandfather, needed someone who knew how to get authors booked on Carson and Merv Griffin, how to engineer stories for the feature pages and how to stir up public interest, book-club interest and movie money. "You movie people are certainly good at it."

Barbara nodded. Joseph Levine, like all the other successful producers, spent enormous amounts of time and money promoting his products. Ned Jared was right in thinking that the same techniques would apply to books.

"What I wondered," said Ned Jared, "was if you might know of anyone who'd be interested in coming over to us."

"Yes," said Barbara. "Me. If the terms are right."

It took Ned Jared a moment to digest the swiftness of her answer and then he described the terms: She would be called assistant promotion director; her salary would be two hundred and fifty dollars a week; she'd have her own office and her own secretary.

"Guess what?" asked Barbara. "The terms are right." The salary was fifty dollars more a week than Joseph Levine was paying her, and besides she had gotten very bored with movie stars, their agents, their business managers and their egos. Ned Jared's timing had been perfect.

Dick Roser was in Washington and Barbara called him to tell him about her new job.

"Two hundred and fifty dollars a week?" He was clearly impressed. "That's terrific for a woman."

Barbara let his comment sink in for a moment, decided not to respond and merely said, "We'll celebrate when you get back."

Her words patched up another wound that Dick didn't even know he had inflicted.

In July, Barbara's life began to turn upside down.

She was looking forward to seeing Dick's parents. It was childish of her, she knew, but she couldn't wait to tell Alex Roser about her new job. She knew that he would be impressed that she had five people working under her—a copywriter, an art director and his assistant, a production supervisor and a full-time secretary. She was curious to have the benefit of his comments about her boss. She referred to Ned Jared privately as the invisible man. He arrived in the office at ten, left at eleven-thirty and, as often as not, didn't show up in the afternoon. She supposed it was a privilege of being related to the founder of the company, and she heard all sorts of weird gossip about him. She was sure that Alex Roser would have a theory and she was anxious to hear it. It was strange, but Dick's father seemed more impressed by and interested in her career than Dick's. She supposed that Alex Roser, like most people, was put off by the mechanical intricacies and incomprehensible technical jargon of nuclear-hydraulic-systems construction and analysis.

As they had done every year, Dick and Barbara drove out to Kennedy to pick up the Rosers for their annual visit. As American Airlines announced the arrival of the plane from Denver, Dick and Barbara were standing in the upstairs observatory watching the jumbo jets landing and taking off. According to a statistic that Barbara had read somewhere, twenty-four planes landed and took off from Kennedy every sixty seconds. It was a staggering number, and every time one of the large planes arrived or departed, the building they were standing in literally shook. Barbara felt sorry for the people who lived in houses nearby. No wonder they were up in arms about the proposed enlargement of the runway area. The constant noise and shuddering of the buildings would be enough to drive anyone crazy.

"Oh, my God!" Dick's exclamation shook Barbara out of her daydream, and she looked to the end of the airstrip where he was pointing. An airplane had split into two parts, the front section careening crazily down the strip heading off to one side, in the direction where another plane was just taking off. The two machines collided, then exploded, and an orange ball of fire ballooned from the mangled fragments of silver metal. The fire trailed off into streamers, igniting portions of the field where oil spills burst into flame. The tail portion rolled forward from its own momentum and stopped only when it came to rest against the forward section of the plane that had been taking off. Barbara saw people standing in the jagged hole that had opened when the jet had broken into two pieces. They were too high off the ground to jump; they stood uncertainly, not knowing what to do, and then their indecision was ended when the flames made a quantum leap into the rear section and engulfed it.

Sirens wailed and trucks rolled onto the strip and began pumping white foam in an effort to contain the fire. Other people in the observatory began to scream and mill around, asking over and over what plane was it that had been consumed.

Barbara knew without having to ask.

Barbara and Dick went to Denver to settle his parents' affairs.

"What do you have to do?" Barbara had no idea of what happened when people died. When her father had died, her mother had been there to take care of whatever legal details had to be attended to.

"Sell the house, make arrangements for his businesses," said Dick. "That's about all, I guess." Dick was very matter-of-fact about the death of his parents, preferring to speak of the practical details that had to be attended to rather than giving expression to whatever grief, loss or anger he felt about it. As always in moments of emotional crisis, Dick withdrew. He worked harder than ever, spending more hours at the office and more time with his blueprints. He dissipated his grief by transforming it into productivity. Barbara wished that he would cry, just once, but she knew him and knew that he wouldn't.

They were in his parents' bedroom cleaning out the closets and packing things to contribute to the hospital thrift shop when Alex Roser's lawyer telephoned and expressed his condolences. He told Dick that his father had left a will and asked if it would be all right if he were to come to the house later that afternoon.

Edward Zeto was young—about thirty-two, thought Barbara; very tall, slightly paunchy and blond. He seemed shy, but Barbara thought that perhaps the circumstances dictated his unusually respectful behavior. He told Dick and Barbara again how sorry he was about the elder Rosers' death and about how much he had liked them. He also told them that he had enormous respect for Alex Roser's business abilities. He spoke with genuine warmth, and Barbara was happy to know that others beside herself appreciated the niceness beneath Alex' gruff exterior.

"Had your father ever discussed his will with you?"

Dick shook his head.

"Did you know anything about the scope of his business?"

Again, Dick shook his head. "My father thought I was too impractical," he said, smiling wryly. "He was probably right."

Edward Zeto took a deep breath and Barbara could tell that he didn't quite know how to say what he had to say next. She was afraid it was something terrible. All she could remember was that her father had left no insurance and a virtually bankrupt business. Could Alex Roser have left behind huge debts that would impoverish her and Dick for the rest of their lives? She felt she was going to gag.

"Your father's will is a simple one," Ed Zeto said, having apparently figured out a way to break the news. "It divides all his assets in two. One half goes to you, Dick, and the other half goes to your wife."

"To *me*?"

"You are Barbara Drooten Roser?" Ed Zeto saw the humor in her stunned response.

Barbara nodded. She didn't know what to say. What, exactly, had the old man left to her? And why had he singled her out?

"Why me?" she finally said.

"He liked you," said Ed Zeto. "And he had plenty to go around."

"Plenty?" asked Dick. He looked confused and pale.

"Your father was worth, gross, one and one-half million dollars. You each get half. After taxes, of course."

No one said a word. They sat around the shabby kitchen table in the old-fashioned room and looked at each other. Ed Zeto seemed to wait for a reaction. There was none. Both Barbara and Dick were shocked beyond sense. Both at the size of the estate and by the way it had been equally divided. All Barbara could think was: I'm rich.

The thought she wanted to repress but couldn't was its corollary: I'm rich—and I'm free.

"What are you going to do with your money?" Dick asked when they got back to New York. He had been very angry with Barbara ever since Ed Zeto had told them about the will. Barbara didn't know why. Was it because his father had cared as much for Barbara as he had for his own son? Or was it because she was now totally independent?

"I don't know," said Barbara. "I'll put it in the bank until I get used to it. Then maybe I'll decide what to do with it. What are you going to do with yours?"

"Leave it in the bank. You know I'm not that interested in money. I have enough for what I want."

Neither of them was aware that they talked of the money as "I" or "mine." The words "we" and "ours" had never been pronounced.

In October of 1966, Ned Jared shut the door of his office. "I'd like to tell you about myself," he said to Barbara, "now that you've been doing my job for several months." It pleased Barbara that he admitted that she was in actuality running his department. She scheduled work and saw that it was done, she settled everyday crises and everyone in the department considered her the boss rather than Ned. Nothing official had ever been said, but the fact that Barbara Roser was now running the J&S promotion department was unofficially acknowledged inside and outside the company.

"I'm an asthmatic," said Ned Jared. "I have been since childhood. The condition has never been cured, but it's controlled via drugs and psychotherapy. I leave every day at eleven-thirty for an appointment with my analyst. If I don't return it means that I've had an attack. I can't breathe. I have to get a shot and check into a hospital with a special room flooded with sterilized air."

"I'm sorry," said Barbara. "I didn't know . . ."

"I know there's a lot of gossip about me," Ned continued.

"I haven't heard any," said Barbara, who had heard that he was an alcoholic, a homosexual, a heroin addict. Also that he liked threesomes, that he dressed up in women's clothes and that he had been seen hanging around the Grand Central men's room looking for some action.

"But I'm not here to tell you my problems," said Ned. "I want to tell you that I appreciate the way you've taken over and that I've told Leon Kravat that you deserve more money and more prestige."

Barbara wanted to ask what Leon Kravat's response had been, but she was too afraid of seeming ballsy and ambitious. She had never met Leon Kravat, although she had seen him once or twice in the elevators. His office was on the floor above Barbara's, and she thought he looked remarkably like the Duke of Windsor—small, impeccably groomed and rather weak.

"He said that several authors had mentioned your work to him, and he also said that he was impressed with the kind of publicity that J&S has been getting." Barbara couldn't hold back a smile. She had done well: there had been a story about a J&S cookbook writer in the *Times* Thursday food feature, several J&S authors had been booked on the David Frost show and the ABC evening news had done a featurette on the Erotic Exercise manual that was doing so well.

"Did he tell you when I'd be made a vice-president?" Barbara made a joke out of the question, hoping to take off the hard edge.

"He said that you would get everything you deserve. I wouldn't be at all surprised if you got my job when I retire in a few years." Ned got up from behind his desk and walked around and patted Barbara on the shoulder. "He asked me not to tell you, but I couldn't resist. Can it be our secret?"

"Our secret," said Barbara, and touched her right index finger to her heart to seal the bond.

Ned smiled his sad, defeated smile. "Thanks," he said. "Thanks very much."

Barbara's secrets were multiplying. Eugene's secret made her feel powerful. Ned's secret made her feel invulnerable.

A few weeks later, as Johnson's credibility gap began to widen and as the Singles Scene was recognized by sociologists as a subsociety worthy of study; after a sniper had killed fourteen persons and wounded thirty-one in a spastic orgasm on top of a tower at the University of Texas and the Supreme Court tightened up the procedures surrounding self-incrimination, Dick Roser dropped his bombshell. Barbara had just put dinner on the table.

"Well, kids, how'd you like to go swimming all year round?"

"Wow!" said Christiaan, who had won a swimming medal at camp the previous summer.

"Are there big waves?" asked Annette, who was a born conservative.

"What do you mean, swimming all year round?" Barbara was furious. What was Dick talking about? And why did he spring it with no advance warning in front of the children? He hadn't bought a horrible house in some ghastly suburb without telling her, had he? A house with a swimming pool purchased with the money he had inherited?

"What do you think, honey?" The tone of his voice made it clear that he was afraid of Barbara's reaction. That was why he had brought it up in front of the children. Dick could not tolerate conflict and would go to any lengths to avoid confrontation. He was a coward in a way that Barbara found contemptible.

"I don't think anything," said Barbara.

"That's reasonable," said Dick almost sighing in relief. "I just found out myself today. Officially, that is."

"Officially, what?" What was going on? Why hadn't Dick warned her?"

"We got the contract. One hundred and seventy-five million dollars' worth. To redesign all the existing hydraulic systems in the nuclear fleet. The whole goddam fleet." It was rare for Dick to swear, and Barbara was surprised at how excited he let himself seem. He was so much like his parents, always hiding his emotions. "The thing is, we have to move to Pensacola. I have to be there by next week."

Barbara just stared at him.

He had no choice but to go on.

"You'll have to get the kids out of school and the apartment sublet; we do have a sublet clause, don't we? There's no rush. You can wait until January, the beginning of the new term. McLaughlin has a house waiting for us, so all you have to do at this end is put our things into storage."

"Can I have a diving board? I can almost do a backflip," said Christiaan.

"Hush," said Barbara. She could not believe that Dick was so callous, so selfish and so uncomprehending of her life. She didn't even know where to start. "What about my job? What about the kids?" Eugene Stannett, Ned Jared and Leon Kravat flashed through her mind. "What about my goddam *life?*"

Annette began to cry. She had never heard her mother scream at her father.

"You don't have to work," said Dick. "We have plenty of money."

Annette had left her chair and was crying hard, her head cradled in Barbara's shoulder.

"It's not a question of money." Barbara didn't know how to talk to Dick. Her life, her Self had no reality to him. If you weren't real to someone, how could you make him understand?

"You'll have a good time. The weather's beautiful. There are lots of McLaughlin wives. . . ."

"McLaughlin wives still set their hair in pin curls. I go to Kenneth. Don't you understand? There's a million light-years between my life and theirs." What she meant was that there was a million light-years between her life and Dick's, but she couldn't say that. She couldn't bring herself to the acknowledgment. Not yet.

"Don't be mad, Mommy," sobbed Annette, not sure that she too wasn't a target of her mother's anger.

Barbara kissed Annette on the neck, feeling the softness of her skin and the layer of baby fat just beneath.

"But you'll try, won't you, honey? It means a lot to me."

Barbara didn't have the heart to refuse him, so she said that she would try. That she and the children would visit Pensacola over Christmas vacation.

"And you'll do it with an open mind?" asked Dick.

"Of course," said Barbara, who despised herself for lying.

She knew what Dick thought. He didn't have to spell it out. He was involved with defending the nation. Her job was trivial: she was peddling a few hours' worth of cheap entertainment. Later that night, when they got into bed, Dick held Barbara in his arms.

"I love you, you know that. I love you more than anyone in the world," said Dick.

"I know," said Barbara. The separate directions of their lives were more than either of them could control. Barbara felt an overwhelming wave of love and sympathy for Dick. He had been her husband for a long time; he had been a good husband, faithful and true. He was a valuable person. He would do anything in his power for her. The trouble was that his power, like everyone else's, was limited. With a great flood of wistfulness at all she knew she was about to give up, Barbara took the initiative and began to make love to him.

"The Imperial Summons," as Barbara called it, arrived in the interoffice mail. Leon Kravat requested Barbara's company at lunch on November the seventeenth. One o'clock. The Italian Pavilion.

Barbara pretended she wasn't excited and called a friend at Time-Life and asked if she could have a Xerox of its

77

file on Leon Kravat. It arrived the next morning by messenger.

Who's Who in American Business.

Leon Kravat was born in North Carolina in 1910. His father was a successful textile manufacturer and Leon went to the University of Miami and emerged with a law degree. His intention was to return to Ansonville and run the family mills. However, the Depression intervened and the mills went bankrupt. Leon went to New York and got a job as house counsel with Revlon, at that time a small company which made only lipstick and nail polish. Leon lasted in the legal department for a short time only, because Charles Revson discovered that Leon had an innate talent as a merchandiser. By the time the phrase "matching lips and fingertips" became a household slogan, Leon was valuable enough to be wooed away by Coty, at that time an independent and prestigious company with a Paris cachet. Under Leon's direction, the balance sheets at Coty improved until it was bought by the Pfizer pharmaceutical company. A "personality conflict" between Leon Kravat and the Pfizer management was resolved when Leon's management contract was purchased by Pfizer for a large sum.

Coincidentally, at that time, in the early fifties, J&S was in financial trouble. It had zero liquidity and virtually no cash flow. It had been incompetently run by descendants of the original founders who cared more about indulging their inclinations toward philosophy and belles lettres than about the message on the bottom line. The board of directors quite naturally looked for outside talent to repair the financial damage. After a six-month search, they settled on Leon Kravat, who, although he had a reputation as a man of ice, also had a reputation for being a magician when it came to money.

Leon Kravat negotiated his deal for himself—he had, after all, originally started out as a lawyer. The terms he received were an indication of the desperation of J&S's situation: he had absolute discretion over all hiring and firing; he had final authority on all editorial, sales, distribution, promotional and advertising questions. Additionally, his contract called for a place on the board and for part of his compensation to be paid in J&S stock. Leon Kravat was the first outsider in the history of the firm to own stock.

Leon Kravat lived up to his reputation for icy flamboyance at his very first meeting with the board. He informed them that it would take him three full years to show a profit. He further informed them that if at any time they were dissatisfied with the way he ran J&S, they could have his resignation immediately.

Calmly, he opened a manila envelope and handed around Xerox copies of his letter of resignation, undated and unsigned.

"I will sign and date the original at any time the board wishes," he said in his uninflected voice.

His gesture was dramatic enough to make the financial pages of the next day's *New York Times*. When a reporter called to ask for further details, Leon Kravat told the *Times* that it was his policy to keep a letter of resignation in his desk drawer at all times.

It was the ultimate corporate weapon, and Leon Kravat had never had to use it. The profit picture at J&S was exactly as Leon Kravat had predicted: the first year there was a loss, the second year the company broke even and for the third year there was a profit. Every year there were higher and higher profits and eventually J&S bought its own press in suburban Chicago and built computerized warehouses in California and Maryland.

In the mid-sixties, J&S went public. Wall Street called it "sexy," its stock price spiraled, and several conglomerates, anxious for diversification, made overtures. All their blandishments were rejected. Leon Kravat's stock was worth a fortune; he still had his letter of resignation unsigned and undated in his desk drawer and the board of directors in his hip pocket.

The Time-Life file concluded with the information that Leon Kravat was married, had two children and resided in Oyster Bay, Long Island. He had no known hobbies or outside interests.

The curt tone of Leon Kravat's summons had put Barbara on her guard and she forced herself to arrive at the Italian Pavilion ten minutes late. What was this lunch all about? A raise? A promotion? After all, he had told Ned Jared that he was impressed with her. Leon Kravat was already seated at a corner table, a bottle of San Pellegrino water opened in front of him. As the waiter seated her, Leon Kravat looked at his watch. Barbara saw him and forced herself not to make an excuse about crosstown traffic.

So far, it was a draw.

Without any of the usual business-lunch chitchat, they ordered: the mozzarella omelet for Leon Kravat and the poached bass for Barbara. She waited for him to make the first move. He did, and it came out of left field.

"How much do you think we pay Ned Jared a year?"

"I don't know." Leon Kravat's boldness had jolted her into a spontaneous reaction. It was exactly what Leon Kravat wanted.

"Thirty-five thousand dollars," said Leon Kravat. "And he's not worth it." He paused and ate some of his omelet. "The fact is that you're doing his job."

Barbara was speechless. How did Leon Kravat know? He was isolated in an executive suite on another floor. He wasn't clairvoyant. No one was.

"You are, aren't you?"

"Yes," said Barbara. It would be stupid of her to lie to him, yet betraying Ned's sad secret made her ill. She looked at the corpse of the fish on her plate and pushed it away.

"Do you think you're worth thirty-five thousand dollars a year?" Leon Kravat's icy eyes appraised her.

"Are you offering me Ned's job?" she asked. If he could be brutal, she could be blunt.

"No," said Leon Kravat.

"Then why did you invite me to lunch?"

"I wanted to meet you."

"So you could find out if I might be worth thirty-five thousand dollars a year?" Barbara had decided that it was better to lay all the cards on the table. It was Leon Kravat's method and, therefore, the best weapon to use on him.

"You handle yourself well," he said.

"Thank you," said Barbara. Apparently Leon Kravat wasn't going to give her a direct answer. She knew better than to press him.

As if the previous exchange hadn't taken place, Leon Kravat asked her if she thought J&S ought to fire its advertising agency and make a switch.

"If we want to change our image, it would be a good idea," she said. "If not, not."

Leon Kravat didn't react to her comment and signaled for the check. Barbara watched as he signed it with a gold Mark Cross pen. His hands were very small for a man, smaller even than hers, and they had been professionally manicured. The manicure, however, did not hide the fact that Leon Kravat bit his nails. For a moment, Barbara wondered what it would be like to be in bed with him, but her imagination couldn't get past the image of those small hands with their bitten nails on her breasts. It was exciting and repellent at the same time.

Leon Kravat escorted her to the street. He flagged a cab and put her into it. He closed the door and walked off in the other direction.

Barbara felt that she had taken a test. But she didn't know what the subject had been and she didn't know whether or not she had passed. She only knew that Leon Kravat was a teacher from whom she would learn a lot.

Barbara took the children to Pensacola for Christmas. Annette was so excited about seeing her father again that she threw up twice on the plane. Christiaan acted very cool, seemingly more interested in the design and engineering details of the Boeing 707 than in the prospect of seeing his father. Barbara was so preoccupied in caring for Annette that she had no time to wonder what it would be like to see Dick again, this time on strange territory.

Dick was standing there, in the glary sunshine, as they got off the plane. He looked tired and Barbara noticed that he had gained a few pounds; there was a soft, blurry roll just over his belt. The kids ran over to him, climbing all over him, and Dick grinned and picked up Annette and punched Christiaan in the shoulder. Barbara had always been touched by the way Dick's natural reserve melted with his children. He was very nice with them, very comfortable.

"Hi, darling," she said, and kissed him on the cheek.

Dick smiled at her, squinting a little in the sun. "The car's over here."

Annette talked about school and Christiaan talked about the Knicks while Barbara looked out the window and wondered how she'd get through two weeks in Pensacola. There were a bank and a gas station on every corner. The all-American preoccupations, thought Barbara: cars and money. Dick swung the car through a galvanized-iron gate and showed a plasticized identity card to an armed guard, who ran it under a futuristic machine that emitted a blue light, then waved them through. The black tar road led through a maze of identical stucco houses. They were painted yellow, pink and blue in some predetermined rotation. There was no grass; the sandy soil inhibited growth. A few scraggly palm trees poked through the sand here and there.

"We're almost home," said Dick.

Home was a house that the Navy Department had assigned to Richard Roser and family. It was a pink one. There was a living room furnished with a fake early-American sofa covered with a scratchy medium orange wool tweed, two barrel chairs upholstered in the same fabric, a piece of green carpet bound with tan tape, a wrought-iron-and-glass coffee table and two scenes of the Everglades hung on the wall behind the sofa. There were a small kitchen, two bedrooms and one bath.

"You've put on a little weight," said Barbara as she unpacked.

"Can't resist the coffee wagon," said Dick. He looked embarrassed. Barbara knew that he was as uncomfortable as she was. She thought that in a day or two their discomfort would vanish. It was simply a result of their having been apart for two months.

That night they went to a hamburger drive-in for dinner and the children gorged on hamburgers and coconut popsicles. They were looking forward to going to the beach the next day. They couldn't get over the novelty of being able to swim at Christmastime.

That night Dick, as Barbara knew he would, began to make love to her. But the act was never consummated because, for the first time in their marriage, Dick was impotent.

"It's just nervousness," said Barbara. "Everything will be all right in a day or two." She spoke for her benefit as much as for his.

"Oh, boy," said Christiaan. "I'm going to dive right in. I'm a real water rat, aren't I, Dad?" They were driving to the beach and Christiaan was squirming with excitement.

"You sure are," said Dick. "Ever since you could crawl."

"*I'm* not a water rat," said Annette. "I hate rats."

"Christiaan doesn't mean a real rat," said Dick. "It's just a way of speaking. It means someone who loves the water."

They rented a green-and-white-striped beach umbrella and Dick helped Barbara carry the picnic she had packed: cold chicken, cole slaw, fruit and cookies and iced tea in a thermos.

"I thought you liked the Knicks better than anything," said Annette.

"I like the Knicks for watching, but I like swimming for

doing," said Christiaan, rising to his sister's challenge. Dick participated in the relentless childish conversation and Barbara tried to blot it out. He was escaping being with her by focusing on the children. She fussed with the towels and wondered why one night of impotence was so humiliating to Dick. After all, she had read that all men occasionally suffered bouts of impotence. It wasn't a sign of disappearing virility.

"Oh-oh, slugger," said Dick, as they walked toward the water. "Man-of-war signs are up."

"What's that? I never heard of that."

"You rarely get them up North. Only down here."

Dick took them to the water's edge and showed them the men-of-war, their gelatinous bodies, slimy and transparent, sluggish in the dark green water.

"Yech," said Annette, and curled her lips. She stepped back, safely away from the water's edge.

"They sting," said Dick. "Careful."

"Scaredy-cat," said Christiaan to Annette. "I'm not afraid." He stepped into the water and picked up a man-of-war and threw it at his sister.

Annette began to scream and Barbara slapped Christiaan as Dick grabbed him by the arm and pulled him out of the water. He looked at his parents belligerently. They had promised him swimming and now they had betrayed their promise. This was supposed to be Christmas and there wasn't even a Christmas tree, just a few crummy palms. There were no windows with animated figures like those on Fifth Avenue. In his anger, Christiaan became sullen and withdrawn. Annette, terrified by the men-of-war and disappointed by the tropical version of Christmas, started whining and clung to Barbara.

Somehow they got through the day, and to Barbara's relief, Dick didn't even try to make love to her.

Barbara was afraid that Christiaan's hand would swell up from the man-of-war, but fortunately it didn't, and the next day everyone agreed to stay in the McLaughlin compound and use the pool. Christiaan practiced his backflip and Annette paddled around the shallow end, careful not to get her hair wet. Dick and Barbara sat in aluminum-and-nylon deck chairs and watched. They were uncomfortable with each other, and finally Dick asked Barbara if she would mind if he checked in at the office.

"Of course not," she said, and they both tried to hide their relief.

She spent the afternoon looking at the McLaughlin wives around the pool, playing canasta or reading paperbacks. She felt as if she were in a time capsule. They wore bright red lipstick—they didn't seem to know that pale lipstick was in fashion. Some had their hair set in pin curls, and almost all of them wore cotton dressmaker bathing suits, the kind with boy shorts that were supposed to make heavy thighs look thin. Was it possible that a copy of *Vogue* or even *Glamour* never reached as far south as Pensacola? Didn't they go to the movies? Hadn't they seen *Darling*? Hadn't they heard of the sexual revolution and bikini swimsuits? Yet Dick liked it here. He was comfortable in Pensacola. It gave Barbara a new insight into him.

"You like it here, don't you?" she asked him after dinner.

"Of course. Why shouldn't I?"

"It seems so out of date. So fifties."

"Well, I guess that makes me a fifties person," said Dick.

"I didn't mean it that way." Barbara could tell from his defensive tone that he felt insulted.

"I'm not insulted," said Dick, reading her mind. "I don't happen to think that being a sixties person is such hot stuff."

"You mean me, don't you?"

"At least I know who I am," said Dick avoiding a direct answer. "You think that keeping up with every fad makes you superior."

"It's better than being left behind."

"I think it's better to know who you are. Even if you're

only a fifties person." Dick was sarcastic and emotional. "At least I know who I am and what I want."

"And I don't?"

Dick's response was silence. He went into the kitchen and poured himself a drink.

"I've never seen you drink after dinner," Barbara said, trying to neutralize the static between them.

"I want to tell you," said Dick, sitting uneasily in the hard barrel chair. "I've met someone."

"Oh." They sat in the hideous living room looking at each other, neither sure of what to say or to do next.

"She's a widow . . . three children . . ."

"And she wants to be a wife and mother. She doesn't want a career," finished Barbara, who had heard only phrases.

"I'd be happier married to someone whose main interest was her house and husband."

"You want to marry her?" asked Barbara. She wasn't surprised. Dick wasn't the kind of man who would be happy with an affair. He was domestic and monogamous.

Dick nodded. Barbara realized that when he'd married her in 1957 she had been the right woman for him. The thing was that she had changed. The woman she'd become didn't make him happy anymore.

Barbara got up and went into the kitchen to mix herself a drink. Dick stopped her. "Sit down. I'll get you one." He left for a moment and returned with a Scotch-on-the-rocks.

"Thanks," said Barbara. "We'll want a divorce," she said.

"It would be best," said Dick.

"Should I get a lawyer? I don't know how to go about these things." As long as she could talk to Dick on an unemotional basis, she'd be able to get through this. She could pretend that it was happening to someone else.

"I'd like to see the children," said Dick very tentatively.

"I'm not going to be a bitch."

"No," said Dick. "I know that. I want to support the children. You know that."

"I guess the lawyers can arrange everything," said Barbara.

She suddenly felt terribly tired. She wanted only to sleep. "I'm exhausted," she said.

"I'll sleep in here. On the sofa." Dick was being a gentleman to the bitter end.

"I loved you," said Barbara. "I really did. I want you to know."

"Me too," said Dick. "I loved you more than anything. But something happened. . . ."

"Things happen," said Barbara, and went alone into the bedroom that the night before had been theirs. Dick followed and started to take her into his arms. There was no desire in his gesture, just compassion.

"Don't, please," said Barbara. His sympathy was more than she could bear. "It's been some hell of a Christmas Eve."

The next morning they performed a holiday charade. There were a pretend makeup set for Annette, some new books and a sweater. For Christiaan, there were a Knicks sweatshirt, a new Peanuts book and a subscription to *Sports Illustrated* in his own name. Barbara gave Dick the Gucci belt she had bought for him in New York and he gave her a bottle of Miss Dior.

On the twenty-sixth, eight days earlier than originally scheduled, Barbara and the children got on the plane bound for New York. The children didn't seem the least bit upset by the change in plans: Annette had already begun to miss her friends and Christiaan hadn't gotten over his disappointment in not being able to swim in the ocean. The winds that would blow the men-of-war back out to sea had not yet come.

Dick hugged and kissed the children good-bye and, not knowing what else to do, kissed Barbara on the cheek. As Barbara made sure that Annette's and Christiaan's seat belts were securely fastened, she realized that everyone felt only relief that the visit was over early. She felt that it was the saddest comment possible about the death of a marriage.

5 In April 1968, Martin
Luther King, Jr., was assassinated while standing on a
motel balcony in Memphis, Tennessee. In May 1968, the
Poor People marched on Washington and Andy Warhol was
shot and wounded by Valerie Solanis. In June 1968, Robert
F. Kennedy was shot and killed by Sirhan B. Sirhan and
Barbara Drooten Roser was divorced from Richard Roser
by decree of a court in Juárez, Mexico. Dick had handled
all the arrangements and Barbara found that getting divorced required no effort whatsoever on her part.

The legal fact occurred so long after the emotional divorce, that Barbara felt almost nothing when she counter-
signed the papers. However, the children had behaved dis-
turbingly ever since the return from Pensacola. Annette
refused to see her father and his new wife when they visited
New York, and Christiaan gave the Knicks sweatshirt to the
super's son with the excuse that it didn't fit him properly.
They both had occasional nightmares that sent them to
Barbara's bed for comfort and reassurance. In the early
spring, Barbara consulted a child psychologist, who said that
Annette's and Christiaan's reactions, while upsetting, were
entirely normal and certain to be temporary. Barbara decided to believe him.

"I'm sorry it didn't work out for you and Dick," said
Barbara's mother one weekend when Barbara drove the
children to Pawling to visit their grandmother. "But I won't
pretend that I'm surprised."

"I was afraid you'd be angry," said Barbara. "After all, it
is the first divorce in the family."

"There's only one thing I want to ask and then I won't
pry any more. Are you positive, absolutely certain that you
made the right decision?" Barbara's mother was asking for
the truth and Barbara no longer had anything to hide.

"I made the *only* decision. I didn't have a choice. Dick

knew what he wanted and it wasn't me. He wanted the me of nineteen-fifty-seven. I'm not that girl anymore."

Evangeline Drooten confined herself to one comment: "I think the change is for the better."

As Barbara got older, she had come to appreciate her mother more and more. Her mother was a rare combination of practicality and understanding. She accepted reality, aware that there was no point in trying to change the unchangeable. At sixty-seven, Evangeline Drooten seemed younger than she had at fifty-four. It was astonishing how much she had changed since her husband's death. She had been transformed from a small-town society woman, dependent and passive, into an involved and active adult. Barbara wondered fleetingly if her mother had ever thought about remarrying, and she wondered about herself and how divorce would change her.

"Tell me, how would you and the children feel if they spent the summer with Bamma?" Bamma was a childhood mispronunciation of "grandmother" that had stuck.

"I'll ask them," said Barbara. It was a decision she didn't want to have to make. She already felt enough guilt over the divorce.

It turned out that Annette and Christiaan were overjoyed with the idea of spending the whole summer in Pawling. It was a big novelty and therefore highly exciting. For Barbara it was a happy compromise: after the painful months of getting accustomed to living without Daddy, they had a treat to look forward to, and she didn't need to feel guilty about it. It was their choice.

"You need some time alone," said her mother. "You need to think about yourself, your life."

As Barbara drove back to the city, she recalled the conversation she had had with her mother in the fall of 1959, just before she had gone to meet Dick in Montauk. Her mother's advice to put herself first for a change had worked: it had glued her marriage back together again. And now that the marriage was over, the advice seemed more valid than ever. She did need to be selfish, to devote time to herself, to thoughts about *her* life, *her* future.

Barbara decided that it was time to stop being so passive. She decided that it was time to take conscious control of her life.

The Gramercy Park apartment depressed Barbara. It was filled with too many memories—good and bad. They lurked there to attack her unexpectedly from unforeseen angles and forgotten hiding places. She realized that, for her anyway, the most important thing in life—after the person you lived with—was the place you lived in. The first major decision Barbara made on her own was to move.

She had never touched the money she had inherited from her father-in-law. It was still in savings accounts, drawing interest. From time to time Barbara had thought that she ought to invest it more aggressively, but she didn't know how and she didn't know whom to ask. Now she was glad she hadn't. She finally had a use for the money.

Barbara spent eighty thousand dollars for a five-room cooperative apartment on East Seventy-seventh Street between Park and Madison. Eugene complimented her on the way she had handled the negotiations, and since he had a fearsome reputation as a tough negotiator, Barbara was impressed that he was impressed.

The moment Barbara took possession of the new apartment, she made a second major decision: she donated every single possession she had acquired during her marriage to the Sloan-Kettering Thrift Shop. She gave them the Paul Stuart sofa they had bought in the late fifties, the set of Lenox china Dick's parents had given them, the children's furniture they had bought together at Furniture in the Raw; she gave away draperies, rugs, mixing bowls, radios, two television sets, an adding machine, Dick's drafting table and gray metal chair, her entire summer wardrobe, their double bed with sheets, pillowcases and blankets.

She then went on a six-month shopping binge, buying her

way out of depression. She bought a new bed for herself, new rugs, new linens, new dishes, new sofas, new tables, chairs and mirrors, bunk beds for the children's rooms so they could have sleep-over visitors. She spent all her free time in Bloomingdale's, Porthault, W. & J. Sloane and Lord & Taylor. Every day she bought new things and every night when she got home from work there were more packages for her to unwrap. New possessions for her to own. Ironic, she thought, but Alex Roser's money had purchased her freedom from his son. It had, in addition, bought her a new Self.

All of her bold and dramatic decisions, so far, had worked out splendidly. Little by little, her depression, pangs of guilt and regret disappeared. Gradually, she began to feel stronger and more confident. The thing she regretted most was her passivity. She had known long before Dick that their marriage was over and yet she had done nothing about it. She had allowed it to drift until circumstances forced a divorce. Looking back, she couldn't understand why she had lacked the courage to be the one to get out first.

Barbara, in the past, had always prided herself on being in the mainstream of events. She realized now that she was capable of being in the forefront of them. In the very late sixties, women began to talk about liberation. Barbara understood their complaints in a way that went beyond words: she had had to struggle at underpaid and underappreciated jobs, she had put her wants after Dick's and the children, she had been falsely self-effacing and passive and she had been sitting on a volcano of energy and rage.

As the old decade faded in a snarl of unfulfilled promises about the quality of life, of national cynicism and bitterness over Vietnam, Barbara realized that a fundamental alteration had taken place in her: she had changed from passive to active.

Barbara couldn't take her eyes off Leon Kravat's bitten nails. She was mesmerized by them. He noticed that she was staring and he forced himself not to hide his hands.

"Stanley Bairman," he was saying. "Do you know him?"

"I know of him." Stanley Bairman was the sales manager at Viney, Newton—the General Motors of American publishing. Barbara wondered why Kravat had dragged his name into the conversation. Now that Ned Jared had retired, she was in Kravat's office to discuss her new responsibilities. Leon Kravat had already told her that she would be raised from fifteen thousand dollars a year to seventeen five and that she would have a new title: promotion manager.

"He's joining us here," said Kravat. "He'll add a lot of strength to J&S." He stopped, and he obviously expected Barbara to congratulate him on his coup.

"That's nice," said Barbara. She was wondering where Bairman was supposed to fit in and how it would affect her. Leon Kravat wasn't the kind of man to tell employees his plans unless he had a motive.

"He'll be named promotion director," Kravat continued, slightly off the beat.

"Whom will I report to?"

"Why, to Stanley Bairman. He'll be on the steering committee."

"And I won't?" Barbara saw it all: they were giving her a raise to calm her down and a new title to shut her up. They were giving her more responsibility and yet they were bringing in someone who knew nothing about the department to run it.

"Only heads of departments are on the steering committee," said Leon Kravat, as if he were talking to an idiot.

"I thought I was supposed to be head of the department. After all, I've been running it for two and a half years."

Leon Kravat made a bridge, touching the raw quicks of his fingers to each other. "We're aware of your contributions," he said. "But we feel that the men in the department will resent taking orders from a woman."

"They've been taking orders from me for two and one-half years. They happen to *like* me," said Barbara. "What you mean is that *you* wouldn't like to take orders from a woman."

"I didn't say that."

"You didn't have to." Her hands began to shake and she didn't bother to try to control them.

"Now, don't get emotional," said Leon Kravat. He was condescending and patronizing. "Try to see things our way."

"I will *never* see things your way."

Leon Kravat began to say something, something to placate her, but Barbara never heard what it was. She got up and walked out on him, leaving him alone with the middle of his sentence.

Emotional? In five minutes in Leon Kravat's office Barbara had turned into a mass murderer.

The famous unsigned, undated letter of resignation that Leon Kravat held like a guillotine over the Board of Directors was in the Time-Life file still in Barbara's desk. It took her less than sixty seconds to find it, to obliterate Leon Kravat's name with a red grease pencil, type her own in its place and sign and date the letter. Barbara then put it in the interoffice mail and wrote *Personal* on the envelope.

She threw her duplicate makeup kit, her phone book and her datebook into a Bendel's shopping bag and left her office for the last time. She went straight home and in the space of exactly one phone call, she had a new job. In a week she would go to work for Palisades Press, a paperback company, as promotion director with a thirty-five-hundred-dollar raise. She had turned down the same offer from Palisades six weeks before, and they were happy to learn that she had changed her mind.

At five-thirty, Leon Kravat telephoned Barbara.

"Your behavior was very unprofessional," he said. He obviously didn't like being decapitated with his own guillotine.

"So was yours."

There was silence. Leon Kravat's second-favorite weapon.

Finally: "We wish you'd reconsider," he said. "You know how much we think of your work."

Sure, thought Barbara. Enough to hire someone else to

take the credit for it. So let the opportunity for the wise-crack pass.

"Do you really want me to reconsider?"

"That's why I'm calling." Barbara noticed that he had changed from the imperial we to the impersonal I.

"All right. On the condition that my title is promotion director, that I'm on the steering committee and that I get a thirty-five-hundred-dollar-a-year raise."

"I'm sure you're aware of the J&S policy on increases," said Kravat. Barbara loved that euphemism: increases. "We're only permitted to give a ten-percent increase once a year. After the executive board reviews the request." He was spouting the official line, hiding behind the executive barricades erected to spare management the hassle of dealing with dissatisfied employees.

"Fortunately Palisades Press hasn't heard of your policy," said Barbara.

Another silence. One that Barbara could interpret: Leon Kravat hadn't known that she had another job. She waited for his reaction.

Again, finally: "We want to wish you the best success in your new position," he said, reverting to the imperial we.

"We thank you, Mr. Kravat," said Barbara, and hung up.

That was that, she thought.

The Barbara Roser–Leon Kravat chapter had come to an end.

Or so she thought.

Barbara began her new job on April 2, 1969—the day Eisenhower was buried in Abilene, Kansas. The symbolic implications of the coincidence did not escape Barbara. With Ike, his golf scores, Sherman Adams, the mink coats and Deepfreezes, the end of the "police action" in Korea, circle pins and circle skirts was buried a part of Barbara. Her innocence together with America's innocence had died, along with God, somewhere in the sixties.

Innocence, unlike the Phoenix, would not arise from the

ashes of disillusion and maturity. Barbara regretted its passing, but she, like her mother, was a reluctant realist and accepted that what was over was over. America's innocence was replaced, as the years of Vietnam, Johnson and Nixon dragged endlessly on, by bitterness, by contempt for authority and by a jealous and self-destructive hedonism. Barbara's innocence was replaced by the acquisition of knowledge: by 1969, at the age of thirty-two, Barbara had begun to find out what she wanted—and how to get it.

Going from J&S to Palisades Press was like going from Tiffany's to a used-car lot. At Palisades twenty-two books of miscellaneous description appeared each and every month. At J&S the trade list had consisted of fourteen hand-picked and meticulously edited titles twice a year: spring and fall. Palisades Press, a multimillion-dollar property, had been founded seven years before by the man who still owned it, a maniac named Jay Berg.

In 1962, with money advanced by a men's-magazine distributor, Jay had started publishing four pornos a month. In the classic tradition of paperback publishing, they had hard-core covers and soft-core contents. In those years, porno was an excellent business if the publisher knew how to walk the fine line between being raunchy enough to separate the customer from his seventy-five cents and being socially redeeming enough to stay out of jail. Jay Berg turned out to be a genius at walking this fine line. Palisades prospered and grew until Jay had no choice but to go legit. Palisades began issuing a motley collection of popular fiction and nonfiction that grew in numbers every month. Legit, it turned out, made almost as much money as porno, and so Jay Berg found himself being introduced as a "publisher" at parties, a designation that fed his primitive sense of snobbery very well.

Jay bragged to his staff that he had never read a book that carried a Palisades Press logo. He felt he could sell a book better if an editor gave him a brief oral description of the plot so that he, Jay, could devote himself to the important business of selecting a cover. This division of labor worked out satisfactorily for everyone: Jay never had to waste his time reading the junk that Palisades published and no editor ever had to hassle with a publisher who had literary delusions.

Jay Berg, in addition to his other characteristics, was a full-fledged paranoiac whose office walls were decorated with ancient and modern weapons and tools of warfare. A suit of armor stood in one corner of the room and crossbows, bows and arrows, handguns, knives, machetes and poison rings were arranged in show cabinets. A hand grenade served as a paperweight. When asked about the offbeat decor, Jay Berg said, "It makes me feel safe."

Apart from his interest in weaponry, Jay missed the porno business. Porno was his true calling and he continued to run Palisades Press only because it made so much money. His heart was in a new company he had formed with his brother-in-law. It was called Blue Movies, Inc., and produced cheapie skin flicks. Featuring a minimum of plot and a maximum of nudity, they made money hand over fist and gave Jay the satisfaction that he had missed since Palisades had become semirespectable. All in all, Jay Berg was a lucky man. As he himself said: "I can have my cake and eat it too."

Few Americans could make that statement.

The Sexual Revolution had been fought and won when Barbara found herself, at the age of thirty-one, divorced, attractive and available. At the beginning, she was one of the victors of that Revolution. Although the youth culture announced that life was over at thirty, Barbara found that New York in the late sixties was a festival of men and that she was one of the principal celebrants.

New York was filled with men: all kinds, ages and sizes of men available for every taste, occasion, activity, position and experiment. There were married men looking for a little action on the side. There were widowers with and without children; there were professional bachelors; divorced and separated men; men who wanted to be rescued from homosexuality by one magic night in bed and homosexuals who wanted to use an angry and hostile woman as proof of the superiority of their tastes. There were stockbrokers whose erections followed the Dow Jones averages, jock sniffers who hung around P.J.'s and Elaine's and had trouble getting it up, studs whose emotional attention span was just as long as and no longer than their penises.

Barbara met men at work, at parties, at conferences and conventions. Twice she allowed herself to be picked up at the bar of the Regency Hotel, and early one Sunday morning she permitted herself to be picked up in a deli on Third Avenue. On one occasion Barbara took the initiative and picked up a marketing manager on the Eastern Airlines shuttle flight to Washington, D.C. Barbara was also fixed up by married friends, she was introduced to friends of friends at small dinner parties and her phone number was given out by people she barely knew to men who were complete strangers.

The rules had all changed. No longer was it a question of holding hands on the first date and kissing on the third. In the late sixties, if a woman accepted an invitation from a man, it was generally understood by both that she was also accepting an invitation into his bed. In reality, the system worked out well, because Barbara discovered very shortly that if she liked a man well enough to go out with him she liked him well enough to go to bed with him.

In the two years after her divorce Barbara slept with a producer of TV commercials who smoked so much marijuana that his libido was a borderline case; a high-powered political media man who proclaimed eternal love and adoration after a torrid weekend in bed and was never heard from again. She had a brief affair with a lawyer deep in psychoanalysis who fell madly in love with her and later confessed the reason: he was irresistibly attracted to divorced women and one of the goals of his analysis was to rid himself of this strange obsession. She had a matinee with a famous film writer who told her that he really preferred threesomes and asked her if she would mind if he invited another girl. When Barbara turned him down, he shrugged and asked if, in that case, she would mind rinsing out his socks and underwear, since the Carlyle, where he was staying, charged exorbitantly for laundry service.

Twice Barbara thought she was in love. She lived for several months with Alex Proschka, a fairly well-known minimal artist who moved from his Union Square studio into Barbara's co-op and announced after a few months that she was ruining his work. He moved out leaving her one of his one-inch-square dotted canvases as a good-bye present. At the time, it was worth five thousand dollars.

Half a year after Alex disappeared, a lawyer named Len Coloner came into Barbara's life. Len was divorced, he was attractive and he was stable. He proposed to Barbara and two weeks after she accepted, Len, without warning, re-married his former wife. Barbara was devastated by the rejection and set about repairing her torn emotions with the attentions of more men. That was the occasion on which she picked up the marketing manager on the Washington shuttle. She swore that she had had it with love.

She had a number of one-night stands and a variety of two-week affairs. She would fall into bed with any remotely attractive man who asked her, and there were occasional mornings when she woke up with a vicious hangover unable to remember the name of the man next to her. She had simultaneous affairs, juggling two men at once, excited by the attention and competition, thriving on the subterfuges necessary to conceal one's existence from the other.

For a while it was glamorous, like a glossy movie, and Barbara was in love with herself. In love with the image she was projecting, in love with the woman who could attract so many men. But then Barbara began to realize that the image she was in love with didn't love her back. She realized that she was in a state of constant arousal, which depended for release on the next man, the next phone call, the next encounter. It was an arousal incapable of satisfaction.

Barbara learned that she was emotionally incapable of promiscuity. Going from one man to another, from one bed to the next didn't work for her. She found that after she'd been to bed with a man several times she became attached to him, dependent on him, wanting more and more from him. Paradoxically, the life-style she had established for herself prevented her from getting the more and more, the satisfaction, the return on her commitment.

She was skin-popping sex and she was starving inside. She discovered that underneath her Op-Pop-Mini-Maxi life, there was no one at home. It was corny, but she missed having an old-fashioned monogamous relationship and she missed her children. The interesting thing was that as much as she missed the sense of being part of a family, she didn't miss Dick. In fact, she had trouble remembering him and the quality of their life together. When she did think about him, all she could recall for sure was how tired she had been all the time: tired from juggling a marriage, a career and children. Tired from schedules and shopping lists, tired from trips to the dry cleaner and the pediatrician, tired from going nonstop from seven in the morning to midnight, tired from being a wife, mother, hostess and career girl. She hadn't realized it at the time, she had probably been too tired to, but she had spent her twenties in a state of exhaustion. Now, in her early thirties, she was in a state of exhilaration and it had a manic edge to it that was tinged with a sense of despair.

But Barbara ignored the despair and went on with her life.

In life, some things are circular. Events repeat earlier episodes and ricochet in the mind with conscious and unconscious allusions. Other things are linear: that is, they have a beginning, a middle and an end. It is impossible, as we go along, to know which experiences will fall into which category. By the time Barbara was into her thirties, she had had both experiences: the linear, such as her marriage and the unexpected inheritance from her father-in-law, and the circular.

That Annette and Christiaan went to Barbara's old grammar school in Pawling was circular. It seemed quite natural, after the first summer of separation, to agree that it would be best for the children to stay with their grandmother. In the fifties, when Barbara had envisioned a *McCall's* life of Togetherness, such a separation would have horrified her. But now, in the seventies, divorced, living alone, deeply involved in a career, it seemed merely sensible. Perhaps, thought Barbara, she was rationalizing, but it was a way of dealing with the fact that it was her mother, and not she, who was raising her children.

Both of them loved the country: Christiaan loved outdoor sports and Annette loved being able to walk to school without fear. A life for Barbara's children without muggers, juvenile gangsters and dope pushers was an easy choice over the hazards of an urban upbringing.

It had turned out to be an easy decision to make. It was easy to introduce Christiaan and Annette to Mr. Melina, who had been principal of the Pawling Grammar School when Barbara had gone there and who, whether he was lying or not, said that he remembered an essay she had written that had won a Lions Club civics prize. It was easy to be a weekend mother. It was easy to arrive on Friday night with boxes from Creative Playthings and F.A.O. Schwarz filled with educational toys and tied with ribbons of guilt.

It was hard for Barbara to believe the warnings of the experts—they had led her down the garden path so many times before. Hard to imagine Christiaan a future homosexual, Annette a solitary alcoholic. Hard to conceive of Substandard Egos and Lowered Self-esteem. Yet, according to the experts, Barbara was risking all of these and more.

She was allowing her children to grow up without the presence of a strong father figure, and was herself too often absent.

Not that Barbara didn't love her children. Not that she wouldn't have done anything for them, including providing the masculine role model the experts said was vital to healthy emotional development for adolescent boys and girls. But Barbara had no choice. Both grandfathers were dead. Dick was living in Pensacola being a father to another woman's three small children and Barbara had not yet met anyone she'd consider marrying. Barbara's own emotional life consisted at that time of a series of lovers all taken on a trial basis, and sleep-over boyfriends, according to the experts, were an absolute no-no. A multiplicity of male figures, according to them, was even worse than none at all.

And so it was easy to follow a policy of minimum resistance and maximum practicality and let her children live with her mother, and it was hard to accept the guilty consequences of the easy decision. Barbara was upset when she admitted to herself that she thought her own life was more interesting than her children's lives. She had never heard or read of any other woman who put herself first. She accused herself of being callous and selfish; she wondered if her maternal instinct had been perverted, and she hoped to God that the few experts who said it was the *quality* of time spent with a child that was crucial rather than the quantity knew what they were talking about. Only later, with the advent of Women's Liberation and the discovery that other women found child raising boring and tedious and with the prospect of a second, lasting marriage, was Barbara finally able to admit her guilt out loud and thus be freed of it.

In January of 1970, Biafra surrendered after thirty-two months of war, famine and futility. The Cowboys, who had a rep of always losing the Big One, lost 16–13 to the Baltimore Colts in the Orange Bowl. Everyone was predicting that *Love Story* with Ali MacGraw and Ryan O'Neal would be the biggest movie of the year, fashion designers considered the fifties a fit period for revival and Barbara went back to work for J&S—on her terms.

Leon Kravat, whom she had never expected to lay eyes on again, called and invited her to lunch at the Italian Pavilion.

"How about the Brussels? It's nearer my office," said Barbara. It was time she conducted her life on her own turf. She knew the maître d', the wine steward and the waiters there. It would be like having the troops on her side.

"One o'clock?" asked Kravat.

"One o'clock."

Barbara didn't go to the trouble of being late. She had already made her point with Leon Kravat. She wondered what was on his mind. It didn't take long for him to tell her.

"Would you consider returning to J&S?" he asked. He had already informed her—confidentially, of course—that Stanley Bairman was "not working out." Barbara could have told him that a year ago. But a year ago Leon Kravat hadn't bothered to ask.

"My terms haven't changed," said Barbara. She could afford to be indifferent. She was—to a point. She liked Palisades; Palisades liked her. She was treated well and she was given almost total freedom to conduct her job the way she pleased. If J&S wanted her back, they'd have to go all the way.

"We're prepared to meet them," said Leon Kravat. His voice was totally uninflected. He was so calculated that Barbara could read the four paragraphs that lay behind every five-word sentence. If IBM could have produced a computer that bit its nails, it would have produced Leon Kravat.

"Title, salary and status?" asked Barbara.

"Everything," said Leon Kravat. "We made a mistake in letting you go."

How nice of him to admit it, thought Barbara. She let

him wait while she decided to answer. She stirred her demitasse and nibbled on the lemon peel that lay on its small saucer. Leon Kravat's right hand was lying on the white tablecloth. She was sitting right next to him on the banquette. Impulsively, she took his hand in both of hers and examined it closely.

"You know, Leon," she said. "You're really too old to be biting your nails."

Triumph was an endless high. Barbara was interviewed by a reporter from the *Times* who was preparing an article on the progress of women in the executive suite from coffee servers to policymakers. She addressed the Ad Club on book promotion and advertising. *Publisher Weekly* quoted parts of the speech, and *Writer's Newsletter* ran a rave piece on Barbara's charm, competence and brilliant future.

Barbara had money and status. She had learned to be defiant and she had learned to win. Her life went on, phone calls and deals, best sellers and authors' publicity tours, lovers and loving, her children and the indulgences that money and power could buy—until the summer of 1971.

That August, she met Nat Baum.

6 IN THE BEGINNING, IT WAS just like the fifties all over again. Nat didn't suggest a matinee on their first lunch date. He waited a whole week to call her again; they met for drinks at the St. Regis bar and had such a good time that they both canceled other dinner dates and had dinner together. As he put her in a taxi, he kissed her on the forehead. It was the first time they had touched. On the third date he arrived at Le Manoir with a single yellow rose and took her home. He kissed her on the mouth in the foyer of her apartment, wished her good night and left.

By the time they went to bed together, on their fifth date, it was by mutual consent and mutual desire. It was an orgasmic adventure of lust and necessity. It was well past midnight when Nat dressed to go home.

"Tomorrow?" he asked. Barbara loved the way he dressed: he was wearing a silk Art Deco printed shirt from Saint Laurent with a coordinated tie in a contrasting but complementary pattern. She thought he had the best taste in clothes of any man she had ever met.

"What about your wife?" asked Barbara. It was the first time since they had met that either of them had referred to Nat's marriage. He took it in stride.

"We have an arrangement." He was stepping into his trousers: dove gray, flared leg, no pockets. Everything he wore was like cream. Cashmere and silk and the softest flannel. He was the most sensuous man Barbara had ever met.

"You go your way and she goes hers?"

"Something like that." He was slipping into his shoes: soft loafers, almost like bedroom slippers. Not by Gucci; Nat Baum was too hip to be wearing Gucci at this late date.

"It's very Continental of you," said Barbara.

"I'm just a nice Jewish boy from the Lower East Side," said Nat Baum. "And besides, all I asked was if I could see you tomorrow."

"Touché," said Barbara.

She liked being put in her place. Her success had made her too assertive. She came on very strong and she was conscious of it and didn't like it and was powerless to control it. It was probably corny of her, a hang-up left over from the fifties, but she considered it unfeminine and she was happy to have someone tell her to knock it off when he was right and she was wrong. She had overstepped the unspoken agreement they had made. All they had signed up for was a good time.

"Tomorrow?" asked Nat as he kissed her one last time and made her wish that the evening were just beginning instead of ending.

"Tomorrow."

September. October. November. They were possessed by each other. Possessed and obsessed.

"I can't stop thinking about you," said Nat. "I think about you twenty-four hours a day. Do you know that I walk around with a perpetual hard-on. It's embarrassing. I'm going crazy. You're driving me crazy."

It was the same with Barbara: "You're like heroin," she said. "Addictive and forbidden. I can't get enough. I'm a Nat Baum junkie."

They were fascinated with each other: Older Man/ Younger Woman.

"How can you be almost twenty years older than me?" asked Barbara. "It's not possible."

"It's a mistake in the calendar," said Nat. "They'll have to rewrite it."

"Maybe I see you as a father figure," said Barbara, teasing him.

"Better than a mother figure," he answered, and they dissolved.

Nat made no bones about being impressed with Barbara's money. He, like most men Barbara had known, had been intimidated and turned on by her apartment, obviously expensive, and her clothes, also obviously expensive. Barbara had observed that men liked the idea of going to bed with a woman who they thought might possibly be richer than they were. She supposed it added to their sense of conquest.

"I like rich women," said Nat. "They're independent. They can always tell you to go to hell."

Barbara knew that Nat's wife had money. She wondered why *she* hadn't told Nat to go to hell. She would if her husband carried on as blatantly as Nat.

"Behave," said Barbara, "and I won't tell you to go to hell."

"Suppose I misbehave?"

"If you misbehave, you can go to hell. Consider yourself warned." Barbara loved the tension between them, the being on edge, the heightened nuances, the constantly shifting balance of power. It escalated the eroticism.

"Right now, *you* behave," he said, and made her docile with his kisses.

Then there was religion. He was Jewish and she was Gentile.

"Funny," said Barbara, "but you don't *look* Jewish."

"Funny," said Nat, "but you do." They thought it was hilarious.

"Jewish men are warm and passionate. Not uptight like WASP men," said Barbara. "There's only one unfashionable thing about you, Nat Baum: you're not the least bit 'cool.' "

"Not the least bit," said Nat. "Come here," and she did and they dissolved again at the wonder of it all.

Often he'd call her from his office and say, "I want to fuck you," and they'd both leave their offices and meet in Barbara's apartment and make love until they were breathless and limp and dizzy and go back to work to meet again at five-thirty and fall on each other like cats in heat.

They couldn't keep their hands off each other, and they dabbled in semipublic love. Once, driving back from Emily Shaw's restaurant in Pound Ridge, Barbara went down on Nat while they were driving seventy miles an hour on the New York State Thruway. Once they did it standing up in the passageway that led to the lounges in the Beekman Theater. Once they did it on a folding chair in the room that held the mineral collection of the Museum of Natural History, hiding behind the entrance doors just out of sight of the guard who was patrolling the foyer outside.

One Saturday, early in November, Nat told his wife that he had an important business meeting and he sneaked away from home and spent the day in bed with Barbara. They tried every position they had heard of or imagined. They even made up a few that they were sure no one had ever thought of before. They explored every inch of each other's bodies with fingers and tongues and toes. At six, cross-eyed with fatigue and passion, Nat reluctantly said that he had to leave.

"That was fantastic," said Barbara as they stood at her door.

"It was OK," said Nat. "For openers."

They explored all their fantasies with each other. They had an agreement to go all the way, to place no limits on the extent of their odyssey. They were explorers on an uncharted realm of pleasure and indulgence. They marveled that they were on the identical wavelength. They could finish each other's sentences, read each other's thoughts. When they looked at each other, they saw only their own reflections. It was incredible, it was magical. How could it be? With all their differences, they were the same person: one-half male, one-half female.

They saw each other every day except on weekends and holidays. It was part of the price of being involved with a married man, and Barbara paid it without complaint. Whatever Nat Baum could give her satisfied her. She censored all fantasies of the future, content to live only in the present. Nat was married and he had no intention of doing anything about it.

"After all," he said, "I've been screwing around for years."

"And I've had affairs with married men before. Big deal."

They were adults. They knew what the score was. They were both positive that they could handle it.

Just after Thanksgiving, which Barbara spent in Pawling and Nat spent in East Orange, New Jersey, with his wife, her brother and his wife, Nat asked Barbara if she could get away for a week in January and spend it with him in Eleuthera.

Barbara accepted the invitation calmly.

She expressed her excitement in a buying orgy. She bought French bikinis, chic terry beach robes, jeans for deep-sea fishing and white pants for free-port shopping, forty-dollar cotton tops to go with the pants, long dresses of voile for dinner and dancing and cashmere sweaters (they had been revived from the fifties) to throw over them. She bought new underwear and new nightgowns, sneakers and thong sandals for day and platform sandals (revived from the forties) for evening. She bought new luggage at T. Anthony, had her legs waxed at Arden's and her hair put into condition at Don Lee's. She ordered new makeup in darker shades to go with her suntan, après-sun moisturizing lotion and a portable hair dryer that worked on American and European current.

It never dawned on Barbara that she was, in fact, buying a trousseau.

On a Friday afternoon, the New York skies dark and dirty, Nat and Barbara took the flight via Nassau to Rock Sound. They took a taxi to the house that Nat had rented for the week. It was owned by a British designer of home furnishings and was set back from a curve of white beach. The sea was transparent emerald, the palm trees were carefully tended and the immaculate swimming pool had a floor of Portuguese hand-painted tiles. The interior of the house was white—the bleached wood floors, the walls—and the ceiling was painted a blue that matched the sky. The furniture, a combination of native rattan and English antiques, was covered in a white-and-blue geometric print designed by the owner. A large collection of blue-and-white Delft formed the only other decoration.

The house was equipped with every conceivable luxury: a staff of four who were rarely seen and never heard; a sauna bath and exercise room with mirrors and a ballet barre; a white marble bathroom with double everything: sinks, bidets, tubs and toilets. It had a small refrigerator stocked with champagne, gin, tonic and limes. The towels were the big ones from Porthault. There were sunlamps fitted into the ceiling, air conditioning and a tap for bath oil fitted next to the ones for hot and cold water. There was even a special round tub which provided sea water if you wanted to bathe in the ocean without leaving the house.

The rental for the house also included two automobiles: a gaily striped Jeep and a chocolate Rolls. There were a sailboat, a motor yacht rigged for deep-sea fishing, water skis, a tennis court, a bowling alley, a boathouse with all sorts of fishing tackle and even a small tarmac landing strip.

It was paradise on earth, and Nat and Barbara availed themselves of none of it. They spent the entire week in bed.

They made love every way they had in the past and a few new ways they hadn't gotten around to yet. They had oral, anal and vaginal intercourse. They did it on the bed and off the bed; they did it sitting up and standing up and lying down. Vertical, horizontal, right side up and upside down. They would have done it swinging from the chandeliers had there been chandeliers.

They didn't waste time eating or drinking—although they ordered an occasional rum punch from the butler, who had never had it so easy.

Neither of them could believe that seven days could have passed so quickly when they dragged themselves apart on Sunday afternoon. Barbara was taking the flight back to JFK, and Nat was taking a later flight to Miami to a record distributors' convention. They said and kissed their good-byes, and Barbara walked off toward the Pan Am gate where the plane was waiting. She heard Nat before she felt his touch.

"Barbara!"

She stopped in her tracks. All she could think of was that he had figured a way to stretch their week into two weeks.

But no.

"Will you marry me?"

She was sure she hadn't heard him properly.

"I said, will you marry me? I mean it. I'm serious."

The loudspeaker announced the last call for the JFK flight.

"I know you're serious."

Before he could answer, Barbara passed through the departure gate. She had no memory of boarding the plane, of fastening her seat belt, of landing, of going through customs, of getting back into Manhattan, of returning to her apartment.

She wished she were dead.

No.

She wished he were dead.

Goddam him. It wasn't fair, thought Barbara. They were having an affair. They had agreed on that. No divorce, no marriage, no heavy scenes, just an affair. No responsibilities, no commitments, no future. Now, without warning her, Nat had broken the rules. He wanted to convert their linear relationship into a circular one.

She'd tell him to go to hell. Marriage was dead. This was the seventies. No one got married anymore. Nat Baum could take his proposal and shove it.

Barbara raged and fumed. She almost exploded. And the worst thing was that the son of a bitch was in Miami, out of reach of her anger. He had dropped his bombshell and split. Since her rage had no target, it burned out on its own fuel. Barbara was embarrassed at her overreaction and was glad that Nat had to be away for the week. It would give her time to think.

She had known that sooner or later the question of a second marriage would undoubtedly arise. She had been sure, though, that the time was safely off somewhere in the distant future. Whenever her mother had brought up the subject, Barbara had replied that she'd worry about it when the time came. Until someone proposed, there wasn't much point in speculating.

It had never occurred to her that Nat Baum would propose. He had said, hadn't he, that they were having an affair? That affairs, by their very nature, were finite, with a beginning, a middle and an end? They had also agreed that the end was still somewhere in the future; that they would get sick of each other and their feelings would die a natural death. Meanwhile, they had agreed to live in the present and enjoy each other without thinking about consequences or permanent commitments.

Now all of a sudden Nat had made a serious proposal and Barbara knew that he expected a serious answer. Well, she knew what the answer was: the answer was no. She wouldn't marry him. She wouldn't marry anyone. There were too many good reasons not to marry again.

Most obviously, Nat Baum was already married. He would have to get divorced first and that might take a long time. Barbara knew a couple who had lived together for four years while the man waited for a divorce from a wife who fought every step of the way. Finally, though, he had won and they were married. Barbara wondered why, after all that time, they had bothered. Their relationship, now that they were legally wed, was for the birds. The waiting, the stress, the uncertainty of the four years seemed to have left them weary and beaten, and now that they no longer had the wife to blame for all their problems, they blamed each other. Having dinner with them was a nightmare, a scene out of *Virginia Woolf*. Barbara wasn't going to end up like that, exhausted and disenchanted. She didn't want to live through a degrading settlement fight and a drawn-out separation. She couldn't stand being "the other woman."

Something else bothered Barbara that she tried to ignore but couldn't. She was, deep down, afraid that if Nat left one woman, he would leave a second. The second would be herself. She felt guilty about having such ignoble thoughts about him and she tried to suppress them as much as she could. But still they bothered her—she could see herself at forty-five, deserted by a bored husband. And a divorce at forty-five was infinitely worse than a divorce at thirty-one. She'd be a two-time loser, and who would want her then?

Barbara was surprised and upset at how important it was to her to be considered marriageable. It made her uneasy to realize how dependent she still was on the acceptance and approval of men. Was she still as basically unselfconfident at thirty-plus as she had been at minus-twenty? The realization threatened her.

And the children. What about the children? Annette and Christiaan had been jerked around enough. They had just begun to settle down. They were both doing well in school, making friends, accepting a father who saw them on vacations and a mother who visited on weekends. They had adjusted to the upheavals in their lives and Barbara felt that it would be cruel and unfair to ask them to make yet another major adjustment. Would it be fair to thrust a stranger on them and expect them to accept him as their new father? And what about Nat's daughter, Joy? She was approaching twenty and, according to Nat, a with-it kid. She was only a dozen-plus years younger than Barbara. What would it be like to have a stepchild who was almost a contemporary? There was more to think about than just herself and Nat. There was more than just the wants and needs of two people to consider. There were five individuals to think about. Six, if Barbara included Nat's wife.

Nat's wife. Evelyn.

Evelyn Baum had no reality for Barbara. Nat didn't speak of her often, and Barbara, out of a combination of courtesy and indifference, never asked. Barbara had no idea of what Evelyn Baum looked like or what she did with her time or how she rationalized Nat's flagrant infidelity. Evelyn Baum, as far as Barbara could see, was a woman who wasn't. As far as Barbara could tell, she never argued with Nat, never made demands and never accused him of his adulteries. Maybe, thought Barbara, Evelyn Baum just didn't give a damn.

Yes, Barbara had a lot of reasons not to marry Nat Baum.

They were all good and they were all bullshit. The real reason that Barbara didn't want to marry Nat Baum, despite the fact that she was madly in love with him, was that she associated marriage with failure.

Barbara had grown up at a time when marriage was thought to be the whole reason for a woman's existence and when marriage was, literally, to endure "until death do you part." Making the painful discovery that she had fallen for a lie had made Barbara infinitely wary and deeply cynical. When she had married Dick Roser, she had never dreamed that she would one day be divorced from him. No one in her family or his had ever been divorced. Divorce was for movie stars and heiresses. Divorces occurred in a never-never land that had nothing to do with Barbara and Dick Roser. And now she could barely remember Dick, what he looked like and how his voice sounded.

Marriage? It scared her. The odds were that it wouldn't work out. Look at the statistics. Marriage? It meant failure, and Barbara couldn't bear failure. Marriage? It was too risky.

The thought of it, though, had made Barbara face herself, and she hated Nat Baum for forcing her to do it. The problem was that loving Nat made it easy to hate him and impossible to reject him.

If she did, if she rejected him, she'd never see him again and that would be impossible. Nat Baum had become part of her. They were so much alike it was as if they were the same person. They were both refugees from other times and other places. They had left their roots, defied their destinies, and they had won. If she killed Nat, she'd be killing herself, and she wanted to live.

It took Barbara the week that he was away to come up with the solution to their dilemma. When she thought of it, she was astounded that it had taken her so long. It was obvious. Nat ought to leave his wife and then he and Barbara could live together.

After all, the sixties and the Sexual Revolution were a

fait accompli. People were shacked up together all over the place with different names on the mailboxes, and doormen were no longer the least bit shocked that the occupants of an apartment didn't have the same last name. Barbara was faced with a seventies problem and she had been approaching it with a fifties mentality. The solution, the obvious solution, was a seventies solution.

Live together. Screw marriage. Marriage was dead.

Barbara couldn't wait to tell Nat.

Their reunion was champagne and caviar and lilies of the valley.

"I never thought I'd miss anyone the way I missed you," said Nat.

"You mean not even the wholesalers and the Fontainebleau made up for me?"

"Not even the dog races," said Nat. "And I won." He pulled a stack of bills out of his briefcase and let them drift down over the bed. There were tens and twenties and an occasional fifty. "Eleven hundred dollars," he said.

"Is that how much I'm worth to you?"

"More. Come here and I'll show you."

She did and he did and they made love among the money, rumpling and crushing it beneath them. It was decadent and whorey.

"Like Berlin in the thirties," said Barbara who had just seen *Cabaret*.

"If this were Berlin in the thirties, I'd be on my way to Buchenwald."

"Oh, God. I couldn't stand that." Barbara tried to absorb him into her body and protect him from Nazis who didn't exist except in their fantasies. "I wouldn't let them have you."

Nat spent his first night back in New York with Barbara, and she interpreted it as a victory over Nat's wife. Proof that Nat preferred her. Barbara realized that it was also proof of her insecurity: she still needed tokens and reassurances despite the fact that Nat Baum had asked her to marry him. How old do you have to be, wondered Barbara, to be truly confident?

"What did you tell your wife?" Barbara was curious about the how-to's of his adultery.

"Nothing. She doesn't know I'm back yet."

"Oh."

Barbara admired Nat's cool. When she had cheated on Dick, she had concocted elaborate lies to explain away her absences. Half the time Dick never noticed them and Barbara had offered the excuses without even being asked. Lies of omission, she realized, were much better than lies of commission. They made life simpler. There was less to remember, and if you had any luck at all, the issue might never be raised.

"But don't you feel guilty about cheating on Evelyn?"

"Did you, when you cheated on Dick?"

It was hard to remember. It had been so long ago and she had been a different person then.

"Sometimes I felt guilty. Sometimes I felt proud. You know, triumphant. Having my cake and eating it too, I suppose."

"It's the same for me. Men and women aren't that different," said Nat. "Only the anatomy is different; the emotions are the same."

Barbara felt that way too. Even though she would never join a consciousness-raising group, she agreed with most of Women's Lib. Certainly with the part that stated that the only differences between men and women were physical.

"Do you know why I love you?" she asked him.

"No. Why?"

"Because you make me feel equal."

The next morning they had orange juice and coffee in bed. Later they went to Rumpelmayer's for brunch. They ordered eggs and bacon and toasted English and they were both thinking about Nat's proposal. Neither wanted, for different reasons, to be the first to refer to it until, finally, Barbara could stand the suspense no longer.

"I've been thinking about what you said at the airport."

Nat made a noncommittal noise—an analyst's *mmmmm* signifying encouragement but not approval or disapproval.

"It's not fair. You're making me do all the work."

She swallowed hard, and he swallowed his coffee.

"I love you and I want to marry you," he said when the coffee had gone down. "Does that make it easier?" He smiled, and his suntan made the crinkles around his eyes even deeper and more appealing than usual. Barbara melted and he took her hand. "Will you marry me?"

Barbara almost said *yes. Yes* was what she felt, but *yes* was asking for trouble.

"I'll live with you," she said. "I have it all figured out."

She began the speech she'd been rehearsing and thought it went well. She explained all the reasons for living together rather than getting married.

"We'll live together," she concluded. "That way we can enjoy each other and there won't be all the hassle of divorce."

She waited for Nat's agreement. Everything she had said made such good sense. It was so logical and she had been so persuasive.

"Bullshit."

"It's not—"

"Bullshit. I'm too old to shack up. That's kid stuff. It's good enough for Joy. Not me. I'm an adult and I want an adult relationship. Marriage. All the responsibilities, all the commitments. All the hassles, as you put it."

"I am making a commitment," said Barbara. "I just don't see any point in getting married. No one does any more."

"I do," said Nat. "So I'm old-fashioned. I'm not interested in a let's-try-each-other-out-and-see-how-we-like-each-other, thirty-day-returnable deal. I want everything. Or nothing. I'm too old to play house."

"I didn't say anything about playing house." Nat's ultimatum had frightened Barbara. "I'm willing to make any commitment you want."

"Then marry me."

7 IN FEBRUARY OF 1972, while the United States stepped up bombing raids over North Vietnam and the Irish Republican Army killed seven and wounded seventeen on Bloody Sunday in Londonderry; while Clifford Irving faced the music and Nina van Pallandt signed contracts for a singing engagement at the St. Regis; while President Nixon visited mainland China and signed legislation ending the West Coast dock strike, Nat Baum argued, persuaded, cajoled, pleaded, harangued, threatened and wooed.

In the beginning, Barbara fought him every step of the way.

"If your marriage is so terrible, why didn't you get divorced a long time ago? Before you met me?"

"There was no reason to," said Nat.

"You told me the marriage was dead. Wasn't that enough of a reason?"

"There was Joy to consider. She was younger then. It wouldn't have been fair to her."

"Do you think it's better for a child to grow up in a divided household? I don't. Look at my kids; they adjusted. It would have been worse for them if Dick and I had stuck it out for their sakes."

"I didn't see it that way. At least Joy had a mother and a *father*. Joy is OK. You still don't know how yours are going to turn out."

Nat had hit home with the remark about Annette and Christiaan. Barbara changed the subject.

"I don't want to be the reason for breaking up your marriage. I don't want to be responsible for anyone else's life."

"Don't be such an egomaniac. I'm not getting divorced because of you. I'm getting divorced because my marriage is dead. You had nothing to do with it."

"Then why didn't you get divorced a long time ago?"—and they were right back at the beginning, arguing the same points, endlessly, getting nowhere.

Nat showered Barbara with attention and gifts. He called her several times a day and they saw each other once and sometimes twice a day. He sent her a pound of Persian caviar and twin bottles of Joy—"the costliest perfume in the world." He gave her a valuable collection of seventy-eight-rpm Benny Goodman records, quince branches, bunches of daffodils and a gold wristwatch engraved with one word: FOREVER.

Nat's campaign was effective. He kept Barbara off balance: one minute attacking and accusing; the next, smothering her with words and gestures of loving compassion. At a certain point she stopped counterattacking and began evading. She didn't realize the subtle shift—but Nat did and he saw the change for what it was: progress.

"What I want to know," he asked, "is why you can't make a commitment."

"Are you implying there's something psychologically defective about me?"

"I'm just asking why you can't make a commitment."

"I *can* make a commitment."

"Then why won't you marry me?"

When she didn't answer, he changed tack and became her ally: "What are you afraid of?"

"I'm not afraid."

"Yes, you are. If you weren't, you'd marry me."

"I'm not afraid. I'm really not. I just don't believe in marriage."

"You're lying." He made his accusation in gentle, understanding tones. "You are afraid. Tell me what you're afraid of."

It took her a long time to utter the words.

"I'm afraid you'll leave me."

She was crumbling, and he kept after her.

"Are you really afraid that I'm going to leave you?" He could be so tender. Now that he had said the words, the sting was gone. He was disarming her worst fears.

"I think about it," she admitted.

"Well, I won't," he said.

"Promise?" The tone was very intense. That in itself frightened her. She wanted to lighten things, to increase the distance between them. The closeness affected her thinking.

"If you have a Bible, I'll swear on it." He raised his right hand.

Barbara smiled. "Your word is good enough for me."

He relented and let a day pass before he mentioned the subject again: "Why does the idea of marriage terrify you?" He was very sympathetic, the way Barbara thought a first-class analyst would be. He wanted to help her understand her fears and thus to overcome them.

"My divorce did me in. I lost faith," said Barbara.

"But that was years ago," he pointed out. "You're not going to let one failure ruin the rest of your life, are you?"

"Then there were the affairs. I had some disasters. Too many. Men rejecting me. Me rejecting men. I'm callused."

"No, you're not. You're defeated."

Barbara thought his words over. He was right, of course. She *was* defeated, too scared to try again.

"I guess I should fight back."

"Not fight back," said Nat. He knew that fighting upset Barbara: she identified strength with a lack of femininity. "But dare to live. Be bold. Boldness isn't unfeminine."

Once again he was right. It was strange how he knew more about her than she did herself. He had an unerring instinct about her deepest feelings. She felt that she could totally depend on him and the effect infinitely soothed her.

"You're letting fear dominate you."

"I guess you're right."

"You don't guess I'm right. You know I'm right."

"I know."

Barbara was resigned to his being right; to his knowing more about her than she did. She was tired of being wrong all the time. She was tired of conducting two battles at the same time: one against Nat Baum and the other against herself. It was wearing her out. She was sick of fighting with him. She was sick of fighting with herself.

Nat Baum was everything she had ever said she wanted in a man: sensitive, intelligent, humorous, compassionate. She thought she must be crazy to keep putting him off. What more did she want? What more could she expect?

The fact was that she loved him and she wanted to marry him. It was time for her to stop making them both miserable.

The minute Nat arrived the evening of the last day of February—leap year: the twenty-ninth—the second Barbara opened the door to him, she embraced him and said, "You win."

He held her as if she were as fragile and elusive as mercury.

"And so do you," he said. "I'm not such a bad catch."

The next day Nat arrived carrying a Tiffany's shopping bag.

"I've been doing some shopping for you," he said, and handed it to her. Barbara opened the pale blue box inside. It contained engraved writing paper: MRS. NATHAN BAUM was centered in navy blue ink, block letters, on the top of each creamy sheet and on the back flap of the matching envelopes.

"They said they could add the address later," said Nat, "once we decide where we'll be living."

"You knew I'd say yes!"

All Barbara could think about was that it took at least six weeks to have stationery engraved. That meant that Nat must have been thinking about marrying her since at least December. It meant that long ago he had gone into Tiffany's and ordered the paper, choosing the style of the lettering, the color and the finish of the paper itself, making all those decisions as if he had already proposed and she had already accepted. His self-confidence had apparently been unaffected by inner doubts or sudden clutches of insecurity. Barbara wished she were more like that. Perhaps if she lived with him long enough, she too would develop that kind of confidence. Maybe, like measles, it was catching.

"I thought I had a fighting chance," said Nat, teasing her.

"Suppose I had said no? I did, you know, in the beginning." His gift, with its implicit assumption of permanence and its bland taking-her-for-granted, both pleased and upset her. She needed to assert herself. She didn't want to be swamped by him. "I might have turned you down. What would you have done then?"

"I would have waited."

"You wanted me that much?"

"Not wanted. Want."

"I love you."

"Ditto."

That evening, Barbara and Nat indulged in future euphoria. She planned menus for the dinner parties they would give; she asked him about the marvelous and romantic places they would visit; she consulted him about the furnishings of their apartment and she even asked him how he would feel about legally adopting Annette and Christiaan.

He told her that he liked no more than eight at dinner parties, since that number permitted optimal conversation; that they would visit Turkey and Marrakech; that their apartment should be an eclectic blend of contemporary and antique and that if she wanted him to and Dick Roser wouldn't object, he'd be happy to adopt her children.

Barbara felt that she was one of the luckiest women in the world. She was young, she was rich, she was free and above all she had the love of a man she loved.

She was glad, now, that she had been married before. She would learn from her earlier mistakes. All the things she had done wrong in the past she would do right in the future.

Now she was mature enough to be able to create a marriage that would be emotionally, sexually and intellectually fulfilling. And the wonderful, the incredible part of it was that all they really needed for total fulfillment was each other.

In the past six months, as Barbara had become more and more involved with Nat Baum personally, she had become more and more involved with him professionally. He had given her virtual carte blanche and she, in fact, was running Alpha's promotion and advertising departments. All copy and art, every ad, both to dealers and to consumers, each mailing piece was routed through Barbara's office at J&S. She had final OK on everything that went out from Alpha and Nat no longer even bothered to look at work in progress, so implicitly did he trust her judgment.

She teased him about the free labor and told him he ought to put her on the Alpha payroll. Despite her teasing, she loved doing the work. It brought her even closer to Nat, if that was possible. She felt that the more a couple shared, the better their relationship would be. There was that much more to cement them together. She felt, in retrospect, that one of the failures in her first marriage was the total separation of her and Dick's professional lives. They came together every night without the slightest idea of what the other had experienced during the day; in a sense they had to identify each other all over again every night of their marriage. This time, that wouldn't happen. She and her husband would share a professional life as well as a personal one. The result could only increase their identification with each other's goals, problems and interests. In fact, from time to time, she and Nat had even discussed whether she ought eventually to leave J&S and work full-time at Alpha.

Barbara was one of the lucky ones: she had a second chance—and Nat Baum had given it to her.

Early that morning, at two A.M., just after Nat left, Barbara sat down and wrote him a love letter, her first to him, on the stationery he had chosen for her from Tiffany's. It was, in a symbolic way, thought Barbara, the real beginning of their marriage.

It didn't seem the least bit strange to her that she addressed the envelope to him at Alpha Records and marked it PERSONAL.

"Reality strikes," said Barbara, three weeks later. "I'm telling them tomorrow." It was the second Friday in March and the past weeks had been a honeymoon. Never in her life had she loved more completely than she loved Nat Baum. He had replied by asking if it wasn't rather sad that he had had to wait until his early fifties to meet the love of his life. Barbara had answered that it was better late than never and they retreated into their cocoon of bliss.

But bliss was finite and Barbara, who had put off telling her children about her remarriage, knew that she couldn't and shouldn't put it off any longer. Besides, she was anxious for Christiaan and Annette to meet their new father.

"Will you call me Sunday night?" she asked Nat, still seeking reassurance.

"You know I will. You don't have to ask," he said.

It bothered Barbara more than she admitted that she couldn't call him. He was still living with his wife. Nat had consulted a divorce lawyer, who had told him that under no circumstances must he be the first to move out. It would prejudice his rights in a divorce action. It would open the way for Evelyn to accuse him of desertion and thus give her leverage in financial negotiations and child-visitation privileges. It seemed inhuman to Barbara that the quirks of the law forced people to live together even though both wanted out.

"When will you be able to move out?"

"When we reach a settlement. I don't want Evelyn to turn Joy against me."

"She wouldn't go that far, would she?" Nat adored his daughter and it was inconceivable to Barbara that Evelyn would prevent him from seeing Joy.

Nat shrugged. "I don't know," he said, and shook his head. The expression on his face was infinitely sad and Barbara held him close until the moment had passed.

Nat had told her that the strain of living with Evelyn had become almost literally unbearable. He had been very jumpy and was drinking more than usual. Sometimes when Barbara met him at five, she realized that he had already had a few and when she pointed it out to him he got very edgy and told her that he had always enjoyed drinking and that he intended to continue to enjoy it. It was against Barbara's nature to nag and she dropped the subject. It was a temporary problem, one that would disappear as soon as Nat was able to move out. In the meantime, he needed understanding, not more hassle.

"I'll call you Sunday," he said. "If I can get away, I'll come over. I love you."

"I love you too," said Barbara. She hated the constant partings and she couldn't wait until the day came when she and Nat could be together all the time. She understood his edginess because she felt it too. The constant upset of meetings and separations was like being dragged through a shredder. The moment he left her apartment that night, she began looking forward to Sunday night and seeing him again. It was a horrible way to live and Barbara wondered why no one ever spoke of the pain of love. Maybe it was one of America's best-kept secrets: that love *hurt*, too.

The next day, in Pawling, Barbara told Christiaan and Annette about their new daddy. Their reactions reflected the differences in their characters.

Annette, now approaching fourteen, was too old for David Cassidy and in a symbolic gesture had given away her collection of a hundred and thirty-eight David Cassidy pictures to a ten-year-old girl down the street. She had outgrown her earlier dreams of becoming a ballerina and dancing with Nureyev and a more recent ambition of marrying David Frost because she liked his funny accent. Annette's current ambition was to be like Jane Fonda. Jane Fonda, said Annette, was the ideal woman, liberated and committed. She too wanted to give speeches against wars even though it meant that she might be arrested.

Christiaan, nearing thirteen, was as old-fashioned as his

sister was contemporary. He was obsessed with sports and manliness. Perhaps, thought Barbara, living in a household of women had made him insist more strongly than normal on the prerogatives of manhood. Annette accused him of male-chauvinist piggery, and Barbara tended to agree with Annette. He showed all the signs. He reacted to Barbara's announcement with rage.

"One man in a family is enough," he had said. "Besides, I've already got a daddy. I don't need another one."

His anger shocked Barbara, and then she realized that maybe he was just fearful of the competition.

"Don't you think it would be nice to have a man to talk to? He'd be on your side," she pointed out.

Christiaan thought it over. "He can't have my chair," he announced. Christiaan sat at the head of the table at meals in what Evangeline Drooten referred to as "the daddy's chair." Christiaan wasn't about to give it up.

"He doesn't want your chair," said Barbara. "He wants to be your friend. Wouldn't you like a new friend?"

Christiaan sensed that he had his mother on the defensive, and he refused to talk to her for the rest of the weekend. Barbara blamed herself. It was her own fault. Christiaan had been spoiled, with Barbara's consent, by his grandmother, by her own guilty indulgences and by the flirtatiousness of his sister. His lord-of-the-manor attitude was her own doing.

Annette's reaction was paradoxical. The first thing she asked about Nat was what he did. When Barbara told her, Annette said: "A businessman. Yuch. I hate businessmen. All they think about is money."

"What ever makes you think that?" Barbara wondered where Annette got her ideas.

"All businessmen are capitalists and capitalists are bloated pigs," said Annette. "Angela Davis says so."

Barbara said nothing. How on earth was she supposed to deal with a thirteen-year-old Communist? She decided on the spot that some problems were better left unfaced.

Barbara had already told her mother about Nat. The good news—he was intelligent, honorable, sensitive, compassionate—and the bad news—he was married but in the process of getting divorced; he was Jewish but never went to synagogue and certainly didn't believe a word of it and, last, and most anxiously, that he was almost twenty years older.

"There are a lot of problems," Evangeline Drooten had said.

"I know," said Barbara, "but we love each other enough to work them out."

"If you're sure . . ." said her mother. Her mother had not been the least bit unkind, but Barbara wished she had been more enthusiastic. But she supposed she was too old to look to her mother for support. After all, she was a mother too, and look at her doubts, grave ones, about her children and their future.

"Anyway," said Barbara, "You'll love Nat. I know you will."

Evangeline Drooten nodded. She wished her daughter well and she intended to keep an open mind.

As Barbara left Sunday evening, Annette pulled her aside.

"When are we going to meet Nat?"

"Soon. Very soon."

"Well, I wanted to know . . ." began Annette haltingly, for she was about to betray Jane Fonda. "What I wanted to know is what I should wear."

Barbara smiled for the first time that weekend. "You know what? I love you. You're just great!"

"I love you, too, Mommy," said Annette. Then she turned serious: "Wouldn't you say that Jane Fonda cares about clothes too?"

"I'm sure she does," said Barbara.

Although her last exchange with Annette sweetened the weekend, reality seemed very depressing, and it caved in on Barbara as she drove back to Manhattan. She was bothered by her mother's obvious reservations. She was disturbed by Christiaan's overt hostility to the idea of a stepfather. She wondered for the first time in a month of euphoria if she had made the right decision. So much pain was involved that Barbara had a sudden impulse to turn the car north and hide someplace in Vermont where no one could find her. But the impulse lasted only a moment; it was a psychic safety valve, and she thought about Nat and what they had together and she knew that she was right. It was worth every bit of pain, and as long as she had Nat, she could cope with anything.

By the time she left her car in the garage in her building and let herself into her apartment, she was in a glorious mood. It was just seven. She would probably hear from Nat any moment and he would probably be able to spend a few hours with her. She turned the radio on to a rock station to match her upbeat mood and made some shrimp salad. She put some white wine in the refrigerator, got out some brie, sliced some cucumbers and put some watercress in ice water to crisp, all the time knowing the phone would ring any moment.

By eight Nat hadn't called, and by eight-thirty Barbara was considering calling him. So what if Evelyn answered?

Barbara knew Nat's number by heart, although she had never once called him. She had looked it up in the Manhattan phone book after their second date and considered it an omen that he lived at Eighty-first and Fifth, just a few blocks from her. She picked up the phone, listened to the dial tone and almost began to dial the sequence of numbers. If Evelyn answered, she'd hang up. It was a switch on the old joke: If a man answers . . .

Only it wasn't funny.

Barbara put back the receiver wondering why Nat hadn't called. Something must be preventing him from getting to a phone. She tried not to speculate. Instead she flipped through the Sunday *Times Book Review,* clipping J&S ads and reviews of J&S books; she glanced at galleys for a spring book on creative indoor gardening; she considered having a glass of white wine and rejected the idea. She was nervous and distracted and couldn't keep her mind on anything. She kept replaying the weekend; she kept wondering what was keeping Nat. It was sheer torture and there was nothing she could do. She was helpless.

Finally, at nine-thirty, the phone rang. It was Nat and he was drunk and depressed.

"I can't stand this," he repeated over and over. "I can't stand living like this."

He was calling from a bar on Third Avenue and he ripped Barbara's heart out, and she did all she could to comfort him but he was beyond comfort.

"I'm miserable. I can't stand being away from you. I can't stand this," he kept saying. She could hear the noises of the bar, the talking and the laughing and the clinking of glasses, an ironic counterpoint to the pain in his voice.

"Do you want me to come by and pick you up?" Barbara was worried about him. Worried that he'd be mugged or beaten in his unsteady state. Worried that he'd get into a sordid bar fight. Worried that something terrible would happen to him. She wanted to protect him.

"You must hate me. I'm so drunk. I'm disgusting." Barbara assured him that he wasn't and that she didn't hate him. But she did feel abandoned and he was too drunk for her to be able to say it and get a comforting response and so she dropped it. She wondered what had happened that weekend. She wondered what was going on between him and his wife. Whatever it was, it was bad news. What had Evelyn Baum said—or done? For the first time, Evelyn Baum was beginning to seem real. A real person who had power over her life and her happiness. Barbara had to know and so she asked the question she dreaded.

"Did something happen with Evelyn? Something bad?"

"I hate myself. I can't stand this," Nat was slurring and it was hard to hear him over the background noise. "I love you. I worship you," he said.

"I love you too," she said. It was the response that was called for. Barbara had never heard Nat this drunk. She was afraid he'd stay in the bar until closing time—three A.M.? four A.M.?—getting drunker and drunker. She thought about getting into a taxi, picking him up and delivering him to his building. But she decided against it. She didn't want to treat him like an infant. She didn't want to be his keeper. She wanted to be his mistress. She wanted to be his wife.

She buried her pain in caring for his, and when she went to bed she couldn't sleep. Christiaan, her mother, even Evelyn Baum—Barbara's mind wouldn't stop, and she knew that not sleeping would only make things worse. Finally, at two-thirty, she got up and swallowed a Seconal with a big slug of Scotch right out of the bottle. She knew it was a foolish thing to do, but it was just for this once and it would guarantee her six hours of oblivion.

Tomorrow she would tell Nat about her weekend and find out what had happened to him and what, if anything, Evelyn had said.

The next morning the only thing that was real about the night before was the barbiturate hangover. Barbara's mouth was dry and her head ached. She drank two Alka-Seltzers, a glass of orange juice and an ice-cold Coke while she dressed for work. Her skin looked gray, and she used extra blusher and an extra spray of Le De to cheer herself up. By the time she had got to the office, drunk a cup of black coffee out of a plastic foam container and eaten half a toasted corn muffin, gone through the mail, returned the calls left from Friday and dictated a memo to the art director about off-register color reproduction in the creative-indoor-gardening book, she felt practically human. She called Nat just before she left for her lunch date and they decided that he would come to her place for dinner. Neither of them referred to the evening before. They had decided, by mutual unspoken consent, to discuss the weekend face to face. It would be easier, and more civilized, that way.

Nat arrived with a potted red tulip in an antique basket from Parrish-Woodworth, a chic Madison Avenue florist.

"What can I say? How can I apologize?" he asked. He looked almost as if he were afraid that she might hit him— or throw him out. His vulnerability touched Barbara.

"You don't have to. Remember: I love you."

They decided not to go out but to order up Chinese food. They both wanted to be alone that evening without the distraction of a restaurant, of menus, ordering, waiters and the conversations of other diners. Barbara told Nat about the weekend: about her concern over her mother's clear reservations and Christiaan's overt hostility.

"I didn't think they'd be so . . . negative," she said. "I didn't think it would be so hard."

"It'll work out," said Nat.

"Do you think so?" Barbara saw herself as liberated and independent, but there were times she needed help. Thank God for Nat: he was always there to help.

"I know so," he said. "It just takes time for everyone to get used to the idea of a stepfather, of a new son-in-law."

Put that way it seemed so reasonable. Of course things would work out. They always did in life, didn't they?

"I adore you; you always fix everything, don't you?" asked Barbara. "I know I can count on you. Whenever there's something wrong, all I have to do is ask Nat. Nat, the Fix-it Man."

The irony was in his smile and in his words, too. "I wish I were."

"You are," said Barbara. "You are to me."

They shared steamed dumplings, shrimp with Chinese vegetables and beef Szechuan. Neither of them wanted anything with alcohol, and they shared some Coke from Barbara's refrigerator.

"I had a murderous hangover this morning." Barbara didn't know how to bring up the subject of last night, of her anger at Nat for getting drunk and failing her, of her sense of being abandoned. She was much angrier at him than she wanted to admit, even to herself, and so blaming herself was an easy, nonthreatening way to begin. "I couldn't sleep. So, dumb me, I took a Seconal and some Scotch."

"There's a name for that," said Nat. "Suicide."

"I only took one Seconal," said Barbara. She didn't want to tell him that she had washed it down with almost six ounces of Scotch.

"Promise me one thing: that you will never, ever, mix booze and pills."

"I promise," she said. She said it meekly and she rather liked his stern tone. It was a way of being punished for her anger at him without ever having to admit it. It was very satisfactory.

"Drink yourself to sleep," he was saying, "Or take a Seconal. But please, don't mix them. You can die from it. Really. People do, you know, all the time."

"I know." His concern moved her, enveloped her in its protective warmth.

"I promise. It's just that I couldn't sleep. I couldn't turn off," she said. Then, hesitantly: "I was worried about you."

"I was an ass. An idiot. I sort of remember calling you. Did I? It's humiliating not to be able to remember."

Barbara was shocked. She hadn't realized just how drunk he had really been.

"Yes. We had a whole conversation. You mean you really don't remember?"

"Did I say . . . anything?"

Her involuntary nervous system sent signals and she ignored them.

"Anything about what?" she asked carefully, making a pile of crumbs out of a fortune cookie.

"Oh," he said, "anything—you know—stupid?"

"Of course not." She wondered what he could be thinking about. "What could you have said that was stupid? You're the least stupid person I've ever known."

Nat shrugged. "I guess I'm sort of paranoid."

"Isn't everybody?" Barbara laughed and her involuntary nervous system gave up. The alert was over. They were lovers again and nothing had changed. The static had ended. Things were back to normal.

"It bothers me when you drink like that," said Barbara. "I feel very left out. I can't reach you."

"It bothers *me* when I drink like that," said Nat. "Although you have to admit I don't do it too often."

"No. Last night was the first time."

"And the last," he said. "Talk about hangovers . . ." He put his hand to his head. "I couldn't see straight this morning. Like, awful."

"Well, at least we were suffering together. I guess it's good for the Alka-Seltzer company. Maybe we ought to buy some stock."

"Maybe we ought to stop abusing ourselves."

"You're absolutely right."

Now she felt lovely again. Wonderful because everything between her and Nat was the same as ever, as warm and tender and as loving as ever. Maybe more so. Going through hell together brought people closer. There was no question about it.

That evening, they made exquisite love, becoming poets with their bodies.

The name Evelyn Baum had never been mentioned.

8 APRIL WAS A CRUEL MONTH.
The world seemed to shatter and so did Barbara Roser's life.

April began with a North Vietnamese drive, the largest in four years, proceeding directly across the technically neutral DMZ. President Nixon counterattacked with heavy air and naval bombardments and, in Paris, the peace talks ground to a halt. In southern Iran, earthquakes wiped out thirty villages and the death toll was put at four thousand persons. In Northern Ireland, Protestants and Catholics waged warfare in the streets and Belfast's soccer stadium was rocked by a bomb blast.

Whether the planets were awry in their courses or whether, that month, human folly prevailed, death and destruction and endings, rather than beginnings, were in the air.

April was the cruel month when Barbara learned that Nat Baum was leading a double life—and that she didn't even add up to half.

The truth came out when Nat reneged on his third promise to spend the weekend in Pawling meeting Barbara's children and mother. When Barbara pointed out to him that it was his third cancellation, he got irrationally angry. He accused her of keeping count on him. She denied his accusation. She just wanted him to meet her family, and time was slipping by. He had told her over and over, hadn't he, how anxious he was to meet them and to have them like him? Why the repeated delays?

She could understand that he'd be nervous. After all, look how nervous she'd been at having to tell them about Nat. But she'd done it. And she'd lived through it. It hadn't been nearly as bad in reality as it was in the imagination.

She pointed out all of that to him.

"It really isn't that bad," she said. "Let's just go this weekend and get it over with."

"I can't," said Nat. "I can't get away this weekend."

"Why not? You've done it before." What could be simpler? thought Barbara. He'd stolen weekends with her before. Hot, intimate stretches of time, the sweeter for being stolen. "And that," she said, "was before you told your wife about us."

Nat looked at her and, fully conscious of what he was about to do, he told her the blunt truth: "Barbara, I haven't told her yet. She doesn't know."

Numb. Hurt. Humiliated. Raging and burning and impotent.

The emotions fused in Barbara like a nuclear chain.

She called him every vile name she could think of. She accused him of every crime her imagination could conjure up. She threw one of the bottles of Joy, "the costliest perfume in the world," the perfume he had given her, into the Karl Springer mirror in the foyer, shattering both the bottle and the nine-hundred-dollar mirror.

He let her rage on until her fury burned itself out.

When she was exhausted, limply sitting in the corner of the sofa, as far away from him as she could get, he took her in his arms, where, after a token movement of protest, she meekly went.

"But I will tell her," he promised. "Just give me time."

And she did. She was too much in love with him, too hooked on him, too obsessed with him to have a choice. She had gone too far forward to go back. She was committed.

When they made love that night, they were as clumsy and vulnerable as sixteen-year-olds.

The next morning, when Barbara woke up, the apartment reeked of Joy. For the rest of her life she would identify its scent with betrayal.

She forced herself not to ask him. She bit her tongue every time she wanted to know whether he had said anything yet. She exerted superhuman control; but by the end of endless April she couldn't control herself anymore and she asked him whether or not he had spoken to Evelyn.

"It's not just Evelyn," he said. "It's Joy too."

Barbara hadn't thought of that. She had two enemies: the wife and the daughter. It had never occurred to her that the daughter's wishes had to be catered to as well. She knew that Joy was nearing twenty and living on her own. What the hell did Joy care whom her father married? She was too busy living her own life. Wasn't she?

"Leave Joy out of it," said Nat. His voice carried a warning.

"I didn't mean . . ."

"Just don't bug me," he said.

"OK," she said, and dropped the subject.

She didn't want to bug him. She didn't want to make him angry. Whenever he got angry, he withdrew from her, let a few days go by without seeing her or even calling her. She couldn't bear being without him and so she didn't ask, she didn't press, she didn't pin him down.

She didn't know what to do and, in the end, did the worst thing of all: she did nothing.

All the time, cruel April slid into the murderous month of May.

Ninety-one miners died in a silver-mine fire in Kellogg, Idaho. Governor George Wallace was shot at a Laurel, Maryland, shopping center and paralyzed from the waist down. A madman brandishing a hammer disfigured Michelangelo's *Pietà* in St. Peter's. The Duke of Windsor, who had given up his throne for the woman he loved, died at the age of seventy-seven and at the Tel Aviv airport three Japanese gunmen threw hand grenades into a crowd, killing twenty-eight and wounding seventy-two.

And still Nat Baum said nothing to his wife.

It all came to a head, late in May, in the Oak Room of the Plaza Hotel.

They had finished the main course, veal for her and a steak sandwich for him, and Nat had just ordered a second bottle of wine. They were both a little high.

"Nat, let's stop playing games. I want to marry you. You want to marry me. Just be brave and tell your wife. It'll only take a few minutes." Barbara hated the pleading tone in her voice, yet she was powerless to control it.

Nat sipped from his glass and fidgeted and refused to look at her.

"Please, Nat, don't make me plead. It's humiliating."

"So don't plead," he said.

"I'm not. I'm asking." *Asking*, she thought: it left her with dignity. Pleading made her a beggar; asking made her an equal. Barbara gently took his hand away from the stem of the wineglass and held it in her own and, one by one, kissed each of his fingers. He took his hand back as soon as she had finished and drank some more wine. He still hadn't said a word. He was forcing her to do all the work. To do everything.

"If you don't, do it, I will," said Barbara. "I'll write to

her. On my stationery. The stationery you got me at Tiffany's. It's engraved 'Mrs. Nathan Baum.' " It was a brilliant idea. Barbara wondered why she hadn't thought of it before. She began to compose the letter.

" 'Dear Mrs. Baum,' " she began, then changed her mind. "Or should I say, 'Dear Evelyn'?"

Nat finished the glass of wine and poured himself more before the waiter had a chance.

" 'Dear Evelyn,' " she began again, " 'This is to inform you . . .' "

Suddenly, moving so fast that no one else in the Oak Room noticed, Nat broke Barbara's empty wineglass with the edge of the heavy ashtray and held a splintered edge of glass to Barbara's face.

"Stop that shit!" He spoke through clenched teeth, and for a split second Barbara was physically afraid of him. They stared at each other, terrified at what they had driven each other to, and then the moment was over. He grinned and put the shard into the ashtray and asked the waiter to take it away.

"A little accident," he said.

As the waiter walked away, Nat leaned over on the banquette, tilting his body closer to Barbara, and she leaned into him, making everything all right. He reached into his pocket with his far hand, dipped down into it and came up with a dime. He held it out to Barbara.

It took her a moment to understand his meaning.

Then she got it, and like conspirators, they went to the phone booths. None of them was in use, and Barbara chose the one farthest from the door. She put the dime into the slot and heard the dial tone. She looked at Nat and handed him the phone.

"The least you could do is dial," she said.

Nat dialed the seven digits. When the phone began to ring, he handed the receiver back to Barbara just in time for her to hear Evelyn's voice.

"Hello?"

"Hello, Mrs. Baum."

"Yes?"

"This is Barbara Roser. I'm with your husband and we have something to tell you. . . ."

PART THREE

THE FORTIES

The Traditional Woman

"I want to be a wife and a mother.
Isn't that what every woman wants?"
  —Evelyn Baum
  June 1946

1 "NAT WANTS TO DIVORCE you," said the voice on the other end of the line. It stopped, paused, waited for an answer and when there was none, went on. "He wants to marry me." It was a feminine voice, soft-pitched, assured.

"Who . . ." began Evelyn, and then she thought better of it. She didn't want to hear any more. Before the voice could begin again, Evelyn hung up the pale blue Princess phone on her night table. She had always liked the color, liked the way it blended with the blue-and-white floral-printed wall-paper and matching fabric she had used in the master bed-room of the Baum's apartment. Everyone had always said that Evelyn had such good taste, that she would have been a fine decorator. Evelyn liked compliments; she was the kind of woman who hadn't received many and she cherished them, piling them up in her memory and pulling them out when they might buoy her up. But they didn't help, not now. She began to cry and reached for a Kleenex.

Although it was only nine-thirty, Evelyn Baum was al-ready in bed. She wasn't sick, but in the last few years, now that Joy was living away from home and Nat was out so often, she had taken to eating an early dinner—an omelet and a salad or perhaps a lamb chop and some spinach—tak-ing a long bath and getting into bed with a book. Evelyn Baum was one of Doubleday's best customers, buying all the new books as they came in and reading four or five a week. Books were Evelyn's narcotic.

Her book, *The Salzburg Connection*, had slipped off her lap as she had stretched to reach the tissue, and now she picked it up. She wanted to get involved in the story again, to lose herself in the life and emotions of another woman. It was a spy adventure set in Austria. The heroine was caught in a perilous situation, pursued by secret agents, but Evelyn couldn't remember who was on what side and who the double agents were and who the American CIA man was.

Evelyn tried to read, tried to remember the plot. She didn't want to think about the call. She had spent the last ten years not thinking about it.

It. Her situation. Her and Nat's situation. Nat's, really. Nat and his whatever-you-called-them. Girls. His stewardesses and secretaries, Evelyn supposed. Young, with long straight hair like Joy's. Girls who were sexually liberated, girls on the Pill not worried about getting pregnant, available for a good time, for a one-night stand, no commitments, no guilt, no hangover the next morning, never giving a thought to the wife who was alone in bed with a good book. Just a bit of healthy fun in bed with Evelyn's husband.

Evelyn had been aware that Nat was cheating on her. He had never made a point of denying it, of telling Evelyn that he was different from his friends. His friends who sat around Evelyn's dining-room table and bragged about their conquests, their nights on the town, their twenty-year-old chicks with the bodies that wouldn't quit. They joked and laughed and strutted around outdoing one another with tales of their capacity, letting Evelyn in on their spicy secrets, flattering her by including her.

Evelyn knew, all right. She knew that all of Nat's friends, men in their late forties and early fifties, rich and successful stockbrokers, lawyers, insurance men, advertising executives, all did it. They all cheated on their wives and they seemed to do it for one another's benefit as much as for anything. They teased each other about their sexual prowess, feeling expansive enough with Nat's martinis and Evelyn's wine and food to let her in on their buddy-boy conversations. Evelyn listened, not saying much. She laughed if a story was particularly funny and concealed her embarrassment if it was too risqué. The truth was that their flattery *did* get to her. It was implicit in their manner that they trusted her; that they knew she wouldn't rat to their wives. It was the ultimate compliment: they treated her like one of the boys.

Evelyn knew, all right. She knew for a fact that all of Nat's friends were screwing around. Kid stuff, really, and, she supposed, basically harmless. Only Evelyn never really let herself think about Nat's doing it. She never pictured him on a narrow bed in the messy bedroom of an Upper East Side apartment shared by four stewardesses, kissing some young girl with his mouth open and wet. And she never thought about his thick chest hair, sticky with sweat, crushed against anyone else's younger breasts.

So Nat screwed around. Evelyn had known it, but she had done her utmost to repress the knowledge. She had forced it to remain in its hiding place in the bottom of her consciousness. She had repeatedly accepted and believed his absurd excuses when he showed up half drunk at three in the morning with an inane expression on his face. She had forced herself not to question him—afraid of an argument, afraid of his anger. She had accepted it. When women grew older, their men became unfaithful.

But it was a sliver of Nat's existence that wasn't particularly important. It had nothing to do with Nat's real life. Those little bimbos, those stewardesses and secretaries, were barred from the citadel Evelyn Baum had erected around herself and her marriage.

The Salzburg Connection fell noiselessly to the carpet as Evelyn writhed on the bed. This time it was no bimbo. This time it was no one-night stand to be explained away by a lie they both pretended was the truth. Their fortress was an edifice of deceit, and now, with one phone call, it had begun to crumble.

2 NINETEEN-FORTY-FIVE WAS
a year of endings. On April 12 of that year, Franklin Roosevelt died. Americans, according to their political convictions, cheered or cried, and Harry S. Truman, the ex-haberdasher from Independence, Missouri, was sworn in as the thirty-third President of the United States. Less than a month later, in early May, Berlin fell and Germany surrendered. That summer, on August 6, the *Enola Gay* dropped an atomic bomb on the Japanese city of Hiroshima, and three days later, on August 9, a second atomic bomb fell on Nagasaki. On September 2 the Japanese signed the papers of unconditional surrender on board the battleship *Missouri*.

The war, at last, was over.

Nineteen-forty-five was also a year of beginnings. On October 24, the United Nations, created in San Francisco, came into existence, and while the Allies divided Germany and created occupied zones in Berlin, the world had abandoned war and turned to peace in a thousand ways. Jack Benny was back on NBC on Sunday night with Mary, Phil Harris, Don Wilson and the whole gang. Fabric rationing was over, hemlines went down and dress manufacturers gleefully predicted that women would splurge on clothes for the first time since the war began. Henry Ford II, twenty-eight years old, took over as President of the Ford Motor Company, whose profits during the war years had slipped far behind those of General Motors and Chrysler. Two brand-new miracles were introduced to the American housewife: foam rubber and Pillsbury's instant pie and cake mixes. A brilliant athlete from Southern California, Jackie Robinson, was signed to a major-league contract by Branch Rickey of the Brooklyn Dodger organization, but not before Rickey called Robinson a nigger to his face to test Robinson's reaction to the vocabularies of his fellow pros. The child movie star Shirley Temple, now seventeen, married John Agar, twenty-four, an Air Force sergeant, at Hollywood's Wilshire Methodist Church before five-hundred invited guests and thousands of screaming fans. The Woodbury Deb promised to love, honor and keep him just as carefully as she kept her Woodbury complexion; the movie of the year was *The Lost Weekend,* directed by Billy Wilder and starring Ray Milland, and *Harvey,* a gentle fantasy about a man and his invisible rabbit, won the year's Pulitzer Prize for drama.

In 1945, America forgot the war and went to a party. It was at this party that Evelyn Edwards met Nat Baum.

The specific party was a freshman mixer held on a Friday night in October in the auditorium of Briarcliff Manor Junior College in Briarcliff, New York, where Evelyn Edwards, nineteen, was a student and to which Nat Baum, twenty-five and just back in civvies, went to meet the kind of girls he liked best: rich girls with class.

"We're going to have beautiful children" were the first words he said to her, this slick, handsome guy who cut in on Evelyn's date, Ernie Coffman.

Evelyn blushed. She wasn't used to fresh guys and didn't know how to handle a smooth line. She was flattered and awkward, although she was, by the standards of the forties, an attractive girl with clean-cut, all-American good looks. She had not been born that way. Her parents had changed their name from Epstein to Edwards. They had had Evelyn's teeth straightened and her nose fixed and her hair straightened so that she could wear a smooth pageboy parted on the side just like the Gentile girls. Evelyn was pretty on the outside, dressed fashionably in a red-and-green block-plaid wool dress with short sleeves, a scoop neckline, a wide skirt and gold kid ballet slippers. On the inside, she was still slightly plain Evelyn Epstein, a shy and modest girl, anxious to please, fearful of offending, with a slightly hooked nose and hair that got frizzy every time it rained.

"Where do you go to school?" asked Evelyn, knowing it

was an inadequate question, feeling that she was inadequate.

"Columbia," he said, and pulled her closer so that she could feel his chest against her flat breasts. It made her uncomfortable. It made her even more uncomfortable when he leaned his cheek against hers, and she pulled away and he took his hand from her back and adjusted her head just where he wanted it, so that they were dancing cheek to cheek.

"What are you majoring in?" She wished she would shut up. She didn't want to betray her inadequacy to him.

"Shhh," he said and she had no choice but to listen to the record. It was "Till the End of Time," and it was Number One on the Hit Parade. Its intimate, romantic lyrics made Evelyn feel even closer to this handsome, older man whose name she didn't even know and embarrassed at the hot feelings they gave her inside.

"We'll have a boy and a girl," he said. "Two children are perfect, don't you think?"

"Oh, no," said Evelyn, not thinking about what she was saying and too flustered to stop. "I want to have a big family."

"All right, then," he said. "We'll have *two* boys and *two* girls. Will that please you? I want to please you."

Before she could say anything, before she could collect her wits, Ernie cut back in, even though it was against the rules to cut in on someone who had cut in on you. The record changed to "If I Loved You," and Evelyn danced with Ernie and thanked God that she didn't have to dance this song, so tender and romantic, with the neat stranger and at the same time wished she were still in his arms, with his cheek pressed to hers. She wondered how old he was. At least twenty-four, and she was sure he was a vet. She wondered if he'd been overseas, if he'd been wounded, if he had any medals. Fruit salad, they called those clusters of decorations. She wondered if he wore fruit salad and tried to picture him in his uniform jacket. He had to have been an officer. She was sure of that. He was so confident, so sure of himself.

Ernie danced sedately, holding Evelyn at a distance acceptable to them both. They had grown up together in East Orange, New Jersey, and when they were children, Ernie had shown her his pee-pee and she had shown him hers. It was an incident that neither of them ever referred to and that, by now, both had almost forgotten. The Coffmans and the Edwardses approved of each other, and the two families assumed that young Evelyn and young Ernie, who was studying law at Penn, would get married. Therefore, they gave Ernie and Evelyn more freedom than they would have otherwise, both families being conservative and disapproving of the wild behavior of the young—cutting up all over the place, using the war as an excuse for hasty marriages, two day honeymoons, seven-month babies and God knew what else.

Ernie and Evelyn fox-trotted through "If I Loved You," and when the next number came on—it was "The Atchison, Topeka and the Santa Fe"—Ernie, as usual, led Evelyn toward the folding chairs arranged around the edge of the dance floor.

"Those fast dances." He shrugged and went to get them both some punch.

Suddenly the stranger appeared again and held out his hand to Evelyn, and she shook her head no.

"I don't know how to Lindy," she said.

"I do, and I'm a good teacher." He took her hands, both of them, and pulled her to her feet.

"Really," she began, blushing again, a deep crimson in the bright lights that had been specially set up by the Drama Department now that blackouts were a thing of the past, "really, I'd be too embarrassed." She fidgeted with her wide scoop neckline, suddenly afraid that her slip strap might be showing.

He took her hand away.

"Don't worry," he said. "It's not showing."

Evelyn wished Ernie would come back. She was more ill at ease than ever with this aggressive man who had the nerve to talk about her underwear.

"Come on," he said. "I'll teach you to Lindy. You wouldn't want our children to think their parents were squares." He made the sign of a square with his two index fingers.

"Oh, here's Ernie with the punch."

"All the more reason to jive." This time he pulled Evelyn to the center of the dance floor and encouraged her gently to follow him, not to be afraid. He put his left arm around her waist, holding her side by side to him with their two hands out in front of them, and they began to Lindy. Suddenly, he spun her out and twirled her around and she laughed, she was so proud of herself. She couldn't wait for him to do it again. It was such a dizzy feeling, and the dance floor was hot and giddy with girls in ballerina skirts and flats outdazzling one another with the intricacy of their improvisations. Even though Evelyn could never hope to compete with them, she began to feel like one of the crowd.

The boys were all wearing dark suits with ties, and Evelyn was a little embarrassed that her partner—his name turned out to be Nat Baum—was wearing hepcat clothes. His trousers were draped and pegged, and his double-breasted jacket had wide lapels that opened to show a lavender shirt. It was practically a zoot suit, and Evelyn had never met anyone who dressed like that before. It added a touch of daring, and she was even more agitated when the next song was "You'd Be So Nice to Come Home to" and Nat Baum held her much too close.

Evelyn wished the dance would never be over, but when it was Ernie came to get her and Nat Baum disappeared. Evelyn spent the rest of the evening peering over Ernie's shoulder looking vainly for him. She made Ernie stay until half-past twelve, when the chaperons cleared out the few remaining couples.

Afterward she thought bitterly that he was probably out in the parking lot making time with some girl who was just as smooth as he and who didn't mind being fast. They were probably even French-kissing, something that Ernie wanted to do but that Evelyn thought was repulsive with all the spit and germs. She told Ernie that you never knew what it could lead to and that they might not be able to handle it. Ernie accepted her excuses and contented himself with chaste, closed-mouth good-night kisses, and Evelyn began to think that maybe French kissing wasn't so repulsive after all. Now that she had met Nat Baum she wondered what it would be like to be French-kissed by him and she just knew she'd never find out. Romantic, daring things like that never happened to her.

Evelyn did everything she could to make Nat Baum call. She doodled his name all over her notebooks with Waterman's violet ink, and once she even wrote "Evelyn Baum" on the inside of the little address book she kept in her purse just to see what it looked like written down. It was damning evidence of her desire, and she guarded her secret with her very life. She looked at the address book only when she was positive that she would be alone. It was a special and tantalizing treat that she saved for private moments.

One day in English Lit while the teacher was droning on about the symbolic parallels between the three witches in *Macbeth* and the three sisters in *King Lear,* Evelyn printed Nat Baum's name in block letters on the title page of *The Collected Works of William Shakespeare* and, just beneath his, printed her own. She crossed out all the vowels, and when she counted she discovered that, between them, their names contained seven vowels. Seven! That meant that it was fated: she and Nat Baum were destined to fall in love. Then she counted the remaining consonants. There were thirteen. Thirteen was a jinx. She would never see him again.

Evelyn's moods seesawed as wildly as the conflicting meanings of the numerical portents.

Some nights Evelyn stayed in her room so that if Nat called she'd be right there when the housemother came for her. On other nights, Evelyn made a point of getting into bridge games in other girls' rooms and purposely forgot to Scotch Tape a note to her door saying where she was. If he called, he'd be told that she was out and maybe he'd wonder with whom and get jealous.

Phone messages were posted on the bulletin board outside the housemother's room on the first floor of Evelyn's dorm. As the days went by, the board became her tormentor. Her heart beat faster every time there was a message for her. But the messages were always from her mother or Ernie, and Evelyn, her heart still pounding, dragged herself up the two flights of stairs, depressed and disappointed. She began to make pacts with destiny: if she had enough willpower not to peek at the bulletin board until six P.M., fate would reward her with a message saying that Mr. Baum had phoned.

Nothing worked. Destiny ignored her pleas and threats and bargains, and even though Evelyn tried to force herself to forget about Nat Baum, her stubborn emotions wouldn't obey her will. She couldn't understand how meeting someone for one night could have had such an impact on her. She wondered about herself. She felt that it was a sign that she was extremely neurotic, although she wasn't exactly sure what neurosis was. No matter how much Evelyn castigated herself for acting like a high school kid, thoughts about his sharp suit, his smooth line, the way his cheek felt against hers kept coming, unbidden, into her mind. He never called, and even if Evelyn had known where to reach him, she would never have dreamed of being so forward. By Thanksgiving, Nat Baum seemed as remote and as unattainable as a movie star.

Thanksgiving, the most American of holidays, was a tradition in the Edwards family. Simon Edwards had changed his name from Epstein to Edwards in the early thirties when Father Coughlin's bitter anti-Semitic diatribes echoed the doctrines set forth in *Mein Kampf*. Although Simon had never been a religious Jew and although he did what he did for his family's sake, he felt guilty about abandoning the name his father had handed down to him. He balanced the guilt with the realization that he was sparing his family the cruelties, deliberate and capricious, that Jews, even in America, faced: being barred from certain hotels and country clubs; being mocked in private and sometimes even in public. To fill the void created when he denied his heritage, Simon had turned his faith to America, and America had rewarded his conversion well.

Simon's business—importing fine bristles for toothbrushes, hairbrushes and industrial and medical use—had been inherited from his father. Edwards' (once Epstein's) Fine Bristles had survived the Depression and had grown through the treacherous war years with their enormous demands for goods to supply the best-equipped army ever sent forth to do battle. Simon's friend and lawyer, Walter Coffman, had advised and counseled him, and now both the Edwardses and the Coffmans were prosperous, middle-class Americans looking forward to enjoying the peace.

The Thanksgiving of 1945 was a particularly festive one for two reasons. The first was that the war was over and Evelyn's older brother, Pete, who had been stationed in Hawaii but who had never seen actual combat, was safely back home. He had already begun going into the Newark office with his father every day, learning the business, just as Simon had learned from his father before him. The second, but no less important, reason was that both the Coffmans and the Edwardses were looking forward to Evelyn and Ernie's announcing their engagement.

Ernie was due to graduate from law school in June of 1946 and he was going to join his father's firm. When he and Evelyn married, it would symbolically cement the close relationship that had sustained and enriched the elder men and would, with the birth of Ernie and Evelyn's first child, complete the circle.

It was thus that everyone looked forward to Thanksgiving. Everyone, that is, except Evelyn, who knew what was expected of her and who didn't know how to say no. She couldn't disappoint her parents, and she didn't want to upset Uncle Walter and Aunt Bea, whom she had loved since she was a child. She was afraid to defy them and terrified of rebelling—and at the same time, she didn't want to marry Ernie. At nineteen, she didn't want her life to be all planned out in advance. Not knowing how to express herself and fearful of ridicule at confiding the deep emotions she felt for a man she had met only once, Evelyn was even quieter and more self-effacing than usual that weekend.

Ernie and his parents arrived at two-thirty on Thursday, and after sherry in the living room, they all sat down to an enormous meal of turkey and cranberry jelly, sweet potatoes and string beans, hot biscuits and gravy and ice cream frozen into turkey-shaped molds for dessert. Dinner was served by a colored maid who came from Newark for the day to help Evelyn's mother with the cooking, serving and washing up.

Conversation was a mixture of business and politics, gossip and trivia. Simon and Walter speculated about the impact on Simon's business of the nylon bristles that were being used increasingly in cheaper brushes. They agreed that the synthetics would certainly affect the cheaper lines that Simon imported, but they also agreed that there would always be a market for better-quality goods: for the rare bristles from boar and ox, camel and llama. In fact, as the economy boomed, it was likely that business at the luxury level would soar to higher levels than ever before. They went on to talk about Truman's version of the New Deal, the Fair Deal; the fight against postwar inflation; the burgeoning black market in everything from wheat to automobiles.

Everyone was very proud of the ruptured duck in Pete's lapel, and Evelyn was trying to remember whether or not Nat Baum had worn one when Uncle Walter put his arm around her and hugged her affectionately and asked her out loud and in front of everybody when she and Ernie were going to name the date.

"It's high time you young folks made it official," he said. Walter Coffman was a genial man, tall and thin, and Evelyn always ducked away from his kisses because his bushy red moustache tickled. "I'd like to see a sparkler on that third finger, left hand."

Evelyn blushed. Being the center of attention made her very uncomfortable. Everyone was looking at her—her mother and her father, Pete and Aunt Bea and Ernie and Uncle Walter—waiting for her to say something. She had known them all her whole life, and still she blushed and stammered until her father came to her rescue.

"Yes, sir," he said. "We could use a lawyer in the family, all right. We'd save on Walter's fees."

They all laughed, and this time it was Ernie who turned beet red. Finally, it was Fanny, Evelyn's mother, who played the diplomat.

"Leave them alone. I think a girl's proposal is something she wants to hear in private."

"You're right, as usual," said her husband. Simon smiled at Evelyn to relieve her of the embarrassment he had caused her. He kept forgetting just how sensitive his quiet and shy daughter was, how deep her feelings ran. She was so unassertive that it was easy to forget that she had any feelings at all. But Simon knew that she did, and he cherished his daughter's sweet vulnerability.

Simon went to the sideboard and got out a box of fifty-cent Cuban cigars that he saved for special occasions and passed the box to Pete and Ernie, careful to treat them equally now that one was out of the Air Force and the other was about to become a son-in-law.

As they lit up, Simon looked around the big reproduction-Sheraton table, highly polished, with its center leaf fitted in to make room for the extra guests, and he was pleased with himself and with the life he had created. His father's worst predictions about the Germans had all come true. Millions of Jews had been exterminated in Nazi concentration camps. The horrible pictures of gas ovens and piles of clothes and starved skeletons hanging on the barbed-wire fences of places like Dachau and Bergen-Belsen were just now being printed in the newspapers. Even H. V. Kaltenborn, a German himself, spoke with horror of the atrocities committed by the master race in behalf of "racial purity." Night after night, Kaltenborn's NBC newscast was a reminder of the vulnerability of Simon's people.

Simon realized that if his father hadn't left Bremen at the turn of the century, it was entirely possible that none of them would be sitting here now in the sunny dining room with the damask draperies and the bone china and the colored maid in the kitchen cleaning up after the feast. Simon was a man with no particular politics of his own. He distrusted zealots of any kind and, to play it safe, contributed equally to local Democratic and Republican causes. It was his way of buying protection for his family against excesses from either the right or the left.

But the threats were in the past now, and Simon Edwards looked forward to the future. He looked forward to letting Pete gradually take over the business and to seeing Evelyn happily married to a good husband with some fat, bouncy babies to keep her busy. Simon had enjoyed being a father and now he joyfully anticipated being a grandfather. He led his guests back into the living room, where the coffee was to be served.

"Let's go for a drive," Ernie said to Evelyn.

He borrowed his father's Cadillac and took Evelyn to their usual necking spot. They parked where they always did: on a dirt road on a wooded hill overlooking the football field of West Orange Public High. The stadium was deserted. This year the traditional Thanksgiving Day game against East Orange was an away game. As Evelyn knew he would, Ernie put his arm around her and kissed her.

"Don't you think Dad is right? About setting the date?"

Evelyn didn't say anything, and Ernie was nervous about actually proposing. Blindly, he went on. "We could announce our engagement at Christmas and marry in June just after I graduate. Dad offered to give us a honeymoon in Havana for a wedding present," he said, saving the best for last.

When Evelyn still didn't say anything, Ernie assumed she was overcome with emotion. He was unable to speak anymore himself. Instead, he cradled her head against his coat, taking her silence for acceptance. He didn't know what to do when suddenly she moved away from his embrace, cradled her arms against the Cadillac's dashboard, buried her head and broke into sobs.

There was no way for him to know that she was thinking about a brash young man who had talked about her slip strap and about the beautiful children they were going to have.

On Sunday afternoon of the Thanksgiving weekend, Evelyn caught the one-fifty train from Grand Central to Briarcliff. The train was almost empty and Evelyn had a window seat all to herself. The conductor helped her put the small suitcase on the overhead rack and she waved good-bye to her parents, who had driven her into New York and walked her through the station down to the lower level where the Westchester trains departed.

Evelyn stared out the dirty windows, feeling as bleak and gray as the tenements of One Hundred Twenty-fifth Street. She loved her parents and, by her silence, had lied to them. She knew just how much they were looking forward to her engagement, to the June wedding, the trip to Havana and the babies that would follow soon after. She didn't have the heart to tell them that she didn't want Ernie. Instead she had said nothing, and they had assumed her silence meant assent to all the plans they had so lovingly made for her. She had repaid the trust of people who loved her with evasion and dishonesty. Evelyn was inexperienced at deceit, and she felt soiled. She hated herself for her indecisiveness and cowardice.

When the train finally slowed down and pulled into the Briarcliff station, Evelyn got into the long black limousine that the college provided. Briarcliff took excellent care of its students—they were girls from wealthy families, accustomed to protection and luxury. The car was available to take them to the station on Fridays when they left campus for the weekend and it faithfully waited on Sundays to pick them up on their return.

The limousine set Evelyn down in front of the administration building, where she signed in at the desk and walked through the rear doors to the path that led to her dorm. She switched her suitcase from her right hand to her left and began to think about Ernie. She had been cruel to him all weekend, refusing to give a definite answer to his request that she meet him at Tiffany's to pick out a ring. It wasn't so much deliberate stubbornness on her part as an inability on the one hand to tell him that she didn't want to marry him and a fear on the other that no one else would ever ask. Evelyn knew that her dreams of Nat Baum were just that: dreams.

Evelyn recognized the truth about herself. She wasn't the kind of girl that drove men wild. Her datebook wasn't filled up weeks in advance. She had been to one and only one football weekend, and it had been a disastrous blind date arranged by a friend who lived in her dorm. Not for Evelyn were tulle and taffeta dresses, proms and phone calls, bouquets and books of poetry. Not for her were dancing at the Stork Club, getting high on Scotch out of a flask at the Army–Navy game. She wasn't one of the girls who made and broke engagements as casually as they wore their sloppy Joes, returning diamond-solitaire rings and acquiring new ones as if it were all a jolly game of Monopoly.

Despite the nose job and the orthodontia, the hair straightening and the stylish wardrobe from Best and Altman, Evelyn was still a plain girl, because she felt like one; and because she felt like one, she acted like one. Men picked up the scent very quickly and they left her alone in search of the belles, girls who know how to flirt, how far to go in the back seat of a car, girls who had known how to get along with men from the time they were five and had already learned how to manipulate Daddy into buying them a forbidden strawberry ice cream cone between meals or a big bottle of pink bubble bath.

The truth about herself didn't depress Evelyn. She wasn't afraid to admit or accept it. It was just that in meeting Nat Baum, she had had, for the first time in her life, a dream. Something, someone to aspire to. She knew how foolish, how unrealistic it all was. It was just that it was hard for a dream-starved girl to give up the only fantasy she'd ever known. Yet it was the sensible thing to do.

As she walked across the campus, Evelyn paid no attention to its attractions. Even in the thin December sun it was pretty. The stone buildings were ivy-covered, and an artfully landscaped gazebo was 'set in the center of the carefully tended main lawn. In the spring, when the weather turned warm, the girls took their textbooks and sat around it, studying and enjoying the pleasant air and the smell of freshly cut grass.

As she turned right on the fork that led to her dorm, Evelyn made up her mind to call Ernie that evening. She would make a date to meet him at Tiffany's and they would pick out the ring. It was time to stop dreaming and come back down to earth. She began to compose the sentences in her mind. She wanted to sound warm and gracious. She wanted to do the right thing and she wanted to do it the right way.

When she arrived at the dorm, Evelyn put down her suitcase. The double oak doors were very heavy and she always needed both hands to open them. As she tugged on the heavy wrought-iron latches, someone took her arm. Evelyn turned in surprise.

"I thought before we had our children, we ought to get to know each other."

Nat Baum stood there, holding the heavy door open for her. He motioned to her to go through. As if he had done it a thousand times, he picked up her suitcase and brought it inside and put it down just in front of the housemother's door.

"I've been standing here waiting for you. I'm freezing," he said. Evelyn noticed his cloth coat and suddenly felt embarrassed about the warm beaver she was wearing, a high school graduation present from her parents. "She"—Nat motioned toward the housemother's door—"wouldn't let me come in. She said the rule is that no men are allowed inside the dorms without a date. Can I be your date?"

Evelyn nodded. She was too flustered to say anything. She couldn't believe this was happening to her.

"Will you have dinner with me?" Nat Baum asked, quite formally.

"Thank you," said Evelyn. "I'd love to." There was a moment's pause and then she asked, "Is it all right if I take my things upstairs first?"

"Sure."

She wanted time to think. As she headed up the stairs, Nat Baum called up to her:

"Bring a scarf."

A scarf? What on earth would she need a scarf for?

Nat Baum's car was a brand-new tomato red Hudson convertible. Evelyn wondered how he had managed to get it— the waiting lists at auto dealers' were endless. Her father had ordered his new Oldsmobile last March and he was still waiting for delivery. Car manufacturing had still not swung into full production and anyone who drove a new model was someone with pull.

"Let's put the top down," said Nat.

"But it's almost December," said Evelyn. She had never heard of anyone who drove around with the top down in the middle of winter.

"So what? The sun is still out and we're together."

Without really waiting for her answer, Nat Baum snapped out the clamps that held the canvas top to the windshield frame and pulled back the top. He tucked it under the flap behind the rear seat and snapped the heavy fasteners that held it securely down.

Now that Evelyn had had time to think about it, it seemed a marvelous idea—so adventuresome and so imaginative. As Nat put the car into first, Evelyn tied the scarf around her head. That was what it had been for!

They drove to White Plains, to a small Italian restaurant in a seedy section of town. It was dark inside; there were candles stuck in chianti bottles, red-checked tablecloths and sawdust on the floor. The jukebox was playing unfamiliar songs with Italian lyrics. A waiter in a worn but immaculate red jacket came over.

"What would you like?"

Evelyn hesitated. She had never before been in a restaurant that didn't have menus.

"Spaghetti," she finally said, unable to think of any other Italian dishes. She was sure that they'd have that.

"Spaghetti? You really want spaghetti?" asked Nat.

"It was the only thing I could think of," Evelyn admitted.

"Why don't you let me order for the both of us?"

"I'd love that."

He turned to the waiter and ordered a dinner of antipasto, lobster Fra Diavolo, linguine with oil and garlic and a bottle of chianti. Most of the food was completely unfamiliar to Evelyn, but she tried everything and discovered that it was delicious.

"Were you in combat?" she asked.

"Hell, no," said Nat Baum. "That's for suckers. I ran jazz shows for the Negro troops. I had an office, a secretary. I wasn't going to get my head shot off."

Evelyn was shocked at his sacrilege. She had had images of him storming the beach at Guadalcanal or taking a fortress at Anzio or breathing the desert dust at El Alamein. She had never once imagined him sitting in an office, shuffling papers.

"Shooting a gun isn't the only way to win a war," said Nat, reacting to the expression on her face. "As a matter of fact, I consider it murder and I consider murder immoral."

"I never thought of it that way," said Evelyn, and she hadn't. Her attitudes toward war had been formed by the movies and bond rallies. The fact that real people bled and died and hurt never occurred to her. War, for Evelyn, was a Technicolor extravaganza. Not murder. Nat Baum had opened the meal by serving a revelation. "But I guess you're right. I guess killing people *is* murder."

"You know," said Nat, veering away from a philosophical discussion of murder, "most people have no idea how much Negroes have to offer."

"They certainly contributed a lot to the war effort." Evelyn had read about the success the Army had had when it began to draft colored men. At first, a lot of people had predicted that they wouldn't make good soldiers, that they were lazy and lacked discipline, but that had turned out to be wrong. Negroes were not only fine soldiers but good Americans too. The experiment had turned out a complete success, although early in the war it had been considered daring and even risky.

"I produced jazz shows. Bird Parker, Dizzy Gillespie, Bunk Johnson, Louis Armstrong even." Nat Baum reeled off a list of names Evelyn had never heard. "It was a way of showing the Negro troops that the Army appreciated them. It was terrific for morale. We gave shows in London, Paris—the French are wild for American jazz—Naples, Guam, Midway, the Aleutians . . ."

Evelyn's initial disappointment at Nat's revelation that he hadn't seen combat or fired a gun had turned into admiration verging on awe. She had never given a thought to things like troop morale except for conscientiously writing V-mail to Pete once a week in care of his APO address.

"Have you heard much jazz?" asked Nat. He sensed that Evelyn was impressed and he was kind enough not to make her feel inferior.

"No," said Evelyn. "I've never heard any." His kindness and the red wine conspired to permit her to risk the truth.

"We'll have to do something about that," he said.

His easy assurance that they would be seeing each other again made Evelyn's heart race. She could feel it bump under her breast. She was afraid that he might be able to see it, but he went on talking as if nothing had happened.

"You know, jazz is an art form, an expression of raw unconscious." He went on to trace the African roots of American jazz; its journey to the New World in the sweltering holds of slave ships; the way Negroes who worked in the Southern cotton fields sang the ancient rhythms to make their days bearable; the birth of jazz in New Orleans, where it was played in the honky-tonk bordellos of Basin Street. Originally, said Nat Baum, jazz had been considered an inferior form of music, nothing but a seamy product of the whorehouses. He described its trip up the Mississippi to Chicago, its eventual ascent to respectability and its acknowledgment, by critics and musicians the world over, as an authentic American art form.

Nat Baum explained the psychic importance of music and its significance as nonverbal history. He quoted Freud on creativity, Jung on the collective unconscious; criticized Spengler on the decadence of the colored races and their threat to Western civilization; mentioned meeting Yves Tanguy and Henry Miller at Village parties.

Evelyn listened, barely able to follow. They finished the first bottle of chianti and Nat ordered a second. He used words out of books that Evelyn hadn't read and referred to people whose names she had never heard. He was introducing her to a world of excitement and vitality that she hadn't even known existed. She wondered how she could ever reciprocate.

By the time dinner was over and she had had her share of the two bottles of wine and ridden back to Briarcliff in the red convertible with the top down and the stars out and the cold wind whipping her face, she was in love.

Nat Baum dropped her off at the big iron gates.

Without a word about when she'd see him next—and with her first French kiss.

3 NAT BAUM DROVE UP TO
Briarcliff six times in the next three weeks. He was attending Columbia on the GI Bill and shared a four-room apartment on Morningside Drive with five other vets. Although
Nat had officially registered for credit courses in economics,
he soon found that the study of economics consisted of text-
book Keynes, modern accounting procedures and analyses
of fluctuations in the gold standard. He had naïvely assumed it taught one how to make money. Nat soon dropped
his ec course and instead audited psych, sociology and philosophy. He told Evelyn that as long as Uncle Sam was paying the bill, he preferred being stimulated to being bored.
He admitted to her that he had no idea how he was going to
earn a living once he left school. He said that he had two
ambitions: one was to be a twentieth-century Renaissance
man and the other was to get rich. He also swore that he
would never join the nine-to-five rat race. Like getting shot
at, it was strictly for the squares.

He took Evelyn to the Stuyvesant Casino to hear Louis
Armstrong, and to a no-name joint on West Fifty-second
Street to hear the Joe Mooney band. He took her to a dem
sum parlor in a basement in Chinatown, then dancing at
an all-black nightclub called the Zanzibar, and lent her his
copy of *Strange Fruit*. He got her to give up her pageboy
and wear her hair in a ponytail; he gave her an old sweater
of his that was sizes too large for her and that she wore with
a tight, short skirt, bobby socks and saddle shoes. He gave
her a Bessie Smith record of "Down Hearted Blues" which
he said was a collector's item and teased her about her
preference for "Bell Bottom Trousers."

He told her that he was determined to make her hep, and
she was his willing creation. The sixth time he took her out,
Nat informed Evelyn that he had stopped seeing his other
girls.

"I've kissed them all good-bye."

"Oh," said Evelyn. She had refused to see Ernie ever since her first dinner with Nat in White Plains. She was in love with Nat and she couldn't stand the thought of Ernie and his law degree and his junior high kisses. She had blithely taken it for granted that Nat Baum felt as deeply about her as she did for him.

"Oh," she said, trying to conceal her sharp sense of betrayal. Nat Baum interpreted her "oh" as cool indifference.

"I want to stop fooling around," he said. "Don't you?"

For the first time Evelyn heard a tentative note in his voice. She had never seen Nat unsure of himself. He wanted her encouragement before he went on, risking himself. Evelyn nodded, not understanding how or why the balance of power between them had changed so suddenly.

"I'd like to go steady," he said. They were sitting in the Hudson, parked in the lot opposite the iron gates that guarded the campus. Nat fidgeted, lighted a Lucky Strike. Evelyn could hear him swallow. "Would you like to go steady?"

Evelyn was unaccustomed to power. She wasn't used to people's asking her for favors or courting her opinion. The feeling frightened her; she liked it better when someone else made the decisions. She sat there in the front seat, trying to think of how to say yes. It was taking her a long time.

"It's OK if you don't want to," said Nat.

The hurt in his voice hurt Evelyn.

"I want to. I love you," she blurted out before she could stop herself. She knew, just the way everyone else did, that the man was supposed to say "I love you" first and then the girl was supposed to say it second. Evelyn had broken a rule for one of the few times in her life.

"Will you go steady with me?" he asked, quite formally.

"Yes, I will," said Evelyn and she lifted her lips for the kiss that would seal the promise. It was, she felt, a sacred moment.

"Then we can spend the weekend together," said Nat. "I can borrow a friend's place in New Hope."

The brief moment when he had been in her power was

gone. He kissed her lightly on her nose. His casual confidence had returned intact. The uncertain twenty-five-year-
old boy, worried about rejection and afraid of admitting his
feelings, had disappeared. Now that he was gone, Evelyn
wished he had stayed a little longer. She had loved him very
much.

"How about it?" He asked. "You'll dig New Hope."

He wanted to go all the way. The quick caresses he had
won in the erotic battle they had been fighting no longer
pacified him. If she wanted him, she'd have to give in.
Evelyn had been dreading this moment and dreaming of it.
If she agreed, and her parents ever found out, she'd never
be able to face them again. On the other hand, if she
turned Nat down, she was sure she'd never see him again. It
took her no time at all to make her decision.

"I'll ask Amy if she'll tell my parents I'm spending the
weekend with her." Evelyn was sure that Amy would. Amy
lived in Evelyn's dorm and Evelyn had lied frequently to
Amy's fiancé, a Yale junior, on nights when he called and
Amy was out with the driver of the Briarcliff limousine—a
townie, greasily handsome in a sinister way that reminded
a lot of the girls of John Garfield.

"You fix it with Amy. I'll pick you up Friday, about four."

It was almost ten, time for Evelyn to sign back into the
dorm, and Nat walked her to the gates and kissed her with
an open mouth in front of the night watchman, who had
seen the same scene a thousand times before. He wished
they'd hurry it up so he could lock up for the night and
sneak out for a few Rheingolds.

"Friday," said Nat, as the watchman cleared his throat
loudly for the second time. "We'll pick up right where we
left off."

They all knew what he meant.

Even the watchman.

Sex was a mystery to Evelyn.

When, in 1939 at the age of thirteen, she had started

to menstruate, her mother had given her a slim blue book called *Strictly Confidential* which, her mother told her, would explain everything. It explained nothing.

There were diagrams of the male and female reproductive systems, neatly drawn and conscientiously labeled. They had nothing to do with the reality Evelyn had experienced.

A U-shaped penis flanked by two symmetrical ovals called testicles didn't look like Ernie's nine-year-old penis and it didn't look like her father's penis. Evelyn had seen it once when she had walked into her parents' bedroom without knocking. Her father was naked, just about to put on a pair of undershorts. He yelled at Evelyn to get out and she did, but not before she saw that his penis seemed loose and that it wobbled when it moved. The dark hair surrounding it obscured the testicles that *Strictly Confidential* insisted existed. Evelyn sketched hair over the diagram in an attempt to reconcile the picture with what she herself had seen, but no matter how many times she erased and drew it again, the penis in the book was still neatly U-shaped and not wobbly and the two little ovals still curved out on either side of it. Evelyn didn't know if the book could be lying or if her own eyes had deceived her.

The diagram of the female reproductive system showed the labia, vulva and hymen. It confused Evelyn even more because the penis was at least visible and Evelyn could always justify the gap between what she had seen and the diagram by imagining that either she or the book had made a mistake. But the labia, vulva and hymen were invisible. When Evelyn looked down all she could see was the beginning of a slit, and when her pubic hair grew in, even the slit was invisible.

Two times, when curiosity prevailed over terror, Evelyn tried examining herself to see if her anatomy corresponded to the diagram in the book. Her explorations were abortive and unenlightening. Pee was dirty and she was afraid to get any on her hands. Her mother had warned her of the dangers of touching herself down there because of the possibility of infection. Her mother had also told her that touching herself down there was a crime against Nature. Evelyn was even more terrified of Nature than she was of her parents.

And so Evelyn's body remained a mystery to Evelyn.

By the time she went away to college, Evelyn had acquired some playground knowledge of the facts of life. Once, one of the girls in her gym class had asked her if she knew what rape was. Evelyn, at fifteen, had never heard the word. The girl informed her that rape was when a boy stuck his tail into your thing. When Evelyn asked for a clearer explanation, the girl got very angry and walked away from Evelyn, leaving her alone and embarrassed and confused. Later, in study hall, she got a pass to the library and, making sure that no one was watching what page she turned to, she looked up rape in the dictionary. It defined the word as "carrying away by force."

Sex, according to the playground sophisticates, was something that boys liked and girls didn't. Sex was dirty and a girl had an obligation to stay clean for her husband. A girl had to be on constant guard that a boy wouldn't catch her and drag her into an empty lot or into a cloakroom and make her do it. According to the same information, if a boy did do it to you, it was likely that you would bleed to death.

Sex, Evelyn also knew, was the way you got babies. The man's seed joined with the woman's seed and a baby grew. Although she spent a lot of time wondering about it, Evelyn was never able to understand just how the two seeds got together since sex was dirty and no woman would ever let a man do it to her.

Evelyn had small breasts and she was thankful. She felt sorry for a girl in her class named Kendall Kennedy who had large ones and whom the boys teased until she cried and who, finally, begged her parents to let her go to another school. At the same time, Lana Turner was the Sweater Girl and one of the most popular of all the movie stars. Again, Evelyn couldn't reconcile the differences between the pictures she had seen and the reality she was experiencing. Lana Turner with her boobs thrust out was the object of admiration and adoration and Kendall, whose breasts were just as big as Lana's, was the object of derision and she tried to hide them under a baggy woolen jacket which she refused to take off even in the summertime.

By the time she got to Briarcliff, Evelyn knew that there was more to sex than vulvas and labia and she knew that girls liked it too. She wanted to know what went on at frat parties at Yale and at big weekends like the Dartmouth Winter Carnival, but she was too shy to ask and not popular enough to be invited to participate. Dorm conversations about sex were shrouded in allusions and unfinished sentences and bouts of hysterical giggling.

Ernie never brought up the subject of sex and so, once, Evelyn did. Ernie told her that he respected her too much. He meant it as a compliment and, at the time, Evelyn accepted it as one and she still didn't find out all the things she wanted to know.

In 1945, when she was nineteen, Evelyn's body, Evelyn's emotions and Evelyn's questions were still unsatisfied. Her sexual education had been typical. Her ignorance was typical, her confusion was typical and her pain was typical. In the forties, no one talked about sex. Women didn't talk to women, and men were the enemy except if they were like Ernie and respected you.

Nat Baum had never mentioned the word respect. He had touched Evelyn's breasts and when she told him to stop he hadn't listened to her. Once he had tried to feel in between her legs, but she had been quick enough and had closed her thighs and stopped his hand from moving until she wrung from him a promise that he'd behave. It was one of the few arguments that Evelyn had won in her life.

She thought about it later and wondered exactly what it was that she had won. By Friday, at four o'clock, she was prepared for the same argument and, this time, she was prepared to lose.

New Hope, in Bucks County, Pennsylvania, was a picturesque little town, a mecca for artists, successful and unsuccessful; writers, published and unpublished, and a cliquish population of rich divorcées, homosexuals and professional bohemians. Nat and Evelyn arrived there at nine-thirty, having stopped for dinner in a Greek restaurant in Princeton. The restaurant was another of the exotic spots of which Nat Baum seemed to have an inexhaustible supply. Evelyn followed Nat back into the small, hot kitchen where two men in high white hats opened the lids on a variety of large pots to let them see what was cooking inside. They chose lamb with eggplant and lamb with scallions, both steamy and delicious in a garlicky tomato sauce greasy with olive oil. They had salads with black olives and feta cheese; loaves of thick, crusty bread and a bottle of retsina wine, which Evelyn hated at first and then got used to. There was rich homemade yogurt for dessert, followed by small cups of the bitterest, blackest coffee Evelyn had ever drunk. It was like molten lava.

"Helps keep the grease down," said Nat as they went back to the red Hudson.

"I knew there had to be a reason," said Evelyn, and Nat laughed.

One of the amazing things that Evelyn had discovered in herself since meeting Nat was that she had a sense of humor. She was able to make him laugh, and every time she did she felt as if she had just grabbed the gold ring from the merry-go-round.

In New Hope, Nat stopped the car in front of a small building made of weathered gray shingles with a peaked roof and a small courtyard in front with a cobblestone path up to the front door, which was painted a dark burgundy.

"We'll go in the back way," said Nat, and Evelyn followed him around to a door on the side of the building. Nat had the key ready and opened the door and reached inside and flicked on the lights.

"It's sort of spooky in here," said Evelyn as she stepped

in. The whitewashed walls were bare of paintings, which were with Nat's friend in Arizona, where he was spending the winter. The floors were plain wooden planks spattered with paint; there were a desk made from an old door laid across two sawhorses, a folding metal chair, an empty easel and a big brick fireplace that covered the entire back wall of the gallery.

"I wish you could see Alexis' work," said Nat. "He's an expressionist. A very talented cat. He's got the same kind of setup in Arizona: a gallery on the first floor and living quarters upstairs. Come on, let's light a fire and go upstairs."

Evelyn had been feeling jumpy and nervous. Afraid of sex, afraid of Nat, afraid of herself. She didn't know what to expect and she veered between a desire to flee and a desire to hurry up and get it over with. In the activity of getting logs from under a tarp behind the building, laying them over the kindling just so and crumpling up pages from a stack of yellowing copies of *The New York Times,* Evelyn's nervousness disappeared. As they lit the newspaper, the fire began to take; it flamed up, lending pastel orange and pink reflections to the white walls, and what had been empty and cold now seemed warm and romantic.

"Let's go upstairs," said Nat, and took her by the hand. Evelyn followed, curious to see how a painter lived. There was no conventional railing on the staircase. Instead, a thick, twisted rope, the kind used to tie up boats to docks, was threaded against wooden posts sunk into every fourth step. The upstairs apartment was really a balcony that looked down over the gallery and directly faced the big brick fireplace. There was a kitchenette with a hot plate, a half refrigerator, a sink the size of a shoe box and a bathtub. It was the first time in her life that Evelyn had been in an apartment where the bathtub was in the kitchen. She thought it extremely exotic.

A large double bed was covered with a rough colorful spread that Nat said was a Mexican serape. There were bookcases made of orange crates, a pine bureau with three drawers and a samovar on a wooden pedestal. Evelyn couldn't keep her eyes away from the bed. It lured her and threatened her.

"Come on, let's look at the fire. I'll tell you your fortune." Nat sat down on the foot of the bed and Evelyn sat down next to him, not touching him.

"Can you tell fortunes in a fire?"

"The colors reveal your true personality," said Nat. He extended his arm, put it around Evelyn's shoulder and gave her just a small tug, enough to bring the side of her body against his. They had sat in this position so many times before that it didn't frighten Evelyn, it comforted her. "You see," he said, and pointed with his other hand, "it's blue at the bottom, then orange, then yellow right at the top."

"I never noticed that," said Evelyn. "What does it mean?"

"If you put your head on my shoulder, I'll tell you."

She relaxed against him.

"Well," he said, "the blue is for fidelity. The orange is for passion. The yellow is for the sun. The sun represents tomorrow. The future."

"That's very romantic," said Evelyn.

"The fire tells the truth," said Nat, and he kissed her, gently at first and then with passion that reflected the colors of the fire until the fire that burned in the room burned inside them.

He was very gentle with her. Very tender. Very thoughtful.

"Do you want me to?" he asked, as he took the first step.

"Yes," she murmured.

"You're sure? I want you to be sure."

She nodded.

"And this too?" he asked, going on to the next stage.

"This too," she answered.

"I'm not hurting you?" His mouth was so close to her ear that he barely had to speak. She could feel the words rather than hear them.

"No, not hurting me."

"Am I pleasing you?"

"Yes."

She wasn't aware of his techniques, only of her ecstasy.

"More?" he asked.

"Yes, more."

"Now . . ." he said.

"Don't!" She was suddenly rigid, suddenly fearful.

"Why not?" Gently.

"Don't. I'm afraid."

"Afraid of what?" Again, gently.

"I'm afraid to tell you."

"Don't be."

"I'm afraid of getting pregnant."

"Why?"

She was afraid to tell him that too.

"It doesn't matter," he said.

"How can it not matter?"

"We're getting married, so what difference would it make?"

"Oh," she said. "I didn't know."

"We are, aren't we?"

She nodded and he continued to do what he had been doing and Evelyn forgot everything except her ecstasy. Why hadn't anyone ever told her about this? Or even hinted? Why had she had to wait to meet Nat Baum to find out? Suppose she had never met him? If she had never met him, she would never have known. She would have gone her whole life without knowing.

They spent the night wrapped up in each other, and the next morning Nat showed her how to make tea in the samovar and they ate the bread they had smuggled out of the restaurant the night before.

"Thank you," said Evelyn as they ate.

" 'Thank you' for what?" asked Nat.

"For giving me myself," she said.

They spent that Sunday in bed, making love to each other, and went out for a walk in the bitter December cold and

171

bought cheese and fruit to go with the wine that Nat had in the car. They had picnics in bed instead of proper meals at proper restaurants at proper times.

Finally, early in the evening, it was time to leave. They drove back to Briarcliff, Evelyn sitting close to Nat, but rather quiet, thinking her own thoughts. She didn't understand what he saw in her. She was plain, she was provincial, she was inexperienced. He was handsome, he was hep, he was knowledgeable. What on earth did he see in her?

But Nat couldn't believe his good luck in meeting her, this girl sitting next to him, her hand on his thigh, wearing an expensive beaver coat that she just accepted and never thought about twice. She was sweet, she was docile; all her life she had had the things he had had to fight for. The things she took for granted were the things his very dreams were made of. She was a creature from another world—a world he wanted to belong to more than anything else in life.

As they kissed a final time in front of the gates that guarded Briarcliff, Evelyn finally spoke her thoughts.

"I just don't know what you see in me," she said.

"I see the world in you," he said, and he was telling more truth than she was capable of understanding.

The story of Nat Baum's life moved Evelyn to tears.

He had grown up in a tenement on Essex Street on Manhattan's Lower East Side. He had shared a room and a lumpy bed with his two brothers—David, two years older, and Eddie, two years younger. The room, an all-purpose living, dining and bedroom, faced an air shaft, and its brown-varnished walls were sticky in the summer and dank in the winter.

Nat's father, a Russian Jew from Kiev, was addicted to chess and allergic to work. He considered himself an intellectual and grudgingly went off to the handbag factory where he sewed the handles on ladies' purses twelve hours a day. Nat's mother, who listened to the old man's laments, cooked and washed and sewed, and when Nat was seven, she died of tuberculosis.

On David's twelfth birthday, Nat's father announced that he was quitting his job. At twelve a boy was able to get working papers, and Nat's father announced that he had slaved long enough to support his children and that now it was their turn to support him. David got a job in a drugstore, sweeping out, making deliveries and dispensing medicine, although he had no license and no training.

Nat, in his turn, also went to work when he reached twelve. After school and on weekends, he delivered groceries, carrying bags and boxes up five and six flights of tenement steps, happy when a generous housewife gave him a penny tip. At thirteen, Nat worked as a busboy in a restricted club in Wall Street. He cleared dirty dishes and empty whiskey glasses from the linen-draped tables of men who smoked big cigars, talked in millions and gave nickel tips. At fourteen, Nat went to work for Wanamaker's. He worked for a tough Irish foreman in the receiving room, unloading heavy cases of merchandise in July's steamy heat and February's bitter cold. There were no tips, but there was an informal understanding that whatever Nat could steal Nat could have. He acquired warm coats for himself and his brothers, lined gloves, underwear, sweaters, scarves, bathing trunks and shoes. At fifteen, Nat janitored a building in the fur district and made the first real money of his life running bets for the bookie who operated out of a luncheonette on the corner of Eighth Avenue and Thirty-third Street. Nat's father suspected that Nat was holding out on him and beat him every Friday night in an attempt to force him to disgorge more money.

In 1936, when he was sixteen, Nat had had enough. He quit school, lied about his age and enlisted in the Army. It was steady work and steady pay, and it took him miles away from the tyrannical oppression with which his father had ruled their impoverished household. Nat did well in the Army, reenlisting at the end of his first three-year hitch.

He liked the discipline; he liked having a bed he didn't have to share; he liked the freedom of weekend passes and having enough money in his pockets to spend at the movies or at a whorehouse.

He showed an early talent for getting along with his superiors, he knew how to get around the rules without causing any trouble and he knew how to accept favors from grateful officers without fawning. His interest in jazz, born in Southern whorehouses and soldiers' bars, became a career when the war began and Negroes were drafted.

By 1941 Nat was a first lieutenant, and he was attached to a Special Services unit based in Fort Myer, Virginia. The Army put on jazz concerts to entertain the black troops who were waiting to be shipped out to Europe. Nat was assigned to assist a colonel who had been an executive with Victrola in civilian life. Nat coordinated the shows, organized the programs, set up the lighting and sound systems and made sure the musicians showed up, more or less sober, in time to play their gigs. He got along well with the musicians, who introduced him to marijuana, and he amused himself by wire-recording the performances of his special favorites. The shows were enormously popular with the troops, Nat did all the work and loved it and the colonel, who was shacked up off-base with his girlfriend, was happy to take all the credit. Later on, Nat would ask the colonel, Jack Saunders, for help and Colonel Saunders, remembering past favors, would be only too happy to oblige.

By the time the war was over, Nat had made captain, and although he told no one, including Evelyn, he already had an idea of how he would make his fortune. He had hated being poor. Poverty was humiliating and poverty precluded freedom and mobility. Nat swore that whatever else, he would never again be poor.

His energy and his passion for life fascinated Evelyn. His hunger had been born in a background far removed from the middle-class affluence in which Evelyn had been raised. She wept for the poverty and the struggles that Nat had

had to bear. He kissed away her tears and comforted her.

"That's all in the past," he said.

"You're going to be very successful, aren't you?"

"Very," he had said.

"You're extremely honest," said Evelyn. She didn't know any other boys who admitted their ambitions so openly.

"It's one of my greatest charms," said Nat. "My honesty."

"Everything about you is charming," said Evelyn.

"Oh, no. I have some very unappetizing qualities."

"Such as?"

"I'm too aggressive. I need everyone to like me and that's a serious character flaw," he said. "And I'm also insensitive. I care more about my feelings than other people's."

"I don't believe that," said Evelyn. "You've never been that way with me."

"You're different," said Nat.

"I'm glad," said Evelyn.

They kissed. It was Tuesday, the first time they'd seen each other since their weekend at New Hope, and they were necking in the front seat of the Hudson, which was parked, as usual, in the lot across from Briarcliff. Nat made a move for Evelyn's skirt, slipping his hand underneath.

"Not here," she said, all too conscious of the big arc lights that surrounded the lot.

"I want to," said Nat.

"I do too," said Evelyn.

They both paused, wanting to and knowing that this wasn't the place.

"We're too old to be necking in cars," said Nat. "We should be curled up in a big bed together."

"I know," said Evelyn, "but there's no choice."

"Yes, there is."

"There is?"

"Sure. We'll make it legal. Is it OK if I talk to your father?"

It was as much of a formal proposal as Nat Baum ever made.

4 On Saturday, Evelyn and Nat took one look at each other and burst out laughing. Evelyn had told her parents about Nat, and her mother and father had invited him to dinner that Saturday night. Although Evelyn had feared that her parents would disapprove of Nat's zoot suit and knob-toed shoes, she didn't have the courage to suggest that he tone down his wardrobe for the occasion. She loved Nat and she was going to stand by him, zoot suit and all.

For the momentous dinner, Evelyn herself had abandoned the ponytail, sloppy Joes and bobby socks that she wore to please Nat. Instead, she had gone to the hairdresser and had her hair set in a pageboy, parted on the side, and she was wearing a conservative navy blue suit, a white shirt and a belt and Capezios that she had bought with her mother's approval that September in Altman's.

She couldn't stop laughing at the sight of Nat, whose mind had so obviously worked the same way hers had. He was wearing a conservative navy blue suit, a white shirt and a subdued tie. He had even gone to the extreme of having his long pompadour barbered to a conservative business-man's cut.

"The two of us are wonderful!" said Evelyn.

"Like they say, great minds work in similar directions," Nat responded, and they were pleased as Punch with themselves as they walked out to the red Hudson and began the drive to the Edwardses' home in East Orange.

When Evelyn had told her parents about Nat Baum, the first thing they had asked her was if she loved him. Once she assured them that she did, more than anything else in the world, and that marrying him was her one and only desire in life, they asked her about Ernie.

"We always thought you and Ernie . . ." they had said.

Evelyn had shrugged.

"I know," she said. "But I don't love Ernie. I like him. That's different from love. It's Nat I love."

Her parents were amazed by the news and they were struck by their shy daughter's decisiveness. It was so unlike her to assert herself, to know so definitely what she wanted. It made them realize that their little girl had grown up.

Evelyn's mother began to weep. She wept wistfully at the thought that her little girl was a woman now and she wept happily because that woman had found a man to love. Although she had never said anything to Evelyn, Naomi Edwards had worried from time to time that her daughter, who was already nineteen, might never find a husband. She had sensed Evelyn's reluctance to make a commitment to Ernie and she was afraid that no other man would recognize Evelyn's sweetness, hidden as it was behind her modest manner and rather plain looks. Whoever this Nat Baum was, Naomi Edwards felt that if he was perceptive enough to love Evelyn, he must himself be a sweet and lovable young man.

Simon Edwards was more reserved; he had his daughter's future to think about.

"What does this Nat Baum do for a living?"

"He's going to Columbia now. On the GI Bill."

"How is he going to support you? He can't support a wife if he's a student."

"He'll support me, Daddy. I know he will. He's going to be very successful."

Simon was not convinced.

"You can't live on love, you know," said Evelyn's father.

"Oh, Daddy, I know. But we'll be all right. I just know we will. Wait till you meet Nat. You'll see what I mean."

"If you say so," said her father.

Simon had never known Evelyn to be so certain of what she wanted. He knew that if he forbade the marriage, Evelyn would, for the first time in her life, disobey him. The realization startled him. Besides, he reasoned, there was every probability that Evelyn might be right. This Nat Baum might be a young man with a future, a young man who would be a good husband and a good provider. Simon decided to suspend his decision. He'd wait until he had met Nat Baum and then he'd make up his mind.

After all, Simon thought, the war had been over for only a few months and many vets, just out of the Army, had had to go through a period of readjustment to civilian life. Stories about the problems of settling down again were in the newspapers every day. Not having a job or even any prospects was nothing to hold against a young man, especially a young man who had been honorably discharged with the rank of captain. After all, if a boy was ambitious and hard-working there was nothing to hold him back. Come to think of it, Simon's own father had started with nothing but the clothes on his back and some gold coins sewn into the lining of his overcoat. Not everyone was as lucky as Simon or as his son, Pete—lucky enough to have a thriving family business to walk into. Besides, more than anything, Simon loved his daughter and wanted her to be happy, and if this Nat Baum would make her happy . . .

"If you love him, honey, I'm sure he's all you say he is."

"You'll love him, Daddy. I just know you will!"

"You'll like my parents, I know you will," said Evelyn, repeating herself, as they drove south to New Jersey. "And they're just going to love you."

Evelyn gave Nat directions until they reached the Edwardses' home. It was set back from the road, a substantial but not ostentatious middle-class house, painted white with gray shutters, the bronze door knocker immaculately polished. It was a house that Norman Rockwell would have been happy to paint.

"You must be Nat," said Simon Edwards as he opened the front door. He shook the young man by the hand and said, very gravely, looking Nat over, approving of his suit and tie and neatly cut hair, "Welcome to the family."

"Thank you, sir," said Nat. He looked so handsome and so serious standing there shaking hands with her father that

Evelyn felt that there wasn't enough love in the world to express how she felt.

Evelyn's mother said nothing. There were tears in her eyes, and after a moment of not knowing what to do or say, she simply leaned forward and impulsively kissed Nat on the cheek.

As they took seats in the living room, Evelyn's mother served small glasses of sherry from a silver tray. For an uncomfortable moment, there was silence.

"Evelyn tells me that you and she want to marry," said Simon Edwards, breaking the tension. "I remember how hard it was when I asked Naomi's father for her hand. I was shaking in my boots. I want to spare you that," he said, making a joke of the classical situation. Everyone laughed in relief. When they stopped, Nat spoke.

"It's very kind of you," he said. "To tell you the truth, I was terribly nervous. I didn't know what I was supposed to say."

"All you have to tell me is that you love my daughter and want to take care of her."

"That makes it very simple," said Nat. "I love Evelyn and I want to spend the rest of my life caring for her."

Over dinner, Simon treated Nat as an equal, asking him his opinion of how Truman should handle the massive series of labor strikes that were threatened for early in Forty-six. They talked about Dorothy Shaver's appointment as president of Lord & Taylor and her enormous seventy-five-thousand-dollar-a-year salary, and Simon asked Nat if he had yet seen the new Swedish film sensation, Ingrid Bergman, who was starring in three films that year: *Saratoga Trunk*, *Spellbound* and *The Bells of St. Mary's*.

Nat responded graciously and intelligently to Simon's comments, and he ate everything on his plate and asked for seconds. He complimented the crispness of the skin on the roast chicken and the lightness of the mashed potatos in such a way that Naomi Edwards felt it was the best meal she had ever prepared.

Evelyn barely said a word, watching Nat and admiring him and seeing how much her parents responded to him. He was mature and self-confident but without a trace of the cockiness that she liked but knew her parents would disapprove of. Above all, she marveled at the dirty things they had done with each other the weekend before and was sure that her inflamed thoughts were engraved on her face for everyone to see. But apparently no one noticed.

By the time the meal was over, Nat Baum had been accepted as a member of the family. Naomi Edwards invited him to stay over. He could sleep in the guest room. Nat accepted the invitation, and shortly, Evelyn's parents, delighted with the young man Evelyn had chosen, went up to bed, leaving Nat and Evelyn alone.

Evelyn was in a joyous mood. All the people in the world she loved best loved her and loved each other. She felt that their love was a fortress; nothing bad could happen to her, not ever.

"They loved you. Just like I knew they would," said Evelyn.

"They're wonderful people," said Nat.

"They'll be just like real parents to you," said Evelyn. "They'll treat you like their own son."

"I'd like that," said Nat. He had only a few memories of his mother and they were sad ones. Of his father, now dead, he remembered only the tyranny and the beatings. "It would be nice to have a family."

They were on the sofa in the Edwardses' living room, and Nat was conscious of the heavy lined draperies, the thick wall-to-wall carpeting, the fresh flowers in the cut-glass bowl on the coffee table. It wasn't his taste—he wouldn't have furnished the room in quite the same way—but he recognized what it represented: wealth and comfort. He ached for both. He ached for Evelyn, who represented them. At this moment, knowing that soon she would be his, but not yet officially possessing her, he loved her more than he ever had.

"There's something I feel bad about," said Nat.

"What?"

"I want to give you an engagement ring." Nat paused, embarrassed at the admission he was about to make. "But I can't afford it."

"I don't care," said Evelyn. "I want you. I don't care about a ring."

"But I do."

"It doesn't make any difference to me," said Evelyn. "I love you. That's all that matters to me."

"One day," said Nat, not hearing her, "I'm going to give you a big, beautiful diamond ring."

"Nat, you don't have to."

"I know I don't have to. I want to," he said.

By the time Nat and Evelyn left East Orange on Sunday, a June wedding had been agreed upon. Nat and Evelyn were starting a new life at exactly the same time that America, unconditional victor in the biggest, costliest and most destructive war in history, was dreaming golden dreams of the future.

The months rushed by for Nat and Evelyn in a blur of decisions, shopping lists, wedding plans and the pervasive musk of sex. Spring of 1946 was the season of *Open City;* of bebop, whose suggestive lyrics shocked parents, and of the housing shortage. The first thing returning veterans did when they got home was to get married and the second was to have babies. The postwar baby boom put enormous pressure on the American housing industry and changed the tenor and texture of American life.

Men like William Levitt saw opportunity in the problem, built Levittowns and grew rich. Apartment living became a new factor in American life, and the growth of urban complexes centering around major cities like Los Angeles, Chicago and New York spilled out for hundreds of suburban miles in every direction. The traditional American rural ideal faded in a stampede to population centers and sociologists studied the new phenomena of depersonalization, anomie and isolation. Reverberations of the new life-styles of millions of Americans in a highly volatile and mobility-centered society were felt in every area of life—social, economic, political and artistic. Police departments noted a sharp rise in violent crime, the Dow Jones average soared to a new high of 212, Winston Churchill made the Iron Curtain speech in Fulton, Missouri and artists and sculptors like Hans Arp, Vasili Kandinsky, Constantin Brancusi and Marcel Duchamp had smashed all connections with the aesthetic past.

Simon Edwards told Evelyn and Nat that he would buy them a house as a wedding gift. For a time, Evelyn had wanted to live in Greenwich Village; she had liked the taste of bohemian life to which Nat had introduced her in loft parties and smoky jazz clubs. But the dark basement apartments with mildew and cockroaches that Evelyn found picturesque only reminded Nat of the tenements in which he had grown up. Evelyn quickly acquiesced to Nat's preferences and they accepted her father's offer.

The purchase of the house was a dramatic object lesson to Nat in the power of the checkbook. Although "the housing shortage" consumed millions of words in newspapers and magazines, it miraculously disappeared as soon as a buyer with a substantial bank balance appeared. It was a demonstration of economic power that Nat was never to forget.

After five Sundays with real estate agents, Nat and Evelyn decided on a twenty-thousand split-level ranch house on a shady road in Great Neck. Split-level was the most modern concept in housing, an avant-garde breakaway from the Victorian and Colonial designs that had dominated American housing since the turn of the century. Split-level ranch houses were the latest thing, and Nat and Evelyn, conscious of style and status, were thrilled.

Once the papers were signed and the deed handed over, Evelyn began to furnish her new home. Although she had never decorated a room before in her life, her combinations of patterns and color, texture and shape were original and distinctive. Everyone who visited paid her compliments. Evelyn had never been aware that she possessed a talent of any kind, and she consciously and unconsciously linked the emergence of her new talent with the fact that Nat Baum was in love with her and was going to marry her. Somehow, in Evelyn's mind, it was really Nat who inspired the talent, and she shrugged off the compliments convinced that she had done nothing to deserve them.

In addition to the shopping and planning and dreaming, there was sex. Those months of Evelyn's life between her engagement and her wedding were constantly imbued with passion and physical lust. The tentative explorations that Evelyn and Nat had begun that weekend in New Hope blossomed into obsession.

They returned often to the balcony in that house for nightlong bouts of lovemaking that left them purged and exhausted. They made love in the red Hudson, and once they unlawfully entered an unlocked beach house on the Jersey shore. They never knew who owned it, and the off-season mustiness and a lumpy bed that belonged to strangers added an illicit and poignant edge to their lovemaking.

Evelyn gave herself over entirely and with abandon to her sexuality. She felt alive, aware of every nuance of the weather and the things and colors and people around her. She was existing on a heightened plane where the world literally glowed and there was only one worry to mar her perfect happiness.

She was afraid of getting pregnant.

The Pill had not yet been invented. Unmarried girls in the forties did not go to birth-control clinics for diaphragms. There was no foam and no IUD. There was only folklore which recommended a Coca-Cola douche.

Each month Evelyn anxiously watched the calendar and her own body, alert for signs of suspicious thickening or morning sickness, the only two symptoms of pregnancy that Evelyn knew about. If her period was a day or two late, she panicked. She wondered desperately what she would do, whom she would tell and whether Nat would still love her and still want to marry her. Sex was her dirty secret and the fear of pregnancy was the price she paid for ecstasy.

But she got through the six months, and as far as she knew, she wasn't pregnant on her wedding day.

About six weeks before the wedding, late in April, Simon Edwards invited Nat to have lunch with him. He asked Nat if he would pick him up at the Edwards Bristle Company's office and factory in Newark. Simon had a surprise up his sleeve and he couldn't wait for Nat's reaction.

The idea had come to Simon in early March. It was such an obvious brainstorm, he couldn't understand why he hadn't thought of it before.

The more Simon had seen Nat, the more impressed he was with him. Nat had done well in the Army and it was obvious that Nat was going to go just as far in civilian life. Even though he didn't have the legal training that Ernie did, Nat Baum would be a big asset to Edwards' Bristles.

Simon asked Pete how he would feel about taking Nat in as a full partner. It would be a way, said Simon, of dividing his estate. Since Simon had already informed both his children that he intended to divide everything down the middle, Pete had no reason not to agree. Besides, Pete liked and admired his future brother-in-law. He thought of himself as competent but slightly plodding; he saw Nat as self-assured and bold, two qualities Pete wished he had more of. Simon's proposal wouldn't cost Pete a cent and it would give him the benefit of a strong partner. Pete was quick to agree that his father's idea was a good one.

Having Pete's full concurrence, Simon went ahead and had the office next to Pete's repainted. He had wall-to-wall carpeting installed and he furnished the room with a desk and big leather chair identical to the ones in Pete's own office. Simon wanted to make sure that Nat felt like a complete equal and not merely a son-in-law who had married into the family business.

The morning of their lunch date, Simon had the porter vacuum Nat's office, dust it carefully and polish the glass top of the desk. When the receptionist announced Nat's arrival, Simon went out to greet him personally and he escorted him back to his own corner office and shut the door. Simon had everything planned: he'd make the offer, Nat would accept and as a final surprise, Simon would take Nat down the corridor and show him to his brand-new furnished office. If he wanted to, he could start work that same afternoon.

"I thought it was time we had a man-to-man talk," said Simon as he gestured Nat to a chair. Nat was struck with the commanding air Simon assumed in the office; at home, he was genial and easygoing. It was an interesting contrast. "Just us men, without the women around."

Nat nodded.

"Women, I love them," said Simon, "but not around an office, you know what I mean?"

Nat nodded.

Having dispensed with the preliminaries, Simon got down to business. He talked about the future. He spoke about it in terms of the Edwards Bristle Company's balance sheets— balance sheets that made better and better reading as time went on. Business was so good now that orders far exceeded stock on hand. The company had representatives in Europe, the Far East and South America, outbidding competitors for the raw bristles that would be finished in the Edwards factory and sold, in turn, to various manufacturers. Simon discussed the breadth of the bristle business. It went far beyond the obvious items like hair- and toothbrushes, al- though, of course, those markets created a solid base to work up from. There were, Simon explained, many uses for bristles not generally known to the public. There were medi- cal uses and industrial applications, in both light and heavy industry. Gold finishers and diamond polishers both required extremely delicate brushes; companies like Hoover and Electrolux needed medium-weight bristles, and heavy-duty bristles were used by manufacturers like Boeing, Ford, Gen-

eral Motors, Chrysler and U.S. Steel. As far as the future
was concerned, Simon concluded, the sky was the limit.

"There's room for you in that future," said Simon, finally
getting to the point.

Nat nodded, saying nothing.

"Believe me, it's not because you're marrying my daughter, either. If you were a stranger off the street, I'd hire you."
Simon went on to describe the offer in detail: the same salary
as Pete's—ten thousand dollars a year—and equal ownership
of stock. Nat would be a full partner and he and Pete would
divide the responsibilities as they saw fit. Tentatively, Simon
said, Pete and he had thought that perhaps Nat might excel
at sales and promotion, while Pete would oversee the running of the finishing plant and the internal aspects of the
company.

"Of course," Simon was quick to add, "if you and Pete
decide to carve things up some other way, it's fine with me.
Hell, Nat, I want to retire. To enjoy life. I want to turn the
whole thing over to you and Pete. Lock, stock and barrel."

Simon had finished his speech and he sat back in his big
chair and waited for Nat's reaction. He knew that the young
man would be stunned at the generosity of the offer. Very
few men in their twenties made salaries of ten thousand
dollars in 1946. You could live like a king on ten thousand
dollars a year.

"Thank you very much, sir."

Simon got up and began to walk around his big desk. He
wanted to shake hands with Nat. Then he would take him
down the hall and show him his new office. Simon couldn't
keep the satisfied smile off his face. He couldn't wait to see
the look on Nat's face when he got a glimpse of that office.

"I appreciate your offer, I really do," said Nat. "But I
can't accept it."

It took a moment for Nat's words to sink in. At first,
Simon thought he hadn't heard right.

"You have another job?" He'd find out what the other
offer was and match it, that was all.

Nat shook his head.

"No, I'm going to go into business for myself."

"Oh."

That alternative had never occurred to Simon.

"Besides," Nat added, "although I appreciate your offer, I couldn't possibly accept it under any circumstances. It would make me feel like a parasite."

"I'm not handing out charity," said Simon. He was uncomfortable on the defensive. He wasn't used to it.

"Let's have lunch," said Nat. "And I'll tell you what I have in mind."

They sat in a dark taproom, and over Dewar's-and-water and rare-steak sandwiches, Nat told his father-in-law about his plans.

After lunch, Simon walked Nat to the red Hudson, which was parked in the lot outside the Edwards Bristle Company's offices and factory. The two men shook hands and Nat got into his car and began the drive back to Manhattan.

As Simon Edwards walked back to his corner office, he realized that he had never even gotten the chance to show Nat the office that had been so carefully prepared for him. His little daughter, thought Simon, had picked herself quite a man. Simon hoped she'd be woman enough to handle him.

For Evelyn's sixth birthday, her Aunt Bea had given her a music box shaped exactly like a wedding cake. When the top tier was lifted, it played "Here Comes the Bride" until the top was put back down. That Christmas Evelyn asked for and received a doll with golden blond hair and a bride's long white dress. As with most girls, Evelyn's favorite game was "Bride," and she played it whenever she could persuade her brother to play "groom." Like most girls, Evelyn thought that being a bride was the pinnacle of a girl's existence, and like most girls, Evelyn dreamed of the day when she too would be one.

She had pictured it in a thousand ways, embellishing and revising the details. She spent hours trying to decide on the exact shade of white for her gown—oyster, champagne or candlelight. She knew that she definitely wanted long sleeves with pointed tips that came over the hands. She was undecided between various styles of veils and different lengths of trains. She dreamed about single ring versus double rings, flower girls, ring bearers, bridesmaids, best men, something old, something new, something borrowed and something blue. She imagined her wedding day over and over, seeing herself as the bride, the fairy princess, the most beautiful girl in the world marrying the handsomest man in the world.

When the day came, the reality of Evelyn's wedding surpassed every girlish excess of her imagination.

The eleventh of June, 1946, was a perfect day, with blue skies, a gentle breeze and an indulgent sun. The wedding was held outdoors, on the lawn of the Edwardses' home. The pink and white dogwood were in full bloom, and tubs of pink and white roses had been set around in front of the leafy green shrubbery. The florist had created an altar of more white and pink roses and a perfect bouquet of white orchids with baby's breath for Evelyn to carry. The service itself, a civil one, was performed by a judge of the New Jersey Supreme Court. He was a dignified white-haired man whose demeanor added the proper degree of solemnity to the occasion. The reception afterward was a caterer's delight. A white tent had been set up, and tables were lavishly spread with caviar and champagne, lobster in Newburgh sauce and filet with Stroganoff sauce, sherbets in three flavors, chocolate mousse and a four-tiered tower of a wedding cake, a confectioner's extravaganza, frosted in white sugar icing with a bride and groom perched on the very top.

The mother of the bride was dressed in a dusty rose gown and she cried, touched by the gravity with which Evelyn and Nat pronounced their vows and the tenderness of the long kiss that sealed them. The father of the bride beamed with pride. He was proud of his daughter, who looked so beautiful in a Hattie Carnegie gown; proud of his new son-in-law and proud that he was able to provide the kind of wedding that everyone would talk about for weeks.

The guests, one hundred and fifty of them, were enchanted. The women got giggly on champagne and children threw up from excitement and then went to sleep in the guest room. The men gathered in little tuxedoed groups and talked of business and politics and Bob Feller's pitching. A quartet of musicians strolled around the garden playing all the romantic songs from *Oklahoma!*, *Carousel* and *Showboat*.

Evelyn barely noticed any of it. All she thought about was the words of the ceremony and how she would spend every day of the rest of her life living up to them. She would love Nat, honor him and obey him.

After standing in the receiving line and accepting the good wishes of friends and relatives, being kissed and exclaimed over, Evelyn went up to her bedroom and changed into the powder blue going-away suit that had been purchased at the same time as the wedding gown. It had shirred, padded shoulders and a peplumed jacket, an enormously full skirt that reached to the calf and a pillbox hat with a veil to match. Like her wedding gown, it was an original Hattie Carnegie design. It was in the height of style, an American adaptation of Christian Dior's sensational New Look.

Evelyn's parents walked the newlyweds to the waiting limousine that would take them to Idlewild airport. Evelyn's mother cried and kissed them, and Evelyn's father kissed her and shook Nat's hand and gave them a sealed envelope that contained a check for one thousand dollars.

Nat and Evelyn took a Pan Am Clipper on the new semiweekly service that flew to Bermuda. The flight took five hours, and Nat and Evelyn drank champagne and ate filet mignon for dinner. When they registered at the hotel, the clerk who signed them in called Evelyn "Mrs. Baum." It was the first time anyone had called her by her new name and Evelyn blushed and knew that she would remember the moment forever.

Bermuda was gentle and romantic, the days were bright and the nights were soft and Evelyn learned how to enjoy making love with the lights on.

Their week was over in a second. On the flight back to New York, Evelyn thought about the freshly painted nursery, empty now and waiting, and Nat thought about business. The first person he would call on Monday morning was Jack Saunders. Colonel Jack Saunders, his superior officer in the Army, now a civilian, was back at his old job with Victrola and he owed Nat Baum a favor.

5 "WHAT YOU NEED," SAID Jack Saunders, after Nat told him about the wire recordings he had made backstage at the troop shows, "is a kid and a garage."

Saunders ordered his third martini. In the nine months since Nat had seen him, Jack had gained twenty pounds and a new wife. He informed Nat that he had divorced Number Two in a Cuban divorce mill and that he had just married the babe he'd been shacked up with outside of Fort Myer. She had been giving him a hard time about making it legal and so, Jack said, he figured what the hell. His alimony was murder but that was the price you paid. He told Nat that he had some blue-chips which had been left to him by his father, who had been a stockbroker in St. Louis, and his salary at Victrola plus fringe-benefits like kickbacks from booking agents and "consultant fees" from starving musicians who were eager for backup jobs on singles by big-time singers. If you wanted a third wife, said Jack, it was nice to know that you could always afford one.

Jack was an upper-class St. Louis WASP with the accent and manners that even money couldn't buy. But he wasn't a square. He dropped names like Frankie Laine and Vaughn Monroe and the Andrews Sisters. He had taken Nat to "21" for lunch, and Jack Kriendler had greeted him as if he owned the joint.

Jack Saunders, thought Nat, really had it made.

"I see big things for you, Nat," said Jack, expansive on the gin and impressed with Nat's ideas.

"I've got big plans," said Nat, declining a third martini and noticing that Jack barely touched his "21" Burger, rare.

Jack took a three-by-five pigskin notebook out of his breast pocket, with a gold pencil scribbled a name and phone number on a slip of paper, tore it out and handed it to Nat. The name was Eddie Schmidt.

"Eddie'll make you a master."

A master was a disk from which hundreds of identical records could be pressed. Once you had a master, you were in business, provided, of course, that you had something people wanted to buy. And thanks to the United States Army, Nat Baum had the best: Yardbird Parker, Dizzy Gillespie, J. C. Higginbotham.

"Eddie's an electrical genius. A kid who was born with a wiring diagram where his brain ought to be. Pay him fifty bucks and he'll think it's the moon."

Jack signed the bill, commenting that Victrola would be happy to pay for the lunch. Part of Jack's job was expanding a circle of contacts in the record and music businesses, and now that Nat was in the trade, it was a legitimate business expense.

"I always believe in throwing a few legit names on every swindle sheet," said Jack as they stepped into the hazy July day on Fifty-second street. "Keeps the IRS boys off balance."

Laughing, Jack strolled back west to Victrola's offices just off Times Square. Nat went into a drugstore on Fifty-second between Fifth and Sixth and dialed Eddie Schmidt.

Eddie Schmidt was nineteen, of German descent. He lived with his parents in a heavily German part of Queens Village and had a job he hated in the mailroom of CBS. His ambition was to be a sound man, and he had thought that by getting a foot into CBS that he would be able to work his way into the control room. During the war he had taken a lot of shit in high school because of his parents' German accents and Eddie wanted to see himself in a position of dominance. He pictured himself wearing a headset, giving directions to actors and announcers through a heavy glass window, surrounded with banks of wires and mikes and tubes. Nothing would happen without Eddie's say-so. Meanwhile, he was delivering and picking up mail in a wire cart such as housewives used in grocery stores and it was a thirty-five-dollar-a-week pain in the ass.

"I have some wire recordings. Jack Saunders said you could cut masters for me," said Nat Baum.

Eddie said, sure, he could handle it, only he wanted to know how much Nat Baum was going to pay for the favor.

"Jack said you'd do it for fifty."

"Plus expenses."

"Plus expenses," agreed Nat.

They made an arrangement for Eddie to rent a garage that he knew of. It would cost ten dollars for the evening and Nat said that he would, of course, pay the ten dollars. Nat figured the garage was probably Eddie's and that the "rental" was a way to chisel a few extra bucks. In Eddie's position, Nat would have done the same thing, so he agreed without an argument.

That evening at five, Nat picked up Eddie in front of the CBS building at 485 Madison and drove out of Manhattan via the Queens–Midtown tunnel. Following Eddie's instructions, he passed through the unfamiliar streets of Queens until Eddie said, "Stop. We're here."

The garage was attached to a dingy yellow house in need of a paint job. A few scraggly trees groped for life and a sullen patch of crabgrass overgrew the driveway to the garage. Eddie pushed up a wooden latch and they were inside. Eddie flipped a switch and three bare bulbs hanging from rubber-insulated heavy-duty wires lit up the area over a nicked and scarred workbench. Sophisticated-looking recording equipment, meticulously clean in contrast to the grubby surroundings, stood on the bench. There was no car in the garage and Eddie told Nat that the workbench stood in the acoustical center of the place.

The equipment looked expensive, and although Nat said

nothing, he realized that he wasn't the only one with the same idea. Eddie evidently had a good sideline going in making bootlegged masters.

Nat handed over the reels to Eddie, who fitted them into sprockets on a gray wire recorder, a much more technically advanced one than the portable model Nat had used to make the originals. Eddie ran the wire backward until the entire spool was rewound on the spool already in the recorder, which was hooked to a machine that Eddie called an equalizer. Eddie turned on the recorder and listened critically. He adjusted a series of dials on the equalizer in order to modify sound so that it could be transferred from the wire to an acetate with the most accuracy.

"There's a lot of crap in the background," said Eddie. It was his only comment about the contents of Nat's reels.

Nat had been worried about questions as to where and how he had obtained the recordings, but since Eddie didn't ask, Nat didn't bother to tell him that they had been made, live, at Fort Myer. The "crap" in the background was the applause, screams and whistles of the audience. It was none of Eddie's business.

"You want to get a good balance between bass and treble," explained Eddie as he made minute changes in high and low frequencies on the equalizer. Finally, he seemed satisfied with the quality of the sound. Nat realized as he watched Eddie work that for all Eddie cared he could have been working with recordings straight from the death house of Sing Sing. He was a technician and the problem as far as Eddie was concerned was acoustical and not ethical.

Now that Eddie was happy with the sound mix, he took one of the blank acetates he had asked Nat to buy at a record-supply house on West Forty-seventh Street and put it on the turntable of the cutting lathe. He switched on the lathe, dropped the cutter head on the outside perimeter of the acetate disk and started the wire recorder. Eddie stepped back from the workbench and sat down on an ancient slatted wooden chair and listened.

"You want the sound level to be as exact as possible," said

Eddie. "Otherwise you'll get so much distortion you won't know what you're listening to."

When the first master had been cut, Eddie removed the disk, now covered with grooves, from the turntable. Except that it had no colored label printed with the name of the song and the performer, it looked like any record you'd buy in a record store except that it was slightly heavier and thicker. Eddie repeated all the steps with each of the wire recordings that Nat handed him, transforming the smooth acetates into grooved seventy-eights until, at one A.M., Nat had masters of live performances given by the top jazzmen in the world.

Nat added up the overhead: fifty for Eddie, ten for the garage and a few bucks at the record-supply store for the blank acetates and paper sleeves to protect them. It had cost him sixty-odd bucks to go into business.

All he had to do was find customers, and that, he knew, would be easy. The hard part was behind him.

He dropped Eddie off at a nearby saloon and drove home to Great Neck. Evelyn, as she had said she would, was waiting up for him. Together, they listened to the records.

At first, the noise in the background—the cheering and clapping—bothered them. They were accustomed to studio-produced recordings. Once they got used to it, though, they realized that it added a sense of excitement and immediacy that was lacking on professionally made recordings.

"It's terrif," said Evelyn. Nat had taught her slang and she loved to use it, although she was always afraid of making a mistake.

"It's a good selling point," said Nat. "A real novelty. A performance recorded live in front of a real audience. I bet the kids will really go for it."

"I bet you're right!" Evelyn couldn't get over how energetic and enthusiastic Nat was. "You'll probably end up a millionaire," she said.

"That's what I'm shooting for."

"One thing," said Evelyn as they turned off the lights and

snuggled toward each other in the big bed. "Isn't it going to cost you a lot of money to get started?" Evelyn had heard enough business conversations between her father and brother and Walter Coffman to know about things like capital, overhead and operating expenses.

"Don't worry," said Nat. "I'll take care of the money."

He was elated and excited that night, and it lent a vibrant note to their lovemaking. As she was about to fall asleep, Evelyn wondered if they'd made a baby. It would be very romantic. A new business and a new baby in the same night.

Nat's sense of timing was nothing short of genius.

The Teen-ager, like victory gardens, bond rallies and margarine, was a wartime creation. Before the war, people between thirteen and eighteen were culturally invisible. No magazines were edited for them, no Acnomel was manu-factured for them and no music was created for them. How-ever, during the war, all the grown-ups disappeared. The men turned into GI Joes and went overseas and the women, like Rosie the Riveter, spent their days inside factories. Ex-cept for the old folks who never did anything anyway and certainly never spent any money, the most highly visible group of Americans were those just under draft age.

It was the particular genius of the American free-enter-prise system to discover that teen-agers constituted a separate and highly cohesive group with special interests, etiquette, tastes—and plenty of money. It took only simple arithmetic to come up with the fascinating observation that millions of teen-age allowances added up to millions of dollars' worth of purely discretionary income. Once that observation had been made, it didn't take any brains at all to observe that while adult Americans were preoccupied with winning the war at home and abroad, adolescent American boys were preoc-cupied with meeting adolescent American girls.

There was no better place to meet someone of the same age and the opposite sex than on the dance floor. Teen-agers in bobby socks and saddle shoes, dungarees and sloppy Joes danced during lunch hour in high school auditoriums, after school in local sweet shops and Saturday nights in teen canteens. American teenagers Lindyed, jitterbugged and bunny hopped through World War II. They swung and swayed to Sammy Kaye, they swooned over a skinny kid from Hoboken named Frank Sinatra and they thought that jazz, bop and Dixie were the living end.

Jukeboxes gobbled up five billion nickels a year and they needed to be filled. Disk jockeys needed records so that Linda Sue in Homeroom 314 could dedicate "Mairzy Doats" to the gang and "On a Slow Boat to China" to Gary. The Lucky Strike *Hit Parade* needed new hits every Saturday night at nine P.M. When the dust settled and all the numbers were added up, the results were staggering: in 1946 alone, RCA Victor and Decca *each* sold one hundred million seventy-eights.

The record business was into the big time and the big money, and Nat Baum was right there to cash in.

The end of July and the beginning of August were hot and humid. The *Daily News* carried front-page photos of eggs being fried on sidewalks, up in Harlem little colored kids opened fire hydrants and Coney Island reported record-breaking crowds each and every weekend. The miserable weather slowed everyone down; in those days, before air conditioning, people were happy to draw the shades and settle down with an electric fan and a pitcher of lemonade. Nat Baum never noticed the temperature or the humidity.

Every morning, early, he kissed Evelyn goodbye and got into the red Hudson with his masters. Using the classified directories as a guide, he methodically visited every retail record store in Manhattan, the Bronx, Queens, Brooklyn, Nassau and Suffolk, Westchester and northern New Jersey. For fourteen hours a day, every day of the week except Sundays, when the stores were closed, Nat played his masters for record-store owners and took orders.

By the middle of August, Nat had commitments for almost eight thousand records. One Sunday he took his stack of orders out to East Orange and showed them to his father-in-law. Simon Edwards knew nothing about jazz, he hated teen-agers and their submoronic fads, but he knew a good business deal when he saw one. Nat didn't even have to ask. Without a word, Simon pulled out his checkbook, and Nat left the Edwards house that evening with twenty-five hundred dollars.

The next morning at nine, Nat took the check to a processing plant in Long Island City and had ten thousand records pressed. They were ready on the Wednesday after the Labor Day weekend, and Nat picked them up at the plant and turned the living room into a stockroom. He traded in the sporty red Hudson for a more practical station wagon, loaded it up with records and delivered them to the stores.

By the beginning of November Nat had a company, Hep Cat Records, Inc., and an office, two rooms overlooking an air shaft around the corner from the Brill Building, and by the end of the month he was able to begin paying his father-in-law back. The magic of the big-name stars plus the patriotic appeal of Army-base performances clicked, and Nat had a hard time keeping up with orders.

He worked an eighteen-hour day. He visited the retail stores constantly, making notes of which platters were selling and which were dogs. He got good display on the counters and he made sure that fast-selling items were reordered. He fought with the processing plant for faster deliveries. He brushed off aspiring no-talent musicians who wanted to record for Hep Cat. He paid bills, filed invoices, ordered labels and sleeves, argued about prices and juggled income and outgo so that the money was always working, making more money.

For Nat, the eighteen-hour days passed in a flash. For Evelyn, they dragged by, minute by minute.

She was bored and lonely in her beautiful split-level in Great Neck and she finally asked Nat if she could help him out in the office. He was delighted.

Every day Nat and Evelyn drove into the city together, and Nat taught Evelyn how to run the office. He taught her the rudiments of bookkeeping; he taught her which bills had to be paid right away and which could wait; her hunt-and-peck typing became faster and more accurate with practice. It was fun and it was challenging—in the beginning.

When Nat was in the office, he was invariably on the telephone, gossiping, yelling, cajoling, threatening, placating and bargaining. When he wasn't on the phone, he wasn't in the office. He visited the record stores, cultivating owners and buyers and clerks, eating lunch with them and getting loaded with them after work. When he wasn't with store owners, he lunched in the deli in the Brill Building, getting to know the A&R men with the big labels, the wholesalers and distributors and promoters and talent agents and the musicians who hung around between sessions.

Business was an all-male world that included Nat and excluded Evelyn. It didn't take her long to decide that she preferred eating a sandwich alone at her desk to feeling like an intruder in a Turkish bath.

After the novelty of coming into the city every day wore off, Evelyn discovered that an office could be as lonely and boring as an empty house. Nat was always busy—too busy to talk to her; too busy to take her out for lunch, just the two of them, alone. The office was dingy and depressing, and the furniture, abandoned by a previous tenant, was battered and ugly. The location was too far west for Evelyn to be able to shop on Fifth Avenue at lunchtime, and the work itself, once she had mastered it, was no longer challenging and satisfying. It was mechanical and repetitious. Instead of counting the hours until Nat came home to Great Neck, Evelyn counted the hours until he came by the office to pick her up and drive her home.

Evelyn tried not to complain. After all, Nat was working so hard for her—for them, really: for their future. She felt guilty over the resentment and anger that she felt because he paid more attention to his business than he did to her. She felt that if she were really a good wife, she'd be proud of his success rather than jealous of it.

Then, one day, the truth dawned on her: her boredom

and resentment had nothing to do with Nat's eighteen-hour days and her menial office chores. What she needed—what every woman needed—was babies. Babies were proof of a woman's success just as money and power were proof of a man's.

Instead of counting the hours in the day, Evelyn began counting the days in the month.

Nineteen-forty-six turned into 1947. The Marshall Plan for the economic recovery of Europe was proposed, and the Cold War began in earnest. Best sellers ran the gamut from *Peace of Mind* to *I, the Jury*. Marlon Brando, an unknown Method actor, electrified Broadway in a torn T-shirt as Stanley Kowalski in *A Streetcar Named Desire* and, in the fall of 1947, the World Series was telecast for the first time. Jackie Robinson was elected Rookie of the Year, the strapless bra was invented, Savarin was the coffee served at the Waldorf-Astoria and late in September, Evelyn skipped her period.

She had been waiting so long that at first she thought she had counted wrong. She decided not to say anything, not to start up any false hopes. She crossed her fingers and kept counting. In October she skipped again, and in November her gynecologist, Dr. Martin Kallmann, confirmed the diagnosis: Evelyn was expecting.

Now that the doctor had made it official, Evelyn permitted herself to believe it was really true: she was, at last, going to have a baby. Although she had never precisely admitted it to herself and though she had certainly never discussed it with Nat, there had been moments when she was afraid that there was something wrong with her—something that would prevent her ever from having children. Now that her tiny, unspoken fears had been dispelled, she couldn't wait to tell Nat about the marvelous thing that was happening to her, to them.

When he got home that evening, Evelyn gave him time to shower and change and then she mixed him a martini, seven-to-one and icy cold, just the way he liked it. She took time with everything: chilling the glasses and plumping the cushions on the sofa, heating some cheese sticks and getting out cocktail napkins of Madeira linen that had been a wedding gift—elated with her secret, wanting to drag out the delicious anticipation. She savored the moment of the telling, imagining the look of love and pride and surprise on Nat's face, and she held in her excitement until she couldn't bear the tension a second longer.

"Guess what?" she asked. She was proud of her casual tone. She hadn't known she was such a good actress. Never in her life had she felt so important. Never in her life had she been so important.

"How many guesses do I get?" asked Nat.

"The usual," she said. "Three." She enjoyed their little game and wondered what he'd guess first. She couldn't begin to imagine.

"You're pregnant," said Nat and he counted on his fingers. "We're going to have a baby in June."

She was going to surprise him and he had turned the tables. It was she who was struck silent.

"You haven't had your period since September," said Nat.

"But how did you know?" Did she have no secrets from this amazing man she was married to?

"I can count," said Nat. "You're as regular as clockwork. Every twenty-nine days. Besides," he said, wickedly grinning, "you're sexier than ever."

Evelyn blushed.

"Your nipples are more sensitive. They harden the minute I touch them. Your breasts are bigger; they're bulging out of your bra. And you get wetter faster."

"Nat!"

Evelyn could feel her cheeks turn scarlet. She wasn't used to that kind of dirty language. Their bedroom talk had always been endearments and baby talk. It had never been clinical, it had never been blunt. Nat's matter-of-fact recitation caused Evelyn's nipples to harden and her vagina to become moist even though they weren't touching.

They never did have dinner that evening. Their lovemaking had a new tenderness and sensuality. It had never occurred to Evelyn that pregnancy not only would be the answer to her dreams but would renew the sexual excitement of her marriage. For the first time in her life, Evelyn felt womanly.

The next week, Nat suggested that Evelyn stop coming into the office. He could afford to hire a secretary and he wanted her to take it easy and enjoy her pregnancy. Now that Evelyn was about to become a mother as well as a wife, Nat wanted to assert himself as man of the household. He had hated his own childhood; he had missed the love of a mother and the alliance with a father. He didn't want his family to suffer the bitterness his father had created in walking away from the traditional male role. Nat was pleased that he had learned from the mistakes of his parents. It was a sign, he knew from his psychology courses, of maturity.

Now that she was pregnant, Evelyn enjoyed staying home in Great Neck. She wasn't lonely anymore now that she had her baby to wait for. The days passed quickly. She listened to Arthur Godfrey, made lists of names for girl babies and boy babies, Christmas-shopped and waited, in tune with herself, her husband and her destiny.

Thanksgiving passed and so did Christmas, and Nat and Evelyn wondered what the holidays would be like next year. At Thanksgiving their baby would be five months old and at Christmas, six months. Their baby would be fat and affectionate and it would laugh a lot. Their baby would never cry at night or whimper like ordinary babies. Their baby would be like the ones in the magazines, cuddly and dimpled and sweet-smelling. It was corny and Nat and Evelyn knew it and they kept on with their dreams.

Their baby, their first baby, would add richness to their life. It would bring them closer and it would bestow upon them and their love immortality.

"Do you want a boy or a girl?" asked Evelyn as they drove back from her parents' house on Christmas afternoon.

"It doesn't matter. Our second will be the opposite sex

of the first, so it really doesn't make any difference, does it?"

Evelyn agreed. "Only," she said. "I hope the first one is a boy."

"If it's a boy, we'll love him, and if it's a girl, we'll love her," said Nat, taking one hand off the steering wheel and patting Evelyn's not yet bulging stomach.

"Did you ever think that we might have twins?" The thought had suddenly occurred to Evelyn.

"Oh, my God!" said Nat and he laughed like the happiest man in the world.

It snowed heavily on the night before New Year's Eve and Evelyn woke up in the middle of the night feeling chilled. She wondered if she had forgotten to close all the windows. She turned on her night light, and as she pulled back the covers to get out of bed, she realized that her nightgown was wet. It was glued to her thighs with blood. The bed where she had been lying was drenched and Evelyn reached out and touched Nat's hand.

"Nat" was all she said.

She lay there shivering while Nat called Dr. Kallmann, forcing herself not to think about what might be happening to her.

Dr. Kallmann asked one question. It was about the color of the blood.

"It's bright red," said Nat.

Dr. Kallmann told him to call an ambulance and said that he would meet them at the emergency entrance of the Nassau County hospital.

Evelyn was placed on a stretcher covered with a protective rubber pad. Blood poured out of her and she was hardly aware of the screaming sirens as the ambulance sped through the dark, snowy night.

Dr. Kallmann was waiting as the two orderlies moved the stretcher next to the examining table.

"Can you save our baby?" asked Evelyn as they moved her onto the table.

The bright overhead lights blinded Evelyn, and if Dr.

Kallmann answered her question, she didn't hear. Her legs were spread and her ankles were fitted into the stirrups and she wondered why she didn't feel any pain. She saw pools of bright blood on the white tiles. She was embarrassed about messing up the immaculate floor, but before she had a chance to apologize, she fainted.

When Evelyn woke up, it was two A.M. of the first day of 1948 and she didn't have to be told that she had lost her baby. Without words or questions or explanations, she knew.

6 THREE WEEKS AFTER EVELYN miscarried, she went to Dr. Kallmann. He examined her thoroughly, probing, feeling, palpating as she lay spread on the cold metal examining table, her heels in the stirrups, her body modestly draped with a sheet, a watchful nurse hovering, at the same time soothing the patient and guaranteeing a witness in case the doctor was accused of improper behavior by a hysterical patient.

After Evelyn was dressed again, her blouse tucked in, her seams straight, the nurse led her to Dr. Kallmann's office and shut the door, leaving doctor and patient alone. Dr. Kallmann's office was as shabby and comfortable as he was. The room was wood-paneled, and two walls were solid with sets of medical books in sedate dark red, dark green and dark blue bindings. One wall was obscured by floor-to-ceiling oatmeal-colored draperies, and on the doctor's cluttered desk an old-fashioned student's lamp cast a pool of soft light. The room, like Dr. Kallmann, made no threats.

"You wouldn't have wanted that baby," said Dr. Kallmann.

"Not wanted it?" It was inconceivable to Evelyn.

"Miscarriages are nature's way of protecting the species."

Dr. Martin Kallmann was short and paunchy. He looked like a rumpled penguin and not like one of the top ob-gyn men on the East Coast. He taught at Lenox Hill and maintained offices on Park Avenue in the Eighties and in Great Neck. The women who filled his waiting room referred to themselves as Kallmann's girls and they invariably fell in love with him. Evelyn was no exception. He was reassuring and Evelyn had complete confidence in him. Their relationship was exactly what the books and magazines said the ideal doctor–patient relationship should be: implicit trust by the patient and complete control by the physician.

"Is there something wrong with me?" It was the one question that had haunted Evelyn since the miscarriage. She had asked herself, over and over, why had she lost the baby? What was the matter with her?

"Nothing's the matter with you. Absolutely nothing. Your plumbing is in superb condition."

"Then why—"

Evelyn didn't have to finish the question. Dr. Kallmann had been asked it hundreds of times before in hundreds of identical situations. What was a unique and earth-shattering experience for a woman who had just lost a much-wanted baby was commonplace for the doctor. His job was to reassure her, to put things in their proper perspective.

"Sometimes fetuses don't develop properly. It happens much more frequently than you think." Dr. Kallmann avoided being too specific, too clinical. He found that it upset his patients.

"You mean my baby wasn't normal?" Evelyn was horrified by the thought. She wanted to know everything, no matter how terrible.

"I don't know," said Dr. Kallmann.

"Don't know? Couldn't you tell?"

"Not without an autopsy." He wanted to stop her morbid line of questioning. It would accomplish nothing.

Evelyn shuddered. "An autopsy? On a baby?"

"Circumstances sometimes warrant it, although on a baby as young as yours it would most likely be inconclusive."

Evelyn thought over the doctor's words. She wondered what had happened inside her, without her knowing about it, without her being able to do anything to help.

"What went wrong, then?"

"You are asking a question that is unanswerable. You know, Mrs. Baum, we doctors aren't superhuman. Sometimes, we just plain don't know what went wrong."

"Tell me some of the things that could go wrong."

Evelyn would not be placated. The doctor began the recitation.

"The possibilities are literally infinite. For a fetus to grow to term, to be born healthy and whole, millions of cells must develop in the proper way and in the proper sequence. Some of the most common things that go wrong are that hearts or lungs fail to grow. Sometimes infants are strangled by the umbilical cord. Sometimes they drown, literally drown, in the amniotic fluid . . . Do you really want to hear more?"

"Just one thing," asked Evelyn. "Was it my fault?"

That was the question that had tortured Evelyn. She was sure that she had done something wrong. She was convinced that there was something wrong with her. She felt guilty. She was certain that the loss of the baby had been her fault. She had no way to know that almost every woman who miscarried felt the sense of guilt and responsibility. In the late forties, women didn't talk to each other about things like that. They suffered in anguished isolation. When their doctors told them that guilt was a common reaction, women tended to feel that the doctor was simply trying to make them feel better. Without knowing it, they felt that their doctors, whom they trusted, were lying to them and they usually nodded in agreement and continued to feel guilty. Dr. Kallmann was not a cruel man; he knew that his words, true though they were, didn't comfort, but he said them anyway because it was the best he could do. Doctors, like the men and women they treated, were prisoners of their times.

"Was it my fault?" Evelyn whispered.

"No. It was most definitely *not* your fault. You have got

to get that idea out of your head. A miscarriage is not the end of the world."

"It feels like it to me."

Evelyn had let everyone down—Nat, her mother, her father. Everyone had been so pleased with her and she had failed them.

"Well, it's not the end of the world and it's not your fault." Dr. Kallmann could be surprisingly brisk.

"What should I do?" Evelyn could hear the whine in her voice and was ashamed of it. She wanted to be told what to do. If someone who knew more than she did told her what to do, she would do it and everything would turn out all right.

"What you should do is forget the whole thing. Go home and go about your business. Get pregnant again just as soon as you can. It's the best remedy."

Evelyn smiled for the first time.

"Is it really that easy? Just go home and get pregnant?"

"It's that easy." Dr. Kallmann gestured toward the waiting room outside filled with women in varying stages of pregnancy. "Women do it all the time."

Dr. Kallmann's advice was easier given than followed.

It was three years before Evelyn conceived again. She had been pregnant for only nine weeks when, early in March 1951, she aborted spontaneously. There was no warning, just an attack of severe cramps. It was over in ten minutes in the privacy of her bathroom, with no dignity and no sirens in the middle of the night.

In the days that followed, Evelyn refused to eat, she refused to leave the house and she refused to get dressed. She refused to tell anyone why, but the sight of a pregnant woman or the sight of a child—in a supermarket, in a drugstore, walking on a sidewalk—was unbearable to her. She was afraid to pass a school, a playground or even a shop window displaying children's clothes. She was afraid of the world around her, because everywhere she looked she saw accusation in a child's smile, a mother's frown, an empty baby carriage.

Nat was worried about Evelyn and her parents worried about her. She grew thin, fearful and anxious. Together, they finally persuaded her to see Dr. Kallmann. Her mother drove her to the doctor's office, walked her inside, sat with her in the waiting room. Evelyn would have done none of it had she been alone.

Dr. Kallmann examined Evelyn and told her, truthfully, that there was nothing wrong with her that he could discover. Her ovulation was regular, and even many women with irregular ovulations had healthy babies. All Dr. Kallmann could say was that it was harder for some women to conceive than others. It was harder for some women to carry to term than others. Unfortunately, Evelyn seemed to be one of those women. All Dr. Kallmann could suggest was that she keep trying.

His words failed to reassure Evelyn or to restore her confidence. Although he hesitated, he finally prescribed a tranquilizer. It was a brand-new drug at that time and the research on side effects wasn't complete. However, considering the paralyzing extent of the patient's anxiety, Dr. Kallmann felt the benefit justified the possible risks.

The tranquilizers seemed to work a miracle. Evelyn's acute anxiety vanished, and by May of 1951 she was pregnant again.

She was happy and elated. Dr. Kallmann had been right after all and she was sure, absolutely positive, that nothing would go wrong this time. Her earlier miscarriages had been cruel and capricious mistakes of nature. This time, she was going to present Nat with a beautiful baby and she settled down to wait, convinced of a happy ending. She was, unfortunately, wrong. In July she miscarried once again.

Dr. Kallmann, whom she now saw as her enemy, put her back on the tranquilizers, but this time they didn't work. Evelyn took them but she didn't believe in them. She didn't believe in her doctor and she didn't believe in her husband.

She was convinced that Nat was lying to her when he told her that things would work out, that they would have a baby, that there was nothing wrong with her and that he loved her and always would, no matter what.

She was unable to do what millions of women were doing every day. In 1947, over three million eight hundred thousand babies were born; in 1948, over three million six hundred thousand—and the statistics continued year after year into the fifties. The postwar birth rate, as scientists had predicted, soared.

Evelyn looked inward and found herself wanting. She was inadequate and barren while Nat and his business were thriving. Her brother, Pete, had married three years ago and already his wife had one boy and was pregnant again. Ernie Coffman had married a girl he'd met at Penn and they had three children under five. All around were portents of richness and fecundity and inside herself she found nothing but sterility and barrenness.

Sex, which had once been a source of joy, now became a procreative necessity. Evelyn's desperation to conceive was expressed sexually. She remained frozen after Nat ejaculated, not wanting her inadequate body to destroy the healthy cells he gave her. She stopped having orgasms.

Finally, in September of 1951, Evelyn was pregnant for the third time that year. Upon Dr. Kallmann's advice, she remained in bed for the entire nine months. She gained forty pounds from the inactivity, but in June of 1952 Evelyn was delivered, by caesarian section, of a healthy, perfectly formed daughter. The child, in celebration of the circumstances, was named Joy.

7 THE FIFTIES REALLY BEGAN
in 1952 when Eisenhower was elected in a thirty-three million-vote landslide, when the poodle cut and toreador pants
were the latest fashions and when *I Love Lucy* and *Dragnet*
were the shows that Americans stayed home to watch.

While Evelyn had been obsessed with gynecology, Nat
was obsessed with business. Although he never told Evelyn,
things were not going well. Jazz, with its hard, grinding
rhythms and funky blue notes, had been the music of the
frenzied forties. The times had changed, though, now that
the war was over and the postwar celebration had ended.
Americans turned to suburbia, babies, gray flannel suits
and gray flannel music. They wanted Eddie Fisher to sing
"Any Time" and they wanted to hear Mario Lanza and
Tony Bennett and Perry Como. People paid for Patti Page
and the "Tennessee Waltz," for Jo Stafford and Kay Starr
and Teresa Brewer; for Les Paul and Mary Ford and "How
High the Moon."

Jazz was dead and Hep Cat was dying. In 1952, for many
reasons, Nat Baum folded his company. It was a business
decision that saved him money, difficulties and his reputation.

During the six years of Hep Cat's existence, Nat had never
paid a cent to the musicians whose work he was selling. He
didn't have to because he had no contracts with any of
them. The only way a musician knew that his work was
being sold was if he accidentally happened to come across a
Hep Cat record. Nat justified his behavior because what he
was doing was very common. The smaller labels just couldn't
compete with the bigger labels, and one way around the
dilemma was not to pay the talent. It was, Nat thought,
possibly unethical, but since everyone did it and since everyone in the industry knew it, he didn't see why he shouldn't
do what everyone else did. Hell, he had a right to live too.

Besides, the odds were that you'd never be caught. Most of the performers were colored; they felt powerless, and therefore most of them did nothing. They were accustomed to being screwed by nightclub owners with Mafia connections, to being cheated by record companies that kept crooked or nonexistent books, to being mistreated by a country that still called them niggers and made them use separate entrances and separate facilities and separate waiting rooms in the South. By 1952, their music no longer popular, they were either drunk or drugged or dead and most of them didn't bother. They accepted having their talent stolen and abused. It was too much effort to stay alive, never mind to fight.

Some, though, or their estates if they were dead, hired lawyers, accountants and muscle. Nat was called a bootlegger, a pirate and a thief. He was threatened with suit, with jail or with having his legs broken unless he paid up. Eventually, a financial settlement was reached, but the period was an ugly and frightening one for Nat. The solution, he decided, when he added up the harassment and subtracted the shrinking sales, was to shut down Hep Cat. There was no way on earth to collect from a company that didn't exist.

Concurrent with the shift from jazz to pop came the revolution in equipment. The old seventy-eights were phased out by forty-fives, which in turn were made obsolete by the long-playing thirty-threes. The entire pricing, manufacturing and distribution structure of the record industry was in upheaval. For a while, Nat didn't know which way to jump. He had enough money to live on, enough to play the stock market, and he bided his time. He couldn't touch top talent and he didn't want to risk hard-earned money on unknowns. Promoting an unknown cost a fortune in publicity, plugs and payola and the odds were that you'd lose. Inevitably, Nat came to the conclusion that he'd have to find something besides music to put on his records. He knew that he'd form a new company, with a new product, and that he would play it absolutely straight. He never again wanted to be called a crook. His problem was that he couldn't figure out the angle.

The solution, the beginning of Alpha, came to him the first time he cheated on Evelyn.

The girl was Jack Saunders' daughter by his first marriage. Her name was Pam and she had just graduated from the University of Missouri, where she had been the Homecoming Queen. She wanted a job in the record business but not, she insisted, in a big company. She wanted to learn everything, and the best place to learn everything was to be a gal Friday in a smaller company. Jack called Nat and asked if he could use any help.

"If she's got big tits and good legs, why not?"

"Hey," said Jack, half proud and half insulted, "take it easy. She's my only daughter."

The appointment was for four, and when Pam Saunders walked into Nat's office, Nat was stunned. She was tall and cool and blond and stacked. She had blue eyes and fluffy hair, and Nat got a hard-on just looking at her.

"You ought to be making a million dollars a year modeling," he said. "What do you want to bury yourself in an office for?"

"Because Dad does," she shrugged. "Besides, I need the money. Dad spent all his on his wives. I've got to support myself."

"On forty-five dollars a week?" She was an expensive-looking girl, in the same way that her father was an expensive-looking man. Nothing flashy, just generations of solid money and WASP self-assurance. They owned America and they knew it. "You could make forty-five an hour posing for magazine covers."

"Listen," said Pam. "Are you interested in hiring me or making me?"

Her bluntness took Nat off guard. He wasn't used to women who were so direct. He had forgotten how much fun flirting was. He remembered that he used to be very good at it.

"Both," he finally said. "It's the way I prefer to work."

"Dinner?" she asked.

"Dinner."

While Pam sat there and listened, Nat called Evelyn to tell her that he had a business dinner and that he'd stay overnight in town. As he spoke, Nat realized that he had been setting up a convenient precedent for several years now. Every other time he had stayed in town, it had been for a legitimate business reason: usually dinner and a nightclub and bed, alone, at the Astor Hotel. The pros preferred by Nat's business acquaintances weren't for Nat. He liked his women with class, and besides, he had vowed when he was seventeen that he would never, not ever, pay for it. Those nights had been boring, most of them, with business types and stale dirty jokes, but well worth it in dollars and cents. Nat decided he owed himself a good time for a change.

Dinner led to Pam's apartment, a small two-room flat on the parlor floor of a brownstone on Perry Street. The furniture was authentic antique Hepplewhite and, Nat would bet, had been in Pam's family for generations. It had that deep, rich patina that was achieved only by years of faithful polishing by well-trained maids. It was the kind of look that only generations of money could buy. It was the kind of money that impressed Nat the most.

Pam began stripping off her clothes as soon as they shut the door, and Nat decided that if she could do without preliminaries, so could he. They were both naked by the time they got to the small single bed in the rear bedroom, and as Nat was positioned over Pam, about to enter her, feeling the scratchy pubic hair with the tip of his erection, it remotely registered on him that this was the first time he had been unfaithful to Evelyn. He was proud of himself—not for his adultery but for the six years of fidelity. It was much more than most men could say for themselves.

It was strange and exciting to wake up in an unfamiliar bed the next morning.

"Does your father know you sleep around?" asked Nat.

"Who says I sleep around?"

What she was telling Nat was that what she did was none of his goddam business. He took the cue and let it drop. While she made coffee in the kitchenette the landlord had jammed into a former closet in the living room, Nat lay in bed, smoked a cigarette and noticed a French-English phrase books on the night table.

"*Avez-vous du sucre?*" he asked, reading from the phonetically spelled translation.

"*Et voulez-vous du lait?*" she asked, putting the two cups down on the night table.

"*Oui*," said Nat, still reading. "*Tous les deux, s'il vous plaît.*"

She disappeared back into the living room and returned with the cream and sugar.

"I'm thinking of maybe going to Paris if I can't find a job," she said. "I thought it might be a good idea to learn some French."

"Don't they teach French at the University of Missouri?"

"They teach it but I didn't learn it."

They both laughed. Pam was a beautiful girl and her beauty was a valuable commodity, one that had allowed her to pass a required French course without cracking a book. It was a commodity that permitted her to do and say as she pleased. Her beauty was a passport to freedom; it was better than money. Nat thought that beautiful women were the luckiest people in the world. Everything came to them. They never had to make an effort, never needed to feel insecure, never needed to ask.

Nat flipped the book back onto the night table, and when they had drunk their coffee, they made love.

"I love it in the morning," said Nat, thinking that he and Evelyn never made love in the morning. He was always rushing to get up, get dressed, swallow some coffee and catch the goddam Long Island.

"Morning, noon and night," said Pam.

She was responsive and hot and young and soft and firm

and perfect. Nat wanted to see Pam again. He wanted to, fuck her again. But he sensed that she was danger. There was something provocative and bitchy about her that appealed to him. She also made him feel clumsy and inadequate. Even though he was now tailored by Brooks Brothers and had left his zoot suits and sharp shirts behind a long time ago, he felt Jewish and unsure in the face of her cool WASP confidence. Girls like Pam, bluntly sexual and insistently independent, were more than Nat was willing to take on. He was attracted to them and afraid of them and the fear always prevailed.

Besides, he thought, he didn't want to hurt Evelyn. He loved her, he adored Joy, he didn't want to rock the boat. On the other hand, he was only thirty-two years old and he wasn't supposed to fuck just one woman for the rest of his life, was he? He decided that a one-night stand here and there was the perfect solution.

He left Pam with a kiss and a pat on her fanny, bare beneath the man's silk dressing gown she wore. He got into a taxi going up Seventh and gave the driver his office address. The cab got stalled in a traffic jam in the middle of the garment center, and while Nat sat there in the back seat waiting for the taxi to move again, he suddenly began to think about the phrase book.

He remembered that a few weeks ago he had read an article in the Sunday *Times* travel section about the boom in tourist travel. Planes were bigger and faster—the flight from New York to London took only ten hours and they were solidly booked. Americans were going to Europe to visit museums, to shop, to sight-see, to taste new foods, to get laid and to see what the foreigners were really like. A spokesman for the travel industry predicted that every year the number of Americans visiting Europe would rise. Air fares were bound to decrease, and the jet, not yet a reality but certainly on the horizon, would make the trip in a mere six hours.

Every single tourist going to the continent, Nat realized,

would be up against a language barrier. Unless their parents
had been born abroad, few Americans spoke a word of any
language other than English. It occurred to Nat that it
would be easier to learn a few basic phrases from a spoken
lesson than from a phrase book. It occurred to Nat that if
people bought phrase books, they'd probably buy records to
practice with at home before they even left.

He leaned forward and told the taxi driver that he'd
changed his mind about his destination. He asked to be
let off at Brentano's.

In February of 1953, the papers officially incorporating
Alpha Records, Inc., were drafted by Nat's lawyer, Victor
Helden. Alpha was registered with the State of New York,
and the Internal Revenue Service added its corporate identity
number to its records. Once again, Nat Baum was in business.

Nat chose the name Alpha because it represented a beginning. Nat wanted a new self. The outward signs of his rest-
lessness were obvious: sleeping with Pam Saunders; buying
his clothes—his gray flannel suits and oxford-cloth button-
down shirts—at Brooks Brothers and J. Press; closing down
Hep Cat with all its implications of pop, payola and the
slangy, sleazy world of Tin Pan Alley. The inward signs
were visible only to Nat. He wanted his old self to disappear.
He wanted to obliterate all traces of the poor Jewish boy
on the make. He wanted to smooth away the rough edges
and the memories of struggle and hunger. Perhaps it was
the aura of solidity of the Eisenhower years—but Nat Baum
wanted to grow and to change, and Alpha was to be the
vehicle of his transformation.

That morning of his first adultery, after leaving Pam,
Nat had bought one copy of every phrase book that Brentano's had in stock. Using them as a guide, Nat wrote a
script that ran from "Hello" and "Thank you" and "You're
welcome" to "Where is the nearest hospital?" and "May I
see you again tomorrow night?" What Nat had realized in

his moment of insight was that anything that could be taught in a book could be taught, more easily and with less effort, on a record.

Alpha began with a base of three records in the three most popular tourist languages: French, Italian and Spanish. Nat quickly discovered that Alpha freed him from the tyranny of retail record stores. No longer did he have to offer bribes to get good display; no longer did he have to provide booze and broads to persuade a store owner to write a larger order; no longer did he have to hustle. The bulk of his new business was through the mail. Nat's largest expenditure in getting Alpha started was paying for full-page advertisements in all the women's magazines—*McCall's* and the *Ladies' Home Journal* and the *Companion*. When Alpha began to show a profit, Nat bought full pages in the mass-market magazines—*Life, Look* and *The Saturday Evening Post*.

The smallest expense involved in Alpha was making the records themselves. Nat interviewed professors of languages from Hunter and Columbia and NYU until he found several whose voices and diction were particularly pleasing, and he paid them a flat fee of two hundred dollars to read the scripts into a microphone in a rented studio. Their contracts stipulated that Alpha could use their names and degrees in its advertising and promotion and that they had no further financial claim beyond the two-hundred-dollar fee.

It was a completely legitimate business, a long way from the world of seedy garages in rundown neighborhoods and bootlegged wire recordings. Nat Baum liked the feeling that never again would he have to look over his shoulder.

Hep Cat had served its purpose. It had been a way to cash in quickly when Nat had needed to create a financial base. Hep Cat had been a product of the forties. Alpha, on the other hand, was a creation of the fifties. It was the foundation for a long-term capital gain.

As the first three records established Nat's market, he began to branch out. He haunted the nonfiction departments of Brentano's and Doubleday and noticed that Americans seemed to be insatiably interested in self-improvement —in losing weight, in improving memory and posture, in slimming down and building up through exercise, in self-hypnosis to cure everything from alcoholism to insomnia. Americans were interested in becoming gourmet chefs, in their destiny according to the astrologers and in winning friends and influencing people. The future of Alpha, like the future of America itself, was boundless.

Nat began to be more daring. He ran test ads on any subject that seemed as if it might sell. If enough responses confirmed Nat's hunch, he would go ahead and cut the record. He hired professional writers, for flat fees, to write the scripts and he hired actors, always hungry, to read them, again for flat fees. If a subject didn't pull, he simply ignored it. Alpha was virtually a foolproof business. Nat knew ahead of time which records would sell and which wouldn't. Alpha was immune to the fads of teen-agers, the tastes of Dick Clark and Murray the K and pressure for a cut of the receipts from the Mafia thugs who controlled the jukeboxes. Alpha was a clean business. It had been Nat's single-handed creation. All the risks belonged to him and so did all the profits.

By 1957, Nat Baum had made it. No one could point a finger and call him a Sammy Glick. He was established, respected and respectable. To complete the image, Nat left the two rooms around the corner from the Brill Building and moved Alpha into a suite of offices on the third floor of a conservative building on the corner of Madison Avenue and Fifty-fourth Street.

For Nat, Alpha was the real beginning.

For Evelyn, Alpha marked a disturbing transition. She sensed that Nat had changed and that she had been left behind.

The worst thing that happened to Evelyn was that her husband didn't talk to her anymore. Nat used to talk to her by the hour when they were first married and he confided his dreams and ambitions, his fears and insecurities. They would stay up half the night holding each other and talking about themselves and their future, but now, if Nat had any dreams or ambitions, fears or insecurities, Evelyn didn't know what they were because he didn't tell her about them. When Evelyn asked him why he didn't talk to her anymore, Nat simply denied that he had stopped.

"I talk to you all the time," he said.

Evelyn was lost for an answer. Yes, they talked. They exchanged words. They talked about whether the car needed servicing, whether it was time to have storm windows put up, if they should buy a new tube for the old Dumont or buy a new television set altogether, how many times a month the service should mow the lawn and what train Nat would be taking. The things they talked about did not make Evelyn feel that she was intimate with her husband. Slowly and surely and helplessly, Evelyn saw that their lives were separating.

She didn't blame it on Nat. In fact, if anything, she blamed it on herself. Dr. Kallmann had told her that it was very unlikely that she would have any more children, although, of course, it was all right to "keep trying." Evelyn allowed herself to become obsessed with Joy, with two A.M. feedings, toilet training and with her first steps, and first words, with her health, safety and happiness. Evelyn knew that she was ignoring her husband in favor of her child, but she rationalized that Joy's baby years were short and precious. They would be over all too soon. Later, Evelyn promised herself, she would make it up to Nat.

The small, subtle signs of decay in her marriage disturbed Evelyn, but they were easy to ignore as long as Joy was a baby, in need of constant attention. Joy made Evelyn feel needed. Joy made Evelyn feel indispensable. Joy filled Evelyn's life.

In 1957, when Joy was five, she went to kindergarten. That was the winter when Evelyn was unable to ignore the fact that her marriage and her husband had drifted away from her. It was a painful reminder of the earliest period of their marriage when Nat had been working eighteen-hour days to get Hep Cat started and she had been alone, all day long, waiting for his return. In the eleven years that Evelyn had lived in Great Neck, she had discovered that her only real interests were domestic. She had gone to League of Women Voters meetings and failed to get interested in addressing envelopes or canvassing by telephone. She had tried the Garden Club and the Women's Reading Club and she found that she had no talent for small-town politicking and little talent for making friends with women whose lives and interests were as narrow and isolated as her own. She didn't enjoy afternoon bridge games and kaffeeklatsches and there was nowhere, in that expensive ghetto of wives and children, that she fitted in comfortably.

The only people who really mattered to Evelyn were her child and her husband and her immediate family. In 1946, she had looked forward to Nat's coming home, to the sex that invariably followed. Now, in 1957, after more than ten years of marriage, the initial eroticism had, quite normally disappeared and Evelyn was once again home alone all day long, only now there was nothing to look forward to except Joy's safe return from kindergarten.

Without her having really noticed it, Evelyn's life had shrunk around her. When she went to New York, she felt impossibly dowdy and out of style. Nat, as he grew older, was becoming more attractive, more distinguished. She, on the other hand, had lost the glow of youth and was turning into a middle-aged lady with no waistline and no future. Sometimes, Evelyn sipped Dubonnet all day long. She told herself that since it tasted more like soda pop than liquor, it wasn't really serious. But she knew that it was, and it scared her.

So in the spring of 1958, when prosperous Americans were fleeing the cities to the green suburbs with "good schools" and "all the benefits," Evelyn made a strange request. She asked Nat how he would feel about moving into New York.

Evelyn had her arguments marshaled.

"We'd see more of each other. We could go to concerts, to the theater; we could entertain more. You wouldn't have to commute—you know how much you hate the Long Island. And besides," said Evelyn, "there'd be more for me to do. I'd like to take a cooking course and I'd like to go to a gym."

Evelyn stopped, having run through her arguments. She waited for Nat to answer. She didn't know what to expect. She thought, bitterly, that that was an indication of how far apart they'd grown. Ten years ago, she would have known.

If he said no, Evelyn was prepared to fight. She had fought for very few things in her life; Nat had been one of them, and now that she had married him she was prepared to fight to keep him. She couldn't have said why, but moving out of Great Neck into New York City would help save her. She knew that she was being left behind. She saw herself in the women around her. Too many pregnancies had taken their physical toll. Being housebound had taken its intellectual toll. Being isolated had taken its emotional toll. Evelyn was thirty-two, and she looked tired and ten years out of style. She didn't want to stand passively by while she lost her looks, her husband, her self. She knew that if they moved, she had a chance.

She waited for Nat's answer.

"I think it's terrific," said Nat.

"You do?" She had been so ready to quarrel that she was surprised by his easy agreement.

"We should have done it years ago, but I thought you liked it here. I hate the goddam suburbs. They bore the shit out of me."

"I was afraid it was me. I thought I bored you."

Now that it was coming out into the open, Evelyn found that it was easy to express what had been bothering her, undermining her. She had sensed Nat's detachment, his lack of interest, and she had thought it was her fault.

"You don't bore me. The suburbs do. Stockbrokers in

Bermuda shorts. All they talk about is the Dow Jones and their golf scores and getting loaded on Saturday night. The wives are worse. I haven't had one intelligent conversation around here for ten years."

"I was afraid I was getting boring."

"The minute you get out of here you wouldn't be boring. You'd have a thousand things to do, a thousand interests."

Nat remembered how open Evelyn had been to new things when he had first met her, how she had changed from a plain, shy girl into a girl with style and appeal. He had had something to do with the change in her, but it hadn't all been his doing. She had been receptive. It surprised Nat that she still was. It was sad, he thought, how he had forgotten what his wife was like.

"What about Joy?" asked Evelyn. Joy was the one subject that had bothered her. Was it fair to take her away from the pleasant suburban life and shut her into a city apartment? The experts said no.

"What about Joy?"

"Well, you know what they say about bringing up children in the city?"

"What about it? I was brought up in the city and I survived."

"They say that suburban school systems are the best and that fresh air and trees . . ." Evelyn felt that she should argue her child's rights fully.

"Who's 'they'? The half-assed 'experts' who write for women's magazines? We'll put Joy in private school. She can have all the trees and grass in Central Park and she'll grow up three steps ahead of all the other kids."

"So you agree?"

"I can't wait to get out of here."

Nat gestured at the split-level ranch. At the time that Evelyn's father had bought it, it had been the ultimate in middle-class aspiration. In the years since, Nat Baum had left the middle class and its aspirations far behind.

"When should we start looking?"

"I'll call some agents tomorrow."

They had some wine with their dinner that night and they made love, and just before Evelyn fell asleep she realized that the reason that she was so happy was that for the first time in years she and her husband had had a conversation. A real conversation.

Evelyn spent that summer looking at apartments and watching her father die. She spent her mornings with real estate agents and her afternoons at Sloan-Kettering Memorial Hospital.

Her father had cancer of the stomach. There was nothing that could be done, said the doctors, when an operation showed that the cancer had metastasized. That meant that the disease had spread beyond the point at which the malignant cells could be surgically removed or excised with radium treatments. What they didn't say, what they let Evelyn and her mother and brother find out for themselves, was that cancer was to eat Simon Edwards up, little by little. They didn't say that it would stink, stink so much that the room he lay in was hardly bearable. They didn't say that he would shrink and wizen before their very eyes and that he would be in almost constant pain. And they didn't say that, at the end, he wouldn't even know who they were.

By the time, in late July, when Simon Edwards died at the age of sixty-two, it was a relief for all the members of his family. Their suffering had already been endured and their grief already inwardly acknowledged and accepted.

8 IN OCTOBER OF 1958, NAT and Evelyn bought an eight-room apartment at number 934 Fifth Avenue, between Seventy-fourth and Seventy-fifth

Streets. Its large, light rooms faced Central Park, and at Nat's insistence, it was on the third floor.

"You've got to remember, I grew up in a walk-up. I feel trapped on a high floor. Suppose the elevator breaks down? Or there's a fire? On the third floor you have a chance. On the twelfth, you're dead," he explained.

"I never thought of it that way," said Evelyn, and she, whose life had always been secure and who therefore never thought about survival, was surprised, as always, at how close to the surface concern about survival was to her husband, whose childhood had been so different from hers.

"You can take the boy out of the tenement," said Nat, "but you can't take the tenement out of the boy."

"And you still have the best sense of humor of anyone I ever met."

It took Evelyn over two years to make her apartment perfect. To find the right fabrics and papers, the most comfortable sofas and handsomest coffee tables, to hunt down the right accessories and most compatible antiques. She spent her days in the D&D building at Third Avenue and Fifty-ninth street; she haunted the auction rooms at Parke-Bernet and the antique shops on Madison Avenue as well as the ones in the Village. Her talent for decorating hadn't deserted her, and she had forgotten how satisfying it was to see a room take shape as she added and edited and re-arranged. She had also forgotten how nice it was to be noticed and complimented. Everyone who visited commented on what an outstanding job Evelyn had done, and Nat echoed their praise. Some people even told her that she was so good that she ought to become a decorator and get paid.

"Me? Paid?" she asked, and she laughed.

Except for the problems with Joy, the sixties were on the whole a very happy time for Evelyn. She attended to her apartment; she hired and trained a maid, something she had never done, finding it awkward at first to give instructions and then becoming accustomed to it. She drove out to East Orange once or twice a week to visit her mother. She took cooking lessons at James Beard's and then at Michael Fields's and learned how to make *poulet a l'estragon, estouffade de boeuf, saumon poché avec hollandaise, rillettes de porc, crème brûlée* and *marquis au chocolat.* She gave dinner parties to show off her skill and Nat was at least as impressed as their friends.

There were things that Evelyn tried but didn't succeed at. She tried to force herself to go to a gym. Although she wasn't the least bit overweight, she had a chunky body with a flat chest, no waistline suppression and boyish hips. She was told that with the proper exercise that she would develop her bustline and achieve a waist. The best gym, she had been told, was Kounovsky's, just off Fifth Avenue on Fifty-seventh Street, and she went there and signed up for a ten-lesson course. She bought a leotard and was issued a floral-printed bag with her name taped to it, but although she tried to force herself to keep on with it, she was intimidated by the other students. They were either flawless fashion models or society women whose pictures were in *Women's Wear Daily.* The models talked about agents and photographers and the society women talked about gallery openings and the best brands of panty hose. Evelyn felt inferior to both groups, sleek and svelte and self-absorbed, their conversation filled with references to people and parties that she only read about in the papers, and so she left and never returned after her fourth lesson.

Evelyn's second failure was fashion. In the early sixties she welcomed the constructed, cookie-cutout shapes that Jackie Kennedy made popular and the flattering bouffant haircut that the First Lady wore. The sleeveless dresses showed off Evelyn's pretty arms and hid her stubby midsection, and the bubble-shaped coiffure was flattering to her small, oval face. When the so-called Youthquake erupted in the mid-sixties, when Mary Quant designed the mini and Vidal Sassoon the geometric haircut, Evelyn was suddenly cut off from fashion. She was almost forty years old, and fashion was for people under twenty. Like many women, Evelyn couldn't get used to skirts that barely covered their thighs, and the harsh angular haircut was unbecoming to a face with crow's feet and parentheses lines bracketing nose and mouth. Like many women, Evelyn clung to the little gabardine dresses of the early sixties, knowing that she was out of style and not knowing what to do about it.

Evelyn saw her failures in perspective: after all, a woman of forty shouldn't be expected to have the body of a twenty-year-old or to wear a twenty-year-old's clothes or hairstyles.

Evelyn's successes as a homemaker and wife far outweighed such trivial failures. She was a gracious hostess to her husband's friends and business associates; she ran an immaculate, attractive household; she saw to it that the meals were delicious, that the laundry and dry cleaning were always done and that her husband, busy with his successful business, was never disturbed by the boring details of housekeeping.

The real proof that Evelyn was a good wife—and that Nat thought so too, and appreciated it—was that their sex life revived. Although it hardly burned with the intensity of their courtship and honeymoon, the sexless period following Joy's birth had given way to a new sexual rhythm: one that included lovemaking once or twice a week; one that made Evelyn feel, more than anything, that she was indeed as attractive to her husband as he was to her.

Evelyn was less sure that she was a good mother. Joy, now an adolescent, was moody and defiant and Evelyn wondered what she had done wrong. She couldn't communicate with her daughter, who at times was openly contemptuous of her. She worried at various times that Joy might become a drug addict, an unwed mother or even a jailbird. The school counselors assured Evelyn that it wasn't her fault: the difficulties she was having with her daughter were being shared by most parents of teen-agers. The generation gap was at fault, they said, not Evelyn.

Nat agreed with the school counselors and psychologists.

When Joy was openly insulting to Evelyn, Nat told her to let it roll off her back. It was, he said, merely a stage, and he told her not to take things so seriously.

Evelyn wondered often if Nat, somewhere down deep, didn't really want a son. She had asked him that question a thousand times and a thousand times he had answered that he didn't, that one Joy was worth any number of boys.

Joy and her father were very close. There was a bond between them that excluded Evelyn. They had private jokes and liked to spend time alone together—at the Plaza for Sunday brunch; shopping at far-out boutiques with loud rock and flashing lights; going to James Bond movies and having hamburgers later at Daly's Dandelion.

Evelyn was jealous of Joy's relationship with Nat, but since there was nothing she could do about it and since she didn't want to risk further alienating her daughter, she did nothing, taking comfort in the wisdom of the psychologists who said that Joy was "just going through a stage. All kids do."

Evelyn decided to believe that they knew what they were talking about. After all, they were the experts. She was only a mother.

In 1964 the Baums bought a house on Pleasant Street in Nantucket, Massachusetts, partly because Ned wanted a summer place to escape to and partly because Joy's best friend's family had a house there too.

The house was a luxury they could easily afford. The Baums were, by any standard, quite rich. Nat was drawing eighty thousand dollars a year from Alpha and he was a shrewd trader in the bull market of the sixties. Evelyn's own income, from the trust her father had set up for her, gave them an additional twenty-five thousand dollars a year.

"Money," said Nat, "is to spend."

And spend it they did. They bought an eighteenth-century house of enormous charm and didn't care that it needed plumbing, electricity, a brand-new foundation and a total renovation of all exterior and interior surfaces.

Evelyn spent two summers supervising the work on the Pleasant Street house, living with Joy in a rented house on nearby Milk Street. Nat spent every weekend in Nantucket, arriving even when the airport was fogged in and the flights canceled and he had to drive all the way to Woods Hole and take the ferry.

With all the ups and downs, life was everything Evelyn had dreamed of when she had been a bride in 1946. She had lived long enough to know that problems were always temporary and that the real foundations of life, her husband and her child, would always be there to protect her and to depend on for comfort and satisfaction.

The happy times lasted through the sixties, and it was not until 1970, when Nat began to talk about the big five-oh, about selling Alpha, about cutting out to a Polynesian island, that everything began to blow up.

Nineteen-seventy was the year of *Love Story*, Kent State and Nat Baum's fiftieth birthday. Nat had been born on July 12, and Evelyn spent the week before planning an elaborate surprise birthday party. She had bought lobsters down at the Straight Wharf lobster pound and made green mayonnaise with chervil and parsley from her own herb garden to serve with them. She had ordered two large roasts of beef; she had bought tomatoes and scallions and cucumbers and lettuce fresh from the trucks that pulled up every morning in front of the Hub on Main Street piled with produce from the truck farms in the center of the island. She had made a birthday cake, layers of genoise with a mocha frosting; she had ordered champagne and extra ice; she had restocked the bar with Scotch, gin, vodka, lemons and limes and cases of club soda and tonic. She had bought dozens of candles in colored-glass holders to put out in the garden or on the screened-in porch in case it rained. She had bought several dozen red geraniums in pots and bouquets of asters and daisies and black-eyed Susans to welcome Nat for the big weekend.

She had mailed invitations to Nantucket friends—people

from New York and Boston who had summer houses; she invited local painters and gallery owners; she asked Nat's buddies from the boatyard on Lower Washington Street where he kept an outboard that he used for bluefishing; she invited Nat's lawyer and best friend, Victor Helden, and his wife, Francine, to fly up from New York and spend the weekend as houseguests.

Evelyn realized, as she made her plans, that this year was Nat's fiftieth birthday and that next June would mark their twenty-fifth wedding anniversary. It was nice, she thought, to have two major milestones to celebrate in sequential summers. She already began to wonder what she could do in 1971 to outdo the gala preparations she had just completed.

Evelyn had gone through the charade of swearing everyone, including Joy, to the utmost secrecy. Nat, officially, was to know nothing about the party until Saturday night when the guests would start to arrive. But, of course, Evelyn knew that he would be expecting something. All year long he had been talking about it.

"It's staring me right in the face. The big five-oh," he'd say. "Old. I'm getting old."

"You don't look it," said Evelyn, and he didn't. He had thick dark brown hair that showed no signs of thinning or receding, his sideburns were fashionably long and his clothes were youthfully sporty, mostly from Saint Laurent, where he spent a fortune. He had no paunch, no excess fat—he carried his hundred and fifty-five pounds on his five-ten frame as lithely as a young man. In fact, thought Evelyn, Nat had never been more attractive. "You're aging beautifully."

"But I'm aging," he'd answer.

"I didn't mean it that way. What I mean is you're not getting older, you're getting better."

"I'm getting older. Don't spout clichés at me."

"Darling, I didn't mean . . ."

There had been variations of the same conversation several times over the past six months and they all had ended up with Nat admitting that no, of course he wasn't really bothered by turning fifty. He was just joking.

"After all, it happens to the best people," he'd say, and then they'd both laugh.

On Friday afternoon, the eleventh, Evelyn drove out to the airport to meet the three-thirty plane. Nat always left his office early on Fridays in the summer. For a change, the Delta flight arrived more or less on time, and Evelyn stood in the bright sunshine just behind the galvanized-iron fence that separated the passenger area from the blacktop landing strip. She watched the passengers disembark and cross the small airfield. There were the usual Friday-afternoon faces, husbands whose wives and children spent the summer in Nantucket while they spent the weeks in the city and joined their families for weekends. Evelyn greeted them; she knew almost all of them by sight if not by name, and many of them had been invited to Nat's birthday party. Usually Nat was one of the first off the plane—he liked to sit near the front; but this time, she didn't see him. Sometimes he got to La-Guardia late and had to take a seat farther back in the plane.

More passengers walked down the steps, carrying flight bags and attaché cases and tennis rackets, and she watched as the ground crew unloaded bicycles, suitcases and golf bags from the baggage compartment.

Finally, the passengers stopped descending, and although Evelyn was sure that Nat would appear at the top of the steps any second, he didn't. He had obviously missed the plane.

It was strange, she thought, this weekend of all weekends. But she supposed that he had had a late meeting or a business lunch that had dragged on longer than usual. She drove back to the house and asked Lydia if Mr. Baum had called and the maid said that no, he hadn't.

Evelyn then called Nat's office. She spoke to his secretary, whose name she didn't know. The secretaries changed constantly: Nat said it was impossible to hire a good one. Either he fired them or they quit. The current girl said that Mr.

Baum had left for lunch at twelve and hadn't returned.

"Is his briefcase still there?" Nat always brought his briefcase up to Nantucket—and he never opened it. It was a long-standing family joke.

"It's still here," said the secretary.

"Thank you," said Evelyn. "Please ask him to call me when he gets in."

Evelyn hung up, mystified but not worried. On an impulse, she dialed their apartment. Maybe Nat had gone there to pick up something he'd forgotten—a new sport jacket, perhaps, or the expensive Blaupunkt shortwave radio he always meant to bring with him but kept forgetting. Evelyn dialed 212 and then their New York number. Evelyn counted eight rings and was about to hang up when someone picked up the phone.

"Hello?"

There was no answer.

"Nat?"

Silence.

Then there was the sound of the phone being quietly hung up.

Now Evelyn began to worry. Suppose there was a burglar in the apartment? But no, a burglar wouldn't answer a phone. Or would he? Evelyn drove from her mind the memory of the horrible Janice Wylie murders. The Career-girl Murders, they had been called, and they had happened in an elegant building not too far from Evelyn's. As far as Evelyn knew, the apartment was supposed to be empty. The cleaning woman came in every morning to pick up for Nat, but it was past four—she left at one. Nat was the only other person who had keys, so it had to be Nat, didn't it? Only Nat wouldn't pick up the phone and then hang up. It didn't make sense.

Evelyn called the building and Alec, the nice doorman, the one with half a brain, answered. He told Evelyn that Mr. Baum had come home at two o'clock and hadn't come down yet.

Evelyn sat in the Windsor chair by the phone in the foyer of the Pleasant Street house, looking out through the leaded glass panels that distorted the view, and didn't understand. The refrigerator was filled with lobster and champagne. The house was filled with flowers and she was filled with anticipation and Nat, apparently, was barricaded in their New York apartment, incommunicado.

He hadn't really been seriously upset by the big five-oh. Or had he?

Obviously, he had.

Evelyn dialed every half-hour but, as she had more or less expected, there was no answer. She remembered turning forty. She hadn't particularly liked it. It had come during a decade when people, including her own daughter, were announcing that they didn't trust anyone over thirty. It made her aware that menopause might not be so many years away and, with it, the final inevitability of no more children—although she had, slowly, over the years, come to terms with that too. Forty made her aware of the passage of time, but since there was nothing she could do about it, she accepted it.

That, really, was one of the biggest differences between her and Nat: she accepted things; he fought them. Evelyn didn't know which was better. Sometimes she thought she was right. Why fight the inconquerable? Other times, she wished she were more like Nat. Unless he had fought, there would have been no marriage, no Alpha, no happy life. Still, Evelyn didn't see the sense of fighting fifty. No matter how hard you fought, you could never win.

She kept on dialing, and finally, a little after midnight, Nat answered.

"I've been trying to get you," said Evelyn.

"I know."

"Is it fifty?"

"It's not fifty." His tone of voice shut her out completely.

"You know," she said, not knowing what else to say, "you

could still make the early plane tomorrow. I didn't want to tell you, but I have a party planned. A surprise party . . ." She felt like a fool even as she rattled on. "I've invited all your . . ."

For an answer, he hung up.

The next morning, after calling all her guests and telling them that the party had been canceled, Evelyn left for New York on the eight-thirty plane.

At ten, Evelyn rang the doorbell of 3-B and there was no answer. She rang it four more times and waited and still there was no answer. She was hesitant about barging in. She was scared by Nat's mood. Still, there was no response when she called through the door, and she opened her bag and got out her keys. It was her own apartment and she felt like an intruder. She was irrationally frightened of entering. She wondered what she thought she'd find: mutilated corpses, evidence of unspeakable acts? She told herself that she was ridiculous and went in.

"Nat," she called again as she opened the door. There was no answer. She glanced into the kitchen. Two opened bottles of club soda were on the counter and a jar of instant coffee was spilled into the sink, forming a dark brown puddle where the faucet leaked slowly.

The living room was empty and immaculate except for Friday's *New York Post,* an overflowing ashtray and two empty bottles of Dewar's.

"Nat?"

He wasn't in his study, and Joy's bedroom was untouched. Evelyn proceeded down the hall and went into their bedroom—the master bedroom, the real estate agent had called it—hers and Nat's. The room had been demolished. The bedclothes had been ripped off the bed and the top sheet was torn. Nat lay on top of the mattress cover naked—asleep, passed out, whatever. Evelyn touched his forehead and her hand came away greasy with sweat.

The antique tole chandelier hung crookedly from the

ceiling, and every one of the six candle-shaped bulbs had been smashed, so that a fine rain of glass was strewn over the bed and carpet. A porcelain lamp had been thrown against the wall, and a pool of dried vomit led into the bathroom. Nat's clothes, about which he was ordinarily compulsively neat, were all over. His tie hung from a doorknob. His shirt was half on and half off the dresser. His trousers were on Evelyn's vanity table and his underwear was half kicked under the bed. The windows were shut and the air conditioning was off. In the stale July heat, the room smelled as if carnage had been committed there.

"Nat?" He was leaden, unresponsive.

Evelyn went into the bathroom to get a towel and washcloth. She could at least sponge off the sweat and clean him up. She gasped when she saw the room. Her bottles of perfume, Joy and Arpège and Norell, were shattered on the tile floor. All the towels—bath towels and hand towels—were on the floor soaking up the perfume and shards of glass. Everything breakable in the room had been broken: the mirror over the washbasin, the makeup lights that flanked the mirror, the door on the shower stall, the three glass shelves that held makeup and bath oil and after-shave, a mouthwash bottle and a bottle of Bufferin. A tube of toothpaste had been smeared into the bath mat and face powder had been spilled over everything. Finally, in red lip-stick, in bright red letters, *Fuck You* had been scrawled over the wall that was opposite the bathtub. The pink-and-white gingham fabric that Evelyn had used on the walls and ceiling was completely ruined.

It took her a moment to absorb all the damage, wondering at the rage and violence the room contained. Then she noticed the diaphragm on the back of the toilet. It was smeary with vaginal jelly—and, Evelyn wondered, with sperm? Nat's sperm?

Oh, Nat. Why did you have to bring her here? Whoever it was, why did it have to be here? Why couldn't you just go to a hotel or a motel like the rest of your friends? Why did you have to bring your dirty little secrets home?

Evelyn took a clean washcloth out of the linen closet, held it under the cold-water tap and wrung it out. Stepping carefully around the debris on the bathroom floor, she went back into the bedroom and smoothed it over Nat's face.

He didn't move. He didn't open his eyes and he didn't speak.

Evelyn began to clean up. She picked up Nat's clothes. She found a pair of pale blue bikini panties under the bed. She found the ceramic window-shade pull in front of her night table; it had been ripped off and the cord was left broken. She put everything in the waste can.

She went into the utility closet in the kitchen and with Comet and a dustpan and brush began on the bathroom, picking up the big pieces of glass, mopping up perfume and mouthwash and scrubbing up the powder. She got the vacuum cleaner and heard the glass as it got sucked up into the machine. She scrubbed the washbasin and tub and, picking up the diaphragm with a Kleenex, threw it into the waste can with the panties and the shade pull. She worked on the lipstick *Fuck You* with spray dry-cleaning powder and succeeded only in smearing the letters and bleaching out the color of the fabric. It would have to be ripped out and replaced.

Evelyn carefully picked up the towels and washcloths and threw them into the waste can and took everything out to the incinerator. There was no one in the hallways. On July weekends, 934 Fifth Avenue was almost deserted. She heard the ceramic shade pull bump along the chute as it fell three stories to the basement.

She wished she could throw her mind and memory away as easily.

Evelyn went back and straightened up the kitchen and made herself a cup of coffee. She took it back to the bedroom and sat on the chaise, watching Nat, as if by looking at him she could understand him. He had slept through the noise of the vacuum cleaner, the sounds of water running, the sound of her voice. She wondered what, besides liquor, he had put into his system.

At three that afternoon, he woke up.

"What are you doing here?" he asked.

"I could ask you the same thing."

"I don't want to talk about it."

"I do."

"Later," he said, and passed out—or fell asleep, or whatever it was—again.

"It didn't mean anything." Nat was talking about the girl. "I wish I could make it unhappen."

"Who was she?"

"I don't know. I picked her up at a bar."

"Why did you bring her here?" Evelyn hated herself for acting like the betrayed wife, for giving Nat the third degree. But she was entitled and he knew it and he went along with it. It was her right. "What did you have to bring her to our home for? Into our bedroom?"

Nat shrugged. "I don't know. I don't know why I did any of it." He gestured around the bedroom, the signs of destruction still apparent—the twisted chandelier, the spotted carpet, the broken window shade.

"Did you have a fight?" asked Evelyn. "What went on in here?"

"I don't know. I don't remember." Nat didn't know if he had wrecked the room or if the girl had or if they had done it together. He wondered what kind of monster lived in him. He wondered how that monster could be there without his knowing it and being able to control it. He was afraid of the monster. He was afraid of himself.

It was eight-thirty now and Evelyn had scrambled some eggs and made some toast, which Nat washed down with two Cokes. They were eating off trays in the bedroom.

"I was pretty drunk . . ."

"And you got drunker?"

Nat nodded.

235

"I just don't remember. I blacked out. I feel terrible."

"Hangover?" Compassion pulled Evelyn one way, anger the other.

"Worse," said Nat. "Guilt. Remorse. I don't know why I did it. Any of it."

"I wish you hadn't brought her here."

"I know."

"You could have taken her to a hotel."

"Evelyn . . ."

"Just keep your whores out of my house."

"Evelyn, it was one time. One night. It didn't mean anything."

"It means something to me." Evelyn had known or anyway guessed that for years now Nat had screwed around a little on the side. All his friends did. As long as he didn't rub it in, she could pretend that it didn't happen or that, if it did, it didn't matter that much to her.

"It won't happen again," said Nat. "I mean that."

"What won't happen? You won't pick up girls or you won't bring them here?"

Nat looked at her.

"Don't torture me, Evelyn. I'm torturing myself enough without your help."

Nat slept through most of Sunday, waking up only to eat a pint of Haagen-Dazs rum-raisin ice cream and drink several bottles of plain club soda. He watched part of the Mets–Cincinnati game, and on Monday morning he announced that he felt semihuman.

"Why don't you spend the week in Nantucket?"

It was blackmail, but it was blackmail with a purpose. It was a way for Evelyn to assert her claim on Nat's primary loyalty and it was a way for Nat to absolve his guilt. If it had been only a business deal and not a marriage, it would have been considered a good one. Both parties won. Evelyn salvaged her pride and Nat bought her forgiveness with his repentance. Neither stopped to realize that pride was only an emotional cosmetic and that forgiveness had no price tag.

Nat phoned his office and said that he was taking the week off. Evelyn called and arranged to have a new shower door put in and the fabric on the wall replaced. She gave the doorman a set of duplicate keys and told him to let the workmen into 3-B.

She was glad that she wouldn't have to be there when they saw the *Fuck You* scrawled on the pink-and-white gingham wall.

9 IN THE NEXT YEAR EVELYN learned something about herself that she had never known before: she discovered that she was alone.

Joy had already been living for a year in her own apartment; Evelyn's mother moved to a condominium in Fort Lauderdale, where she occupied herself with canasta and a yoga class, and Nat barricaded himself behind a bottle of Scotch. He kept a bottle of Dewar's in the refrigerator, and every night when he got home, he read the *Post* and sipped straight, cold Scotch until dinnertime. After dinner, he resumed drinking until it knocked him out.

He wasn't nasty to Evelyn; he didn't abuse, insult or blame her. He simply ignored her.

There were a thousand things Evelyn wanted to talk about that she was afraid to mention: the diaphragm, Joy, Nat's drinking, their marriage, their nonexistent sex life, her desire to help him, the future, the past. There were a thousand things on Evelyn's mind and every one was a booby trap surrounded by barbed wire.

Occasionally, Nat would deliver a semidrunken monologue about what a failure he was. Everything, according to him—his life, his business, his ambitions—had turned sour. Nothing, he said, had worked out the way he had envisioned when he was twenty-five. He hadn't become a force in the world of jazz. He hadn't traveled as much as he had wanted. He hadn't seduced glamorous and sophisticated women. He was just another guy trying to make a buck, producing shlocky how-to records for people who were too poor or too dumb to go to an analyst, a teacher, a guru. He was over fifty now and his whole fucking life added up to nothing.

Evelyn tried to show him how wrong he was. She pointed out how successful he had become, how much money he made, how much she still loved and needed him and how Joy adored him and hung on his every word. He had everything, she said—his brains and his health, enough money to do whatever he wanted; he had looks and energy and humor and charm.

Nat told her that she was full of shit.

Evelyn wished she had someone to talk to. Her daughter, whom she rarely saw, was openly contemptuous of her, and her mother's marital advice had been along the lines of "you've got to take the bad with the good."

The leaders of the Women's Lib movement, Betty Friedan and Gloria Steinem and Shirley Chisholm, were talking about consciousness raising and the sisterhood of women, and Evelyn sometimes wished she were thirty and liberated and not forty-four and alone. Never before had she noticed that she had no friends: she had been too busy to notice, keeping house, raising a child, catering to her husband. She knew other women, of course, but they were exactly like her: wives and mothers. She wondered if they had the same problems that she did and she wondered how they dealt with them. She never found out because women of her generation had been raised not to talk about "personal things." Evelyn was a victim of a conspiracy of silence that kept her isolated and lonely.

Nineteen-seventy drifted into 1971, and without really being able to say why except that she was afraid, Evelyn decided not to open the house in Nantucket. Joy was going to Europe with her boyfriend, and Evelyn told Nat that she wanted to spend the summer in the city keeping him company.

Nat said he didn't care one way or the other.

The crisis points loomed ahead like two jagged mountain peaks: their twenty-fifth anniversary and Nat's fifty-first birthday. Consciously and unconsciously, Evelyn was braced. She had never come to terms with the violence of Nat's fiftieth birthday and she had never discussed his behavior with him: she was too frightened. Now that two more major milestones were ahead, Evelyn feared the worst and yet her imagination couldn't conjure up what the worst might be. She knew better than to plan any big celebrations and cautiously she waited for some indication from Nat to guide her. He continued to be unusually quiet, and when their anniversary, for which she had so carefully braced herself, arrived, Nat's incredible gift was a total surprise.

Joy called from Copenhagen to wish them a happy anniversary, and that night they went out to dinner, alone, to the Côte Basque. As they sipped espresso, Nat took a box out of his pocket and handed it to Evelyn. In it was a five-carat cabochon emerald set in a ring of big, round diamonds.

"You didn't have to."

"Don't you remember? I promised I'd get you a diamond ring."

Evelyn remembered the promise. Nat had made it just after they'd become engaged. They'd been sitting on the sofa in her parents' living room. . . . It was hard to believe that twenty-five years had passed.

"Only I realized that emeralds go better with green eyes than diamonds. I promised you a diamond, but I realized that an emerald would be prettier, so I compromised: I got you both."

Evelyn slid the ring on. It was extremely heavy, and it sadly made her conscious of how much her hands had changed in twenty-five years. The tendons on the backs of them were prominent, as were the large brown freckles. Evelyn resented age for making her hands less beautiful than the ring.

"Thank you," she said. And then she repeated herself: "But you didn't have to."

"You deserve it," said Nat. "For putting up with me."

The guard on his face dropped as he spoke. It was more apology than he had ever made for the pain he had caused her, and it reminded Evelyn for a poignant moment of the unsure boy she'd had glimpses of occasionally years ago. The memory brought tears to Evelyn's eyes and the green stone shimmered and swum. Even Nat, whose emotions were usually so carefully guarded, seemed moved. It was a long time before either of them spoke; and that night, for the first time in a long time, they went to sleep in each other's arms.

Evelyn felt buoyed enough by Nat's gesture to ask what he wanted to do for his birthday. She had always loved occasions and he had always hated them, and they compromised by agreeing to have the Heldens to dinner. The evening was pleasant and normal. Vic Helden, as usual, flirted outrageously with Evelyn, and Francine Helden, as usual, got quietly smashed on old-fashioneds. She had never gotten used to the way her husband was openly seductive with other women, and the liquor helped blot it out.

In a low-key way, the summer passed; and late in August, the miracle happened.

"I've gone legit!" announced Nat. He literally bounded through the front door with a bottle of iced Dom Perignon under one arm and a huge bouquet of red and white roses in the other arm. He was so ebullient that Evelyn wondered if he had already been drinking.

As they celebrated with the champagne, Nat told Evelyn all about his deal with J&S. It was the association with J&S and its old-line established reputation that seemed to transform Nat. Evelyn was amazed, as she had been so many times during their marriage, at how much prestige meant to Nat, and at how hard Nat was still fighting Essex Street and being poor and Jewish.

"Life is *not* over at fifty!" said Nat.

"See," said Evelyn, who tried to resist but couldn't, "I told you so."

"I just wasn't smart enough to listen," said Nat, and they went downtown to El Faro and celebrated some more with Spanish food and sangría.

All winter and fall, Nat's good mood continued; he talked about his plans for the future, about maybe merging with a publishing company, about maybe selling Alpha. There had been, he said, various nibbles, some quite tempting. There was still time to make it big, really big. Nat worked harder than ever, spending more time at the office, sometimes even Saturdays. He seemed to have found a new well of energy and enthusiasm and it was contagious. Evelyn felt alive again, and it was all due to Nat. He talked to her, he made love to her, he made her happy.

Evelyn never dreamed that the joyous event she was celebrating was Nat's conquest of another woman—younger, prettier, more desirable.

To exist, the triangle needs three consenting parties. Nat consented actively by initiating it, Barbara consented with knowledge and Evelyn consented by default. She accepted without question Nat's excuses, absences and explanations. Although Evelyn did, in fact, have questions, she was afraid of the answers and therefore never asked them.

To exist, the triangle demands three complementary elements: love, power and danger. Mixed incautiously, these elements, like those in physics, are volatile and potentially explosive.

Nat Baum, like everyone who is involved in a triangle, began by thinking that he could dominate it.

Nat, like everyone, loved love. He particularly loved being loved by two women. It was simple arithmetic: twice as much love meant twice as much virility. He went from

Barbara's bed to his wife's bed, erotically recharging and sexually cross-pollinating. Barbara's love made him believe in Evelyn's love and Evelyn's love convinced him of Barbara's love until, finally, Nat began to love himself. That love, self-love, transcended the love he received from the two women. Loving himself, for the first time in his life, was the most significant emotional reward Nat Baum got from the triangle.

Nat, like everyone, needed power. The power he exercised at the office—the power to hire and fire, the power to praise or criticize—had long since become stale. He had already proved that he had the power to make more money than his father or his friends and to outperform the Dow Jones. Nat needed more power. He needed absolute power. Power over two women who would fight for him, who would compete for him, was the only arena of absolute power permitted in a democratic society.

Nat, like everyone, found the fact and fiction of danger irresistible. The need for power led inevitably to the risks of danger, and danger is narcotic. It possesses the true narcotic's quality of demanding ever more to satisfy. The power addict's habit grows until only bigger and bigger doses will satisfy.

Nat, like almost everyone, understood little or nothing about the dynamics of the triangle. He knew only that he was excited and interested in life for the first time in a long time. He felt young and puissant and in control. He kept on, pushing further and further, exacting more love and exercising more power and increasing the dosages of danger and discovery until, finally, the triangle that he thought he controlled controlled him.

To Nat, the triangle was a work of art and he was the artist. He found it poetically satisfying to invite his wife and his mistress to share successive weeks in Eleuthera with him on the same day. It was esthetically gratifying to know that as one plane took Barbara away, another would be bringing his wife to him. Not only did he feel that he controlled the triangle; he felt that he controlled the very air through which the planes flew.

He had been toying off and on with the idea of proposing to Barbara. In a playful moment, he had ordered MRS. NATHAN BAUM stationery for her. He loved Barbara, and proposing to her was a way to increase the dosage of danger. He also recognized that a proposal might get him in over his head and so, resisting the irresistible, he did nothing definitive until, on the spur of the moment, at the airport, he asked Barbara to marry him. He did it at the last moment, at a time when Barbara couldn't answer. Her inability to answer, permitted him to gamble without losing. Once again, he had taken a risk—and won.

Because he loved Barbara, Nat meant his proposal at the moment he made it; and yet, three hours later, when Evelyn's plane arrived, he was truly happy to see her.

A week with a wife is different from a week with a mistress.

Nat and Evelyn used all the facilities the lavish house offered. They chartered a single-engine Cessna to fly to a neighboring island with no name and dazzling white beaches, where they sunbathed and skinny-dipped and ate the picnic the cook had packed earlier that morning. They got high on chilled rosé wine and dozed through the return flight.

They used the fishing boat and went bonefishing on the nearby flats. It was superb sport, but Evelyn was disappointed when she was told that bonefish weren't good to eat and that they would be having filet mignon that night instead of fish they had caught themselves.

They water-skied, swam, snorkeled and sailed the blue-and-white Sailfish. They went to Nassau one evening and spent the night at the roulette tables, coming away ahead by eleven hundred dollars.

Nat used the sauna and Evelyn relaxed in the big marble tub, fascinated by the tap that dispensed bath oil. It was the kind of luxury that only movie stars and heiresses could afford. They dressed for dinner every night and ate it off the polished Chippendale table. The food was cooked by a talented West Indian and served formally by a butler who wore white gloves and poured the wine without dripping.

Once they made love in broad daylight on the private beach in front of the house, and every night they made love in the big bed in the master bedroom.

Not a trace remained of the woman who had shared that bed the week before.

10 No trace of barbara

Roser intruded into Evelyn Baum's carefully placid life until Barbara Roser telephoned and said that Nat wanted a divorce. Evelyn hung up before the voice could continue. She didn't want to hear any more—but the voice inside wouldn't stop.

Evelyn wondered how long Nat had been involved with the woman who had called her; she wondered why she had never, not once, said anything about the suspicions she had had but quickly suppressed; she wondered, above all, what Barbara Roser was like: what she looked like, how old she was, where she bought her clothes and under what circumstances she had met Nat and who had seduced whom.

Evelyn decided to stay up until Nat returned home. She would have it out with him. She would spew out her anger, her accusations, her threats. She would find out everything. She would make him answer every question and she would find out just what he planned to do. As night turned into morning and Nat didn't come in, Evelyn alternated between rage she could barely control and, despite herself, worry about what might have happened to him. The fact that he didn't come home at all was the most punishing blow of all.

It exhausted Evelyn. His absence, cruel and blatant, erased Evelyn, obliterated her and, in the end, made her even wonder if the call had been some kind of joke or if she had, in fact, even heard right.

When Evelyn heard the keys in the front door the next morning at ten, she hoped for a moment that it might be Nat. It wasn't. It was the maid, Lydia. For a split second Evelyn considered messing up Nat's side of the bed. She didn't want the maid to know that her husband had been out all night.

She resisted the impulse, feeling cheap and shoddy. Lydia was used to Nat's side of the bed being unslept in and if she thought anything about it, she had never said a word. Those had been the nights when, according to Nat, he had had to be in Philadelphia, Boston or Chicago. The nights, Evelyn now realized, that he had spent with Barbara Roser.

Evelyn didn't get dressed that day. She wasn't going to leave the apartment. She hated herself for it, but she didn't want to miss Nat's call. She didn't know when to expect him and she wanted to be there when he arrived.

That night, at six, she heard his key in the door. She wrapped her robe neatly around her nightgown. She was so tired that she didn't know what she was going to say, although she had been rehearsing dialogue all night and all day. She went out into the living room.

"Jesus," said Nat, throwing his *Post* on the sofa. "You look lousy." He was at the bar, mixing himself a Scotch-and-water. "Want a drink?"

"Where have you been?" asked Evelyn. He was so casual, so offhand, standing there as if nothing had happened, carefully cutting a sliver of lemon peel for his drink.

"Out and around," he said. "You know us boys." He winked at her.

"Do you want a divorce?" asked Evelyn, wanting to get it over with. Wanting to hear it from his own lips.

"Oh, that."

"That."

"We were a little high. You know how it is." Nat settled himself on the sofa, taking off his shoes and putting his feet on the glass-and-steel coffee table the way he always did. Evelyn half expected he'd open the *Post* to the stock-market pages and look at the closing prices.

"We?" she asked.

"Barbara and I," he said.

"She's your mistress." It was a declarative sentence.

"Everyone has one, don't they?" asked Nat. "I mean everyone who can afford one."

"It's not like a Cadillac," said Evelyn. "Something you go out and buy."

Nat shrugged, neither agreeing or disagreeing with her.

"What are you going to do?" Evelyn wanted some kind of answer. She wanted a resolution. It was the suspended animation, the unexpected energy in the room, that was the most unbearable in a sequence of unbearable events.

"What am I going to do?" Nat asked himself out loud. He appeared to think it over for a moment. Then he looked at Evelyn, meeting her eyes for the first time, his face completely blank, and answered:

"Nothing. I'm not going to do anything."

Evelyn's folder was on Dr. Leon Amster's desk when the nurse showed Evelyn into his office. He was a large, square man who wore large, square glasses. Evelyn, although she and Nat and Joy had used him as a family doctor for fourteen years, still wasn't sure whether he actually knew who she was or whether he simply reacted to the notations in the folder.

"Insomnia. I can't sleep," she said.

It was true. It was also true that the real reason was Nat. But how could you ask a physician to treat the effects of a husband's infidelity?

"How long have you been unable to sleep?"

"Two weeks," said Evelyn.

Two weeks since Barbara Roser had called. Two weeks

of never knowing whether Nat would come home. Now that the affair was out in the open and officially known to Evelyn, Nat used it as carte blanche to stay out whenever he pleased. It was the never knowing that was the worst.

"Any other symptoms?" asked the doctor.

"No."

Was the fact that your husband had a mistress a symptom?

"Change in bowel habits? Nausea? Unusual bleeding? Irregular periods? Changes in appetite or eating habits?"

"None of those."

"Let's have a look at you."

He listened to her heart and took her blood pressure and her temperature. He examined her breasts and poked around her abdomen. He looked into her ears; there had been a middle-ear infection he had treated her for several years ago. The nurse took a sample of blood from her middle finger and gave Evelyn a kidney-shaped enamel pan and asked for a urine sample. The simple tests were done right in Dr. Amster's office.

"You're how old?" He looked at the folder. "Forty-six?"

Evelyn nodded.

"You're in excellent health so far as I can see."

"But I can't sleep. I'm exhausted."

"Do you want sleeping pills?" Dr. Amster was used to people who used all sorts of elaborate charades to get prescriptions for barbiturates. Mrs. Baum's wasn't even a charade.

Evelyn didn't know how to say yes. So she said no.

"I don't like to prescribe them. For all the obvious reasons," said the Doctor. "Let's go over one thing: are your periods normal?"

"Right on time." Evelyn racked her brain. "Maybe a little less blood than usual."

"Scanty flow?" asked the doctor.

Evelyn nodded. "I guess you could say so."

Dr. Amster smiled.

What had she said to please him?

"Scanty flow," he half murmured. "This is unscientific, but the odds are that, considering your age, you're premenopausal."

"Premenopausal?" Evelyn had never heard the word.

"It probably means that your system is getting ready for the change. It's quite normal, nothing to worry about. Many women have preliminary symptoms: nausea, fatigue, periods of insomnia." Dr. Amster smiled again. He hated for patients to have symptoms he couldn't account for. He liked to solve their problems. That was what he was there for.

Mrs. Baum began to weep.

Another symptom, thought the doctor, happy that his instinct had been proved correct. Weepiness. Silently he picked a Kleenex out of the box on his desk and handed it to her.

Old. The menopause. It had never dawned on her. She was too young. Only forty-six. Too young for the menopause.

"Don't cry. It's nothing to cry over. Just think, you won't be bothered with that monthly mess."

It occurred to Dr. Amster that depression was another symptom. It was, most likely, a result of the massive hormonal changes going on in the body. It was strange, though, how some women weren't bothered by it at all. Dr. Amster supposed it was just one more of a hundred medical mysteries.

He gave Evelyn a prescription for Elavil. He told her that it would help her over this difficult but normal stage in a woman's life cycle.

Evelyn went to the pharmacy in the Carlyle Hotel, and as she waited for the prescription to be filled, she realized that she liked that monthly mess. It made her feel healthy and whole. She liked it and she welcomed it every month. It reminded her that she was a woman. She didn't want anything or anyone to take it away. Not time. Not age. Not Dr. Amster's words.

The pharmacist handed Evelyn a small round clear vial with the pills. As Evelyn went to the cash register, she impulsively picked up a package of Tampax. Its familiar blue pattern was reassuring. It was more effective than Dr. Amster's words with their kindly intentions and cruel realities. It made her feel that, somehow, everything would be all right.

Everything was not all right.

The Elavil didn't work. Nat was more flagrant, more charming, more invulnerable than ever. Evelyn tried to confront him, to pin him down, to make him make a decision. Nothing worked. If he had a chink in his armor, if he had a soft spot somewhere, Evelyn didn't know where it was. She didn't know how to get at him, and the whole time he was destroying her, day by day, with charm, with anger, with indifference.

The charm:

"What are you going to do, Nat?"

"Do about what?"

"You know. About Barbara or me."

"It's probably a passing fancy," he'd say.

"What's a passing fancy? Her or me?"

"Both of you," he'd say, and try and sometimes succeed in taking her to bed and making her come.

The anger:

"Nat, I can't stand this."

"And I can't stand your whining."

"Nat, it can't go on like this. You can't have it both ways."

"Why not?"

"Because I can't stand it. It's humiliating." She always tried not to cry.

"If you don't like it, you can always leave."

"But I don't want to leave."

(Leave? Where would she go? What would she do? Leave was the one impossible alternative.)

"So get yourself a lover," he'd say. "Just stop bugging me."

Indifference:

"Nat, when is this going to end?"

"Don't ask me. I don't know."

"Nat, why are you doing this to me?"

"I don't feel like talking about it."

He was a master of torment and she had no weapons. None.

May slipped into June and June into July. Nat informed Evelyn that he was spending the Fourth in Amagansett. He also informed her that she wasn't invited.

Evelyn sat on the bed—their bed—watching him pack.

Swim trunks. Striped terry beach robe. White linen trousers.

"You're really going."

"I told you I was."

Suntan lotion. Shaving things. Toothpaste and brush.

"I didn't really believe you."

"That's your tough luck."

"But what am I supposed to do?"

"Anything you want. We have a modern marriage."

"Nat . . ."

Navy blazer. Pale-blue-and-white-striped shirt. Underwear.

"Nat, I'm going to go to a psychiatrist." Evelyn had been thinking about it for weeks. It was a desperate gamble on her part. She wasn't even sure she'd have the courage to keep the appointment. She hoped that maybe Nat would realize how serious things were. How close to the edge he had driven her.

"Mazel tov. Everyone ought to have one."

"Even you?" Evelyn asked cautiously. "Maybe we could go together."

"Me?"

Cashmere cardigan. Blue paisley tie. Tennis shorts.

"I'm not paying to have my head shrunk. I'm so interesting they ought to pay me. Hell, do you realize that I could make some shrink famous?"

"It might help . . . you . . . us."

Nat's back was to Evelyn. He was looking at the rows of shoes on the shoe rack in the bottom of his closet.

"Hon, do you know where my tennis sneakers are?"

In Dr. Craig Leighton's nondescript beige office in the Majestic, an old luxury building on Central Park West, Evelyn began to find out about herself.

Four times a week, beginning in early July, Evelyn took the crosstown bus, got out at Seventy-second Street, walked the few blocks to the Majestic, went to the seventh floor in the old-fashioned elevator with brass and black-iron gates, entered Dr. Leighton's office, lay on his couch and cried. Dr. Leighton had an apparently inexhaustible supply of white Kleenex, an accessory that Evelyn felt sure was essential in his profession, and Evelyn had the impression that she alone was using up at least a year's supply. She had never cried so much in her life, and it was a tremendous relief. The luxury of crying was well worth the forty-five dollars per fifty-minute hour.

Evelyn asked Dr. Leighton if she could please have some tranquilizers.

"Can't you get along without?" he asked. "I'd prefer it if you tried to deal with your feelings."

"Please? I've spent my whole life trying to deal with my feelings and look where it's got me. Here." She motioned at the psychiatrist's office.

The patient had a point and Dr. Leighton wrote out the prescription. The Valium had a calming effect, and on the fourth visit, Evelyn stopped crying and began talking.

"It hurts," she said.

"What hurts?"

"Everything."

They proceeded to unravel the patterns of Evelyn's life. They were patterns of failure.

She was surprised when she realized that her relationship with Joy duplicated the relationship she had had with her own mother. Evelyn and her mother had been, at the most, distant relatives. Never once had they had an intimate conversation. Never once had they confided in each other the realities of their lives. Evelyn's mother was a mystery to Evelyn, and she realized she must be a mystery to Joy. The only difference had been that Evelyn was brought up at a time when children took it for granted that they were to respect their parents and Joy grew up at a time when children took it for granted that they were to hate and openly defy their parents. Other than that, both mother–daughter relationships, with Evelyn in the middle, were characterized by distance, detachment and a complete lack of intimacy.

Evelyn examined her inability to have more children, her consequent frigidity and the effect it must have had on Nat. She was astounded to learn that she expected the same things from her husband that she had taken for granted from her father: total loyalty on his part and complete subservience on hers. She wanted him to be the daddy and herself to be the child. It was the first time that Evelyn had realized that, and she said, in amazement, "But fathers and husbands are different!

"I'm a forty-six-year-old baby," said Evelyn, and they kept at it: finding out why Evelyn was unable to be assertive, why she had failed to explore her talents, why she had failed with Joy, why she had failed with Nat. If the subject, failure, was depressing, Evelyn's discoveries about it came as an exciting revelation to her.

Nat teased Evelyn about having the only WASP analyst in New York.

"All the good Jewish analysts take off in August," said Nat. "I bet this creep goes to some goyish resort in February."

"I would appreciate it," said Evelyn, "If you would stop putting down my analyst."

Nat said nothing.

It was the first time Evelyn had ever had the last word with him. My God, and it had taken only twenty-six years.

One Tuesday in the middle of September, the month that the Black September terrorists invaded the Munich Olympics and the month that Bobby Fischer decisively beat Boris Spassky, Evelyn didn't go straight home after her session with Dr. Leighton. Instead, she took a taxi downtown and went into Henri Bendel. On the first floor she bought two hundred dollars' worth of ivory bracelets, on the second floor she bought a lynx coat for three thousand dollars, on the third floor she bought a black jersey pants outfit from the Sonia Rykiel boutique for four hundred and fifty dollars, on the fourth floor she went into Beauty Checkers and had a ten-dollar makeup lesson and on the fifth floor she bought six sheer bras, six pairs of silk bikini panties, a crepe-de-chine nightgown and a silk robe.

She was oddly pleased at the extravagance of her self-indulgence.

"I'll match my Bendel bills against Nat's Saint Laurent bills any day," she bragged to Dr. Leighton.

Evelyn didn't know and didn't care that it is one of the most typical signs of improvement when the patient begins to spend money on himself or herself. It is, according to the theory, an early sign of a strengthening ego. It is a poignant attempt on the part of the patient to buy a new self. Evelyn wasn't aware of the theory or of its significance. She only knew that for the first time since May she felt something other than pain.

Evelyn wore the pants suit, the lynx coat and the makeup to a party that she didn't want to go to and that Nat did. Jack Eckaston was a stockbroker and once, somewhere back in the sixties, had produced a rock musical based on *Hamlet* that was still paying him royalties. Nat, although he would never admit it, was impressed by Jack. There was something about show business that, even now, still attracted Nat, and the mixed group that attended Jack's parties often included theatrical people.

"Jesus! It's divine!" shrieked Sylvia Eckaston. She fingered Evelyn's coat. "What is it?"

"Lynx," answered Evelyn. Nat kissed Sylvia carefully, knowing better than to disturb her heavy makeup and long false lashes. He headed toward the bar.

"Lynx? I never heard of it. Is it the new thing?" Sylvia was pathetic in her desperation to be "in" and "new" and "with-it." She took the coat from Evelyn. "Do you mind if I try it on?" Before Evelyn could answer, Sylvia already had one arm in the coat.

Evelyn left Sylvia raving over the coat and said hello to Ned and Elaine Brooker. Ned sometimes handled special ad campaigns for Nat, though he looked more like an accountant than a successful free-lance adman.

They talked about the problems they were having with their fourteen-year-old boy. He had a severe reading problem and none of the better private schools would admit him, even though the Brookers were paying private tutors a fortune to help him catch up with the other kids.

"I wonder why we all did it," mused Evelyn. "I mean I sometimes wonder why we had kids." Everyone she knew, including herself, had haunting, seemingly insoluble problems with the children they'd looked forward to so eagerly.

"Who knows?" said Ned. "I was twenty-six and Elaine was twenty-two. What did we know? We just had them."

"I'm Clarence Hussar," said a voice to Evelyn's left. He barged into the small group, his drink held in front of him like a weapon. "I want to meet you." He looked directly at Evelyn, an open, dirty look. Clarence Hussar was as greasily handsome as his photographs. "I'm in real estate," he added. It was the kind of crude socioeconomic label that passed for manners in New York.

"I know," said Evelyn.

Clarence Hussar's buildings were famous for being extremely profitable and extremely ugly. Tall white towers, they lined First and Second Avenues and were filled with singles—bachelors and stewardesses and widows with poodles who complained about the other tenants and the cheap construction of the buildings. Clarence Hussar had come from nowhere, somehow raised financing, thrown up his buildings, advertised them every Sunday in the real estate section with a full-page ad featuring a photograph of himself. Clarence Hussar was one of the richest landlords in the city.

"I like your substructure," he said to Evelyn, candidly examining her breasts, hips and legs.

"This is my husband, Mr. Hussar." Nat had suddenly appeared, a drink in each hand. He handed one to Evelyn and nodded to Clarence Hussar. Hussar returned the nod, acknowledged the sexual challenge and decided not to compete. He addressed himself to Nat.

"First and Second. That's where all the action is."

"We live on Fifth," said Nat. He wanted Clarence Hussar to know that he was at least an equal.

"So do we," said Mr. Hussar, who, although he had backed down on the sexual level, was more than willing to compete on any other plane. "Hell, I wouldn't live in one of my buildings if you paid me. I'm just saying it's where all the action is, expansionwise. What's your line?"

Nat began to answer and Evelyn walked away.

She stopped for a moment to say hello to Francine Helden, who was already slightly high, and then she went toward the back of the apartment to find the bathroom. Horrible as he was, Clarence Hussar's vulgar compliment had been flattering—and it had made Nat pay attention to her. Evelyn wanted to find a mirror. She wanted to see what she looked like.

She closed and locked the bathroom door behind her. Her makeup—the foundation and blusher and shadow and mascara—was all unscarred, unsmudged. For some reason, Evelyn suddenly remembered being fourteen. She remembered the nose job her parents had bought her. For years after, whenever she looked in the mirror, she still saw the old, ugly nose. She remembered the hair straightening and how, no matter how many chemicals were used and how skilled the hairdresser had been and how nice her hair looked when she left the beauty shop, it never lasted. On the first humid day, little kinks showed at the hairline where the beautician had been afraid to use the caustic chemicals for fear of burning the skin. She thought about the clothes her mother had bought her, according to the latest advice in *Seventeen*, and how, no matter how much change was worked on her outside, she had always felt the same inside: awkward, homely, unacceptable. And she remembered how, for a brief period, during their courtship and in the early months of their marriage, Nat had convinced her that she was really attractive.

Clarence Hussar, with his crude pass, had worked the same magic: he had made her feel attractive. Another man, a doctor, a man she paid, had helped: he had encouraged her to spend money on herself, to fight back, to win her husband back. The power that men exerted over her frightened Evelyn. She wondered what she would be—and if she would be—without a man in her life to make her feel real.

She touched on some more lip gloss and left the bathroom. As she opened the door, Victor Helden was standing there.

"You look great tonight. A real knockout." Victor stepped back a pace and held Evelyn's chin in his hand, studying her. "I always said you were my type. Maybe we ought to try a matinee one of these days."

"Oh, Victor!" Evelyn was used to Victor's flirting—the flirting that had driven Francine to drink, the flirting that was probably harmless.

"No, I mean it. You know, Evelyn, I'd really like to score with you."

"Victor, you're drunk." Evelyn could smell the alcohol on his breath as he edged closer to her.

"I'm not drunk. Francine is a lousy lay and I'm horny. I bet you'd be hot stuff in bed, wouldn't you?" Victor moved in closer to Evelyn, pinning her against the wall, cupping his hands over her breasts and covering her mouth with his. His lips were wet, and he opened his mouth and tried to force his tongue through Evelyn's closed teeth. She turned her head.

"C'mon," he said. "You want it just as much as I do."

The kiss resumed, and Evelyn let it go on for a moment. Victor was right: she was excited; and then, suddenly, she was afraid. She pushed him back. He lurched a half step and looked at her, his eyes filled with carnal knowledge.

"You liked it." It was an accusation and a challenge. "You're hot and don't deny it." He came toward her again.

"Get your hands off my wife." Nat had appeared down the hall and was coming toward them. With horror, Evelyn wondered how much of the scene he had witnessed. "Get your fucking hands off my wife!"

Nat was viciously angry. He faced Victor in a boxer's stance, ready to take a swing at him. Victor stepped back a pace.

"Just a kiss," he said. "Just a little kiss is all."

Nat had faced his lawyer down and he was in control again.

"Come on, Evelyn. Let's get out of this dump."

"You looked good tonight," said Nat when they got home. He mixed himself a light Scotch.

"Thank you," said Evelyn. "I'm glad you approved."

"I like my women to look good. It's good for my image." he said.

"Your image?"

"Didn't you know? Single-handed and against the tides of history, I alone am keeping the tradition of the male-chauvinist pig alive and well."

He was half joking and half serious. It was a mood of his that Evelyn never knew how to respond to. If she took one side, he'd invariably take the other. She could never win.

"Nat, are you still seeing her? Barbara?" The moment she'd said it, she wished she hadn't. She and Dr. Leighton had decided it was best not to cross-examine Nat, and most of the time Evelyn was able to keep her curiosity in check. Most of the time. Not all the time.

"Ah, shit, Evelyn. Knock it off." Nat poured himself another drink, a little stronger this time.

Chastened, Evelyn went silently into the bedroom and began to undress. As she sat at the dressing table, removing her makeup, Nat appeared in the doorway and leaned against it, the glass of Scotch in his hand.

"You're hung up on him, aren't you?"

"Hung up on who?" She tried to be nonchalant, but her throat tightened. So he had seen Victor kissing her—and her returning the kiss, even if it was just for a moment.

"The creep. Leighton."

Evelyn was relieved and amazed. "Are you crazy?"

"There's got to be some reason you're looking so good. I figure you're screwing him. I hear all the hip shrinks do it these days. Make it with their patients. Right on the old couch."

"Nat, he's fifteen years younger than I am. He's half bald and he's got a potbelly and he sweats a lot."

"It's a good racket," Nat went on. "Not only do they get laid but they get paid for the privilege. Tell me, does he go down on you?"

Evelyn turned around. She had been watching Nat via the reflection in the mirror. Now she turned and looked at him directly.

"You're jealous," she said. It was ironic and incredible. Nat was the jealous one! "Oh, my God, you're actually jealous."

He couldn't control the expression that proved to her that she was right. But then he forced himself to a grin. The moment had passed.

"Nah, no way," said Nat. "What the hell, everyone ought to get as much as they can. I wouldn't care if you picked up guys in the subway and blew them off in Central Park."

Evelyn didn't bother to answer.

She had finally discovered a weapon that worked.

She wondered if Nat was going to force her to use it.

11 NAT BAUM HAD WHAT
every man wanted: a wife and a mistress. They both loved
him, wanted him and were willing to fight for him.

He had it made, stacked, on ice—and it was a royal pain
in the ass.

Barbara's demands were hysterical, based on promises he
had made and hadn't kept. Evelyn's demands were stran-
gling, based on guilt and possessiveness.

Nat left Barbara's apartment one night in early October
of 1972. She had been demanding that he leave Evelyn and
move in with her. She had, as she had many times before,
threatened to stop seeing him. They had had a bitter, ex-
hausting fight that had ended up in bed. Afterward Nat had
gotten dressed and, on the way home, stopped off for a night-
cap at the Polo Bar in the Westbury Hotel.

Barbara and Evelyn. Evelyn and Barbara.

Evelyn owned him, literally and emotionally. She owned
sixty percent of Alpha, and she hadn't been making an
idle threat when she had told him that if he ever left her
she'd render him penniless. She owned him, too—the part
of him that was loyal and tender and dependent. He needed
her.

He needed Barbara too. She turned him on. She had class
and status and he could get it up longer, harder for her
than for any other woman he'd ever met. He had kept
thinking that maybe the sex thing would fade away. But it
hadn't and the fighting only seemed to intensify it.

Evelyn and Barbara and Barbara and Evelyn: he hated
them and he needed them and it was driving him crazy.

Nat ordered a second Scotch and noticed that the girl at
the end of the bar was cute. Long blond hair, small tits, no
bra, about Joy's age. She smiled at him. Nat motioned her
over and she picked up her drink and walked over to sit
on the stool next to his.

He paid for her drink and one more for the two of them and they left the bar together and went to her studio apartment somewhere way east in the Eighties.

As he undressed, he suddenly remembered Pam Saunders. He realized he had been smarter in his thirties than he was now. He had known then that the one-night stand, sex without emotion, was for him.

As he fucked the girl whose name he didn't know, he felt free for the first time in months. The only cure for women was more women.

Nat wished that his wife and his mistress could see him now.

In October of 1972 Jackie Robinson, who had been Rookie of the Year when Nat and Evelyn had fallen in love, died. Norman Norell, who had designed a strapless evening gown that Evelyn had taken on her honeymoon, died. In October of 1972, Evelyn fought for her life and lost.

The idea had been growing in Nat's head until it was irresistible. On the way home from work, he stopped in at the bar of the Drake Hotel, had a few drinks, picked up a kid who said she was going to Hunter and invited her home with him.

"Evelyn," he said, "I'd like you to meet, uh . . ."

"Jenny," said the girl, who looked confused. She looked from the man she had let pick her up to this woman. She guessed it was his wife.

"Jenny?" Evelyn didn't know any Jenny. Nat had never mentioned any Jenny. Who was Jenny?

"Jenny's a friend of mine, aren't you?" Nat handed her a drink and sipped at the one he had made for himself. He slurred the words very slightly. He was just beginning to get high.

"Well," said the girl, "We just met."

"The fact is," said Nat. "I just picked you up, didn't I?"

The girl looked uncomfortable. She was a member of the

liberated generation. She liked casual sex, especially with attractive strangers. But she wasn't a pro and she didn't go for any weirdo stuff.

"Listen, thanks for the drink," she said. "I'd better leave."

"Hell, no," said Nat. "The party hasn't even started."

The girl got up from the sofa and Evelyn suddenly realized what Nat had in mind. He wanted to go to bed with this girl and he wanted Evelyn to watch.

"I think you'd better go." Evelyn spoke to the girl.

"I'm sorry, uh, Evelyn," said the girl.

"I thought we could have a good time," said Nat as Evelyn shut the door behind the girl. The hurt, the humiliation, the anger made Evelyn want to kill him. She wished she could annihilate him and she was terrified by the intensity of her wish.

"Get out," she screamed. "Just get out of here!"

"Honey," said Nat.

"Get out!" she screamed, and she kept screaming until he left.

Evelyn didn't hear from Nat for a week. Finally, she got a call from Victor Helden. He was, he said, acting as Nat's lawyer and his client wanted to know if Evelyn wanted a divorce.

"Does he? Does Nat want a divorce?" Evelyn felt degraded at having to ask a third person about her husband's wishes.

"He didn't say. He wants to know if you do," said Victor.

Evelyn didn't want a divorce. She wanted Nat. She wanted him back, despite everything, and she hated herself for wanting him. It was asking to be hurt and humiliated and abused all over again. And still, she wanted him.

"Victor, why doesn't Nat ask me himself?"

"I don't know. Maybe he's afraid. You know, you were very rough on him."

"Me? Rough on him?" It was unbelievable, incredible.

Evelyn wondered what in God's name Nat had told Victor.

"He said you threw him out. It hurt him very much."

"Did he tell you how much he hurt me?"

"Look, Evelyn I'm not a marriage counselor, just a law-yer."

"Victor?"

"Yes?"

"You're a friend too, aren't you?"

He hesitated a moment and then said, "Sure. I've been a friend for years."

"Then why don't you come to lunch? I'd like to talk things over with you.

Again, Victor hesitated.

Then he accepted her invitation.

"Tomorrow?" asked Evelyn.

"Tomorrow," said Victor, and Evelyn wasn't quite sure whether or not he understood what she was really talking about. Maybe he'd been so drunk he didn't remember what he had said. On the other hand, he had always come on with her, even sober.

Evelyn gave Lydia the day off, and she prepared the shrimp-stuffed avocados herself and arranged the fruit pas-tries on a rectangular silver tray. She was nervous but she was determined. She wanted Nat back and Victor was the way to get him.

The conversation stayed superficial until, as they finished the avocados, Evelyn asked Victor how long it had been since they had seen each other. She wanted to remind him of the Eckastons' party and the incident.

"A couple of weeks," said Victor evasively. He looked uncomfortable and Evelyn didn't know how to handle the situation. She had assumed that Victor would make all the moves. After all, he had always been very aggressive.

"Would you like some dessert?" Evelyn went into the kitchen and returned with the tray of pastries. She took the coffeepot off the warmer on the buffet and poured them each a demitasse of coffee.

"I guess you and Nat are having your troubles," said Victor.

"All marriages have their ups and downs," said Evelyn. "And anyway, I don't feel like talking about my marriage."

"Oh."

"As a matter of fact, I thought we might, you know . . ." Evelyn was being as direct as she could. "You know. What you said the other night."

"Said what?" Victor gulped the hot coffee and choked slightly. Then he poured himself another glass of white wine from the bottle that was still on the table.

"Indicated that you . . . that you and I . . ." Evelyn didn't know how to say it, what words to use. Instead, she reached out and put her hand on the expensive black silk-and-mohair cuff of Victor's custom-made suit. Then, since he didn't pull away, Evelyn moved her hand down and caressed the back of his hand.

"You're asking me to fuck?" Victor looked like a trapped animal. He jerked his hand away from Evelyn's touch.

"You said you wanted to."

"I say a lot of things."

"That kiss . . . in the hallway."

"For Christ's sake, Evelyn. So I kissed you. Who knows? Maybe I even felt you up a little. That doesn't mean . . ."

"Doesn't mean what?"

"That I want to lay you, for Christ's sake."

"You mean you were just being polite?"

"Something like that." Victor's eyes darted back and forth. He didn't look at Evelyn. "Everyone does it, you know. Talk, I mean."

"I don't."

"Then you're the exception."

Evelyn realized that the conversation had turned back on her. She hated the whiny tone in her voice. She sounded prissy to herself, just the way she had in college when she had told Ernie that she couldn't go all the way because nice girls didn't. He had backed down, relieved, because Ernie's advances had been token. But now it was all upside down and Evelyn had tried to make an advance, a serious one, to a man who she thought wanted her and here he was telling her that *he* didn't want to.

"Victor, I just thought it might be nice."

"Evelyn." He sighed heavily, finished off the glass of wine and poured another, and as he drank off half of it his discomfort seemed to evaporate. "Look, Evelyn, I just turned fifty-six. I can hardly get it up anymore these days and when I do, I want it to be for someone twenty. I like 'em young. It makes me feel young, even if it's only for a little while."

He tipped back his chair and unbuttoned his suit jacket. He hooked his thumbs on either side of his waist and Evelyn could see the beginnings of a roll of flab that the careful tailoring had concealed. She noticed, for the first time, the network of broken capillaries that threaded their way across his cheeks and over the fleshy part of his nose. He was repulsive. The thought of his pudgy, expensively massaged body on hers made her skin crawl. She must have been insane to think that she wanted to go to bed with Victor Helden. Victor Helden and his wet kisses and fatigued penis.

"I suppose when you're sixty, you'll want them twenty-five."

Victor shook his head. "By then, I'll want them fifteen."

"I see," said Evelyn, and the sad thing was that when he was sixty, he'd be able to find someone fifteen. She wasn't even fifty and she couldn't find anyone. Of any age.

"Look, Evelyn. If you're feeling horny, get yourself a young stud. A guy who can go all night. Believe me, you'll feel like a million dollars, getting all that young juice pumped into you."

"I'll think about it, Victor."

"See ya round the block, kid," said Victor as he left. Evelyn noticed that he omitted the usual goodbye kiss.

She was alone in the apartment. She stacked the dirty lunch dishes in the Kitchen-Aid and threw the organdy place mats into the laundry hamper. She removed the wineglass that Victor had left on the coffee table and emptied the ashtray. When she had finished, the apartment looked as if no one had been there.

It wasn't so easy to wipe away the traces that had been left inside herself. Evelyn removed her makeup and took off her clothes and, on impulse, ran a shower. She was used to a bath, but she felt that a shower would make her cleaner. She washed her hair and scrubbed her body hard with a camel's-hair-bristle brush that her brother had given her. When she was done, she dried herself off and went into the big walk-in closet to get a robe. Her clothes hung on one side of the closet and Nat's hung opposite them, on the other. She looked at his expensive suits and sport jackets and trousers, all lined up neatly hung from expensive wooden hangers. Nat adored clothes. He often joked that he was just like a woman: whenever he got depressed he went out and bought some new clothes. They were all expensive and they had the best labels: de Noyer, Saint Laurent, Meledandri, Battaglia. She picked out one of the jackets and held it to her nose. It smelled just like him.

Evelyn went into the kitchen and took the large chopping knife, the one she had bought when she was taking the James Beard course, from the magnetic rack over the butcher-block counter and carried it back with her into the bedroom. She sat on the floor of the closet and began with a tan whipcord jacket from Saint Laurent. It was hard where the fabric turned under and there was a double thickness of fabric, but Evelyn kept at it and finally she had shredded the fabric into a fuzzy pile that stuck to the carpeting.

She cut up a Meledandri jacket and got bored, suddenly, with jackets. She reached up and pulled a pair of gray flannel trousers from a hanger and, beginning at the belt line carefully cut around the zipper. It wasn't too long before she had cut the fly out.

Methodically, she mutilated every pair of pants in Nat's wardrobe. When she was done, she got up, leaving the damaged garments on the closet floor, and shut the door behind her.

She went into the foyer and got an unopened bottle of Scotch and took it into the bathroom. She swallowed the entire bottle of Valium. It was almost full, since she had had the prescription refilled only last week. She had only a dozen Seconal capsules, but she swallowed them. Then she swallowed the remainder of the Elavil. She finished six Ampicillin from when she had had her ear infection; she took Nat's Donnatal and the Compazine that a doctor had once prescribed for nausea. The only other drug in the medicine chest was a half bottle of codeine cough syrup and she drank it down.

Evelyn looked in the mirror as she shut the medicine chest and noticed that her freshly shampooed but unset hair had almost dried. It had been years since it had dried naturally, without rollers and the hair dryer of the salon. It was still as frizzy as it had been when she was fourteen and she still hated it.

Taking the bottle of Scotch with her, Evelyn lay down on the bed and forced herself to drink its entire contents.

Free. She was free at last.

What the hell did a woman of her age need with freedom?

PART FOUR

THE SIXTIES

The Liberated Woman

*"I want to try everything: all the men,
all the highs and I don't even mind
the lows. But I'll kill myself if I end
up like my mother."*

—Joy Baum
May 1968

1 It was quarter to six when the phone rang. Joy was on the sofa working on a macramé belt she'd started over a year ago and Terry was in the kitchen making dinner. Terry was a liberated man and Joy was a liberated woman and they had a liberated relationship. It was Tuesday and, according to the work schedule posted on the bulletin board, his night to cook.

Joy, as usual, picked up the phone. Her father knew that she and Terry were living together but her mother didn't, and Joy didn't want to shake her up.

"Daddy!" Her father was one of the few people in the world, except Terry, whom Joy could talk to. And lately, things with Terry had been tense.

"Baby, I've got some news and it isn't good."

"Oh." Joy wondered what he was setting her up for. Maybe her mother was in one of her assertive moods and was going to try to force her to go to a "decent" college and shape up. Her mother had disapproved when Joy had moved out of her parents' apartment; she had disapproved when Joy announced that she wasn't going to go to college; she disapproved of Joy's hippie friends and the film courses that Joy audited at NYU. Her mother didn't approve of Joy's life-style, she didn't understand it and every now and then, she tried to make Joy change it. Usually, though, she didn't have the courage to speak to Joy directly and got Nat to do the dirty work. Her father was on her side. He said right out loud that if he were her age and had a rich father, he'd be doing exactly what she was doing: sitting around on his ass half-stoned all the time.

"Your mother tried to kill herself."

"What!"

"She swallowed the medicine chest. She's in the hospital now. They pumped her out and they think she's going to be OK."

"She really tried to kill herself?" Joy could barely believe it. Her mother had the most boring life in the world. What could be important enough to make her want to kill herself? Except, maybe, the boredom. Or Barbara Roser?

"Really. It was a serious try, too."

"What happened? I mean, why did she do it?" Joy's mother was a complete mystery to her. She had often wondered why she had the mother she did. They couldn't have been more opposite. They had been at each other from the time Joy could remember. Sometimes, when she was little, she used to think that maybe she was really an orphan and that her parents had adopted her. It was the only possibility she could think of that would explain how come she had the mother she did. "What made her want to kill herself?"

"Me."

"You?" Suddenly, Joy hated her father, even though she really hated her mother. Maybe she hated them both. Maybe she even loved them. She was messed up; that was for sure.

"I was a prick," said Nat.

"Was it Barbara?" Her father had introduced her to his girlfriend once, but Joy didn't know how serious it was or even if her father and Barbara were still going together. Joy and her father made a point of not prying into each other's sexual lives.

"Baby, could you come over? I'll tell you everything. Only in person. Not on the phone. Please?"

"Sure," said Joy. She noticed that her father hadn't answered her question.

"Thanks. It would help to have you around. I need you."

It was nice to be needed.

"At least I'm good for something."

They arranged to meet at the hospital, the Voorhees

Clinic, at seven-thirty, when evening visiting hours began. They said goodbye and hung up.

Only then did Joy begin to cry.

Even though they had made a pact not to smoke until after dinner, Joy asked Terry if it would be OK if she broke the rule and had a joint.

"I need it," she said, taking her first deep drag.

The tears were still running down her face and Terry had brought over the box of Kleenex. He had taken dinner off the stove and was sitting next to Joy, cuddling her and trying to comfort her. Terry liked to take care of her, but she rarely permitted it. She preferred to be independent and self-sufficient and always pulled away when he wanted to cuddle. She said that necking was kid stuff. Only this time, she didn't fight and surrendered to his embrace and leaned her head against his shoulder. Finally, the grass began to work and she calmed down. She was embarrassed that she had cried.

"My old lady just tried to knock herself off. She missed." Now that Joy had stopped crying, she had forced her bottom teeth out against the inside of her top teeth, making her chin tight and hard. It helped her to keep in control.

"Poor Joy." Terry knew that it was better to react to Joy's emotions than to her words. Very often they were in direct conflict, and this was one of those times.

"Can you imagine it? My mother tried to kill herself." Joy was still trying to get used to the reality of it. "I didn't think anything meant that much to her. I guess my old man must have really fucked up this time. He sounded upset. I mean, really upset."

"I should hope so," said Terry. "I'd be pretty goddam upset if you tried to kill yourself."

"Well, I'm not trying." Joy was immediately defiant. Terry knew enough to let it drop.

"I guess your mother's OK now, though."

"Yeah. I think she's sleeping it off."

"You want me to go with you to the hospital?" Terry wanted to go with her, very badly. He hoped it didn't show too much.

Joy shook her head.

"But maybe I could help." The rejection stung. Terry loved Joy, and she was often a difficult person to love.

"You don't want to come. It'll be a heavy scene. Anyway, I can handle it myself." It drove Joy nuts the way Terry always wanted to help everybody. The trouble with him was that he was too nice. He let everyone walk all over him— including herself.

"I love you," said Terry.

"I'm hungry," said Joy. Grass always did that to her.

Terry finished the dinner: chicken and brown rice and organic squash and white wine. As he set it on the table in the sun-room, Joy got up from the sofa, and just before she sat down to dinner, she hugged Terry very hard.

"I love you too," she said. "Even if I am a bitch."

2 JOY OFTEN REFERRED TO HER-
self as a bitch. It was a way of insulting herself and asserting herself simultaneously. She acted like a bitch when she was threatened. It was the only effective self-defense she had learned. The more frightened Joy felt, the harder she lashed out. It was her offense and her defense.

Joy the bitch was also Joy the poet. She was a very sensitively constructed sending and receiving mechanism, extremely vulnerable and extremely wary. Her emotions were close to the surface and she struggled to keep the surface emotion-free. At an early age she had learned that her mother was her enemy and that her father was her friend and she had learned how to manipulate them. She had learned to defeat her mother and seduce her father.

In 1963, when Joy was eleven, the sixties began to reveal their configuration.

The anthem of the sixties was Rock. In 1963, the Beatles came to America, were seen and conquered. John, Paul, George and Ringo evolved as the sixties evolved from bubble-gum rock to art rock to psychedelic rock. The Stones, all the time, howled the counterpart—raunch rock, defiant rock and finally, at Altamont, lethal rock.

Rock was the audio of the sixties and television its visual.

President Kennedy was shot and the TV cameras were there with Instant Replay and Stop Action. The funeral was a TV special, and the murder of Lee Harvey Oswald by Jack Ruby was a live show, not taped or prerecorded. *Ozzie and Harriet, The Flying Nun* and *My Favorite Martian,* the war in Vietnam, Johnny Unitas and Johnny Carson and the Marlboro Man were all transmitted with the same number of kilowatts on the same channels. The tube hypnotized Joy. It bombarded her with instant pleasure, instant pain and instant arousal, fact and fiction all mixed up and blurred together to create an Image.

It was the electronic age, the age of McLuhan and the global village, and Joy, at eleven, was content to listen and watch. When she turned twelve, in 1964, she wanted to participate.

In the fall, Joy would be going to a new school, Ardsley. It had an excellent reputation and it had been hard for her parents to get her in. She had had to go for two interviews, and her parents kept telling her how lucky she was when she was finally accepted. Joy didn't tell them, because she didn't tell them much of anything, but she was scared at the thought of a new school and new kids. She was used to her friends from her old school and she wasn't sure if she'd like the new kids or if they'd like her.

Her mother wanted to take her shopping for some new clothes and Joy acquiesced, although she knew ahead of time that it was going to be a hassle. Her mother hassled her about clothes the same way she hassled her about her hair. Joy had thick dark brown hair that fell to her shoulder blades. She wore it parted in the middle and she washed it every single night and dried it with a hand dryer. The whole process consumed an hour and a half and it gave her mother fits. She told Joy that washing her hair so often was bad for it, that it would begin to fall out and that she'd go bald. She said she couldn't understand how Joy could spend so much time hand-drying her hair and she said that she couldn't understand how Joy could even see considering the way her hair fell over the sides of her face. Why, she would ask, couldn't Joy at least tie it back in a ponytail? A *neat* ponytail?

Mostly, Joy tried to keep her mouth shut and let her mother yap on. But every now and then she'd get into a screaming battle with her mother that would end when Joy would go to her room, slam the door and put an album on the stereo and turn it up as loud as she could. Joy knew that her taste in music drove her mother nuts too.

Joy wanted to go to Paraphernalia. She wanted Mary Quant minis, poor-boy sweaters, colored panty hose and a day-glo vinyl raincoat. Her mother said that the clothes at Paraphernalia were cheap and badly made.

"They have nicer things at Bonwit's," said her mother.

Joy shut up and let her mother drag her to Bonwit's.

They went up to the Young Junior department and to the right of the elevator was a boutique, an area the store had set up featuring flashing lights and rock music and mod clothes. Joy headed toward the boutique and her mother followed. There was a pair of red wool hip huggers with bell bottoms that Joy liked and showed to her mother. Her mother examined them for a moment and handed them back to Joy.

"Why don't we get some clothes for school first and then we'll come back here. If you still like these, why don't you get them for weekends?"

Her mother was trying to be reasonable and so Joy tried to be reasonable too. Her mother hadn't said she couldn't have the bell-bottoms. Just that she couldn't have them until later. Joy followed her mother to the middle of the seventh floor, where racks of skirts, slacks, sweaters and blouses surrounded them. Joy sat on a sofa upholstered in little-girl pink while her mother and an old saleslady picked out a bunch of things: some pleated plaid skirts, some wool sweater sets and a red wool coat, double-breasted with a belt in the back; then they took them, along with Joy, into a dressing room. The saleslady left them alone together.

Joy's mother sat down on a small fake-French chair and arranged her pocketbook on her lap. Her mother had a happy look on her face and Joy could tell that she was looking forward to buying her a whole pile of things.

"That plaid skirt is darling. Why don't you try that on first?" said her mother, handing Joy a Black Watch skirt. Joy reached out to take it and at the last minute, just as she was about to take off the faded jeans she was wearing, let the skirt drop to the floor.

"Joy! Don't throw your things on the floor."

"It's not mine. I hate it."

Joy's sudden violence caught her mother off guard. She looked confused for a moment.

"It's a piece of crap."

"Dear, lower your voice." Her mother's confusion turned to embarrassment. It bugged Joy the way her mother always acted as if she had to apologize for being alive. What was she afraid of? That old crock of a saleslady?

"I will not," said Joy as loud as she dared. Part of her was defiant and part wanted to be disciplined. She was daring her mother to come down on her hard.

"Shhh," whispered her mother. Her mother was blushing and Joy was disgusted.

At that moment, the saleslady stuck her head into the

dressing room. Her smile was a lie. It pretended that she hadn't heard what had been going on.

"And how is everything?" she asked.

"Everything stinks," said Joy.

The saleslady looked to Evelyn for a clue.

"She's premenstrual," said Joy's mother, and everyone in the room knew it was a lie.

"Well, if you decide on anything," said the saleslady backing out, "I'm Miss Ronzini."

Angie Ronzini went back to the floor knowing that this kid would win the fight with her mother and that no sale would be made. Angie saw it happen a dozen times a day: mothers and teen-aged daughters having violent arguments over clothes. And they were always rich people. You could tell by their clothes, by their jewelry, by the way most of them never even looked at the price tags, confident that whatever it cost, they could afford it.

Angie tried not to be bitter, and most of the time she succeeded. She was sixty-one, one year away from retirement, and it helped to keep things in perspective. Angie—Angelina was her given name—had worked at Bonwit's for thirty years, twenty-seven of them in the Better Dress department. In the old days, women knew how to shop. Dresses were presented to them, one at a time, as if they were the most precious jewels, and the customers were called clients and you built a relationship with them that lasted for years. You outfitted them for weddings, parties, cruises, fall, winter, spring and summer, for funerals, christenings, graduations and all the other ceremonies of life. But that was the old days.

Two years ago, when volume in couture had begun to drop, Angie had been transferred to the Young Junior department. It was another world—sleazy, rushed, ungracious —and Angie didn't like it. Every night when Angie got back to Forest Hills, where she lived with her eighty-year-old mother, they would relive the day. Bonwit's was to Angie what television was to Joy—a complete world, one where

276

fact and fantasy merged and where Image was the stock-in-trade.

Angie stayed on the floor, courteously asking clients—no, customers—if they'd like some help. Most of them said no and never looked at her, just went on pawing through the racks. Angie felt sorry for this new generation. They didn't know what they were missing. They didn't know that shopping itself could be an art, exquisite in the doing. It was a lost art, degenerated into a lust for acquisition in which speed and quantity and a hurriedly flashed charge plate were more important than leisure and quality and dignity. Too bad, thought Angie, but it was their loss, not hers.

As she stood watch on the floor, Angie saw the brat and her mother get on a down elevator. The kid stood far away from the mother. If she hadn't known, Angie would have thought they didn't even know each other. It was obvious that they weren't speaking. The elevator doors shut behind them and it made Angie glad that she had never married and never had children. Angie didn't know what shocked her more: the kids with their defiant, foul mouths or the mothers who wouldn't or couldn't discipline them.

All she knew was that she was glad it wasn't her life.

The beefy security man standing just inside the front door of Paraphernalia asked Evelyn to leave her shopping bag with him.

"It's only books," she said, raising the bag to show him that it was from Doubleday.

"It's the rules, lady." He took the bag from Evelyn before she had a chance to surrender it gracefully.

The loud rock pouring out of speakers set around the first-floor selling area made it impossible to talk, so Evelyn followed Joy, who headed past the coats and dresses on the first floor to the stairs at the back of the store. They went up the stairs to where the separates were and Joy pointed to a metal chair that looked exactly like a tractor seat. Evelyn sat down, uncomfortable because the contoured shape forced her to sit with her legs slightly spread. The difference between the reproduction–Louis XIV chair in Bonwit's and the tractor-shaped chair in Paraphernalia was the difference between Evelyn's generation and Joy's. It was the difference between girdles and panty hose, Cole Porter and Mick Jagger, USO shows and antiwar demonstrations.

Evelyn watched Joy pick out some skirts and tops and pants and disappear into a communal dressing room. Evelyn watched the salesgirls, all dressed in extremely short minis, absorbed in the rhythm of the music, frugging alone, their eyes vacant, pointing vaguely when asked a question by a young customer.

Joy emerged from the dressing room with her choices: two hip-slung minis, a pair of jeans and two tops—a white cotton T-shirt with a Donald Duck blowup on the front and the other of a shiny material that looked like satin but wasn't. It had a red body, a green left sleeve and a yellow right sleeve. They went downstairs, where Joy picked out a dark red vinyl coat with metal toggle fastenings and Evelyn went to the counter to pay.

Paraphernalia required three proofs of identification: a license and two credit cards. The woman who stood behind the counter was the only person in the store near Evelyn's age. She carefully checked the numbers of the credit cards against a long list posted behind the cash register. When she nodded OK, Evelyn wrote out the check and said nothing but was struck by the emphasis on security. Obviously, the management was very much concerned about stealing, shoplifting and bad checks. It was a telling comment on the Love Generation.

Evelyn left the store glad to be away from the loud music, glad to have her Doubleday bag back, glad that the clothes crisis was over. She asked Joy if she'd like to stop for a soda.

"Too fattening," said Joy. "I'll have a Tab when we get home."

Joy, who had inherited her father's long, lean frame, was on a constant virtual starvation diet. It worried Evelyn and she tried to keep her concern for Joy's health to herself. Whenever she said anything, it led to another violent argument.

That evening after dinner, Joy went into the kitchen and disappeared into her bedroom with a big blue box of Morton's salt and a bottle of Clorox. At nine, Evelyn looked in; she tried to see to it that Joy was in bed by ten. Evelyn knocked on the door and Joy yelled at her to come in. The room was a combination of little-girl teddy bears and teen-age-girl Beatles posters. Joy's bathroom door was open and Evelyn asked if she could come in.

"Sure."

Joy was sitting in the tub wearing the pair of jeans she had bought that afternoon, and as her mother entered the bathroom Joy poured a large quantity of salt on the wet fabric of the jeans. Joy was sitting in a tub of cold water and Clorox that came to her waist. It must have been extremely uncomfortable.

"It makes them fit right," said Joy.

Evelyn smiled at her daughter.

"You know," she said, "I just remembered that when I was your age we used to set our hair with old socks. It used to drive my father crazy. I wore them all the time, those long ends trailing around my head, and only took them out when I went to school or had a date."

"You mean my generation isn't the only crazy one?"

"No," said Evelyn. She leaned over to kiss her daughter's lovely thick hair and Joy suddenly put her face up and the kiss became a mutual one.

"I'll be in bed by ten," said Joy. "I promise."

"Sleep tight," said Evelyn, and left her daughter's room.

The next day Lydia asked Evelyn what to do about the pair of pants in Joy's bathroom. Evelyn went into the bathroom with the maid. Joy's pants were spread flat on a towel on the floor and the indentations of Joy's hips and thighs and knees were imprinted into the fabric. A big sign propped up on them read: *Danger! Explosive!*

Evelyn smiled and told Lydia that it was just a kids' fad

and not to touch the pants. Lydia shrugged and picked up the Comet and started in on the washbasin.

Ardsley was located on a pretty block on Seventy-seventh Street between Park and Lexington in a brownstone building that had once been the impressive town house of a turn-of-the-century railroad tycoon. It had marble staircases and crystal chandeliers and floor-to-ceiling French doors leading to a rear garden that the teachers opened on nice days in the spring and fall. Before Joy had gotten accepted into Ardsley, she had gone to several schools: one in the Village run on the Montessori method; one on the West Side where black kids regularly mugged the white kids for their allowances, transistor radios and wristwatches and a third one in Gramercy Park that supposedly followed a classic French curriculum and in which the teachers were lay nuns.

All along, Joy's mother had wanted her to go to Ardsley because it had the best reputation in the city for both the prestige of the student body and the excellence of the curriculum. *Life* magazine had done a long article about Ardsley's superlative teaching methods, and other private schools boasted that they too used the "Ardsley method." The method allegedly combined the best features of permissive education, which encouraged the children's natural creativity, and classical education, which provided a grounding in the basic disciplines of language, science, math and philosophy.

It sounded good, but when Joy got there she found out that it was pretty much like the other schools she had gone to: the teachers spent most of their time making the kids shut up and pay attention and the kids spent most of their time resisting their teachers' efforts in their behalf.

The thing that *was* different about Ardsley was the other students. They were the sons and daughters of famous movie stars, politicians and presidents of huge corporations, and there was even a nine-year-old French count. The kids took chauffeured limousines and private planes for granted, they shuttled casually back and forth from Europe and the Coast, they carried book bags made by Gucci and the girls had their hair done at Kenneth and the boys got their own Porsches as soon as they got their driver's permits. Joy figured that she had been admitted so that the school could pretend it was democratic. Joy knew that her father was rich, but she soon found out that there was a quantum difference between the merely rich and the Super Rich.

One other difference between Joy and the others was that she was just about the only kid whose real parents were still married to each other. Most of the other kids had stepmothers and stepfathers and half brothers and half sisters, and they all knew how to play divorced parents against each other for more clothes, a bigger allowance, a sailboat or a new stereo. They also talked a lot about sex. One of the girls swore that she was sleeping with her stepbrother and she also swore that it counted as incest. Some of the kids agreed that it *was* incest, while others said that it didn't count since they were stepbrother and stepsister, not *real* brother and sister.

In the beginning, Joy was very lonely. She had no best friend and no group to belong to. She walked to and from school alone every day and no one asked her to go to Bloomingdale's or King Karol for records on Saturday. She didn't want to do anything obvious like buy grass with her allowance and share it with other kids just to get a friend. That would be buying friendship and Joy was too proud for that. She knew that the cool thing was to wait until someone else asked first.

The time came one Monday morning in October when Ivy Hellman, who sat next to Joy in homeroom, asked if she would mind forging a note to get Ivy out of school on Thursday afternoon. Tickets were going on sale then for the Beatles tour and Ivy wanted to get to the Garden ticket office. Joy agreed, knowing it was the invitation she had been waiting for, and on a sheet of Mrs. Hellman's expensive, engraved stationery from Cartier forged a note saying that

Ivy had a dentist's appointment and could she please be excused from school on Thursday afternoon.

That afternoon Ivy informed Joy that the teacher had accepted the note as genuine and had given Ivy permission to be excused.

Very casually, Ivy asked Joy if she wanted a ticket too.

Joy and Ivy quickly became best friends.

Ivy lived on Park and Seventy-third in a fourteen-room duplex penthouse. Her father was a lawyer who handled divorces for rich and famous people. Sometimes his picture was in the *Daily News* as he escorted a celebrated client into court. He was very distinguished-looking and one of the few lawyers who were celebrities in their own right.

Ivy's mother had been born in Virginia and spent most of her time going to and from Old Westbury, where she belonged to a hunt club. Her picture appeared once in *Town and Country* and she was dressed in jodhpurs and carried a whip. The caption said that she was one of America's best horsewomen and that her favorite dress designer was Donald Brooks.

Ivy's father was really her stepfather. Her real father had been the heir to a paper fortune in the Midwest, and Ivy said that he had turned into a real fag and that was why her mother had divorced him. According to Ivy, her mother had found her husband in bed with her interior decorator one afternoon when her husband was supposedly at his club and the decorator was supposedly supervising the hanging of new wallpaper in the guest bathroom of their Grosse Point mansion. She had immediately placed a call to Jack Hellman, who not only got her a divorce and an enormous settlement but also married her. It was considered quite a coup, since for years Jack Hellman had been considered one of America's most eligible bachelors. He was forty-eight and Ivy's mother was thirty-three when they got married— he for the first time, she for the second. Ivy wondered if her stepfather wasn't a bit on the light side too. After all, she asked Joy, what normal man would stay unmarried until he was forty-eight?

Joy said she didn't know. Maybe he had just had a lot of affairs.

They then had a discussion of exactly what it was that fags did in bed. They knew the term "blow job" but weren't sure what it meant. The conversation was at a dead end and they finally gave up on it and talked about the favorite subjects: themselves and their ambitions.

Ivy said that she wanted to have an affair with Mick Jagger, even though all the fan magazines said that he and Marianne Faithfull were going steady. After she and Mick broke up, Ivy planned to become a poet and turn bisexual, since she wanted to experience everything life had to offer. She also wanted to buy a large house on a deserted beach somewhere, maybe Tunisia, and entertain her lovers there.

Joy had not decided what she wanted to do. She knew only what she didn't want to do: she didn't want to grow up and get married and be like her mother.

She felt sorry for her mother. All she did was tell the maid to be sure to dust the tops of the picture frames, go to the hairdresser and put out ice and lemon peel every night so that when her father got home he could have a drink right away. Even though she was just twelve, Joy could see that her father had a much better time than her mother. He went out to the office every day, he played tennis and had season tickets for the football Giants, he had control over all the money and whenever her mother wanted to change the slipcovers she had to ask her father if it was OK. Whenever the phone rang, it was almost always for her father. No one ever called her mother except maybe Joy's boring uncle, Peter, or the hardware store to say that the special-sized bulbs for the dining-room chandelier had come in.

Joy was also pretty positive that her father had girlfriends.

"What makes you think that?" asked Ivy.

"Sometimes he stays out overnight and I don't think it's a business trip."

"What does your mother think?" Ivy was used to domestic scandal, since it was the cornerstone of her father's success, and she thrived on its petty details.

"Nothing," Joy shrugged. "She believes him."

"If I were your mother, I'd have affairs too. That way I'd be even."

"Anyway," said Joy, who didn't like the thought of her mother's having affairs, "I'm definitely not getting married."

"Well," said Ivy, "I definitely will get married. I'd estimate that I'll have three or four husbands."

"Your father can get you your divorces," said Joy, and they both rolled around on Ivy's bed giggling at the thought.

"Not me," said Joy, when they had stopped laughing and could talk again. "I'll never get married. Not ever. I'd kill myself if I ended up like my mother."

Nineteen-sixty-six was the dawning of the Age of Aquarius. It was the time of Baby Jane Holzer and Andy Warhol, of *Valley of the Dolls* and Paul Simon and feelin' groovy. It was a time of pot, the Pill and promiscuity, and even though there were a few downers, like the riots in Watts and Sandy Koufax' retirement due to arthritis, everyone was making love, not war.

Everyone except Joy.

Joy turned fourteen in June of that year and, like Ivy, a year older at fifteen, was obsessed with sex. Joy was a virgin and Ivy was having an affair with Mr. Kanen, the school psychologist. He was handsome in a tired, thin way and Ivy said that he was a tiger in bed. She had seduced him one day when her math teacher had thrown her out of class and sent her to Mr. Kanen's office. It was a rule at Ardsley that anyone who misbehaved in class had to see the school psychologist. Ardsley believed that understanding the roots of a child's problem was the most effective way of dealing with it.

Joy was envious of Ivy's affair and wished she were having one too. She asked Ivy how she had gone about seducing Mr. Kanen.

"I laid a heavy story on him," said Ivy. "I told him about my lousy childhood and how my father was a faggot and I started crying. Next thing, he had his arm around me, all in the interest of psychology, you know, and the next thing I had my arm around him. When he kissed me, I opened my mouth. After that, it was a cinch."

Ivy, at fifteen, saw herself as a sensuous woman. She had lost her virginity two years earlier and she played a pedagogic role with Joy, instructing and encouraging her. She had told the story of her "first time" often. It had happened at summer camp in Maine.

"Camp was a drag. My parents just couldn't stand having me around all summer watching them and their friends get lushed—I was only thirteen then—so they shipped me off every July. Anyway, he was the swimming counselor. I think he was a junior at Williams, someplace like that . . ."

"How did it happen?" asked Joy. "I mean exactly what did you do and what did he do?"

Joy thought about sex all the time but she could never really picture it. She couldn't see how everything fitted together—arms and elbows and legs and knees. She had even looked at photographs in an illustrated sex manual that Ivy had but it still didn't seem real to her. She always flunked spatial-relations tests and she ascribed her imaginative failure to her lack of three-dimensional perception.

"I knew that he liked me. He kept touching my tits when he was supposed to be teaching me the Australian crawl, and so I made a date to meet him. I sneaked away from my bunk after everyone was asleep and we met down in the boathouse. They kept the canoes and paddles and sailboats and all that crap there. I wore my pajamas. I figured it would be stupid to get dressed, since I knew what was going to happen."

"Weren't you nervous?"

"No," said Ivy. Then she reconsidered. "Well, to tell the honest truth, I was. A little."

"But not enough to make you chicken out?"

"Never. I was just too curious."

"What did he say?" asked Joy. "I mean, how did he bring up the subject?"

"He didn't. He was wearing white ducks and he took them off and he had a hard-on right away. I took off my pajamas and he kissed me a few times and then he just stuck it in and came."

"Was it exciting?" That was the part that Joy was the most curious about. She had read in books about how the earth shook and stuff like that. It was hard to imagine, just like everything else about sex, and she wanted confirmation from a person who had actually experienced it.

"It wasn't too bad for a first time," said Ivy, with the experience of the ages. "I didn't come but I faked it."

"How did you know what to do?" Joy would never have admitted such ignorance to anyone but Ivy. However, since they were best friends, they had a pledge to tell each other everything, no matter how damning.

"My old man—I mean my stepfather, not my real father— shows dirty movies at our country house and I used to sneak in and watch them. It's easy. All you have to do is groan and wiggle around a little."

"I wish I could get laid," said Joy. "I bet I'm the only girl in our class who's still a virgin."

"I bet there are a few more. They just won't admit it, that's all," said Ivy. Ivy was telling the truth as she perceived it and she was also lying in an attempt to make her friend feel better. "You'll dig up somebody."

"I wish it would happen soon. I'd like to get it over with."

It was so sad: they were little girls who wanted to be big girls and they thought that sex was the way to do it. They thought that sex was something to "get over with."

No one—not their parents, not the "dirty books" they bought at newsstands, not the fully illustrated sex manuals they swiped from their parents' bookshelves—told them any different.

What Joy didn't ask, because she didn't understand the feelings and therefore didn't know the words with which to frame the question, was what was sex really about? What did it mean?

Everyone else seemed to know. They all seemed to be so good at it, so accomplished and casual and knowledgeable, and yet no one shared the ultimate secret with Joy. At the age of fourteen, Joy found herself in a world of sexual overkill that she was unequipped to deal with. She was intimidated as she compared her lack of experience, her shyness and fear with the group sex, topless go-go dancers and love-ins that surrounded her. Joy was secretly positive that if it ever happened to her, she'd do all the wrong things and the boy wouldn't come and she wouldn't come and it would be awful. She would know and the boy would know that she wasn't any good.

No one ever told Joy that sex wasn't a competition.

Even though Ivy was the person Joy was closest to, Ivy didn't comfort Joy. Ivy's approach to sex was mechanical and assertively unsentimental. Ivy used words like cock and cunt and tits and going down and was comfortable with them. Joy used them and felt like an impostor.

She kept wishing that her mother would say something about sex. Since Evelyn never said anything, Joy had no way of knowing that Evelyn thought about it as much as Joy did, feeling that she should participate in her daughter's sexual education yet unable to conquer the guilt and discomfort she felt about discussing sex. Evelyn kept telling herself that "tomorrow" she and Joy would have "a long talk."

But "tomorrow" was invariably "tomorrow," and Evelyn's tense silence finally forced Joy to speak first. It turned out to be a disaster.

One thing that Joy had always had fantasies about was the size of her father's penis. She was sure that it was enormous and she thought that it must hurt to have something that big in you. Joy had masturbated with one finger but she never dared two, just as she used Tampax Junior but was terrified of Regular. Joy felt, without knowing quite where she had gotten the idea from, that women were very small down there. She wondered how a man with a big thing and a woman with a small thing could have intercourse, and so she asked her mother.

Her mother blushed a hot, blazing crimson and took a long time before she answered. She finally mumbled, "Well, dear, when a man is ready the woman is ready to accept him."

Her mother's answer was no answer. Joy shriveled up inside at her mother's hideous embarrassment and she never again risked bringing up the subject with her mother.

Joy felt that her mother's generation was hung up on sex —that to them sex was supposed to be dirty and you did it in the dark.

Joy's own generation contended that sex was natural, open and "beautiful." Joy agreed with her own generation—she wanted to be natural, open and beautiful. The trouble was that no one explained to her how you made the transition from feeling shy and awkward and fearful to being open, natural and beautiful.

The mystery became more and more unbearable until, finally, as her fifteenth birthday approached, Joy decided to force the issue. She would make her parents acknowledge her sexuality and she'd get laid even if it meant she had to beg.

Joy used the same technique with her parents that she had used at Ardsley. She kept her cool and waited until they made the first move. In early June, just three weeks before her birthday, Joy's mother gave her the opening she had been waiting for. They were having dinner and Lydia had just served the roast chicken and buttered broccoli and gone back into the kitchen when Joy's mother asked her what she'd like for her birthday present.

"A prescription for the Pill," said Joy. "I'm sick of having to cop the black market."

Joy leaned back in her chair and sucked in her cheeks to make her cheekbones look higher. She thought it made her look like Faye Dunaway in *Bonnie and Clyde*. It made her feel like Bonnie: arrogant, sure of herself, daring.

"You're buying pills on a black market?" Joy couldn't tell which shocked her mother more: that she was buying birth-control pills or that statusy Ardsley had a black market.

Joy didn't answer. Anyway, it had been a lie. Joy had never bought anything on the Ardsley black market except some grass now and then. Of course, you could get anything you wanted—the Pill, LSD, speed, coke, downers—but Joy was afraid of heavy drugs. She was afraid of messing up her head. Grass was OK, though. Once in a while, she and Ivy smoked pot, always in Ivy's bedroom with the windows opened wide, terrified that one of the maids would catch them. There was no problem with Ivy's parents: her father was always working and her mother was always hunting foxes. Ivy's bedroom was by far the safest place. Joy's room was no good at all: her mother was home practically all the time.

Nat was the first one to speak.

"So, the kid's growing up," he said. He looked very pleased. It was hard to tell whether it was with her or with himself for being so hip and taking her bombshell request in stride and not losing his cool.

"But *I* didn't," said Evelyn. She spoke directly to Nat, as if Joy weren't even in the room. "Not at her age."

"You were a slow starter," said Nat. "Think of all the fun you missed."

Her father's tone gave Joy a peculiar feeling. It was the first time she had ever heard anything that sounded the least bit sexy between her parents: like, maybe, they had a secret between them that she didn't know about. For the first time it seemed real to Joy that her parents had actually screwed. She had tried to imagine it lots of times but she just could never make it come true. But the way her father had just spoken to her mother—the tone of his voice and the smile, and the unspoken implication—made it possible. All of a sudden, Joy knew for sure: her parents *had* slept together and it had been pretty hot.

"Dear," said her mother, "Have you . . ."

"I'm a virgin, if that's what you want to know," said Joy. "Pure as the driven snow."

"Well, I guess we'll have to do something about that," said Nat. There was that same tone in his voice: sexy, knowing. It was sort of dirty and sort of exciting.

A week later Joy found herself in the office of a gynecologist whose specialty was teen-aged girls. He was a white-haired man in his sixties, very matter-of-fact, and the whole thing turned out to be about as embarrassing as buying a Beach Boys album. He hardly seemed to notice her. Joy had no way of knowing that he was used to kids with venereal disease and botched abortions and to hysterical pregnant thirteen-year-olds. As far as he was concerned, dispensing birth-control pills to a fifteen-year-old whose own mother had made the appointment was simple humanitarianism.

Joy left his office with her first month's supply of pills. It was just like Ivy's, a round plastic compact with little slots around the edges, each slot containing the pill for the day. Joy couldn't wait to show it to Ivy or to let it casually lie on top of the stuff in her bag so that when she opened it, everyone could look in and see that she was on the Pill.

That night Evelyn, as usual, came into Joy's room at quarter to ten to say good night. Joy was sitting in bed watching a rerun of *The Honeymooners*. Ralph was yelling at Alice and Ethel was trying to intercede.

"Please turn the television off; I want to talk to you."

Joy was positive that her mother was going to ask a million dumb questions about the doctor. She pressed the remote-control switch on her night table and the picture flickered off. Joy was braced. She sat up very straight in bed and crossed her arms across her chest. "Yeah?" She sucked in her cheeks a little. She thought of Bonnie and all the bullets.

"Joy, don't be so tough. I'm not going to stick my nose into your business. It's just that we never seem to have a chance to talk."

"What is there to talk about? I know everything anyway."

"I'm sure you do." Evelyn remembered *Strictly Confidential* and how inadequate it had been. She didn't want Joy to feel the way she had felt: confused and abandoned. "I'm sure that you know all the techniques. That isn't what I want to talk about. You know, Joy, there's more to sex than just falling into bed with someone and going through all the right motions. Your emotions get involved."

"Maybe yours did," said Joy, letting her mother know that she had dug the exchange between her and Nat at dinner, "but not mine." Joy was more embarrassed by her mother's sentimentality than she would have been if her mother were telling her the best way to go down on a guy who couldn't get it up. That she could have stood.

"Yours too. You're no exception." Rarely was her mother so insistent, so positive. "And men's. They have emotions too. People's sex organs and emotions aren't separate. They're joined. What affects one affects the other."

"That's a lot of bull," said Joy. "Sex is a natural appetite, like hunger. Just because I'm hungry doesn't mean I'm going to fall in love with a hamburger." Joy didn't want to squeal on Ivy, but Ivy screwed around all over the place and she never got hung up on anybody. That was how Joy knew what she was talking about. But she didn't want her mother to know. She might tell Ivy's mother.

"Joy, you're still a little girl. You don't know what it's all about. I can't stop you from doing what you want to do. All I can do is caution you. Be careful. Careful with yourself. Careful with your boyfriends. Emotions are powerful. Respect them."

As Evelyn spoke, she watched Joy's little frozen face grow defiant and hard and she wondered how a child of just fifteen could have gotten like that. So vulnerable, so wary, so guarded. The Love Generation. They didn't know the meaning of the word.

"Just remember, Joy," she continued, "there's no such thing as just falling into bed. Not for you and not for the boy."

"Suppose I dig girls? Didja ever think of that?"

Her mother looked as if Joy had slapped her in the face. It took her a moment to recover.

"Oh, Joy," she said, and then there wasn't anything to say and so she tried to kiss her daughter's cheek. Joy pulled away and squirmed down under the covers, leaving her mother to caress the air. Joy stayed hidden, her tears clenched back, until Evelyn left the room quickly, sad and defeated.

Joy didn't know why she had been such a wise-ass. Her mother had been trying, really trying, but Joy didn't know how to unsay something that had already been said. She waited, keeping her cool, waited for her mother to give her the right opening to apologize, but she never did.

3 Summer of sixty-seven was the summer of Haight-Ashbury, the East Village and Flower Power. Ivy Hellman spent the summer in Europe, in a rented villa in Cap d'Antibes with her parents, and Joy, as usual, went to Nantucket with her mother.

Joy had sworn to Ivy that she would come back in the fall relieved of her virginity. She had two possibilities in mind.

One was Boyd Coleman. He was Main Line, a Princeton sophomore and a tennis jock. He had a summer job working on a landscape crew and had chosen the job specifically because it kept him out in the sun and because it was very physical. Boyd had blond hair and the sun had bleached his eyebrows until they were practically invisible. Boyd's father was a stock-market honcho, and his mother sat around the Sankaty Head beach club drinking gin-and-tonic all day long. Boyd had his own Thunderbird, he resembled Robert

Redford and Joy had had a crush on him ever since she had first seen him.

Her second possibility was Dave Davis, who was a townie. Dave's father owned a local construction company and he was considered rich for Nantucket. Dave wore the wrong clothes—a white undershirt with the sleeves rolled way up on his biceps, jeans with tight legs and the cuffs rolled up and engineer boots. He had short sideburns, unheard of in Joy's circle, but if you looked at him the right way, you could pretend that he looked like James Dean.

Dave had a reputation as the town stud. Supposedly he had banged all the girls in Nantucket High—at least, the ones who put out. He worked for his father's company, and Joy would see him riding around in a red pickup with DAVIS CONSTRUCTION lettered on the side panel. She saw him every Saturday and Sunday at Cisco, the best surfing beach. Dave had a surfboard, and although he had no finesse, he was able to get the most out of every wave.

When Boyd invited her to the movies—a revival of *Casablanca*—Joy thought that he'd be the first. Joy didn't care too much which one it would be: they both turned her on. Boyd picked her up in his T-Bird and they sat through the flick and he held Joy's hand. She thought it was a promising beginning and assumed they'd go park somewhere afterward.

"That was a terrific line," said Boyd when the movie let out. " 'Play it again, Sam.' Didn't you think that was terrific?"

"Yeah," said Joy. "Humphrey Bogart was a groove."

"Unreal," said Boyd, as he held the door open for Joy and helped her into the car. She was wondering what he looked like with his clothes off. He had a terrific body.

Boyd started the car and drove to Main Street, over the cobblestones, and parked in front of the Sweet Shop. They went in and Boyd as well as Joy ordered a Tab. He told her that he was very careful about his weight because if he put on even a pound, it affected his game.

At ten-thirty, Boyd drove Joy home, parked on Pleasant

Street and reached over and kissed her with his lips closed. Joy remembered what Ivy had said about opening her mouth with Mr. Kanen and how it had been a cinch after that, but she didn't quite know how to do it. She hoped Boyd would take the initiative, but he didn't. He held her for a moment with her head on his shoulder, and that was all.

"I've got to be in bed by eleven," he said. "I'm staying in training over the summer. I want to make Varsity."

"That's groovy," said Joy. She tried to sound enthusiastic. He wanted to impress her and she didn't want to hurt his feelings.

"You want to go to the movies Tuesday?" he asked. "They've got *In the Heat of the Night*. I really like Sidney Poitier."

"I really dig Rod Steiger. I think he's a sex symbol." Joy thought it was a funny remark because Rod Steiger was old and had a beer belly, and she giggled, but Boyd didn't seem to get it.

"See you Tuesday," he said, and got into the Thunderbird and drove off. Joy wondered if he was shy or what.

The next day Joy was sitting on one of the benches in front of Congdon's Pharmacy talking to some kids from the Rhode Island School of Design when Dave pulled up in his pickup and went into the drugstore. His jeans were very tight and Joy could see the crack in his behind with every step he took.

"Wow, grrroooossssss!" said one of the girls from Risdey, referring to Dave.

Joy didn't say anything, but she thought he was really sexy the way he walked, conscious of his butt.

"Hi," she said, when he came out of the drugstore.

"How do," he said. They sort of knew each other from the time two summers before when her mother had remodeled the old porch into a sun-room. Dave had done all the construction work, sawing the wood, laying the floors and doing some painting. Joy remembered that he drank Bud all day long while he worked .

Joy didn't know what else to say to him and the other kids were watching her, so she felt uncomfortable. They stood there a second, just looking each other over. Finally, Dave turned. "See you around," he said.

"Yeah," said Joy. "So long."

That Saturday, Joy went to Cisco on purpose. She was lying on the sand trying to read *Lord of the Flies* when Dave came over and flopped down next to her. His swim trunks were red-and-yellow-plaid nylon and really hideous. Joy wondered where he had bought them.

"That any good?" Dave indicated the book.

"It's OK," said Joy.

"I never read," said Dave. "Listen, you want to go to the Chicken Box tonight?"

Joy had never been there. It was a crummy townie bar that also served the black help who came with the summer people. Joy knew about it because Lydia went there on her nights off.

"I'm not old enough," said Joy. In Massachusetts, you had to be twenty-one to drink.

"So what?" said Dave. "I've got pull."

"OK," said Joy. She was trying not to look at Dave's legs. They were thick and covered with dark hair.

Dave called for her that night in the pickup and it was groovy to ride high up in the battered vehicle. There were wrenches, paint-soaked rags and a kerosene can on the floor, and the springs were shot so that Joy bounced around on the seat. Dave parked and Joy was surprised at how many cars and trucks were outside the Chicken Box. Dave strolled through the front door and the old, white-haired Negro who stood at the entrance nodded respectfully. Joy realized that Dave was sort of a wheel among the townies. Without asking Joy what she wanted, Dave went to the crowded bar and ordered two rye-and-gingers, and they sat down at a lun-cheonette-type table, the dirty glasses and paper plate of

French fries with ketchup from the previous occupants still littering its marbled formica top. A local rock group was mutilating some Beatles classics, and Joy looked around at the half-white, half-black crowd and didn't recognize one person. She realized that there was a whole other life going on on Nantucket that she had never known about.

It was impossible to talk over the racket of the amplified music and the din of conversation in the square, low-ceilinged room. Joy was used to wine and grass, and she thought the rye was strong and very unpleasant. Still, she drank it down and drank a second when Dave, without a word, got up and went to the bar and returned with two more.

When they had finished their drinks, he put a five-dollar bill down on the table and said, "Let's go."

He drove out on the Sconset Road halfway to the airport and turned off on one of the dirt roads that crisscrossed the island. The pickup bounced and jounced on the rutted, unpaved road. Joy knew that this was it.

Dave braked the pickup to a stop, switched off the ignition and extinguished the lights.

"Ah," he said, and reached over and grabbed Joy.

"You've got nice tits," he said, pulling her T-shirt up. "You don't wear a bra. I go for that." He held one breast in each hand and Joy waited for him to kiss her. She wondered if he would kiss her breasts. Instead, having held her breasts for a moment, he abandoned them and unzipped his pants and, squirming in the front seat, pulled off his pants and shorts with one motion. Joy took her jeans off by herself and the next thing she knew he was inside her.

"Don't you know anything about foreplay?" she asked.

Dave didn't answer. He was pumping in and out of her, completely absorbed in himself.

Joy was a virgin and he wasn't and she realized that she knew more about sex than he did. He had one arm around her and the other braced against the dashboard to give himself leverage. His movements became faster, finally almost spastic, and then, abruptly, he stopped.

"Ah," he said, when he came. He withdrew himself and leaned back on his side of the seat and lit a cigarette.

"Didja come?" he asked.

Joy decided not to lie.

"No."

"Yuh frigid?"

"No."

"Yuh must be."

"Let me show you something." Joy took the cigarette from his hand, flipped it out the window and began to demonstrate some of the things she had read about and some of the things Ivy had told her about. It was a revelation to Dave, and they spent every Friday and Saturday night of the summer parked in the pickup pursuing their erotic education. For years after, Joy identified sex with the odor of kerosene and paint solvent.

Joy waited all summer for her mother to ask her what she was doing with Dave Davis until two o'clock in the morning. Joy knew that her mother was awake because when she got home she could hear her turn over in bed. But her mother never said a word. Ever since that conversation the day she got the Pill, Joy and her mother had been very remote and cautious. They walked around each other on eggs.

Although Joy was getting a lot of sex that summer, she was surprised to find that she felt extremely lonely. She had no one to talk to. She went to the movies once a week with Boyd and they talked about the plot and, late in August, they even screwed. It was a big disappointment. A real nothing compared with Dave. The trouble with Dave was that he was totally inarticulate. He came from a completely different background; he had no ambitions other than to take over his father's construction company when he retired. Dave hated to talk and said that talking was boring. Joy understood that just as she used him for her satisfaction, he was using her for his.

Joy missed Ivy terribly. Ivy was the only person in the

world whom Joy felt close to, but she was in France, and letters weren't ever the same as the four-hour talk sessions in New York.

And so it was that during the summer she had turned fifteen, Joy and her father became best friends.

It began on a Friday in the middle of July. Nat had come up on Thursday, and Friday was bright and sunny, a perfect beach day. Evelyn had a garden-club meeting, and Nat and Joy went to the Jetties Beach alone. They had hot dogs and ice cream for lunch and afterward took a long walk down the beach past the umbrellas and crowds all the way down to the Cliff Beach, which was where the Palm Beach crowd gathered to discuss tax exemptions, divorce settlements and real estate values. The rich talk about money.

"You getting plenty this summer?" Nat asked suddenly.

They had been walking in silence and his question came out of the clear blue.

"I'm getting laid a lot if that's what you mean," said Joy.

"And?"

"And it isn't enough."

"You mean you're getting quantity but not quality?" Nat inflected it as if it were a question, but it was really a statement.

"Sort of. I feel very lonely." It was the first time Joy had ever admitted that to anyone. Of course, she usually had Ivy, so except when she had been new at Ardsley she had never felt lonely before. Sex and loneliness had come into her life at the same time.

Nat and Joy sat down on the bottom step of the steep flight of wooden stairs that led down to the beach from the houses high on the cliff above.

"Is it the same for men?" asked Joy. "I mean, just getting laid isn't enough?"

Nat nodded. "Men are people too."

"Then how come everyone makes such a big deal about sex?"

"The right person makes all the difference," said Nat.

"With the right person you don't feel let down?"

"Right."

"I guess it's one way to tell if it's the right person, then. You don't feel let down afterwards."

"It's as good a test as any," said Nat.

There was something in the way her father spoke that made Joy think he was feeling exactly the way she was. She had the impression that he too was "getting plenty" and that it wasn't enough. She wished she had the nerve to come out and ask him. Even if she had, she wouldn't have. She didn't really want to hear the answer.

"You mind if I ask who you're making it with?" he asked.

"Dave Davis."

"The kid who put in the sun porch?"

Joy nodded.

Nat said nothing.

"Don't you want to know more about it?"

"Only if you want to tell me."

"I guess there's nothing more to tell; I already told you the important part."

"About feeling let down?"

"Yeah." Nat noticed that Joy's head was down. She looked very sad.

"Well, think of it as practice," he said to cheer her up. "So it shouldn't be a total loss."

He made his daughter look at him and they both laughed, sharing their first secret. Then they got up and started walking back down toward the Jetties. It was just past four, and the breeze had died down and it was very still. The water was as shiny and placid as a millpond.

"Did you ever have the right person?" Joy asked.

Nat nodded.

"Mom?"

He nodded again.

"Is she still the right person?"

There was a little pause before Nat answered.

"We're still married."

In response, Joy took his hand. It was their second secret.

Neither of them spoke again. They walked the length of the beach. Joy was thinking about her father. She was wondering what would happen if he ever met another right person.

She crossed the fingers of the hand that wasn't holding his and hoped that he wouldn't.

If he did, she was afraid that she'd lose him.

That summer, Joy and her father grooved on the same things: Mao jackets for men, "Lucy in the Sky with Diamonds," James Bond movies, Richie Havens and Jimi Hendrix, bluefishing on Dionis Beach, fried clams on Straight Wharf and malachite ice cream cones from the Sweet Shop. They flew to Expo 67 one weekend and dug Habitat; they were Doves and not Hawks; they thought the Glassboro meeting was a crock, another widening of the credibility gap; they watched the race riots in Detroit, Birmingham and Spanish Harlem and agreed that if they were poor and black they'd be stealing color television sets too.

In 1967, when the world was on a seemingly endless high, Joy and her father formed a closed corporation that continued into the fall. When the Jets were in town, they went to the Polo Grounds, ate Harry Stevens' hot dogs and drank Bud and cheered even though it turned out to be a losing season. They went to shlocky movies on Eighty-sixth Street and became connoisseurs of vampire movies and bikini-beach films and loved Clint Eastwood in spaghetti Westerns. They ate cheeseburgers and spinach-and-bacon salad at P.J.'s; they went to rock concerts at Fillmore East; they shopped at the Different Drummer and the O Boutique; they frugged in the upstairs back room of Max's Kansas City and in the funky Electric Circus on St. Marks Place and caught the Sunday-afternoon freak scene at the Bethesda Fountain.

It was during that fall that Joy and Ivy made a brand-new discovery: they found out that stealing was a new kind of high.

Joy and Ivy were members of the first generation of Super Consumers. Exhorted by television and magazines, by advertising and promotion, they were programmed to buy, to spend, to throw away in order to buy some more. Theirs was the generation of instant fashion, instantly disposable; of paper dresses and Courrèges boots, of Saint Laurent's Mondrian Look, the Gypsy look and the *Doctor Zhivago* look, of Jean Shrimpton selling Yardley, Twiggy selling dresses and Joe Namath shaving on TV to sell Schick.

By the time they reached their mid-teens, Ivy and Joy were full-fledged Super Consumers. They spent their Saturdays in the stores, going from one to another for the newest paperback best seller, the latest shade of lip gloss and the newest Peter Max poster.

One Saturday afternoon in late October, they were in the Young New Yorker shop of Lord & Taylor buying poor-boy sweaters. Joy had already decided on a red one and a yellow one and Ivy was trying to choose between purple and green. She had already picked the same red one that Joy had. Ivy liked the purple better, but it didn't go as well with things she already had as the green. It was a tough decision. They were in the dressing room and Ivy had put on the green sweater one more time to try to make up her mind.

"Why don't you take all three?" asked Joy.

"My old lady would kill me. My clothes bills flip her right out." Ivy studied herself in the full-length mirror. "I guess I'll take the green," she said. Joy could tell by her voice that she really wanted the purple but had decided to be practical.

Ivy peeled off the green sweater, and in the split second when it was reversed over her head, temporarily cutting off her vision, Joy impulsively stuck the purple one in her tote bag.

They went to the cash register and, with the plastic Lord & Taylor credit cards that their parents had given them, paid for the sweaters. They waited while the salesgirl tore off the tickets, wrote up the sales slips and put the sweaters into Lord & Taylor shopping bags.

"Now what should we do?" asked Ivy as they went out the

revolving doors. It was unusually cold for October, and they were both wearing mid-thigh-length fake-fur coats.

"My knees are freezing," said Joy, pulling her coat around her.

"It's fashionable," said Ivy, and they broke up.

"Let's go to King Karol," said Joy. "I want to get *Alice's Restaurant*. I love Arlo Guthrie."

They walked the block over to Madison and got on an uptown bus. They sat in the seat just behind the rear door.

"I got you a present," said Joy, very casually, once they were settled. She reached into her tote bag and handed the purple poor-boy to Ivy. The tags were still on it.

"You swiped it?" she asked.

"Nothing to it."

"Wow," said Ivy, caressing the sweater. "Outasight!"

That was the beginning of what Joy and Ivy called their "boosting phase." They were very professional about their life of crime and never hit the same store twice. They didn't want to risk being recognized. In the beginning, they were very cautious, taking only small items—scarves, rings; once from a posh drugstore on upper Madison Avenue they took seven different shades of eye shadow off a revolving display rack; they took felt pens, panty hose and pearlized nail polish. Once that began to get a little boring and they had acquired more confidence, they upped the ante. The most expensive thing Joy ever swiped was a vinyl raincoat from Paraphernalia, and Ivy's biggest haul was a Sony transistor radio from Liberty Music at Madison and Fiftieth.

As October turned into November and November into December, they found that the crowds of Christmas shoppers created confusion and made the stealing and the getaway easier than usual. Joy and Ivy never felt the least bit guilty, and they never used any of the things they stole. Their biggest problem was how to get rid of the stuff once they had stolen it. Sometimes they dumped it into garbage cans on the street. Other times they abandoned it on a bus. They never brought it home, because they had no safe hiding places; either their mothers or the maids would be sure to notice unaccounted-for merchandise piling up in the back of a closet.

It never occurred to them that what they were doing was against the law. If the stores were dumb enough to put merchandise within reach, Ivy and Joy weren't so dumb that they wouldn't take it. It seemed to them that the stores were daring them and they weren't about to turn down a dare.

On the Saturday before Christmas, they turned their talents to the gourmet department of Bloomingdale's. They took a can of flageolets, a jar of cornichons, a tin of Scandinavian rollmops and a seven-ounce jar of truffles that was tagged at sixty-five dollars. They went by names, picking the things that sounded the most exotic. They had never heard of any of them. The truffles appealed to them simply because they were so astronomically expensive. They decided to duck out the Fifty-ninth Street side of the store, go over to the Woolworth's on Third, boost a can opener and have a picnic. For once, they had something that could be eaten and that was, thus, undetectable. They wondered why they hadn't thought of it sooner.

They shoved their way through the mob to the outer door of the store, and just as Ivy, who was immediately behind Joy, stepped onto the sidewalk, a man tapped her on the shoulder.

"Excuse me," he said.

"That's OK," said Ivy, thinking he was apologizing for bumping into her.

"I believe you have some of our property in there."

Before Ivy could react, the man had taken her large shoulder bag, the canvas one that was identical to Joy's, and opened it. He pulled out the tin of flageolets.

"May I see your sales slip, please?" He was extremely polite, but his hand on Ivy's shoulder was firm. Joy's first impulse was to run, but then she realized that she wouldn't run out on Ivy for anything in the world.

"We don't have one," said Joy. There was no point in lying.

"Then I'm going to have to ask you to come with me."

Taking each girl by the elbow, he led them back through the delicacies department and to an elevator marked EM-PLOYEES ONLY.

"If you steal the merch, does that make you an employee?" asked Ivy.

Joy giggled, but the man didn't. They got off on the ninth floor and were led through a narrow corridor with glass doors on either side to a big bull pen where people were sitting around on crummy couches and wooden folding chairs. Ivy wondered if they'd all been caught shoplifting too.

"OK," said the man, gesturing to Ivy to follow him. Joy went with them, toward a frosted-glass door.

"Not you," said the man. "You sit down."

Joy went to the cracked leatherette couch with the chrome arms that were beginning to peel and she began to get nervous. It hadn't occurred to her that they would separate her and Ivy.

In a few minutes, Ivy came back accompanied by the man. She looked scared, but when the man asked Joy to go with him, Ivy punched Joy's arm and said, "You'll knock 'em dead, kid."

It made Joy feel a little better, but by the time she got to the unmarked door, her knees were actually shaking and she had to pee. She was terrified about what they would do to her and she had no idea what it might be.

The small office contained an old wooden desk, two chairs and an old-fashioned green filing cabinet. A bunch of half-dead chrysanthemums in a hobnail glass vase stood on top of it. Joy was surprised that the person behind the desk was a woman. The man shut the door, leaving the two of them alone.

"Joy Baum?" The woman was reading from a filing card.

"Yes," Joy said. Actually, she only tried to say it. There was a big blob in her throat and the word got only halfway out.

"Sit down." The woman kept reading from the card.

At least they didn't have rubber hoses. Joy sat down. The

woman read both sides of the card, and finally she looked up at Joy. She was in her forties; she had dark curly hair in an out-of-date style with lots of hair spray and a moon-shaped face. Joy noticed that her eyes, behind hideous pink plastic harlequin-shaped glasses, were quite pretty.

"How old are you?"

The question took Joy by surprise. She thought that maybe they were going to grill her, the way they did in the movies.

"Fifteen."

"What made you steal sixty-five dollars' worth of truffles?"

Their loot was spread out on the woman's desk and she looked Joy right in the eye.

Joy shrugged.

"Were you hungry? You weren't hungry, were you?"

"No."

"Then why?"

"I don't know," said Joy, and that was the truth. She didn't know why. There wasn't any particular reason that she could think of. Not one.

"Do you have anything against Bloomingdale's?" the woman asked.

"Uh-uh." Joy suddenly began to relax. They weren't going to hurt her. They were interested in some bullshit about whether or not she liked Bloomingdale's. She didn't have any feelings about Bloomingdale's, not one way or the other.

"Your family has had an account with us for over twenty years. We've had a good relationship with them." The woman waved the filing card in the air.

You mean, thought Joy, that they pay their bills on time.

"Does your mother know what you and your friend do with your Saturday afternoons?"

For a second Joy thought that the woman had somehow found out about all the other boosting expeditions. And then she realized that it was impossible and she just answered the question.

"No."

"What do you think she'd say if she knew?"

"I guess she wouldn't like it," said Joy. "Are you going to tell her?"

The woman looked at Joy and Joy couldn't tell if the woman was nice or mean. Joy realized that it didn't matter too much. She was just doing her job.

"Yes, of course." The woman looked shocked that Joy could ask such a question. "However, we aren't going to press charges. As I said, we've had a long-standing relationship with your family."

Joy suddenly realized that all the crap her mother had bought in the last twenty years in Bloomingdale's was probably keeping her out of jail. What a joke.

"What are you going to tell her?"

"That you were found shoplifting."

"That's all?"

Joy was relieved. It was a big nothing. They'd give her a slap on the wrist and let her go. Adults were really a crock.

"We will also advise your mother to get psychiatric help for you."

"Send me to a shrink?" Joy was outraged and her voice rose angrily. "I'm not crazy."

"We can only advise and suggest," said the woman, keeping her voice very calm, "but we've had many years of experience with girls like you. You need help."

So do you, said Joy to herself. A lady cop; you've probably got a major case of penis envy. But Joy didn't say it out loud. She didn't want to get the old lady shook up.

"You can go now," said the woman. "But I want to warn you that shoplifting is a serious crime. We don't take it lightly. I don't ever want to see you in here again. Is that clear?"

Joy realized that by "here" the woman meant her office. She wasn't banning her from Bloomingdale's, just from getting caught.

"Yeah, it's clear," Joy mumbled. She was scared, but she wouldn't admit it, even to herself. She left the woman's office and she and Ivy headed for the elevators.

By the time they got down to the first floor and were out the revolving doors on the Lexington Avenue side of the store, they were making jokes about "having a record." It would have been exciting, they thought, to get fingerprinted.

Joy waited until just before dinner to get home. She didn't particularly want to have to face her parents. She knew exactly how they'd react: her mother would get hysterical and her father would play it cool. She got home at seven-thirty and her parents were just sitting down to dinner.

Her mother began screaming at her the second she got to the table, yelling about stealing, about breaking the law. She threatened punishments, swore she'd take her television set away, insisted she go to a shrink. Joy picked at her food and listened to her mother's threats knowing that she'd never do anything. She'd made them all before and never followed through. Joy never paid any attention; she just let her mother rave on. Finally, though, Evelyn calmed down.

"Joy, I don't understand why you stole," she said. "You have a charge plate. You can have anything you want—all you have to do is charge it. I don't understand why you stole."

"If I told you, you wouldn't understand."

"Maybe I would," said her mother. "I could try, couldn't I?"

Her mother seemed to be sincere, so Joy decided to risk the truth.

"It was fun."

"Fun?" Her mother looked shocked. "*Fun?*"

"Fun," said Joy, trying not to get mad. She *knew* her mother wouldn't understand. "You know, kicks. I did it for kicks."

"But it's stealing," said her mother. She didn't know how to make her child understand just how serious it was.

"The way you act, it's murder. I didn't murder anyone," said Joy.

"Stealing is dishonest," said Evelyn. "Doesn't that bother you?"

"To tell the truth, no."

"Nat?" Evelyn turned toward Nat, who had been listening and who hadn't said a word. "Nat, tell her it's wrong."

Evelyn depended on him to help her. He could get through to Joy when no one else could. She waited for him to speak, to make Joy understand what she had done and why it was wrong.

"Joy," said Nat, "tell me, *was* it fun? Was it really fun?"

"It was OK," she said. "I mean it wasn't terrific and it wasn't awful. It was OK."

"Are you going to do it again?" Her father was as cool as if he were asking her if she were going to the movies next week.

"No. I learned my lesson." Joy tried to look very sincere. The fact was that if she had the chance, she probably would steal again.

"Is that the truth? Cross your heart?" Her father was incredible. He could practically read her mind.

"I *hope* so," said Joy, and this time she really meant it.

Everyone was silent while Lydia brought out dessert. Rum-raisin ice cream. She put down the three crystal bowls and brought the coffee and cups and a glass of Tab for Joy.

"You know," Nat said over coffee, "you're a lucky kid. Stealing from Bloomingdale's. That's a first-class place. When I was a kid all I ever stole was apples and secondhand pants from the pushcarts. That's all there was on the Lower East Side. You rich kids have it good."

"Yeah," said Joy, and they both laughed. "I guess it's tough being poor."

"You want to know the best thing I ever stole?"

"What?"

"I was in the deli one day getting some sour cream for my mother and another kid stole a loaf of rye bread right off the counter. The old man who owned the store got furious and ran out into the street chasing him. I was left alone and there was a big jar of rolled, pressed apricots by the cash register. I swiped the whole thing, jar and all. It's funny. I paid for the sour cream. I left the nickel on the counter. I picked up the jar and ran like hell. You know," he said, "it was fun. I know exactly what you mean."

Joy and her father laughed together and Evelyn felt excluded. It was as if they were lovers with a private joke and she the chaperone.

Later, in their bedroom, just after Evelyn turned off the light, she decided to speak up.

"I wish you hadn't told her about the apricots."

"Why not? Every kid steals," said Nat, and he turned over to go to sleep.

Evelyn sighed. What was she going to say? That she had never stolen? That she had been afraid of her father and obeyed her mother? That she had been brought up to respect her elders?

Nat would just tell her that she was old-fashioned.

He'd tell her that she was "out of it."

Evelyn lay there and thought about her daughter. Cruel and invulnerable. Casual and defiant. She realized that she didn't like her. It was an unacceptable realization. Evelyn got up and took a Seconal. It would be the only way she'd get to sleep that night.

4 IN MARCH OF 1968 AT THE Sandy Lane Hotel in Barbados the relationship between Joy and her mother passed the point of no return.

The Sandy Lane is an enormous hotel set on an immaculate crescent of silky white beach in the most exclusive area of Barbados. The villas of financiers, retired movie stars and aristocrats, guarded by iron fences and long driveways, are the only nearby structures. The Sandy Lane is long and low; it has miles of corridors and a maze of entrances and exits.

Maids, chauffeurs, waiters, barmen, cleaning and mainte-
nance staff, cooks, clerks and phone operators, all black,
work day and night to perfect the housekeeping and the
service. The Sandy Lane has a swimming pool, tennis courts,
three bars, two dining terraces, a dancing terrace, a golf
course and sailboat, scuba equipment and water skis for rent.
It costs one hundred dollars a day to stay there, and Joy
spent the two weeks of Spring Recess at the Sandy Lane with
her parents.

Her father had taken a suite, two bedrooms with a con-
necting bath, and Joy was given her own key. She wore
bikinis and sunglasses and read paperbacks on the lounge
chairs that beach boys placed on the immaculately raked
and manicured sand. Joy was a tall, slender girl with her
father's elegant bones, and with her long hair and straight
white teeth she looked like a model in a suntan-lotion ad.
When Evelyn looked at her, she was amazed that she had
given birth to such a graceful goddess and she felt that the
problems she had with Joy were a small price to pay for the
pride and love she felt for her. If she and Joy didn't always
get along, well, Evelyn thought, everyone suffered from the
generation gap these days. It was part of being a parent and
you took the bad with the good.

On the third day of her vacation, Joy signed up for waterskiing lessons. She wasn't interested in waterskiing, but she
was interested in the instructor. Winston was a light-colored
Negro with extraordinarily even and handsome Anglo-Saxon
features. He had a magnificent, sculptured body which he ex-
hibited in tiny pure-white bikinis. When he wasn't giving a
lesson, he skied in the bay in front of the hotel, showing
off—using one ski, performing turns and leaps and tricks.
He was a showboat, Joy realized, but he was still the most
attractive man at the Sandy Lane. The boys her own age who
were there with their parents were too young for Joy, and
the college kids who would have interested her went skiing
in the early spring—to Vermont if they went to school in the
East and to Aspen if they went to school in the West. They

couldn't afford the Caribbean and they were too old to tag along with their parents. Except for Winston, there was no one who turned Joy on.

Waterskiing turned out to be a cinch. Joy got up on the skis on her first try and by the end of the first lesson she was already learning how to cut across the wake left by the boat. It was a moronic sport, she thought, and in the boat shack after the lesson, when Winston was filling out the slip that would be added to her father's bill, Joy let Winston feel her up.

"See you tomorrow," he said, and ground his pelvis against her. It was a joke the way he attempted to look deeply into Joy's eyes. She wondered which movie he'd seen that in. He was so obvious she could hardly believe it.

"Definitely," said Joy. Winston made sure she saw the bulge in his bikini and she knew she could fuck him anytime she felt like it. She supposed if she got desperate enough, she would.

That night after dinner, Joy sat with her parents at a table on the edge of the dancing terrace. Joy and her mother took turns dancing with her father, and Joy was sitting alone while her parents danced, sipping a white crème de menthe with soda, when a guy wearing white flannel trousers and a navy blazer came over to the table and asked her to dance. She hadn't noticed him before and she wondered what he was doing here. He must have been about twenty-six and he had a foreign accent.

His name was Klaus, and the reason she hadn't seen him before was that he worked in the Pan Am office in town during the day. He was the son of the Swiss executive who managed the Sandy Lane. Klaus had grown up in first-class hotels around the world—his father had worked at the Mamounia in Marrakech, the Palacio in Estoril, the Hilton in Istanbul and the Crillon in Paris and had moved his family around with him. Klaus didn't want to be a hotelier. He said it was murder—endless hours, lousy help and an interminable flow of cranky guests. He did, however, like the travel business and was working as a junior executive for Pan Am in the Caribbean and, he said, looking at Joy as they did a sedate frug to "Ruby Tuesday" played by the native band, was lucky enough to be at the Sandy Lane at the same time she was.

When the dance was over they went back to the table and Evelyn began to talk to Klaus, asking him about the travel business and what his ambitions were until Joy thought she'd scream. Finally her father had the brains to stand up and hold out his hand to Evelyn.

"Come on. Time for bed. The kids can get into plenty of trouble without our help."

"Don't stay up too late," said Evelyn as Nat practically dragged her across the dance floor.

"Jee-zus," said Joy, watching her parents disappear.

"Parents," said Klaus, and smiled. "They're all alike. They can't help it."

They danced until the band stopped playing.

"Want to go to a native nightclub?"

"Love it."

They went out to the parking lot and Klaus helped Joy into his MG and they drove through the lovely tropical night to a place in the middle of nowhere that had a few crummy shacks built in a group.

"Welcome to the town of Queen Elizabethville," he said, and they both laughed. He opened the door for Joy and helped her out of the car. His Continental manners were really a groove, thought Joy.

Klaus led her down a narrow dirt path to a shack with no walls, just some wooden poles around the edges to hold up a straw roof. It was pitch-black in there, except for the light of a few candles and a bare bulb over the loud native band. When Joy's eyes got used to the darkness she realized that everyone in the place was black except her and Klaus and that they were all staring at them. She felt scared. It was very ominous and for a moment she wondered if she'd ever get out of there alive. Joy had a BLACK IS BEAUTIFUL button and thought H. Rap Brown knew what he was talking about when he made a fist and yelled about Black Power, but she still couldn't control the pang of terror that rose unbidden from her insides. Klaus didn't seem to pay any attention to the stares and ordered some drinks. Joy pretended that she loved it and stayed very close to Klaus, and after a while no one gave them a second glance. Joy's fear disappeared and she began to enjoy herself. She couldn't wait to tell Ivy about it. A real native nightclub. Not a dumb resort hotel stuffed with a lot of rich Americans.

The band played all native merengues, and once Joy got the hang of the beat, she got very turned on after dancing so close to Klaus for a long time. He had an enormous erection and they both enjoyed dragging out the inevitable. They kept drinking the amber-colored liquor which Klaus said was an illegally distilled native rum. It was an over-proof alcohol that tasted like molasses and Klaus warned her to take it easy. It was, he said, dynamite.

They danced and drank and finally Joy asked Klaus if he turned on.

"Naturally," he said. He told her that he had first smoked marijuana when he was fourteen and his father was working at the Mamounia. "In Morocco it's called kif," he said.

Joy was knocked out by his sophistication, but she said nothing, playing it cool.

"You want some grass? There's a connection in Bridge-town."

"I have some in my room," said Joy.

"Let's go," said Klaus, paying the bill in BeeWee dollars. The time for teasing had ended.

On the drive back to the Sandy Lane, Joy began to feel dizzy. She realized it was the booze and figured the sensation would go away if she stayed still. She sank back into the bucket seat and closed her eyes, letting the dizziness envelop her. It was pleasant and unpleasant at the same time, like a dream of floating that keeps turning into a nightmare of falling.

"You OK?" asked Klaus.

They were back in the parking lot of the Sandy Lane. Joy hadn't realized that the car had stopped.

"A little dizzy," she admitted.

"I warned you about that stuff."

"I know."

They got out of the car and very quietly made their way through the twisty corridors to Joy's room. Joy kept herself from bumping into the walls by trailing one index finger along the cool, rough stucco. At last they came to her room and Joy handed Klaus her small crocheted bag. He found the key right away and fitted it into the lock. Holding Joy by the arm, he steered her into the room. She flopped on the bed on her back, watching the ceiling twirl around, and she couldn't make it stop and she couldn't even control whether it went faster or slower.

Klaus sat down on the bed next to her and in a nice, slow, tender way began to kiss her. He ran his tongue back and forth against her teeth.

"That feels good."

"Then I won't stop."

"I don't want you to."

Joy felt as if she were sinking into a warm sea. She didn't have to do a thing. She loved that feeling, a man making love to her as if she were will-less, letting her body respond to the sensation, with no control and no mind of her own. She realized on the periphery of her consciousness that it was the first time she had had a lover who was more accomplished than she was. Klaus was rolling up her T-shirt.

"Beautiful," he said, and he ran his tongue first around her nipples and then on her belly just above the waistband of her jeans. Then he began to unzip her fly.

Joy moved up on the bed, propping herself up on her elbows to make it easier for him, and the sudden motion of her body made her violently ill. She began to vomit while she was still on the bed. Klaus grabbed a handful of Kleenex from a box on the night table and handed it to her. She held it over her mouth and ran into the bathroom. The vomit was flooding over the sides of the Kleenex, and by the time she reached the toilet she was heaving spastically, her stomach rejecting everything she had consumed that evening. She continued to retch, feeling as if the bottom of her stomach would come out through her mouth.

The door to the bathroom from her parents' side opened and her mother stood there in her nightgown.

"My God, Joy! What's the matter?"

Evelyn could see Joy's back heaving as she knelt on the blue tile floor, her face in the toilet, embracing the bowl with both arms. She didn't see Klaus until her eyes adjusted to the sudden glare of light from Joy's room. His hair was rumpled and the belt and fly of his white flannel trousers were open. Joy heaved again, making wild animal noises. Her T-shirt was rolled up over her breasts, and her long hair trailed into the vomit-filled toilet bowl.

"I suggest you leave," said Evelyn to Klaus.

"She's sick." He gestured toward Joy. He didn't want to abandon her.

"Leave! Just go. Get out of here!"

Evelyn crossed the bathroom and slammed the door on Joy's side in Klaus's face, leaving him alone in the bedroom with no choice but to go. Joy was aware of the scene but too weak and too sick to interfere.

"Joy?" Evelyn put her hand on her daughter's shoulder. "Joy, what did he do to you?"

"He didn't do anything. It was my fault. All my own fault."

Evelyn could barely make out her words. She was out of breath from the violence of her vomiting.

Nat came to the bathroom door.

"She's had too much booze," he said. "That's all."

"But she's so sick," said Evelyn. "Look at her."

"So she had more than a lot. She'll have a helluva hang-over tomorrow and she'll be fine."

"What should I do?"

"Just leave her alone."

Nat could remember a few occasions in his own life when he had been violently ill from alcohol. Once it had resulted from drinking two whole bottles of sweet Passover wine. He had been just as sick as Joy, and his father had whipped him with a carpet beater. A few years later he had experimented with some moonshine in a jazz joint on West Fifty-second Street. One of the musicians had brought it in from southern New Jersey, where his brother-in-law had a still. He had had a hangover that had lasted forty-eight hours. As far as Nat was concerned, it was a normal part of growing up.

"She had a man in there," said Evelyn once they had gotten Joy cleaned up and back into bed.

"She's almost sixteen. Naturally she had a man in there."

"Nat, she's your daughter. Don't you care about her?"

"I care that she's having a good time."

"You call that a good time?" Her daughter stinking of vomit, holding onto a toilet bowl, her breasts exposed, that man standing there with his fly open. "You really call that a good time?"

"I call it growing up," said Nat. "She'll have a vicious hangover and it'll teach her a lesson."

"I'm not so sure," said Evelyn. She thought it would take more than a hangover. She decided there and then that she wouldn't permit Joy ever to see Klaus again. He was too old for her, too sophisticated. It was time, Evelyn thought, that she put her foot down.

Joy woke up at noon with a headache, a stomachache, shaky hands, sandpaper eyes, blotchy skin and weak knees. She couldn't eat and she couldn't sleep. She lay there with the shades drawn against the bright Caribbean sun and tried hard and unsuccessfully to remember whether or not she and Klaus had actually made it.

At two o'clock a bellboy arrived with a big bouquet of bougainvillaea and a card from Klaus confirming their dinner date for that night, saying that he would pick her up at seven. At three-thirty, her father arrived with vanilla ice cream, ginger ale and sympathy.

He told her about his own youthful experiences with alcohol, which he referred to as "Manischewitz and Moonshine," and to her amazement, Joy actually laughed. Considering her condition, it was an accomplishment.

"Your mother is, to put it mildly, pissed off," he said when they had stopped joking around.

"So what else is new?"

"What's new is that she doesn't want you to see Klaus again. She says he's a bad influence."

"That's tough. I'm having dinner with him tonight." Joy crossed her arms over her chest in defiance.

"I suggest you don't."

"Is that a suggestion or an order?"

Her father hesitated for a moment.

"I guess it's an order."

"Why doesn't she do her own dirty work? If she doesn't want me to go out with Klaus, she can tell me herself."

Nat noticed that Joy never referred to her mother as "Mom," "Ma" or "Mother." Invariably "she" or "her."

"Baby, what's with you and your mother, anyway?"

"She's living in the Middle Ages and I'm living in nineteen sixty-eight. That's what."

Nat Baum was fascinated by the two women he lived with. They seemed to be so diametrically opposite, it was hard to believe that they were related, much less mother and daughter. Evelyn was introverted, afraid of conflict, highly conscious of her responsibilities and yet deeply unsure about her ability to carry them out. Joy was rebellious, self-confident, willing to take risks, and her emotions, unlike her mother's, were on the surface. Nat rarely admitted to himself that he felt his daughter took after him and that he was proud of it. And he never admitted to himself that while he needed his wife, he loved his daughter.

"She only wants to protect you," Nat said in Evelyn's defense. He felt he owed her some loyalty.

"Do *you* want me to stop seeing Klaus?"

"Frankly, I don't give a shit who you date. I'm just telling you what your mother said."

"Well, she can tell me herself if she thinks it's so important."

At six-thirty Joy got out of bed, recovered from the night before, and began to dress for dinner.

"Where do you think you're going?" Her mother came in through the bathroom.

"Out with Klaus," said Joy, brushing her hair.

"Oh, no," said Evelyn. "Not tonight and not ever."

"Oh, yes. Tonight. And maybe tomorrow night too, if I feel like it."

"You're getting on that telephone and breaking the date."

Evelyn pointed toward the old-fashioned black telephone on the night table. Joy continued brushing her hair, caressing it and fondling it. She didn't move from her spot in front of the full-length mirror on the back of her closet door.

"No way," she said.

"If you don't, I will."

"You wouldn't!" Joy stopped brushing and faced her mother, daring her to pick up the phone. Calmly, Evelyn picked it up and asked for Klaus's room. When he answered, she told him who she was.

"Joy isn't feeling well and I'm afraid she's going to have to break your date."

"She's lying!" Joy screamed at the top of her lungs so that Klaus could hear. "She's lying!"

Joy crossed the room and tried to pull the telephone from her mother's hand. Her mother quickly hung it up and with surprising strength held the telephone so that Joy couldn't use it.

"You lied! You didn't even have the nerve to tell him the truth! What's the matter? Didn't you like the sight of his cock hanging out?" Joy stood in front of her mother, screaming, "His big, long, purple Nazi cock!"

Evelyn struck Joy. She slapped her face so hard that Joy staggered back three steps and tears involuntarily came to her eyes. Mother and daughter stared at each other, shocked by the hatred they felt toward each other, and after a moment, Evelyn brushed past Joy to leave the room. As Evelyn reached the door, Joy spat at her. Shutting the door quietly behind her, Evelyn pretended not to notice.

As soon as Joy stopped trembling, she called Klaus. She told him that she was feeling much better and that she could keep their date after all. He hesitated for a moment and then he said that he was sorry, but that he had other plans.

"Oh," said Joy.

"I'm sorry. I really am. But I don't see how I can get out of it."

He sounded so sincere that Joy decided to risk the unknown.

"Tomorrow?"

"I'll be in Antigua tomorrow."

"Antigua?"

"It's for my job. I travel all the time."

"Oh. Well, when will you be back in Barbados?"

"In nine days. After Antigua, I go to St. Maarten and St. Croix and then back here."

"I'll be back in New York in nine days."

"I'm sorry. I wish I could see you again. You know that."

"I know," said Joy. "Well, have a good trip, anyway."

"And you have a good vacation."

"Yeah."

"Maybe next year . . ." he said.

"Maybe," said Joy.

There was never going to be a next year and they both knew it. They decided to stop being polite, said good-bye and hung up.

Joy realized that she was too depressed to go to the dining room for dinner. She didn't have the nerve to sit there at a table all alone and she wouldn't sit with her mother if she were starving to death. She ordered from Room Service, and while she waited for it, she smoked a joint. It was funny, she thought, how she and Klaus had never gotten around to turning on last night. She flipped through a *Glamour* magazine she had taken from the plane and she wished she had her stereo. There was no television in the room and she was restless. By the time dinner arrived, she was a little hungry from the grass, and she welcomed the food because it gave her something to do.

Joy forced herself to stay in her room until ten-thirty, when, finally, she couldn't stand the solitude any more. She put on some jeans and brushed her hair and left the room. The corridors were deserted except for a couple of maids giggling and wheeling a linen cart, and she went down one flight into the large, now empty dining room. She went past the tables already set up for tomorrow's breakfast and out the side doors that led to the upper terrace with its two curved staircases that led down to the dance floor. Music from the band drifted upward. The dance floor was on the same level as the beach, and Joy leaned on the wide stucco railing, looking for her parents. They usually sat at a table right by the edge of the dance floor. Palm trees surrounded the outer semicircle and lights were strung up in them. It was very pretty, like the old movies on television, with the music and the faint sound of water gently lapping at the beach.

She saw her parents; they were with the couple from St. Louis they had gotten friendly with. Nat was dancing with the wife, who was blond and sexy in a sort of whorish way, and Evelyn was dancing with the husband, who wore dinner jackets and bow ties and said that he was "in air conditioning." Joy admitted to herself very reluctantly that her mother looked quite pretty in the soft lights wearing a white dress that showed her tan arms. It was strange to see another man's arms around her mother, and Joy wondered if he had eyes for her.

As she watched the dancers, she noticed Klaus. He was wrapped up with some girl—Joy had noticed her at the beach but had never spoken to her. She was wearing a corny Pucci evening dress and her hair was brushed into a fancy upsweep and Joy thought she looked like shit, but Klaus obviously didn't. Not that she could blame him. What did she expect? That he would sit around and mourn because her mother had decided that he was a bad influence?

Joy watched the dancers, everyone with someone. When she looked past the dance floor, she could see the faint shimmer of the white beach in the moonlight and the chairs which had already been arranged into neat rows for the next day's sunbathers. Joy noticed a couple making out on one of them, and as she looked along the crescent of the beach, she noticed the waterskiing shack.

Winston turned out to be a pretty good fuck. A little on the primitive side, but still better than average. They were lying on Joy's bed, their legs entwined, when Nat and Evelyn got back to their room. Joy hadn't bothered to shut her door to the bathroom.

"Joy?" It was her mother.

"Yes?" Joy didn't move, and when Winston tried to, she held him down with her legs. She could hear her mother's shoes on the tile floor of the bathroom.

Since the bedroom was in semidarkness, Joy could see her mother before she saw her. When Evelyn's eyes adjusted and she saw the scene that Joy had arranged for her, she simply gasped, making a choky little sound and not uttering a word.

"You can go now," Joy told Winston. He got up and quickly and quietly put on his white bikini and left the room. Joy wondered how many times he'd been through scenes like this. Probably a lot. He probably thought it was a fringe benefit of his job.

Completely nude, Joy got up slowly, slowly crossed her room and shut the bathroom door deliberately in her mother's face.

"Good night, Mom. Sleep well."

The next day, at Evelyn Baum's insistence, the three of them left Barbados. A week later, Joy, at Evelyn Baum's insistence, had her first appointment with a psychiatrist.

5 DR. RICHARD SPAULDING'S office was in an elegant brownstone on Sixty-second Street between Park and Madison. There was a marble foyer that rose two stories, with a broad curved staircase and sheer curtains stretched across the windows that extended the height and breadth of the back wall.

Joy buzzed the buzzer, got a return buzz and pushed open the door to the inner office. It was a large, well-proportioned room with a high ceiling and ornamental moldings that dated back to the late nineteenth century. Dr. Spaulding's office was freshly painted a soothing off-white, the carpet was a rich navy blue and the furniture well designed and obviously expensive. Dr. Spaulding was beige.

He had olive skin, light brown hair and medium brown eyes. He was wearing a brown tweed jacket and tan whip-cord pants. He was not too tall and very slim and he was about forty years old.

"So you're the shrink," said Joy.

Dr. Spaulding merely closed the heavy door quietly behind her. They were alone in his office. He indicated the couch and he sat down in a leather armchair, crossing his legs and carefully adjusting the crease in his trousers in what Joy thought was a prissy way.

"You a faggot?" she asked.

"You'll find the couch very comfortable," he said.

Deliberately Joy sat down on the couch, even though there was a pillow on one end neatly covered with a fresh disposable paper case and she knew that she was supposed to lie down. Imitating the doctor, she crossed her legs ultra carefully, making sure that her micromini showed the crotch of her panty hose.

"I suggest you lie down," said the doctor. "It's easier to work that way."

"Don't tell me you're going to try to lay me?" Joy yawned. She wondered how far she'd have to go with this creep.

"I'm going to try to help you," he said. Joy noticed that his voice was beige too.

"Well," said Joy. "Lots of luck." She slouched back on the couch and defied Spaulding to tell her to sit up straight or to lie down or to demand to know about her lousy childhood or if she hated her mother or wanted to screw her father. He said nothing until, finally, Joy got bored with the silence.

"Aren't you going to ask me anything?" she asked finally, mad at playing and not winning.

"Perhaps there's something you want to say," said Dr. Spaulding, carefully keeping his voice in neutral.

"Fuck you," said Joy, and she promised herself that she wouldn't say one more word. She was furious that her mother had forced her to go to a psychiatrist like she was some kind of nut. She wasn't crazy, and there was nothing her mother could do to convince her that she was. She could sic all the shrinks in the world onto her and she wouldn't budge. Joy sat there silently, boiling inside. Spaulding could torture her with knives and guns and give her injections of truth serum and he'd never get one word out of her. Not a syllable.

The forty-five minutes went by, some of them fast and some of them slow. Finally, Dr. Spaulding stood up.

"Your session is over," he said. "I'll see you on Thursday."

"I suppose you wonder why I didn't say anything," said Joy. She brushed her breasts against his arm as she left to go out.

"We can discuss it next time," said Dr. Spaulding.

Before she could get in another word he had closed the door, leaving her out in the big marble foyer.

Her mother couldn't control her curiosity.

"What did the doctor say, dear?" she asked the second Joy walked into the apartment.

"Nothing. What could he say? I'm not crazy."

Joy talked as she strode across the living room heading for the hallway to her bedroom.

"No one said you were—" her mother began.

Joy slammed the door to her bedroom so hard that some plaster chips were jarred loose and fell like silent snow to the carpet. Good. Lydia could clean it up.

Joy wished she were a murderer. She sat on the window seat of her bedroom looking down at the people walking on Seventy-fourth Street. If she were a murderer, she'd have a gun. Joy stuck up her right thumb, squinted her left eye and sighted with her right eye along her right index finger. She aimed at a middle-aged, well-dressed woman who was walking two miniature dachshunds. They were peeing on the metal pole that held the NO PARKING sign. Joy aimed carefully and pulled the trigger. The woman looked up in mild surprise and then her legs crumpled under her and, very slowly, she fell to the sidewalk. She made no sound and there was no blood. Just a neat dark hole in her left breast. The dogs didn't seem to notice; they went on peeing. Joy was surprised at how easy it was.

She spent the next hour assassinating a black delivery boy carrying a florist's arrangement, a distinguished-looking man with a white moustache carrying a large painting wrapped in brown paper and bound with white twine and a girl with blond hair and tortoise-shell-rimmed sunglasses who looked like Candy Bergen.

She watched them all die silently. It was like the slow-motion reruns they had had on television of John F. Kennedy's murder. Joy had been eleven when Kennedy was assassinated and his murder was the public event most indelibly engraved on her mind. It was interesting how television didn't show the pain.

"I killed four people," said Joy on Thursday.

"Yes?" encouraged Dr. Spaulding.

"There was a woman, forty-five maybe, walking her dogs. I got her right in the heart. She didn't even scream." Joy thought that that was an interesting detail.

Dr. Spaulding didn't say anything, so she described the black kid from the florist's, the old man and the beautiful girl. She thought she did a terrific job. She was willing to bet that she was probably the most fascinating of all of Dr. Spaulding's cases. She waited for him to compliment her.

"Whom do you think these people represent?" he asked.

His coolness infuriated Joy.

"They don't represent anybody. They're just some people I knocked off the other day."

"Is it possible that the woman might be your mother and the man your father? Perhaps the beautiful girl is the way you'd like to be yourself. Is that possible?"

"Did anyone ever tell you you were full of shit?"

"Often," said Dr. Spaulding, his voice still in neutral.

Joy decided that he must have some group of grateful patients. They probably sent him arsenic for Christmas. But she decided not to say anything. Why waste her insight on him?

The rest of the session passed in silence. Without another word, Dr. Spaulding got up and opened the door and Joy was again abandoned in the marble foyer. She looked at her Mickey Mouse watch and saw that it was four-fifteen on the dot.

That doctor must have a clock for a brain. A cuckoo clock.

Joy hated Dr. Spaulding and she hated going to him. With the help of Ivy, she made up the most outrageous lies to tell him, and he was so stupid that he believed them. He kept asking her serious questions like the one about whether she thought she was as beautiful as Candy Bergen.

Only an idiot would be fooled by her, and Dr. Spaulding was an idiot. Joy decided in June that she had had enough of Dr. Spaulding and his beigeness. She asked her father if she really had to keep going. He said that he'd arrange an appointment with Dr. Spaulding and that then they'd decide.

"Is that OK?" he asked.

"As long as you go and not *her*," said Joy, referring to her mother.

The next week Nat met with Dr. Spaulding and afterward he met Joy for lunch.

"Dr. Spaulding says you're hostile, destructive and blocked."

Nat had ordered a gin-on-the-rocks with cocktail onions, and he and Joy had a table by the windows in the Edwardian Room of the Plaza. It was a corny place, but Joy really loved it. She had a Bloody Mary with no vodka and felt terribly decadent, like an alcoholic who couldn't drink anymore. Like one of those old-time alky movie stars.

"Hostile, destructive and blocked? No shit," said Joy, sipping her drink. "Did he say whether or not I'm crazy?"

"He didn't comment," said Nat, and they both broke up. Joy knew she was home free.

"What did you think of him? I mean, personally?" she asked.

"A shmuck," said her father, opening the menu. "What do you want for lunch?"

"So I don't have to go anymore?"

"I'll talk to your mother."

"A chef's salad with extra chicken. White meat only," said Joy. "Hey, Daddy?"

"What?" said Nat.

Joy thought about her father, about how handsome he looked and how hip he was and how nice. Her mother didn't deserve anyone like him. She only wished she could find someone like him for herself.

"I love you."

"Ditto and double ditto," said her father. "Now let's order."

Nineteen-sixty-eight was the most pivotal year in American history since 1929. It was an Olympic year, a Presidential year, the year of Black Power, of hippies and Yippies, of hawks and doves, of sit-ins, draft-card burnings and Lyndon Johnson's decision not to run again. Martin Luther King was assassinated in April and Robert Kennedy was assassinated in June. It was the year of the Nehru jacket, of Mia Farrow and Ruth Gordon in *Rosemary's Baby*, of Stanley Kubrick's *2001*, of Joe Namath's Jets. It was the year of *The Double Helix*—James Watson's account of the DNA molecule, cracking the genetic code and ego tripping in the world of science. It was the year that the power of the dollar began to erode. It was a year of disaster and division and it was the year the sixties began to end.

In September 1969, two months after Chappaquiddick, two months after the first moon walk, one month after the Tate–La Bianca murders by the Manson Family, Joy, after persuading her father and arguing with her mother, moved out of her parents' apartment into one of her own. It was an anonymous three-and-a-half in a high-rise on Sixty-third between First and Second in the middle of swinging-single territory. To calm her mother down, Joy signed up for some courses in film at NYU. As long as Joy appeared to be doing "something constructive" her mother didn't cause too much trouble.

Her mother worried about Joy: about Joy and drugs, about Joy's getting knocked up, about Joy's having an abortion, about Joy's shacking up with a boy, about Joy and her future. Her mother had been very upset when Joy told her that Ivy was marrying her boyfriend, Dick Noonjian, a guy of Armenian and Lebanese descent. Joy could tell by the expression on her mother's face that her mother was afraid that Joy would follow Ivy and maybe marry a Chinaman or something even worse—although, of course, her mother would never say anything like that out loud.

Ivy's mother and stepfather had separated and had filed countersuits for divorce. When Ivy told Joy that she and

Dick were going to get married, Joy asked, "Is he going to be Numero Uno?"

Ivy had predicted that she would have three or four husbands at least.

"No," said Ivy. "I'm going to stay married to him until I die. I can't stand all the divorces."

Joy's first year of living by herself was the last year of the sixties. It was the year that Joy changed from negative to positive, from destructive to creative, and it was the year that Joy fell in love.

Joy actually liked NYU. Her classmates, like herself and unlike the rich and sheltered students at Ardsley, were rebellious, unconventional and unhappy. They came from rich, poor and middle-class families. They were black, white, Jewish, Protestant, exchange students from exotic countries in Africa and kids who rode the A train down from the Bronx. They were, like Joy, sexually precocious and emotionally immature. They, like Joy, had grown up in the sixties and were confused by the contradictory signals sent out by a society in rapid transition.

It made Joy feel less like a freak and failure to find out that others too were having difficulty finding out who they were and what they wanted. They had been told to "do their own thing," but at fifteen and sixteen they had been too young to know what their "thing" was. At seventeen and eighteen, they groped for an identity. It was in this transitional period that Joy met Terry Bass.

Joy and Terry were in the same film course. Together they studied the history of film, beginning with the silents and ending with the latest films; they analyzed the great classics—Eisenstein, Welles, Capra and De Mille; the reign of the studios—Warner Brothers, MGM, Fox and Paramount—and the "star system"; the Postwar Realists—De Sica, Fellini and Rossellini; the New Wave of the fifties and the emergence of the auteur: Truffaut, Godard, Buñuel

328

and Antonioni; they continued to the present, studying Kurosawa, Bogdanovich and Bergman.

Movies were their pleasure and their passion. They saw everything from *Patton* to *Love Story,* from *Airport* to *M*A*S*H.* They realized that everything they knew, that their fantasies, ideals and aspirations had all been formed by film. They were the first visual generation receiving images, impressions and information from strips of celluloid, from shadows projected on screens. McLuhan was their prophet and their philosopher. They were, according to the theory, inhabitants of the Global Village.

From sharing the same enthusiasms and the same citizenship, it was natural for them to discover that they shared the same past. Just as Joy identified with her father and resented her mother, Terry's mother was his ally; his father, the Chevrolet King of eastern Pennsylvania and western New Jersey, his enemy. They found that Joy expressed her sense of alienation through rebellion and that Terry concealed his by withdrawing into a shell. Once they discovered the truth behind each other's defenses, they trusted each other enough to become friends. As they confided more and more in each other and as they learned not to fear betrayal at the hand of the other, as they shared secrets, humiliations and dreams, it was inevitable that they would become lovers.

It happened on May 5, 1970, the day after the killings at Kent State. Everyone at NYU felt personally endangered. There had been a demonstration in Washington Square Park following the April 30 action in Cambodia, and a petition protesting U.S. military intervention had been circulated and signed by students and faculty and sent to Richard Nixon at the White House. The demonstration had been peaceful and orderly. Special police units had been ordered to the park, and they stood, arms crossed, pistols holstered, while speeches denouncing American aggression in Asia were read; the petitions were passed, signed and returned to the organizers and, when it was all over, the protestors disbanded and went back to their classes or to the library or out for coffee. The police left quietly and the demonstration had been completed without incident.

The killing of the four students at Kent State had stunned the entire student body. It was easy, all too easy, to imagine the same thing happening in Manhattan. All it would have taken was one cop with an itchy trigger finger, one insult too many about long hair, one shout of "fascist pig" over the tolerable limit.

On the evening after the killings, a candlelit memorial service was held in the auditorium. The entire student body and faculty attended, each individual bearing a single candle. Empty beer cans, Dixie cups, cardboard rolls from paper towels, twisted wire coat hangers, china saucers all were improvised as candleholders, and in the darkened auditorium, illuminated only by hundreds of single flames, the president of the student body gave a brief, simple speech about liberty, freedom, truth and the right to dissent. When he had finished, there was a moment of silence—spontaneous, unplanned and, therefore, all the more powerful. Silently, slowly, the community, united by tragedy, filed from the auditorium.

Joy didn't want to go back to her apartment. She didn't feel like being alone, and she saw Terry in the crowd and together they walked over to the Howard Johnson's on Sixth Avenue.

"It could have been us," Joy said, sipping black coffee from the thick, chipped cup. "We could be dead right now. If we went to Kent State, maybe we would be."

"I thought they'd gone as far as they could at Chicago. I thought gassing people was the furthest they'd go. But now they shoot you if you disagree with them."

"Last year they walked on the moon," said Joy, "and this year they're killing on earth. I wonder when they're going to have the first killing on the moon. I guess they'll let us watch it on TV."

"Remember Flower Power?" asked Terry. His question was not a non sequitur. Joy knew exactly what he was talking about.

"And Haight-Ashbury and making love, not war?"

"The last good year was nineteen-sixty-seven," said Terry. "People had hope then. Or at least, I did."

"Me, too. I never thought it would end. Remember *The Endless Summer*? It was like an endless high back then. Now it's hard to even remember it."

Joy thought for a minute and remembered the song about going to San Francisco with flowers in your hair. It was supposed to have been the dawning of the Age of Aquarius and it had ended before it had really begun. Joy felt that she had lost her past before she had fully experienced it. It was one more thing that she had been cheated of.

"It seems like ages ago," said Terry. "It's funny to be our age and nostalgic about the past. I thought nostalgia was for when you got older."

"I thought death was for when you got older," said Joy.

"I haven't been to bed with anyone for over two years," said Joy. They had finished their coffee and were walking east on Eighth Street, the bright city lights now reassuring, now threatening. They walked in silence, not touching, and Joy wondered what had made her say that. She had never told anyone. Not even Ivy. The last man she had been to bed with was Winston, the waterski instructor in Barbados. Since then, she had been totally turned off sex. She thought it was a gyp and a fraud, all promises and no delivery, just like every cheap plastic toy she'd ordered from television commercials when she was a kid. They were bright and prettily packaged and offered visions of infinite pleasure and fell apart as soon as you played with them. She had thought that sex, like a new toy, a new dress, a new shade of lip gloss, was going to change her life—make it better, more exciting, more interesting. Instead, nothing had changed. Just another promise had been broken.

"It's OK if you don't want to," Terry said. "I understand."

Terry too had been let down by sex. He had discovered, when he was seventeen, that going on peace marches was a guarantee of getting laid. The same girls who believed in amnesty, racial equality and the legalization of marijuana also believed in putting out. After every sit-in, march or demonstration, the participants paired off and rewarded their efforts in behalf of a better world with sex. After a while, Terry couldn't remember whom he had slept with and whom he hadn't. He didn't know their names, their pasts, their dreams, and it didn't make a goddamn bit of difference because, in the end, they had all merged into the same girl, mouthing the same slogans, with the same long, straight hair, wearing the same pair of beat-up jeans.

"I *do* want to," said Joy. They were in Terry's apartment on East Tenth Street. He had a Che poster on the wall and a *Free Angela* button stuck in the wooden frame of his bulletin board. Joy laughed and told him that on her wall was a Dylan poster and in the frame of her bulletin board a Poor People's button. They talked about how absurd they were with their fantasies of being rebellious, tuned-in and original when, in fact, they were as conformist as the middle class they said they hated.

They got into bed and made love to each other with a sense of nostalgia, a sense of mortality, a sense of each other.

That summer, the summer of Janis Joplin's death and Nat Baum's fiftieth birthday, Joy and Terry bought youth-fare tickets to Paris and backpacked through Europe, visiting Amsterdam, London, Copenhagen and Madrid, hitchhiking, staying in youth hostels, smoking grass and singing folk songs wherever young Americans gathered. In Madrid, they rented a Fiat; they drove south through Seville to the Costa del Sol, overrun with British and German tourists, and finally to Algeciras, where they took the ferry to Tangier. In Tangier, they explored the souk, drank sugary mint tea and were told that marijuana was called kif. It made Joy remember Klaus from the Sandy Lane. She wondered what had happened to him.

Summer ebbed and was gone, and Joy and Terry returned

to New York. They had decided to live together and, without making a public announcement, moved into Joy's apartment. They told themselves that they chose her apartment because it was bigger. They didn't want to admit that they felt that Terry's neighborhood was creepy. His apartment had been burgled three times in one year, a Puerto Rican woman had stabbed a Puerto Rican man in the foyer of a building three doors away from Terry's, heroin was openly dealt in nearby Tompkins Park. It violated Terry's and Joy's principles to admit that they were afraid of every black and Puerto Rican and so they told each other that they had made their choice because Joy's apartment was bigger.

Terry resumed his studies at NYU and Joy audited the courses that intrigued her, but more than anything else—more than their courses, their parents, their contemporaries—they were interested in themselves: in learning how to live together, how to share without suffocating each other, how to maintain separate identities while building a sense of community, how to achieve a satisfying balance of dependence and, above all, trying not to make the same mistakes their parents had made.

They wanted to free themselves of the rigid role playing that had crippled the nuclear family. They divided domestic chores—cooking, marketing, laundry, cleaning, bill paying, bed making—evenly. They pooled their finances; each received, coincidentally, the same allowance: five hundred dollars a month. Nat gave Joy her check over lunch—they always met at the Plaza—and Milton Bass, Terry's father, sent his check enclosed with a letter typed by his secretary inquiring after Terry's grades and health. All their household expenses came out of the joint fund, and whatever was left was divided equally, with each able to spend as he or she pleased without explanation to the other.

Joy's desires were considered as important as Terry's; her needs for privacy, for expression, for comfort were regarded as equal to his. They obliterated all the old-fashioned preconceptions about "woman's place" and "a man's world."

When either detected a tendency in the other to revert to a preraised consciousness, the lapse was immediately pointed out and resolved.

Playing house made them both happier than they had ever been before.

In September of 1972, Joy decided to tell her father that she and Terry were living together. She was tired of having to pussyfoot around the subject. It was time, she had decided, to get everything out into the open.

"Dad," she said as they sat at their usual table looking north at Central Park, "it's time you knew the truth. Terry and I are living together." She waited, wondering what her father would say.

"I know. I've known it for a long time."

"Why didn't you *say* anything?" It surprised Joy that she felt actual shock at her father's casual acceptance. She hadn't thought that *anything* could shock her.

"It's none of my business."

"Don't you care?"

"As long as you're happy," Nat said. "You *look* happy." He ran his forefinger down the side of Joy's face, and she turned her head just a little so that she could kiss his fingertip.

"Are you going to tell her?"

They both know whom Joy meant.

"It's none of her business either. Besides," said Nat, "why bug her?"

Joy smiled. She was home free. Thank God, she thought, for a father like that.

"Maybe," Barbara Roser was saying, "the four of us could have dinner together. You and Terry, your father and me."

"Maybe," said Joy. She didn't know what she thought.

It was several weeks later, and when Joy had met her father at the usual table for their usual lunch, her father had introduced her to Barbara Roser. So, Joy had thought, she

334

had gotten things out into the open and now her father was doing the same.

"Hi," said Joy, very cool, hiding her resentment. She didn't like having a third person at "their" lunch. She had never dragged Terry along.

"It's nice to meet you," said Barbara. "I've heard a lot about you."

"All bad, I bet," said Joy, testing Barbara.

"Half and half," said Barbara, passing the test.

"All good," said Nat, settling down to his drink. It was a risk, introducing them, but what the hell, it was worth taking. "She's a good kid."

"He's the only person who could call me a 'kid' and get away with it." Joy leaned over and kissed her father on the mouth, asserting her prior claim. "Chef's salad . . ."

"I know," said Nat, "with extra chicken, white meat only."

Barbara watched them. Father and daughter. The same long-boned bodies, the same hidden eyes, the same humorous, wise-ass style. But Joy worked harder at it. Was it her age? Was it the mother's genes? Did Evelyn Baum have those lips with the wide center and fine corners? Did Evelyn Baum have that same kind of hair that never held a set? Did Evelyn Baum have that same vulnerability? Did Evelyn Baum try so hard to hide it? For all the times that Barbara had speculated about "the wife," she had never imagined her with hair that didn't hold a set.

As if Joy were an equal, Barbara and Nat talked about some business problems involving printers and buying paper. Joy had never heard her father talk about business; he never mentioned the office at home. No wonder he was so successful. He got very animated when he talked about Alpha. It was a side of him Joy had never seen. And it made her begin to like Barbara. She was helping her father and she was treating Joy like an adult, not asking the usual dumb questions about what she was going to do, when she was going to get married and how "her generation" saw things. As if Joy knew.

"The kid doesn't know beans about business," Nat said when he and Barbara had resolved the problem.

Joy shrugged. "Why should I? Who needs the hassle?"

"You've heard your father complaining?" Barbara's question was a statement with an edge of knowledgeable humor.

"I gather *you* have." Joy shrugged, not wanting to admit that there was something that Barbara knew about her father that she didn't. Not to mention bed. Not that Joy wanted to make it with her old man or anything like that. She remembered Spaulding and his Freudian double-talk.

"Yes," said Barbara, very poised. "I have. Lovers generally do share their problems."

Joy glanced at her father. She thought that maybe he'd choke, but he sat there cool as a cucumber. "Lovers." Joy admired Barbara for her honesty. It had taken *her* months to tell her father about Terry.

"I wanted you to meet Barbara," said Nat. He took Barbara's hand, the nails immaculately manicured and painted a fashionable shade of red, and held it in his. Right on top of the table where anybody could see.

Are you going to get married? Joy didn't have the nerve to ask. Besides, she didn't want to know the answer, anyway. If she did, she'd have to take sides, and she didn't want to have to do that.

There was a silence, and that was when Barbara suggested that the four of them get together. That meant that she knew about Terry. It meant that her father told Barbara everything. Even more than he told Joy.

"Listen, I've got to go."

Joy got up abruptly, bumping into the table and almost knocking over a water glass.

"Bye, kid." said Nat, slapping her on the fanny.

Barbara's smile revealed nothing.

Joy walked all the way back home from the Plaza.

She stopped in Bloomingdale's and, on an impulse, bought a bottle of Christian Dior nail polish. The shade was called Cuir and the saleslady told her that it meant "leather" in

French and that it was the most fashionable shade of the year. Joy had never put polish on her nails and she wondered what it would look like.

When she got home, Terry asked her how the lunch had been.

"The old usual," said Joy.

Terry thought she sounded angry, but she didn't say any more so he figured it was just his imagination.

"You know what I'd like?" Joy asked Terry one day a few weeks later. "I'd like to make a film together. Coproduce, so we could work together."

Terry was enthusiastic. "It would be terrific."

"Like Dick and Ivy," said Joy, although she was thinking of her father's conversation about the paper shortage with Barbara.

6 JOY ENVIED IVY AND DICK: they seemed to be very together. They were living in a loft in SoHo that they had renovated themselves, and they were running a custom T-shirt business—for three-ninety-eight their company would transfer any photo onto the customer's own T-shirt. Besides the custom business, they also sold T-shirts with photos of all the famous rock groups, underground stars and counterculture heroes and with slogans. They advertised in rock magazines and underground newspapers, and every morning the letter carrier delivered stacks of orders with the cash enclosed. It was, they said, incredible. They were earning more money than they knew what to do with, and a lot of the time they just returned orders because they didn't feel like working that day.

Dick and Ivy were into yoga, encounter therapy and group sex. They talked about the benefits of Transcendental Meditation, a sensitivity marathon that had given them new insights into themselves and their relationship and how they managed to have outside affairs without getting jealous of each other.

One night after dinner when everyone was pleasantly stoned, Dick and Ivy invited Joy and Terry to go to bed with them. They'd tried threesomes, they said, and regular orgies, but never a simple foursome.

"Why not?" Joy said tentatively, looking at Terry. "It might be a groove."

"No." Terry suddenly sounded very sober. "I think sex is a private matter between two people."

"But it might be fun," said Joy. "How will you know if you never try it?"

"I know," said Terry. "I know how *I* feel."

Joy felt torn between her lover and her friend. Too stoned to argue any more, she turned toward Ivy.

"It's cool," said Ivy. "We believe that people should only do what they deeply want to do. We admire Terry for verbalizing his preferences without feeling threatened by the group. Don't we, Dick?"

He nodded his agreement and Joy wished Terry weren't so square.

After the episode with Ivy and Dick, the relationship between Joy and Terry entered a new phase. Tensions that had lain buried beneath the surface, that had been covered over with resentments unexpressed; conflicts hastily patched up; disappointments carefully hidden began to emerge.

They argued, these children of rich fathers, over money. Joy thought that organic food was well worth the extra expense; Terry didn't. Terry wanted a quadraphonic sound system; Joy wanted a color television set. Joy thought that hard-cover books, which Terry bought by the dozen, were a waste of money when you could wait and get soft-cover. Terry thought that Joy's exercise class was a waste when she could have done the same exercises at home for nothing.

They both knew, and agreed, that their arguments were absurd, but they couldn't stop because the feelings that lay underneath weren't absurd.

They argued over housework and who did more.

They argued over having a baby. Terry thought it would be nice. Joy said: "What? And end up like my mother?"

Their relationship had become a time bomb, ready to explode at any moment. Joy was perpetually angry and Terry was perpetually defensive. They didn't like themselves and they didn't like each other but neither of them wanted to break up. Maybe, if they were patient, things would be all right again.

The cruelest thing of all was that on that evening in October when Joy's father called to say that her mother had tried to kill herself, Joy was shocked, guilty—and glad. It was an excuse to get away from Terry.

"Why would she do it?" he asked.

"I don't know." Joy shrugged. She had never told Terry about Barbara Roser.

"I'll go to the clinic with you," Terry offered.

"It's OK. I'll go alone."

"Call me? Let me know what's happening?"

"Sure," promised Joy. She wished he'd stop smothering her. "I'll call you later."

"You're positive you'll be all right?" Terry wished that she'd let him help her, but she kept him away.

"My father and I can handle my mother," said Joy. They were in the foyer and the doorman hailed a taxi. "My father and I can handle anything."

"You know something, Joy?" Terry asked, closing the taxi door. "The relationship between you and your father is sick."

"Yeah," said Joy. "I know. And guess what?"

"What?" asked Terry.

"I love it!"

She didn't even wave good-bye as the taxi pulled away, heading north up First Avenue toward the Voorhees Clinic.

PART FIVE

THE SEVENTIES

Men and Women:
Consequences

1 THE VOORHEES CLINIC WAS
an exclusive establishment catering to alcoholic heiresses,
burnt-out movie stars, jet setters having first-class abortions,
tycoons having deluxe nervous breakdowns and aging inter-
national beauties having discreet face-lifts. It also specialized
in upper-class suicide attempts.

Voorhees was on a quiet block between Madison and
Park and it looked nothing at all like a hospital. It was a
double town house painted an elegant pale gray and with
its windows trimmed in glossy black enamel. The name
Voorhees was discreetly spelled out in Spencerian script on
a highly polished oval bronze plaque set into the front door.
A well-groomed male receptionist wearing a sterling silver
ID bracelet from Cartier sat at an antique Sheraton desk
in the entrance foyer and politely asked Joy her name. He
didn't do a double take at Joy's jeans, T-shirt, sneakers and
thick-knit Guatemalan sweater. At Voorhees, they were apparently used to everything.

Her mother's room was on the third floor and Joy went
up in the elevator, one of the old-fashioned kind they still
have in Paris with a black iron grill and a glass cage. It was
run by an old black man in a meticulous gray uniform who
was efficient, polite and discreet without being in the least
subservient. The joint really had class.

Evelyn Baum's room, 3-F, faced south, looking out across
a courtyard onto the elegant back gardens of the town houses
along Eightieth Street. The room had pearl gray carpeting
and antique French chairs upholstered in gray raw silk.
There were filmy white curtains and immaculately clean

white venetian blinds. There were a glass-topped dressing table with a regular mirror and a magnifying makeup mirror, a gray-and-white-striped settee and a coffee table with copies of *Réalités, English Vogue* and *Town and Country.* Only when Joy walked to the window to get a better look at the view did she see the heavy wire screen that was bolted to the outside frame. Despite the decorations, Voorhees was a loony bin and they had no intention of letting any of the inmates take a dive.

Joy's father wasn't there, and her mother, who had seen her come into the room, merely followed her with her eyes.

"Hi, Mom," said Joy.

Her mother said nothing. She lay there, propped up against the lace-bordered pillows, not talking, not crying, not anything. She looked terrible. Bloated, like a frog. Her eyelids were swollen and her lips were so puffy that you could almost see their fleshy undersides. Her skin looked like an overinflated balloon, stretched thin and ready to pop at the slightest touch.

"How are you feeling?"

Still her mother said nothing. Her hands were on the sheet, and Joy noticed that they too were all puffy, almost as if a large boil had grown between the skin and the bone structure underneath. Joy wondered if her mother's grotesque appearance was a result of all the drugs. Her mother didn't move, not even to blink her eyes, which were tiny little slits between the puffy lids. She just lay there like a cheap made-in-Japan baby doll.

"I'm glad you're OK," said Joy. She choked at the end of the sentence. She swallowed and cleared her throat.

Her mother made no response.

Tears that Joy didn't know were in her eyes began to roll down her cheeks. She tried to pretend they weren't there, but it was impossible. A box of white Kleenex stood on the night table, and Joy reached for one and blew her nose. She swore to herself that she would do it only once and that the waterworks would stop.

Her mother watched her, following her across the room with her eyes.

"Yeah," said Joy. "I'm really glad you're OK."

Joy stood between the bed and the windows. She had an impulse to rush over and hold her mother in her arms, but she didn't know how to handle the impulse, so she did nothing.

"You look terrific," said Joy. "When do they say you can come home?" Joy was just talking now, to fill up time, saying anything she could think of. She wished her mother would answer. Why didn't she say something? Joy kept on talking and then her mother began to cry, tears spilling out from the little slits. She didn't try to stop and she didn't try to hide them and she didn't try to pretend that it all wasn't happening.

"Don't cry," said Joy.

There was no answer. Joy handed her mother a Kleenex and her mother didn't even take it. The tears fell on the immaculate Voorhees sheets. Joy took another tissue and tried to wipe the tears off her mother's face. Her skin was hot and thin and brittle. It was the first time Joy had touched her mother since she was twelve.

As she tried to wipe the tears away, her mother moved for the first time since Joy had entered the room. Violently, she moved her head so that her face was away from Joy's touch.

Joy was standing there not knowing what to say or do when the door opened quietly and a nurse looked in. She spoke softly and asked Joy to leave.

"I'll be back, Mom. I'll see you tomorrow, OK?"

Her mother said something, but Joy couldn't hear her. She leaned forward and Evelyn Baum, with great effort, repeated herself.

"Don't bother. It doesn't matter anymore."

Joy wanted to embrace her mother, to show her that it did matter, that she did care, but the nurse pulled her away.

"Come on, dear," said the nurse. "Your mother is very tired. You can see her again tomorrow."

Evelyn was staring into the distance and she didn't even seem to notice when Joy left the room, and Joy had no choice but to follow the nurse out into the hall.

Joy thought that her father might be there and she asked for him.

"Didn't you know?" said the nurse.

"Know what?"

"Your mother refuses to see him."

Joy got a taxi outside Voorhees and gave the driver the 934 Fifth Avenue address. When Joy got home, her father was standing at the bar in the foyer pouring liquor into a glass.

"She's dead," he said, keeping his back to Joy. "The hospital just called."

"Oh, shit," said Joy. "Just shit."

Nat drank and Joy smoked grass and they sat in the apartment trying to think of things to say. Lydia had been told to go home, and Voorhees wouldn't release the body to a funeral home until an autopsy had been performed. There was nothing to do.

At nine, they decided they must be hungry and they called Dial-A-Steak and ordered two steak dinners, which they threw out once they arrived. At eleven, Nat finally got up the courage to say what was on his mind.

"Listen, do you mind if I go out? I don't feel like being alone tonight."

"It's OK," said Joy. "I understand."

He put on his coat and left and Joy *did* understand—she didn't particularly feel like being alone either. But she understood another thing as well. As far as her father was concerned, being with her counted the same as being alone. She realized that on the same day she had lost her mother, she had lost her father as well.

Fortunately, Ivy and Dick were at home, and Joy got into a taxi and went down to SoHo. They were very nice and very sympathetic. They sat on a king-sized mattress on the floor and smoked grass and drank wine and talked about what a shame it was that people never talked about death and the psychic function of mourning and the therapeutic effects of grief. By the time they had smoked a lot and drunk a lot, agreed that Joy would live with Ivy and Dick, said everything they could think of to say and all made love to each other, Joy felt the best she had felt all day. At four that morning she remembered that she had promised to call Terry. He answered on the first ring.

"Hi, Terry," said Joy, lying naked on the bed between her best friend and her husband. "Guess where I am?"

On St. Valentine's Day, 1973, Barbara Roser and Nat Baum were married in the chambers of a justice of the New York State Supreme Court. In view of the circumstances, it was a quiet marriage. The newlyweds spent a week's honeymoon in Antigua and returned to their newly acquired apartment at 736 Park Avenue, both bride and groom having sold their previous residences.

One evening in September of 1973, with a Watergate-wounded President in the White House, the New York football Giants looking surprisingly good for the Seventy-three season and Bobby Riggs, the happy hustler, grabbing all the publicity for his upcoming match against Billie Jean King, Nat Baum stopped at Maxwell's Plum for a drink on the way home from the office. He picked up a pretty blond Delta stew, went to her apartment on First Avenue, laid her and was home for dinner by seven-thirty.

Two evenings later, Nat met Joy for drinks at the Oak Room of the Plaza. He didn't understand why, but as he began his third drink, he told her all about the stew. He could see by Joy's expression that she thought he was a dirty old man and a male-chauvinist pig, but he didn't care. He was fifty-three and he wanted her to know he could still get first-class stuff.

Barbara's office at J&S was really impressive: spacious, beautifully furnished and high enough so that it had a view of both Manhattan rivers. Joy was also impressed with Barbara. She was wearing a tobacco brown cashmere sweater set from Halston with a brown-and-black pleated skirt. Her hair was beautifully brushed and her makeup was fashionable and flattering. She made decisions and gave instructions firmly and confidently, and Joy could tell just by watching her that she liked what she did and did it extremely well. She thought that it must have cost a lot for Barbara to have succeeded the way she had. Joy admired her but she didn't want to be like her.

There were constant interruptions—people coming in to ask questions or get decisions—and the phone kept ringing, and Joy finally asked Barbara if it would be OK to close the door and hold the phones. She wanted to talk to her in private.

"I don't know if I'm doing the right thing," Joy said, and then she told Barbara what Nat had said about Maxwell's Plum and the blond stew from Delta.

Barbara listened quietly and let Joy finish.

"You shouldn't have told me," Barbara said. "I wish you hadn't."

"I'm sorry. I really am. I kept thinking about what I should do. I wanted to do the right thing. I'm sorry."

Joy had thought it over a long time before calling Barbara and asking to see her. She had finally decided it was better for her to know. Maybe her mother would have lived if someone had told her soon enough. Maybe she could have done something—fought back, made Nat pay attention to her. Ever since her mother's death Joy had thought over and over about how she had known about her father and his girlfriends and how she and her father used to keep their dirty little secret to themselves as a way of keeping her mother an outsider. Joy remembered every time her father had put her mother down and Joy had been pleased by her mother's inability to defend herself. She thought about all the private jokes she and her father had shared that they had never let her mother share. She thought about all the times she had gone to her father because she knew that he would contradict whatever her mother had said. She thought about it all and wished she could take it all back—and she never could. Not ever.

Although Barbara was only her stepmother and not her real mother, Joy didn't want the same thing to happen again. She had learned from the past. This time, she was on the woman's side.

"Please, Joy, don't ever tell me anything like that again." Joy could see how deeply Barbara was hurt. She wished she could unsay the words. No matter what choice she made, she always seemed to be wrong.

"Joy, I know you meant well. Let's forget it, OK?"

"Sure."

Barbara walked Joy to her office door and said good-bye and Joy wondered what Barbara was really like. She was so composed, so hidden. She wondered what price Barbara had paid for so much control, so much self-discipline.

As Joy took the elevator down to the lobby of the J&S building, Barbara picked up the private line on her desk and dialed the Plaza.

Elroy Swanson was a former Wyoming cowboy who had once posed for a Marlboro ad. His novel about a psychotic killer and the Texas sheriff who hunts him down was moving up on the best-seller list, and Elroy was in town for promotional appearances. He had propositioned Barbara the week before as they drove down Fifth in a limousine on the way to tape the Cavett show. Barbara had turned him down on the ground that she was married.

When Elroy answered, Barbara asked if his invitation still stood, and they made a date for four that afternoon at his room at the Plaza.

Two weeks before the anniversary of her mother's death, Joy called Terry. He was still living in her old apartment and she had been thinking about calling him for a long time. She hadn't spoken to him or heard from him since the night her mother had died—the night she had called him from Dick and Ivy's bed.

"Terry, it's Joy."

"I know." His voice sounded so familiar.

"I'm sorry," Joy said, and she began to cry. She hadn't planned it that way. It just happened.

"Don't cry. Try not to cry."

"I didn't mean to call up just to cry," said Joy, and she laughed a little.

"What have you been doing?" asked Terry after he had told her that he was in a graduate program in film and had a chance of getting an apprentice's job on a movie that would be shot in Boston.

Joy didn't want to answer. She wasn't proud of what she had been doing.

"What have you been doing?" asked Terry again.

"I'm afraid to tell you," she said.

"Would it be easier in person?"

As she taxied uptown, Joy thought about her mother, her father, Barbara and herself.

Her mother had wanted only the two things that society told her she *should* want: a husband and children. When they had gone, she was gone too. There was nothing left for her. Just emptiness.

Joy couldn't decide about her father. Sometimes she thought he was a total bastard—insensitive, manipulative, selfish. Other times, she thought that he was as much a victim as her mother had been. He had been taught that it was a man's world and that women existed to be laid. The more women a man laid, the more of a man he was. Was it her father's fault that he had never seen beyond that desolate equation or not? Joy didn't know.

Barbara. Barbara had wanted more than Joy's mother had wanted and she had gotten it. But the price had been eternal vigilance. Joy felt that Barbara was always on guard, ready to fight back, afraid that the things she had achieved were so precariously hers that she had to watch over them ceaselessly.

And herself?

Joy had spent every minute of every hour of every day of the past year trying to figure herself out. She had been living with Dick and Ivy. The three of them had tried vegetarianism, biofeedback, Primal Therapy, Quaalude, sensitivity marathons and Tantra retreats; they had consulted gurus and astrologers, psychiatrists and palmists; they had gone to handwriting experts, hypnotists and sex therapists in their search for an answer. Now, a year later, Joy still had no answers. But she had, at least, a question.

"I don't like me," she said to Terry. It was strange to be in the apartment they had once shared. "I hate me. My parents spoiled me but I let them, so I can't blame them for everything. I hurt my mother, over and over, because I mistook her vulnerability for weakness.

"And I admired my father because I mistook his indifference for strength. I didn't want to be like my mother; I wanted to be like my father. Unfortunately, I succeeded."

Terry nodded. They were drinking mint tea, and the late-afternoon sun was slanting through the windows.

"I don't want to be like him," said Joy. "I want to change."

Terry nodded again.

"Terry?"

"Yes?"

It was then that Joy asked the question.

"I can't do it alone. Will you help me?"